The Jinx
and the
Pinkerton

Carolyn Lampman

RED CANYON PRESS

The Jinx and the Pinkerton

Copyright © 2018 - Carolyn Brubaker

Printed in the United States of America

Formatting: Wild Seas Formatting
(http://www.WildSeasFormatting.com)

Published by
RED CANYON PRESS
4530 W. Mountain View Dr.
Riverton, WY 82501

Dedication

To Karen who is the best first reader EVER. You have stuck by me through eleven books and counting. I couldn't do it without you!

To Trish who inspired me to start writing those many years ago, and who was the first to put the idea of a wagon train in my head.

And to Todd who spent countless hours under my desk as I wrote, warming my feet and providing companionship. He, and all the Corgis that came before, are the inspiration for Franklin.

CHAPTER 1

Independence, Missouri 1856

"What do you mean I can't travel with your wagon train?" Charisse asked indignantly. "My money is the same as any man's."

"No single women." The wagon master eyed her with studied insolence, then spit a stream of tobacco juice at a passing beetle. "You'd slow us down. A woman just can't keep up."

"That's ridiculous. My team is as fast as anybody's."

"You've driven a wagon before?"

Charisse crossed her fingers behind her back. "Yes," she lied. "I got here from St. Louis, didn't I? The wagon is loaded, and I'm ready to go."

"Then I suggest you find a man to drive it for you. Evenin', ma'am." He tipped his hat and walked away.

Charisse sighed in defeat. *Drat it all, anyway.* He was the third wagon master to turn her down in two weeks. It was always something. Either she was too young, or too pretty or too inexperienced. To listen to them, you'd think only ugly old men who had driven back and forth to Oregon a dozen times were allowed to travel the Oregon Trail.

Her thoughts were gloomy as she trudged back to the hotel. She'd fully expected to be well on her way by now, leaving Preston and her old life far behind. Instead, she'd run into one difficulty after another. First, it was finding a wagon she could afford and having to settle for a team of evil-tempered mules instead of the powerful but docile oxen she wanted. Then her driver deserted her two days out of St. Louis. Now, wagon masters turned her away one after another. It was beginning to look like her money would run out before she could sign on to a wagon train. By the end of next week, it would all be gone, and she'd have to sell the wagon.

Maybe you really are a jinx. The hateful words popped into her mind, tightening her throat and making her stomach clench. Charisse pushed the thought away in anger. That was Preston's delusion, not hers. Luck, good or bad, had nothing to do with her temporary setback. It was merely time to reconsider her options.

Charisse's thoughts came to an abrupt halt as something flew over her head, ricocheted off a window with a resounding crack and bounced downward. "What in the world...?" She put her hand up to protect her face and something smacked into it. Her palm stung as her fingers reflexively closed around a ball. A small boy came careening around the corner, a charming little scamp with tousled red hair and brilliant blue eyes.

"You caught my ball!" Dried tear tracks streaked his dirty face and one bloody knee showed through a rip in his pants, but his smile was bright as he gazed up at her.

"It found me," she said, looking ruefully down at her hand.

His smile faltered. "Did it hit you?"

"No, but it was going pretty fast when I caught it." She chuckled as she handed his ball back. "Looks like you've had quite a day of it."

The engaging grin returned full force. "It's been the funniest day of my life," he said with conviction.

"I'm glad, because your mother will have something to say about your clothes, I'm sure."

"Don't got a mother, and Pa don't care. He says boys got to get dirty to live."

"You must be living high on the hog then," she said with a smile. "How about if I clean that knee for you?"

He tipped his head to the side. "Don't know. Will it hurt?"

"I expect it might. Still, it's bound to hurt a whole lot worse later if I don't."

"You got any iodine?"

"Not with me, I'm afraid."

"Then I guess it's all right," he said dubiously.

Charisse's lips twitched as she pulled a clean handkerchief out of her reticule. "Why don't you have a seat there on the steps while I get this wet?" She dipped the handkerchief in the horse trough and wrung it out.

"What's your name?" he asked.

"Charisse," she said, kneeling down in front of him. "What's yours?"

"Toby." He made a face. "It's Tobias really, but Pa said I don't have to call myself that unless I want to."

Charisse smiled. "Your father sounds like a sensible man. If you ask me, you look far more like a Toby than a Tobias."

Toby gave her an approving grin, and Charisse's heart turned over in her chest. He was such a beguiling little urchin she just wanted to hug him, to remind herself that innocence still existed in the world, that life could be good, and children didn't always die in their mother's arms. "I'll make this fast," she said abruptly. "It's almost dinner time, and your father is probably wondering where you are."

The boy bit his lip and glanced up the street. "I know, and he's going to be mad."

"Because you're late?"

"No, 'cause I ran away from Molly."

"Who's Molly?" Charisse asked, daubing at his knee. "Your big sister?"

"No, Pa hired her to look after me 'cause he has business to take care of." He sighed. "Didn't mean to, but she was talking to her friend in the park, and a dog ran off with my ball. I *had* to chase it." He hung his head. "Then I found some boys to play with, and I sorta forgot to go back."

"Maybe Molly's waiting for you at the park."

"Nah. That was this morning. She's long gone by now."

Charisse was startled. The boy couldn't be much more than seven or eight, far too young to be on his own all day in a busy place like Independence. He was lucky he only had a skinned knee to show for his adventures. "I'm sure she's looking for you and nearly frantic by now."

Toby considered this for a moment, then shook his head. "No, I think she's glad to be rid of me. Her friend was trying to talk her into going with him when I left. Besides, I heard her tell Pa I was Satan's own imp, and I'd be the death of her."

Charisse's lips tightened. *Stupid woman. Any idiot could see there wasn't an ounce of harm in the boy.* "She was probably just upset. People often say things they don't mean when they're angry."

"Molly's always upset with me, especially when her friend is around. I don't think he likes little boys much." Toby sighed gustily. "Anyway, Pa's gonna warm my backside but good for this one."

"If he does, it will be because he loves you. Running away like that is very dangerous. Your father will want to make certain you know not to do it again." Charisse frowned as she gave his knee a final swipe. "Maybe you should tell him about Molly and her friend. I'm not sure she's the proper woman to take care of you. She seems rather flighty to me."

"Pa said I had to learn to get along with her 'cause he doesn't have time to find me another one."

"Another what?"

Toby didn't seem to hear as he looked over her shoulder, his eyes widening in alarm. "Uh oh," he murmured. "It's Pa."

"Tobias Benjamin McCabe!"

Charisse flinched. It was the most incredible voice she had ever heard, deep and compelling, though right now it reverberated with anger. She jumped to her feet with some half-formed notion of protecting her young companion, but the thought of her being able to stop the man striding toward them was ludicrous. His tall, broad-shouldered frame would have looked at home cutting ties in a lumber camp or driving railroad spikes with a heavy sledge hammer. He could brush her aside as easily as he would a pesky mosquito.

Charisse's stomach twisted in panic as the big hands reached out and plucked Toby off the board walk. In spite of the man's size, there was no way she was going to stand by and watch him hurt the child. Before she could open her mouth, the man enveloped Toby into a bear hug. With eyes closed in relief, he sank his face against his son's neck as though trying to convince himself the boy was all right. A moment later, Toby dangled in mid-air as his father gave him a shake. "Where the hell have you been?" he roared. "I've spent half the day looking for you!"

Toby's lower lip trembled, and his eyes filled with tears. "I-I sorta got l-lost," he quavered.

Before she had time to think better of it, Charisse took another step forward and lay her hand on the man's arm. "Please," she said, "you're scaring him."

Charisse felt like some sort of loathsome creature as he turned his head and stared down at her with the most incredible eyes she'd ever seen. They were startling in the darkly tanned face; a deep blue touched with green, and right now decidedly angry.

"I beg your pardon?" he said in an icy voice.

She stiffened her spine. "I said you're scaring him. Toby's already had a rough time of it today. He doesn't need to be bullied by his father, too."

"It's none of your damn business!"

An involuntary shiver tingled across her skin at the menace in his voice. It reminded her too much of Preston in the final months of their marriage. "Maybe not, but I'll not stand by and watch you terrify an innocent child."

"Nobody's asking you to. This is a private matter between me and my son. We don't need the advice of a nosy stranger."

He glared pointedly at her for a long moment, but Charisse held her ground. No bully was going to intimidate her.

"Charisse isn't a stranger, Pa. My knee was hurt real bad until she fixed it," Toby said, looking back and forth between the two of them with an anxious frown. "And she isn't nosy. I like her."

"You're hurt?" Toby's father was instantly concerned.

"Sorta. I fell off a fence and skinned my knee a little. But Charisse washed it off, and it's fine now.

"If you're worried about him being injured, I suggest you stop shaking him around like a rag doll," Charisse pointed out.

Toby's father gave her another irritated glance, then sighed and gently set the boy down. "Look lady, he put himself in danger today by running away. He needs discipline, not coddling."

"I agree, but frightening him is not the way to do it."

"Charisse said you'll want to make sure I don't run away again," Toby said hopefully. "I know better now, so you don't have to whup me. I already learned my lesson."

"Is that right?"

Toby nodded solemnly. "It's dangerous, and I could get hurt even worser than I did this time. From now on, I'll stay with Molly no matter how boring it is."

"It's a little late for that now. Molly refuses to have anything more to do with us."

"Well, at least something good came of this," Charisse muttered.

"That's all you know about it." Toby's father glared at her again. "I had a hard time finding someone to watch Toby for me. Molly was a godsend."

"From what Toby told me, you're well rid of her. She was apparently more interested in her beau than your son."

"I didn't ask you, and I'm not in the habit of taking advice from strangers on how to raise my son."

"Well, maybe you should. The next time you find a nanny, make sure she's someone who understands Toby and truly has his welfare at heart. Anyone with half a brain can see he's just full of energy and has a tendency to do things without thinking." Charisse raised an eyebrow. "I wouldn't be a bit surprised if he hadn't inherited that from his father. Now, if you'll excuse me, I'll bid you both a good evening." With a toss of her head, she brushed past him and marched down the street and around the corner out of sight.

Luke watched her go, his eyes wide with astonishment. It wasn't often anyone took him to task, especially a beautiful woman with eyes like a stormy sea. He found himself wondering what color her hair was underneath the ugly poke bonnet. Probably bright red, the way she'd ripped into him.

"Don't be mad at her, Pa," Toby said in a small voice. "She was trying to help."

Luke glanced down at his son in surprise. "You really liked her, didn't you?"

Toby nodded earnestly. "She didn't even get mad when my ball hit her, and she fixed my knee. See, it feels lots better now."

Luke looked at the raw, scraped skin. It must hurt like the devil. "Then I'm most grateful to her."

Suddenly the door behind them crashed opened and a wizened old woman hobbled out onto the step. "You there, are you the boy's father?"

Luke raised an eyebrow. "I am."

"Then I demand you pay for my broken window."

"What window?"

"That one," she said pointing her cane toward a cracked second story window. "The brat broke it with his ball."

"Is that true, Toby?" Luke asked, frowning down at his son.

"Kinda." He squirmed under his father's gaze. "It bounced off the lamp post at the corner, then flew up and hit the window before Charisse caught it."

"I see." Luke pulled out his purse and extracted several crisp bills. "If you'll tell me how much—"

The old woman's claw-like hand moved with amazing speed as she snatched all the bills from his hand. "That should do it," she said, then whisked herself inside, her slow, shuffling gait miraculously cured.

As the door slammed behind her, Luke's frown turned to a fierce scowl. It occurred to him that she'd had plenty of time to come out earlier but hadn't bothered until he and Toby were alone.

Toby's hand stole into his father's as they started down the street. "I'm sorry I broke the window, Pa. And I'm sorry about Molly," Toby ventured in a tentative voice. "Do you think it would help if I 'pologize?"

"No, she's even madder at me than she is at you."

"She is? What for?"

"I lost my temper with her." Luke sighed. "I wish you'd told me she was spending so much time with her... uh... friend."

Toby shrugged. "You said I had to get along with her. Who's going to take care of me now?"

"I wish I knew. It's going to be tough to find someone."

"How about Charisse?"

"Charisse?"

Toby nodded eagerly. "My new friend. She'd take real good care of me."

"You can't just ask anybody you meet to take on a job like that. She's probably too busy doing... whatever it is she does. Besides, I've decided to go to Oregon." Actually, Matthew McNesby and Allen Pinkerton had decided for him. For the dozenth time, Luke wondered why his superiors were sending him off on a wild goose chase. If it weren't for Toby, he'd probably be more exasperated than anything else. As it was, he found the prospect daunting in the extreme.

"We're going to Oregon?" Toby asked breathlessly. "In a wagon and everything?"

Luke grinned as he reached down to ruffle his son's hair. "Yep. I'm going to buy the wagon and team tomorrow. We'll leave Friday."

"Maybe Charisse is going to Oregon, too."

Luke snorted. "Women like her don't go traipsing off to Oregon. The exposure to the elements isn't good for their lily-white skin. I'm sure there will be a woman on the wagon train who wouldn't mind looking after you during the day."

"Can we at least ask Charisse?"

It was on the tip of Luke's tongue to say no, but something

in Toby's expression stopped him. The boy had given up everything familiar to go with a father he barely knew. Since then they'd been able to spend very little time together. Luke didn't think he could bear to disappoint Toby. "We'll probably never see her again," he said. "What do you say we go get cleaned up and have some supper?"

"Can we go to Benson's like we did for breakfast?"

"Sure, why not?" Luke smiled down at his son. "It sounds like you had quite a day."

Toby nodded eagerly. "I had a great a'venture…"

Luke felt his heart swell as he listened to his son's story. How he loved this child, this part of himself, this miracle. Maybe bringing Toby along hadn't been the smartest thing he'd ever done, but his only regret was the years they hadn't spent together.

Toby was still chattering half an hour later when they walked through the front door of Benson's.

"Look Pa, there she is!" Toby pointed across the room to where Charisse sat at a table by herself, posture rigid as she ate her lonely meal. "I'm going to go ask her if she'll go to Oregon with us."

Luke reached out in a futile attempt to stop his son who darted across the restaurant, then dropped his hand to his side. *Maybe this is the best way*, he thought. She'd been compassionate to Toby before; surely she'd let him down easy.

As he watched, she looked up and smiled as Toby called her name. Luke sucked in his breath in surprise. He spent a moment fantasizing about what it would be like to have that beautiful smile directed toward him rather than his son. It was a short step from there to imagining her eyes luminous with passion and her lips parted in silent invitation. He could almost feel the long graceful fingers trembling against his chest in sweet anticipation as he bent to kiss her.

With a start, Luke jerked his thoughts back to reality. Damn, he couldn't even remember the last time a pretty face had inspired more than a flash of appreciation in him. Maybe it was the aura of sadness that hung about her as she sat alone in the crowded restaurant, or even the way she'd stood up to him. Whatever it was, he was thankful there was no chance of her accompanying them to Oregon. The unexpected trip into the wilderness was going to be tough enough without a distraction like her.

Toby gave his father an anxious glance then said something to Charisse. With a nod, she stood and followed him across the room. With his impassive mask securely in place, Luke leaned negligently against the door frame and waited for them. He'd be properly disappointed that she couldn't go along, of course, and maybe even invite her to join them for dinner. *That will help soften the blow to Toby*, he told himself.

"We meet again," he said. "Quite a coincidence."

"Not really. I'm staying in the hotel next door. I always eat here." Charisse looked up at Luke doubtfully. "Toby offered me the job as his nanny. He assures me he has your permission to do so."

Luke shrugged. "I told him you probably wouldn't be interested."

"On the contrary, I'm seriously considering his offer." She frowned. "That is, if it comes from you as well."

"To tell you the truth, Miss..."

"Jones," she supplied with a slight hesitation.

"Miss Jones, I'd hire you in a heartbeat if we weren't leaving on a wagon train headed for Oregon in a few days."

"Then you *are* looking for someone to go to Oregon with you?"

Luke managed a regretful look. "I'm afraid so."

A moment later he discovered first-hand how it felt to be on the receiving end of her smile. It was like being wrapped in a sunbeam, warm and sweet.

"That's exactly why I'm applying for the job, Mr. McCabe," she said.

Luke straightened in surprise. "You're willing to go to Oregon with us?"

"Not only willing, but anxious to. When were you planning to leave?"

"Our wagon train is pulling out on Friday." He frowned. "That is, if I can find a wagon by then. I didn't have much luck today."

"I have a wagon."

He raised his brows in surprise. "You do?"

"I bought it in St. Louis and came up the Missouri River by steamboat, like most immigrants do."

"Then I fail to see why you'd want to throw in with us."

"It's quite simple, Mr. McCabe," she said. "The man I hired to drive disappeared about two days out of St. Louis, and so far, I haven't been able to find another driver or a wagon train that will take a single woman."

"But you know nothing about me."

"I know that you need a nanny, and I need someone to drive my mules."

"Mules?"

Charisse raised her chin a trifle defiantly. "They're faster than oxen and can live on prairie grass better than horses."

"I've never driven mules."

"They're a lot like horses," she said with a shrug. "I suspect you drive them the same way. Frankly, Mr. McCabe, you and Toby are the answer to my prayers." She flashed him another brilliant smile. "And it looks like I may be the answer to yours."

The answer to my dreams maybe, Luke thought cynically, *but certainly not what my saner self needs.* Taking off on one of McNesby's crazy adventures that involved a two-thousand-mile trek would be difficult in the best of circumstances. Doing it with his seven-year-old son and a woman who looked like Charisse Jones bordered on insanity. "Do you realize how hard this trip is going to be? A good half of the people who go never make it."

"It's actually closer to a fourth, and I'm willing to take that chance. I'm considerably tougher than I look, Mr. McCabe. The way I see it, you need me to take care of Toby as much as I need you to drive my wagon." She stuck out her hand. "Is it a deal?"

With a feeling of impending doom, Luke shook her hand. "I'd be stupid to say no, wouldn't I?" As Toby danced around them in unconcealed joy, Luke couldn't decide which he wanted to do more, join his son in joyous celebration or run for cover.

CHAPTER 2

Charisse turned her head slightly as she put the finishing touches on the braid coiled around her head, then made a face at her reflection in the mirror. The peculiar color of her hair bothered her more than usual today for some reason. It looked as if Mother Nature couldn't make up her mind between red or brown and had compromised with an odd mixture of both. "Well, Franklin, do you suppose Mr. McCabe has had second thoughts this morning?" She glanced over her shoulder at the dog lying comfortably on the floor. "He wasn't exactly wild about hiring me, you know."

Franklin gave her a canine grin and settled his head back against his paws. A chirp sounded over by the window where a small canary sat on a wooden perch in a gilded cage.

She turned back to the mirror and put on her bonnet. "It's all right for the two of you to take that attitude. I'm the one who has to worry about getting us to Oregon. This is probably crazy, but I have to do something before all of our money runs out." She grinned and bent down to scratch Franklin behind the ears. "Of course, most people would think talking to you was crazy, too."

Franklin sighed and closed his eyes.

Charisse shook her head ruefully. If she wasn't careful she'd end up like her great-aunt Gertrude, an eccentric old maid who talked to her cats. A knock sounded at the door, and she turned in surprise. "Now who could that be this time of day? It's seven o'clock in the morning, for heaven's sake."

Her surprise turned to pleasure when she opened the door, for there stood Toby with a single wilted bloom and a huge grin. Charisse couldn't help smiling back. It had been a long time since anyone other than Franklin had been glad to see her. "Well, hello, Toby. You're up early this morning."

"Pa said I should come stay with you while he goes to look at your wagon. He'll be back by noon." Toby held out the flower. "I brought you a present."

Charisse experienced an almost-forgotten feeling of warmth as she reached out to take the droopy blossom. "Oh, Toby, it's beautiful. Thank you. Why don't you come in while I put this in some water?" As she glanced around looking for something to use as a vase, Toby caught sight of Franklin lying by the bed.

"You have a dog!" he exclaimed in delight.

She smiled. "His name is Franklin. Franklin, meet Toby."

"Can I pet him?"

"Be my guest. He loves children, don't you, Franklin?"

Franklin stretched, then rose from the floor and padded over to Toby as though he'd understood every word. He sniffed at the boy curiously.

"What happened to his legs and his tail?" Toby asked, hunkering down so he could pet him.

"Nothing." Charisse ruthlessly dumped out the last of her spring tonic and filled the bottle with water. "He's a Welsh Corgi. They're born with those ridiculously short legs and they don't have tails. He's from England."

"Gosh." Toby looked at Franklin with new respect. "I never met anybody from England before."

"I don't think there are many Corgis in the United States. He was a gift to my husband, but Preston and Franklin didn't care for each other much. That's how we wound up together. We've become best friends." Charisse stuck the blossom in the bottle and stepped back to admire the effect. "You know, that flower is exactly the touch this room needed. Where on earth did you find it?"

"Growing out back. There's a whole bunch of flowers out there. Is Franklin going to Oregon with us?"

"Of course." Charisse fervently hoped Mrs. Benson from

next door wouldn't miss a single flower from her spring garden.

"You know, Franklin," Toby said with a final pat, "I think we're going to be great friends."

Franklin licked Toby's hand, then plopped down on the floor with his back legs stretched out behind him and closed his eyes as though totally exhausted.

Toby's own eyes widened in shocked surprise. "Look how he's lying."

"Franklin always sleeps like that," Charisse said with a smile. "I think it has to do with his short legs."

Toby glanced up and caught sight of the cage. "Who's that?"

"Oh, that's Petey, my canary."

"Does he fly?"

"Only if I let him out of his cage, and I try not to do that."

Toby turned his bright inquisitive gaze her way. "Why not?"

"Because he'd fly away. Petey isn't tame like Franklin."

"Oh." Toby looked disappointed. "I guess we'd better leave the cage door closed then."

"Maybe you can help me take care of him," she said as she walked to the door. "What do you say, shall we go get some breakfast and then check our supplies?"

"I already ate with Pa," Toby said, putting his hand in hers. "But maybe Mrs. Benson would let me have another sweet roll."

Charisse smiled. "I wouldn't be at all surprised."

Forty-five minutes and two sweet rolls later, Charisse and Toby walked around to the back of the restaurant where Charisse's supplies were stored.

"I thought you had a wagon," Toby said.

"I do—it's with the mules. There's no room here and Mr. Tanner was kind enough to store it for me." She pulled the tarp off the supplies Mrs. Benson had allowed her to store under the eaves of the shed.

"Gosh oh fishhooks!" Toby exclaimed. "You have lots of supplies."

Charisse pulled a list and a short pencil out of her pocket. "We'll need all of this and more. I wasn't planning on three of us."

"Four with Franklin," Toby reminded her.

"Franklin may have to make do with table scraps. Let's see... eight pounds of baking soda." She made a check on her list.

Toby peeked into the sack. "What's that?"

"It makes biscuits rise. Eight pounds should be enough, but we'll need more flour." Charisse made a note on her list and went to the next item. "Are you sure your father will be back at noon?"

"I think so. Course he sometimes gets busy and forgets. He has a real important job, you know."

"Oh? What does he do?" Charisse asked curiously.

Toby wrinkled his forehead. "I'm not sure, but Grandfather says he works for the damn-fool government."

"It's not polite to say 'damn.'" Charisse frowned. Why would a man with a government job be going to Oregon Territory? It wasn't even really part of the country yet. Then again, maybe he'd quit his job and was going to Oregon to start a new life, as she was.

"What's this?" Toby asked, holding up a large porcelain jar.

"It's skin cream. I've heard the climate is very harsh in the West."

"Pa said that's why women don't like to go." He tipped his head to the side. "Will it keep your skin lily white?"

"I suppose it might if I had lily-white skin to start with. Here, put it back in the box so it doesn't get lost."

Toby nodded wisely. "It's probably one of those female fripperies Pa says men don't understand."

"I have no doubt you're right. See if you can find the salt. I think I have two bags of it in here somewhere."

"We won't need this," Toby said, holding a bottle of iodine.

"You fixed my knee fine without it."

"Next time you might not be so lucky."

"I get hurt a lot," Toby confided. "Grandmother says it's because I'm too ram... ram..."

"Rambunctious?"

"That's it. It means I like to run up and down the stairs and slide on the banister when she has the Lady's Aide Society over for tea. What's this?" he asked, pulling a pad of paper out of a wooden lapdesk.

"That's my sketch pad."

"Golly," said Toby in awe. "Can I see?"

Charisse grabbed the book from his hands before he could open it. She wouldn't be able to stand the pain of his questions about the pictures that lay inside. "Let's put it away." The words came out more sharply than she intended, and she felt a pang of remorse at the flash of hurt in his eyes. "We'll never get finished if we stop to look at everything," she said in a milder tone. "What's in that box over there?"

Toby opened the box and peered inside, his hurt apparently forgotten. "Pots and pans. I guess they're for cooking, huh?" He glanced around at the piles of supplies again. "How do you know what we'll need? Have you been to Oregon before?"

"No, but I can read." Charisse opened a box and pulled out a worn volume. "This is my copy of The Prairie Traveler: Every Immigrant's Guide to the West. It's full of all kinds of important information. I just bought what was on the list of supplies."

"Holy cattails!" Toby was distracted by the contents of the crate. "Look at all those books. You must really like to read."

Charisse smiled to herself. Conversing with Toby was rather like trying to follow a bouncing ball. "I love to read. What about you?"

"Don't know how. Grandmother says it's 'cause I don't sit still long enough to learn."

"Maybe you never had the right teacher."

And so it went for the rest of the morning. Toby was a

bright bubbling spring of chatter that never seemed to run dry as he helped Charisse search the pile and take inventory. Finally, the last of the supplies were cataloged, and the list of extras they'd need was complete. Charisse sat on a packing crate with a satisfied sigh. The spring sunshine felt so good she pushed her bonnet back, closed her eyes and turned her face into the warmth. Her mind drifted along pleasantly as she listened to Toby's chatter with half an ear.

"Looks like the two of you have been busy."

Charisse's eyes popped open in startled surprise. Only one man had that gorgeous deep voice that sent gooseflesh darting up and down her arms. Luke stood less than a yard away staring at the mountain of supplies. His clothes were covered with dirt and a vicious scratch was visible through the ragged edges of his torn shirt sleeve. Blood oozed along its entire length from his wrist almost to his elbow.

"What happened to you?" she cried, coming to her feet in concern.

He glanced down at his arm and grimaced. "I found out why your driver quit after two days."

"Y-you did?" Charisse's heart sank to her toes. How in God's name had he found out she was a jinx in less than twenty-four hours?

"Those dad-blamed mules of yours would make the bravest man flinch," he said with disgust. "I spent a good three quarters of an hour being kicked, smashed against the corral fence, and tromped into the dirt. When I finally got them all hitched up, they refused to pull the wagon until I fed them all a pile of grain."

"You hitched them to the wagon?"

"That's the way it works, isn't it?" Luke removed his hat and wiped his brow with his undamaged sleeve. "I know they're faster than oxen, but are you sure the extra speed is worth it?"

Charisse dipped her handkerchief in the rain barrel and began to sponge the blood off his arm. "I didn't have much choice in the matter. There weren't any yoke-trained oxen to be had in St. Louis." Bathing his wound with gentle fingers, she marveled at the well-muscled forearm. It was completely outside her experience and surprisingly attractive. As she touched the warm brown skin, she felt an unexpected quiver deep inside, and called herself seven kinds of a fool. The last thing she wanted was a man, especially one that could flatten her without even breaking a sweat.

"Hopefully the mules will calm down once we get on the trail," Luke said. He winced as her movements became brisker but said nothing. Instead, he focused on the pile of supplies. "Looks like you two went shopping."

"No, we went through what I already had." She pulled the list out of her pocket. "This is what we still need."

Charisse studied him as he read down through the list. Though she found his rugged masculinity intimidating, she supposed there were those that would call him handsome. Those blue-green eyes were by far his best feature, though the thick, dark hair did wave down over his forehead and curl against his neck in a most enticing manner. A slightly crooked nose didn't detract from his looks at all. In fact, it gave him a slightly rakish air, if one found brawlers attractive.

"Are you sure we'll need all this?" he asked with a touch of doubt. "It seems like an awful lot."

Charisse nodded. "Since there are going to be three of us, we will. I only bought provisions for myself and a driver."

"She has a book," Toby put in. "It tells you everything you need to know about going west."

"Is that right?" Luke eyed her with sardonic amusement.

Charisse felt herself flush. "Maybe not everything, but it does have a good deal of handy information."

"And was probably written by some two-bit tinhorn who's never been farther west than the Hudson River." Luke's smile deepened. "You know, I find myself wondering why a young woman like yourself would want to go all the way to Oregon. Surely you could find a husband closer to home."

Charisse's recoil was instantaneous. "I'm not looking for a husband, Mr. McCabe," she snapped. "Quite the contrary, I'm running from one!" The blunt statement seemed to hang between them like a bad smell.

Luke's eyes widened in astonishment. "You're married?"

"Not any more. My husband divorced me over a year ago."

The silence was almost palpable. Charisse wondered why she hadn't tried to soft-petal her sordid past for him. Maybe she wanted to see how he reacted, or maybe she was tired of being apologetic.

Luke cleared his throat. "I still don't see why you think you need to go halfway across the continent."

Charisse sighed. "Divorce is a very difficult stigma for a woman to live with, Mr. McCabe. The last year has been a nightmare for me. In Oregon, I'll have a chance to start over again."

"What's diborsed, Pa?" Toby wanted to know.

"It means Miss—uh, Charisse—doesn't have a husband anymore."

"Oh. You mean he went away like Mama did?"

"Not exactly, but the end result is the same."

A small hand patted Charisse's arm comfortingly. "It's all right, Charisse," Toby said. "Me and Pa will take care of you."

Charisse smiled down at him. "Thank you, Toby," she said, covering his hand with hers. As the small fingers tightened on her arm reassuringly, her conscience jabbed her. "I guess I should have told you about my divorce last night, Mr. McCabe. I'll certainly understand if you change your mind."

"Can't see how it has anything to do with us," Luke said. "Toby doesn't give a damn about your past, and neither do I."

"That's right, Pa," Toby chimed in. "I don't give a damn."

"Toby, a gentleman does not say 'damn,'" Charisse corrected him automatically, then colored slightly as she realized his father had said it first.

"There, you see? You're already doing the job I hired you for."

"That may well be, but if people on the wagon train find out I'm divorced, you and Toby will be painted with the same black brush as me."

"Nobody has to know."

Charisse shook her head. "That particular little piece of information has a bad habit of popping up at the most inopportune times."

"Toby, I left my pocket watch on the bureau in our room," Luke said suddenly. "Would you run and get it for me?"

"Sure thing, Pa." He was off like a shot.

Luke watched him go with a look of satisfaction. "There, we have about ten minutes before he comes back. I have an idea to discuss with you. It will take care of a lot of bothersome little details, like your divorce."

Charisse raised an eyebrow. "I can't say I ever thought of my divorce quite that way before."

"Maybe not, but it really has little relevance to the situation, after all. The fact we're both unmarried and traveling together does. It's bound to cause talk and draw attention."

"I suppose you have a solution."

"Of course," he said with a grin that reminded Charisse strongly of his son. "We could pretend we're married."

Charisse's hands curled into fists. For some reason, it hurt more coming from him than the countless others who had made similar proposals. "I should have known you'd be like all the rest. Divorced does not mean I have no morals."

Luke blinked in surprise. "What are you talking about?"

"I do not intend to sleep with you or anyone else!"

"You thought that was what I meant?" Luke was clearly aghast. "Good Lord, an entanglement with a woman is the last thing I want or need."

"It wouldn't be the first time a man saw my lack of social acceptability as an excuse to make a conquest of me," she said bitterly.

"All the more reason to pretend we're married." His tone of voice was completely reasonable and Charisse narrowed her eyes.

"What exactly do you have in mind?"

"It wouldn't be difficult to act like a married couple," Luke said, warming to his theme. "We'll be traveling together, sharing the responsibility of Toby, and splitting the work. About the only other thing married couples do is fight, and I don't suppose anybody will notice if we skip that part."

"I don't imagine it would be too difficult to have a loud argument occasionally to keep people from getting suspicious," Charisse said caustically.

But her sarcasm was lost on Luke. He gave a satisfied nod. "That's the spirit. I knew you'd see the logic of it. Besides, you've managed to keep Toby occupied for an entire morning without having to resort to violence."

"It's merely a matter of keeping him interested."

"Nobody else has been able to do it."

Charisse glanced at him in exasperation. What he was suggesting was preposterous. They hardly knew each other. How could they convince the world they were married? And yet, the thought of leaving the humiliation of her divorce behind was so very tempting.

Luke glanced around at the piles of supplies. "Are these ready to load?"

"I guess so."

"Good, we should be able to get everything into the wagon before lunch."

"But I thought our wagon train wasn't leaving until Friday."

"It's not. We're moving to a new hotel."

"What in the world are we doing that for?"

"You'll be closer to Toby, for one thing. It will make life a whole lot easier for all of us if I have to leave early in the morning or get back late in the evening. Our hotels are only a few blocks apart, but it's still damned inconvenient."

"Why don't you and Toby get a room here?"

"There weren't any. I couldn't get you one at our hotel

either. Besides, think how this will help our deception. As far as anyone will know, we just pulled into town, and we'll have several days to get used to being Mr. and Mrs. McCabe before we leave for Oregon."

She gave him a sharp look. "Mr. McCabe—"

"Don't worry, I got two rooms. Toby will bunk with me, and you'll have the other room to yourself. The desk clerk assumed the extra room was for our son."

"You're certainly taking a lot for granted! What if I don't agree to this charade?"

He shrugged. "Then you'll register under your own name."

Charisse frowned. If she registered under her own name, there would be little point in changing hotels. Either he was very certain she'd fall in with his plan, or he had an ulterior motive she couldn't even guess.

"Here's your watch, Pa!" Toby called as he rushed around the corner of the hotel and raced across the open ground toward them. "You want me to go check on Franklin, Charisse?"

"Thank you, Toby, but I'm sure he's fine. He's used to being alone in my room."

"Franklin?" Luke raised an eyebrow questioningly.

Toby nodded enthusiastically. "He's from England, Pa, and he's Charisse's best friend. She says he's coming to Oregon with us, and I'm glad 'cause we're friends already."

"Is that so?" The eyebrow raised another notch.

"He has the shortest legs I ever saw."

"That's not a very nice thing to say about someone, son."

"It's all right, Pa. It's on account of him being a wet corky."

Luke blinked. "A wet corky?"

"Yep, and he doesn't have a tail either."

"No tail," Luke repeated faintly.

"He sleeps funny, too."

Luke gave Charisse a suspicious look. "I thought your driver disappeared."

Charisse bit her lip. Preston always said her perverse sense of humor was one of her worst traits. Strange how hard it was to resist that streak of mischief after Luke McCabe suddenly decided to rearrange her life for her. "Oh, I don't think it would be wise to let Franklin drive," she said with a touch of consternation. "He's much too young."

Luke frowned. "Just how old is Franklin?"

"I'm not exactly sure, but I think about six."

"You think six! And you left him alone in your room?"

"He's not alone, Pa," Toby said. "Petey's there with him."

If anything, Luke's frown became darker. "And how old is Petey?"

"Two."

"You left a six-year-old and a two-year-old alone?" Luke said sharply.

She shrugged. "They were tired."

"Of all the irresponsible—"

"Pa, it's all right." Toby gave his father an uneasy glance. "Franklin and Petey can stay by themselves."

Charisse nodded. "They do it all the time. In fact, I think they kind of enjoy the time to themselves."

"How convenient."

"Franklin's a really good dog, Pa," Toby said. "You'll like him."

"A dog?"

"Of course," Charisse said with wide-eyed innocence. "And Petey's a bird. What did you think?"

The corner of Luke's mouth quirked with sudden understanding. "Forgive my ignorance. I confess, I've never heard of a wet corky before."

Charisse gave him a sweet smile. "Actually, Franklin is a very friendly Welsh Corgi."

"Ah, of course, I should have realized," he said sardonically. "Tell me, Miss Jones, is there anyone else I should know about, a pet elephant, perhaps, or a cobra?"

"No, but don't you think you'd better start calling me Charisse? People will think it pretty odd if we don't call each other by our given names."

Luke's face brightened. "Then you'll do it?"

"I have to admit it makes good sense," she said.

"Are there any other little details you've forgotten to tell me?"

Charisse pretended to consider the matter. "None that I can think of."

He gave her a speculative look. "There is one thing I'd like to know, though."

Something in his expression caused her stomach to flutter in the oddest way. "What's that?"

"Just exactly what color are your eyes?"

"I beg your pardon?"

"Your eyes. Last night, I could have sworn they were gray, but now I can't decide if they're blue or green."

"Could be either, or any shade in between for that matter. They change with what I wear. My husband always said they were my least distinguished feature."

"The man was an idiot." Luke picked up her box of books and hoisted it to his shoulder. "I happen to like your eyes."

"I... thank you."

He gazed at her for a moment longer. "Changeable eyes, and hair the color of polished mahogany," he said softly. "Who would have guessed?" With a shake of his head, he turned and walked down the alley toward the waiting wagon.

Charisse stared after him in startled surprise. "Who indeed?"

CHAPTER 3

"How much more do we have to load?" Luke asked as Charisse carried a sturdy oak box to the wagon.

"This is the last of it except for the things in my room, and there isn't much of that." She struggled to hand the heavy box up to him. "Put this somewhere safe."

"I have just the spot for it." He turned the box sideways and shoved it down in a gap between two barrels.

"Be careful with that!" Charisse said, her throat tightening in alarm. "That's my grandmother's china."

Luke didn't even glance her way as he used the heel of his boot and the power of a good hard kick to wedge the box in tighter. "Don't worry, it's not going anywhere."

"But—"

"Look," he said, lashing the two barrels down with a rope. "I've packed wagons with everything from cornmeal to explosives. I haven't lost a load yet." He tied the knot securely and jerked on the rope to make sure it was tight. "Your dishes will be fine."

"For your sake I hope so, because if anything in that box gets broken, I'm holding you personally responsible."

His only response was a grin as he jumped down from the wagon.

"Pa, can we go eat now?" Toby asked plaintively.

"You know, that's not a bad idea, Sprout," he said, ruffling his son's hair. "What about you, Miss—uh—Charisse? Are you hungry?"

"Famished."

Luke glanced at the mules who stood docilely at the front of the wagon. They all looked half asleep in the shade of the building. "I guess the wagon will be all right here for a while. Let's go get a bite of lunch."

The three of them walked the short distance to Benson's Restaurant and made their way to a table in the back. Luke pulled out a chair and gave Charisse an expectant look. Charisse felt herself blushing like a school girl as she took the seat and allowed him to push her chair in. She couldn't remember the last time a gentleman had done that for her, especially one as attractive as Luke McCabe. He took his seat on the other side of the table and scanned the restaurant. Charisse glanced involuntarily over her shoulder. "Are you expecting someone?"

"No, of course not. I think I'll have Mrs. Benson's famous roast beef dinner. What about you?"

Charisse nodded. "It's my favorite."

"How about you, son?" he asked Toby with a smile.

"It's my favorite too," Toby said, then frowned. "Do I have to eat vegetables?"

"Only if you want to grow up big and strong," Charisse told him.

Toby looked doubtful. "Vegetables do that?"

"Absolutely."

"But Pa doesn't eat them."

"I'm as big as I need to be," Luke said. "I ate what I was supposed to when I was your age."

"Of course, you did." Charisse couldn't quite keep the note of sarcasm out of her voice. She doubted Luke McCabe had ever done a thing he hadn't wanted to, even as a child.

He flashed her an unrepentant grin. "Don't worry, Toby, from what I understand there won't be much in the way of vegetables for the next few months. They're pretty hard to come by along the trail."

"Really?" Toby brightened considerably.

"All the more reason for us to eat them today," Charisse said primly, then had to bite back a laugh at the look of dismay that flashed across Luke's face. It made him seem more human somehow, less intimidating. As he ordered three roast beef dinners, her gaze wandered over the rugged planes of his face, down the strong column of his neck to the broad shoulders and wide chest. He was so different from the men she knew. Perhaps that's why he inspired such strange feelings in her, a deep quivery awareness that wasn't altogether unpleasant. There were times when she found herself actually anticipating the long trip to Oregon in his company.

Luke turned to her with a warm smile when the waitress left. "How much do you want for your rig, Charisse?" he asked.

"What?"

"I want to buy the wagon, mules and all the supplies."

She stared at him in shock. "You expect me to sell everything to you?"

"That's right."

Charisse's stomach gave a painful twist. So much for thinking he was different. He certainly didn't waste any time trying to take control. "It's not for sale. I went to a lot of work getting that wagon this far, and it's not going to Oregon without me."

"Without you?" Luke looked confused. "Good grief, I spent all that time making sure your grandmother's dishes would make the trip. Does that sound like I'm planning to go without you?"

"Why else would you want to buy my wagon?"

"So I can transport my son and myself to Oregon. Surely you don't think I'd let you absorb the cost. What kind of man do you take me for?"

"I hadn't really thought of it that way." Charisse frowned as she picked up her fork and rubbed it absently. Manly pride: Lord, but she was sick of it. "If you're serious about this, I could sell you half interest. That way neither of us would have to feel beholden to the other."

"You mean like partners?"

Charisse nodded. "Exactly."

"Partners with a woman," Luke murmured. "Can't say I've

ever done that before."

Charisse raised her chin with a touch of belligerence. "It's the only thing that makes sense. This way we'll both have a grubstake left when we finally get to Oregon."

"You have a good point there. All right," Luke said, after due consideration. "I figure your rig and all your supplies are worth about a thousand dollars, so I'll pay five hundred."

"It's closer to twelve hundred, and I'll take six."

After a moment of stunned silence Luke laughed. "You drive a hard bargain, don't you?"

Charisse sighed and propped her chin on her hand. "It's one of my worst faults."

"I'd hardly call it a fault."

"My husband thought it was unladylike to haggle over prices like a fishwife. He hated it almost as much as what he called my 'twisted' sense of humor."

"The more I hear about the man, the less I like him."

The waitress arrived with their dinners and saved Charisse from having to comment. "Mrs. Benson says she's sorry, but we're out of carrots. She sent you some of her parsnip pudding instead. It's her specialty."

"I—I'm sure that will be fine," Charisse said, trying to subdue the bubble of laughter that rose in her throat. The twin expressions of dismay that crossed Luke's and Toby's faces were priceless. The waitress might as well have announced she expected them to eat cabbage worms and stinging nettles.

"Pa, is parsnips a vegetable?" Toby asked as he stared at the yellowish paste on his plate.

Luke picked up his spoon and poked at the pudding with ill-concealed disgust. "Only to people who enjoy seeing others suffer. Don't worry, son, no one actually eats it." He looked up as a small snort escaped Charisse.

She bit the inside of her cheek and opened her eyes a trifle wider. Luke's own eyes narrowed in response. Apparently, her feigned innocence didn't fool him.

"Are we going to say grace, Pa?" Toby asked suddenly.

"Grandmother says you have to, or else the devil will make you sick."

Luke's eyes narrowed even further. "Your grandmother is an interfering old — "

"I think that's a good idea," Charisse said hastily. "Do you think you could say it for us, Toby?"

Toby puffed out his chest a little. "Course I can." He grasped both his father's and Charisse's hands and waited expectantly.

The two adults exchanged a slightly embarrassed glance, then Luke took her hand and bowed his head.

As Toby's voice rose and fell in a litany of the familiar blessing, Charisse was conscious of the solid warmth of Luke's palm. The quiet strength of his hand and the slightly rough skin beneath her fingers were quite unlike Preston's well-manicured grasp. It was pleasantly stimulating and oddly reassuring. For an instant she felt connected, as if the three of them truly were a family.

When the prayer ended, she reluctantly removed her hands and reached for her spoon. She was vaguely surprised to note it shook slightly as she raised it to her mouth.

"I suppose you like parsnips," Luke said with disgust.

Charisse didn't know what he was talking about until she realized she was eating the infamous parsnip pudding.

"As a matter of fact, I love them. I've never had them made into a pudding before, but it's delicious!"

"I'm sure it is," he said sarcastically.

An expression of amazement crossed Toby's face as he watched Charisse eat her second and third spoonfuls. "How come you can eat your dessert first?"

"My dessert?"

"You're eating your pudding."

Charisse laughed. "That's because it's more like mashed potatoes than a real pudding. Besides, they gave it to us instead of carrots."

"You mean if it's made of vegetables, it's all right to eat it first even if it's pudding?" Toby asked.

"Something like that."

Toby gazed down at his plate for a moment, then cautiously took a small bite of parsnips. A look of surprise crossed his face. "Hey, this is pretty good."

"That just goes to show you shouldn't judge something by the way it looks," Charisse said with a smile.

Luke gave her a speculative look. "I was just thinking that myself."

Charisse knew darn well he wasn't referring to parsnip pudding, but she just smiled and continued to eat her lunch. The rest of the meal passed in pleasant camaraderie with both adults answering a constant stream of questions from Toby.

"How long will it take you to pack the rest of your things?" Luke asked as they rose to leave.

"I don't know. Half an hour, maybe."

"All right. I'll get the wagon, then come back and get you."

Toby looked back and forth between them. "I guess I'll stay with Charisse."

"Good choice, son. You'd be bored to flinders with me." Luke put on his hat and glanced at Charisse. "We'll figure on meeting in front of your hotel in about forty-five minutes then."

"Sounds fine."

Toby asked Charisse question after question as she completed her packing and checked out of the hotel. He carried Petey's cage outside and set it on the bench next to Charisse, then sat down on her other side next to Franklin. The time passed pleasantly enough but after nearly an hour, Charisse began to wonder what had happened to Luke. She was just starting to worry when he finally appeared.

Even halfway down the street, Charisse could see the dark scowl on Luke's face. As the wagon moved slowly closer, it was easy to see why. Every few feet the mules stopped and refused to move until Luke flicked his whip over their backs again. He was at the end of his patience, his anger held in check—but just barely.

Intent on watching Luke, Charisse didn't see Benson's black tom cat strut out of the restaurant next door, but Franklin did. In the blink of an eye, he was after it, barking at the top of his lungs. With a startled yowl, the cat streaked across the street with Franklin in hot pursuit.

The mules shied violently away from the small furry missile and the hysterically barking dog under their feet. As the cat shot up a lamppost on the other side of the street, the terrified mules turned back the way they had come. The wheel caught under the edge of the box, and the wagon teetered precariously for a moment before overturning with a crash. It bumped along behind for a dozen yards, spewing boxes and crates all over the street. The sound of splintering wood filled the air as the front wheels broke free and left the wagon box behind. For one heart-stopping moment, she thought Luke was underneath it. Then she saw him dragging along in front of the wagon wheels, the reins still wrapped around his hand in a desperate attempt to control the runaways.

A man ran into the street to stop the animals. Just when it looked as though the stranger might succeed, the mules swerved away from him, right toward a large water trough. The leaders pulled apart and ran on either side of it, smashing the wagon tongue against the end of the trough. The impact sent a wave of water cascading over the top, drenching everything in its wake, including Luke McCabe.

Dragging the weight of the water trough finally brought the mules to a stop, but not before the trough made a long, wet furrow in the street. Luke lay in the mud, face down and unmoving.

"Luke!" Charisse was on her feet and running down the street with Toby beside her before the word had cleared her lips. She didn't even glance at the wagon or the bits and pieces of her possessions; her only thought was to reach Luke.

As they pushed their way past the curious on-lookers, a string of curse words that would have made a sailor blush came from the depths of the mud puddle. Charisse didn't think she'd ever heard anything more beautiful in her life. "Luke, are you all right?"

"Hell no, I'm not all right." He struggled to sit up and wipe the mud out of his eyes. "I lost at least a yard of hide, not to mention nearly drowning."

"Why didn't you let go of the reins?"

"They got tangled around my hand. Besides, I didn't want to get run over by the wheels. Would you mind giving me a hand up?"

Another string of curses erupted as she helped him to his feet and more of his injuries made themselves known, though he was so covered with mud that it was impossible for Charisse to tell where he was hurt. She glanced down at Toby, who stared at his father with wide-eyed interest. *Probably memorizing all the words he's never heard before,* she thought. "Toby, would you please go find Franklin for me?"

He looked up at her. "But Pa—"

"He's going to be fine, but I'm worried about Franklin. He's never been loose in town before."

"I'll go find him," he said and raced off.

"Don't get out of sight," she called after him, then turned to Luke. "I'm sorry you got hurt," Charisse said.

"Accidents happen," he said, gingerly feeling for broken ribs.

Accidents happen. The words were like daggers in Charisse's soul. *Dear God,* she thought *she'd left her affliction behind with Preston and his criticism. This isn't my fault. There's no such thing as a jinx.* Charisse scrunched her eyes shut, concentrating on the litany running through her head. *Maybe if she said it often enough, it would be true.*

"Talk about lucky!" Luke said.

Charisse's eyes popped open. "Lucky! Are you crazy?"

"I'm in one piece, more-or-less, which is more than I can say for our rig." Luke nodded toward the wheels and tongue which were the only part of the wagon still hitched to the mules. "I must have an angel sitting on my shoulder today."

Charisse stared at him in astonishment. "You call this good luck?"

"Don't know what else you'd call it. By rights I should be dead." Luke rolled his shoulders experimentally and winced. "I'll tell you one thing, though. I've had it with those damn mules of yours. There is no way I'm driving them all the way to Oregon, even if I have to pull the wagon myself."

"I don't think you'll have to worry about it," she said miserably. "The wagon is a complete wreck."

"Not necessarily. There's usually a single pin that attaches the wheels to the wagon box. I suspect that's what broke." He looked up the street toward the wagon. It lay on its side twenty feet beyond the canvas top. "Well, I'll be damned," he said softly, then unbelievably began to laugh.

Puzzled, Charisse glanced over her shoulder at the chaos behind them. Her camp kitchen lay on its side, the contents a jumble of flour, sugar and cornmeal. Dozens of books lay strewn about, the crates they had come from smashed to kindling, and the bedding was scattered everywhere. "I don't find the sight of everything I own strung up and down the street very amusing," she snapped.

"Not quite everything," he said with a big grin. "I'll accept your apologies any time."

"What are you talking about?"

"Notice where Granny's dishes wound up."

For the first time, Charisse focused on what remained of the wagon and her jaw dropped in astonishment. Though supplies covered the street, strewn hither and yon, the wagon box wasn't quite empty. Even from this distance it was easy to see two barrels lashed securely into one corner, and the box of dishes nestled snugly between them.

CHAPTER 4

"Are we really leaving in the morning, Pa?" Toby asked, wiggling around on his chair.

Luke smiled. "Just as soon as I can get the team hitched and everybody loaded."

"Can we go see Bert, Lightning, Elmer, and Polly now, Pa?"

Charisse laughed. "It's almost dark outside. Tomorrow morning will be time enough for that. Right now, I'm going to take my time and savor my last civilized meal."

"Don't worry, son. You're going to see plenty of those oxen. They're going to be with us all the way to Oregon."

Charisse frowned. "I still think you could have gotten a better price for the mules."

"Not after Franklin got done with them. There wasn't a man left in town that didn't know about those knot-headed mules and how they practically destroyed our rig. I was lucky to find a buyer for them at all." Luke resisted the urge to smile as Charisse looked away. She was still mighty sensitive about the part Franklin had played in the accident. Of course, his own body was still rather sensitive about all the abuse it had taken, too. "Did you finish taking your inventory of the wagon?"

She nodded. "As best I could without unpacking the boxes. We really didn't lose much. Other than spilling things like the sugar, flour, and salt, it looked a lot worse than it was. I was even able to save most of that."

"You shouldn't judge things by the way they look," Toby added, mimicking Charisse.

"That's right," she said. "Looks can be deceiving."

And Charisse is a prime example of that, Luke thought as he sipped his coffee. He'd known her less than three days, and she'd already surprised him more times than he could count. Lord, what his wife Elizabeth would have thought if she knew he'd hired a woman with such a scandalous past to take care of their only son!

Of course, she'd be madder than Hades that he'd brought Toby here anyway. Not for the first time, he wondered if he'd been right to take Toby away from Elizabeth's parents because he didn't approve of their overly harsh discipline. If Luke had known this assignment was going to be any different than the last half a dozen others he'd had, he wouldn't even have considered it. Contrary to the popular image of Pinkerton detectives, he spent most of his time investigating ticket clerks and conductors for the railroads. Catching minor employees embezzling from their employers was rarely difficult or dangerous. It wasn't until he'd begun his investigation that he'd discovered this assignment was an entirely different kettle of fish. By the time he realized the danger, it was far too late to send Toby back to his grandparents.

Still, in spite of it all, Luke was pleased with the change he saw in his son. Once Toby escaped his grandparents' oppressive rule, the boy had blossomed. Instead of the small fidgety child who had displeased his grandparents so much, he'd become a spirited little boy filled with boundless energy and insatiable curiosity. Since he'd been spending every waking minute with Charisse, Toby had improved even more, and was the happiest Luke had seen him since Elizabeth's death.

Luke certainly couldn't fault him there. Given half a chance, he might choose to spend all his time with the lady himself. Charisse Jones was easy on the eye. Still, it was more than looks that attracted him to her. Not many women would have the sheer spit-in-your-eye bravado it took to leave everything they knew for an uncertain future in Oregon. After years of dealing with his wife's feminine helplessness, he found Charisse's independence as refreshing as her sharp wit and sense of humor. Of course, she was also strong-willed, obstinate, and more than a little feisty. It all made for an unusual combination, one that intrigued him. She was a woman he would gladly call a friend…or a lover.

The thought gave him pause. *Now where had that come from?* The last thing he needed was a case of rampaging lust. No matter how delectable she was, or how agreeable the thought of bedding her might be, it was a distraction he could ill-afford. Besides, she'd already told him what she thought of men on the prowl. She was more likely to rip his head off and serve it to him on a platter than share his bed.

"I think I'll make one last check before I turn in," he said, setting down his empty coffee cup.

Toby looked up eagerly. "Can I go with you, Pa?"

Luke shook his head. "Not this time, son. It's almost bedtime, and we already decided you were going to spend the night with Charisse since I have to get up early tomorrow."

"Oh, Pa…"

"Don't worry, Toby, you aren't missing anything," Charisse said. "Your father is going to do the boring last-minute things like tighten the canvas over the load. Anyway, our dessert will be out soon and you wouldn't want to miss that. I think it might be chocolate cake."

Toby brightened. "That's my favorite."

"You two enjoy your dessert then," Luke said with a smile as he picked up his hat and got to his feet. "I'll see you both bright and early in the morning."

As Luke walked away, he heard Charisse tell Toby they might as well share his father's cake since he didn't want it. Luke grinned to himself at his son's enthusiastic agreement. Leave it to Charisse to make Toby glad he was being left behind. It was nothing short of amazing how well she managed the boy. If she could keep it up out on the trail, the woman would be worth her weight in gold.

Dawn was an hour away as Luke crept down the alley, a

darker shadow in the inky blackness next to the building. He could barely make out the man ahead of him, but elation flowed through him like the effervescence of a good wine. It was the first time since Luke had started watching him that Joshua Simms had made a move that didn't fit the image of the perfect family man. Proof, at last, that McNesby hadn't sent him on a wild goose chase.

He sank back out of sight as Simms suddenly stopped and scanned the area furtively. There was no reason to think anyone else was prowling around this time of night. Yes indeed, Mr. Simms' behavior was most suspicious. The faint sound of clinking keys reached Luke before the man disappeared into the building.

Luke moved quietly along the wall to the door. He wasn't surprised when the door knob didn't turn. So, Simms doesn't want any uninvited observers. Too bad, Luke thought as he pulled a set of skeleton keys from his pocket and inserted one into the lock. On his third key, there was a barely audible click, and the door opened. He pushed it inward a crack and listened intently. A heartbeat later he was inside.

Luke found himself in a small reception area containing a desk and very little else. This was probably where army personnel came to requisition supplies. With a cursory glance, he made his way silently to the other side of the small room where a sliver of light shone beneath the door. Luke squatted next to it and looked through the keyhole. All he could see was part of a table and a lamp with the wick turned low. No sound penetrated the heavy oak door. There was no way of knowing where Simms was, or what he was doing.

Typical. According to Luke's briefing at the beginning of this investigation, no one had ever known for sure what was going on. When a minor clerk at the army depot in Independence had discovered some discrepancies in the supply records, he suspected foul play. Instead of telling his immediate superiors, who might well be involved, he went straight to his uncle, Matt McNesby. The clerk was young and inexperienced, so McNesby wasn't overly concerned, but had decided to check it out. Reluctant to use his own government agents to spy on other government employees, he'd gone to his old friend Allen Pinkerton. It wasn't the first time he'd used Pinkerton agents to investigate inconsistencies inside the government where he felt his own agents' loyalties might be split, and Luke had worked with McNesby on numerous occasions.

Though McNesby tended to view every situation as a threat to the welfare of the nation, he had an uncanny knack of finding what others missed. Once again, McNesby's instincts had been correct. Luke came to Independence expecting to find a clerical problem and had discovered ledger entries that changed from one day to the next with no sign of tampering. It wasn't simple thievery; the numbers went up as often as they went down, and there seemed no rhyme nor reason to it. It hadn't taken long to discover Joshua Simms was the man behind it, but Luke had never been able to figure out how he was doing it, or why. Since the depot was responsible for the supplies for most of the government outposts west of the Mississippi, McNesby was convinced whatever was going on was a matter of national security.

When Simms announced he was quitting and moving to Oregon, McNesby ordered Luke to continue his surveillance and discover what sort of plot was afoot.

Going to Oregon was about the last thing Luke McCabe wanted to do. Normally he wouldn't have minded, but having Toby along changed things. Through the entire week while they prepared to go, Luke kept hoping Simms would slip up somehow and they could pin something on him. Unfortunately, since Luke had been watching, he'd done nothing that wasn't completely normal. Until tonight.

Now, when it appeared his luck had finally changed, Luke found himself on the wrong side of a door. *Damn, there must be some way to find out what's going on in that room. Maybe I could —*

Luke nearly sighed with relief as his quarry obligingly

walked in front of the door and sat down at the table with a ledger-type book. Using a penknife, Simms carefully removed the first hundred pages or so and laid them in a neat pile to one side. Then he pulled an identical book out of his coat and opened it on the table. Luke watched with dawning comprehension as Simms copied a few lines from several of the pages he'd removed. So that's how he was changing the entries. He was substituting a whole new ledger! The pieces of the puzzle were starting to fall into place.

Elated by the turn of events, Luke smiled in the darkness as Simms returned the substitute ledger. As soon as he got his hands on those pages and compared them to the ones in the book, he'd know what Simms was up to. Maybe there would even be enough to make an arrest. With any kind of luck, they wouldn't have to leave for Oregon after all.

The thought barely had time to flit across his mind before Simms picked up the extra pages, lifted the lantern glass, and set fire to them. Luke ground his teeth in frustration as Simms passed from sight again, and he heard the muffled sound of a stove door slamming. Damn! Just when things looked like they were going my way.

Luke ducked back out of sight as Simms came out of the inner office. Without even a glance around, he made his way to the outside door and disappeared into the darkness beyond. The door to the street had barely closed before Luke was inside the office. Though he knew it was probably futile, he took three long strides across the room to the pot-bellied stove and jerked the door open. Lady Luck hadn't deserted him after all. The pages that should have been reduced to a pile of blackened ash by now still smoldered in the firebox, the flames suffocated by a closed damper. Luke snuffed the sparks along the edges and carefully pulled what remained of his evidence out of the stove.

The left side of the pages crumbled at his touch, but even in the moonlight, many of the entries on the right-hand side were still legible on the scorched paper. He pursed his lips in a silent whistle as he read the figures. There were enough guns and ammunition to supply a small army. Other pages contained equally large quantities of black powder, lead, patches, and spare gun parts. It appeared McNesby's intuition was right. The supplies were either on their way to a buyer who couldn't openly purchase arms from the United States government, or the records had been falsified to show some army outpost had more guns and ammunition than it really did. Both possibilities were equally chilling. Without comparing these pages to the replacements, there was no way of knowing which it was, nor even for which fort the supplies were originally destined.

Luke sighed in frustration and squinted at his pocket watch. There was no sign of the original ledger; Simms must have taken it with him. Even if he knew which was the replacement ledger, he wouldn't have time to find the right pages and compare them. Nor was there enough here to make an arrest. Without all the missing information, there was no proof the records had been falsified. Simms could simply say he had corrected a mistake some clerk had made in figuring the monetary value of the munitions. Ironically, the falsified records would appear to prove his claim.

The best Luke could do was pass the information back to McNesby and keep an eye on Simms. Even with a handful of new information, he was no closer to knowing what was going on than before.

It wasn't until he was halfway back to the hotel that he remembered Charisse Jones and felt a flash of embarrassment. He'd been so focused on the possibility of bringing his investigation to a close, that he'd completely forgotten his commitment to drive her wagon to Oregon. Elizabeth always said dedication to his job was his besetting sin. The same single-minded concentration that made him a good Pinkerton man had also wreaked havoc on his marriage and prompted his in-laws to insist on raising Toby themselves.

It was probably a good thing he hadn't succeeded tonight. He had a feeling Charisse wouldn't let him back out of this trip to Oregon no matter what the excuse. A slight grin tugged at the corner of his mouth as he imagined himself chained to the yoke with the oxen. Though Charisse Jones was the perfect nanny for Toby, she was very likely going to be the devil to live with. Anyone who was foolish enough to tangle with that feisty nature of hers would have a real challenge on his hands. Luke's grin widened into a full-fledged smile. He'd always enjoyed a challenge.

CHAPTER 5

"Time to get up," Charisse said, shaking Toby's shoulder. "We're supposed to meet your father for breakfast, and we don't want to keep him waiting."

Toby yawned and glanced toward the window. "But it's still night."

"It only looks that way," Charisse said. "The sun will be up any minute. Come on now, out of bed. Have you forgotten what today is?"

"Gosh oh fishhooks! It's the day we start our 'venture!'"

Charisse chuckled as Toby jumped out of bed and scrambled for his clothes. While he dressed, she finished her last-minute packing. She put Franklin's dish in her bag as Toby buttoned his last button.

"I'm ready, Mama. Let's go."

An invisible band tightened around her throat. *Let's go, Mama. I don't want my party to start before we get there.* The memory came unbidden, cutting through her defenses, squeezing her heart. "Wh-what did you call me, Toby?"

"Pa said I should call you Mama."

It didn't take a genius to figure out why Luke had suggested it. If she'd been thinking, she'd have come up with the idea herself. Their little charade would never work if Toby called her Charisse, but of all the names for him to use... *'Mama, I'm so hot. Make it stop hurting.'*

"Are you crying?" Toby asked.

"No, I-I just have something in my eye."

"It's all right if I call you Mama, isn't it?" he asked doubtfully. "Pa said I was supposed to ask, but I forgot."

Charisse focused on the serious little face before her and

felt the band loosen a bit. It was only a name, after all. Toby looked so concerned that she bent down and gave him an impulsive hug. "Oh, Toby, I can't think of anything I'd rather have you call me."

As she said the words, she realized they were true. His lively chatter and bubbly personality had completely won her heart. Maybe in time he would help heal it. She stood up and dabbed the extra moisture from her eyes. "Now then, what about breakfast?"

Charisse wiped her hand across her brow and sighed. The stop at noon to eat and rest the teams had been hours ago, and she felt ready to drop. The wagons ahead stirred up a cloud of dust that sifted into her clothes and clogged her throat. She had discarded her hoops during the noon stop, but the relief had been temporary. Her corset stays had rubbed raw spots on her sides, her arms ached from driving, and her fingers were cramped around the reins. If only she could get down and stretch her legs a bit.

She envied Luke who walked next to the oxen, keeping them on the trail and teaching them commands they should already know. Charisse smiled to herself. The oxen had turned out to be less of a bargain than Luke had thought. The first sign of trouble had come when the animals took exception to Petey's cheerful song and tried to bolt. It wasn't until after Luke banished the canary to the back of the load that he discovered the oxen were only green broke and didn't know the first thing about pulling a wagon. Luke said he didn't care; he'd train them on the trail. He'd rather walk the oxen all the way to Oregon than drive those blasted mules another yard.

Charisse's smile softened as her gaze traced his broad shoulders and long legs. Luke moved tirelessly with smooth, ground-eating strides the likes of which she'd never seen before. The urge to capture all that masculine grace on paper was nearly overwhelming. In the eighteen months since she'd put her drawing materials away, she'd forgotten how intoxicating the creative urge was. Watching Luke all day had brought it back full blown. Charisse dismissed the odd little quiver she felt inside as a natural reaction. A man like Luke McCabe was as far outside her experience as a circus elephant. The arousal she felt was simply the artist in her responding to an exotic new subject.

"Mama, I'm hungry."

Charisse glanced down at Toby on the seat beside her. "We should be stopping for the night soon," she said.

"You said that an hour ago."

"Yes, and fifteen times since. I'm sorry, Toby, I can't make the wagon train go any faster than it is." Charisse frowned sympathetically as she watched Toby squirm. The wooden wagon seat was anything but comfortable. Her own backside felt as though it had been pounded with a board. Even Petey had stopped singing from his cage in the back of the wagon. "Maybe you can walk with your father for a while."

"Really?" Toby sat up and cupped his hands around his mouth. "Pa!" he yelled. "Can I walk with you?"

The loud noise sent all four oxen in different directions. A steady stream of curse words filled the air as Luke fought to control the startled animals. Petey sent up a frightened chirping which scared the oxen even more. Charisse had her hands full, hanging onto the reins with one hand and trying to keep Toby in the wagon with the other.

"This is no time to be gazing at the scenery," Luke yelled. "Pull them in, dammit!"

"I'm doing the best I can!" Charisse shouted back. "Toby, if you move one inch before I say you can, you're riding the rest of the way to Oregon in the wagon."

Toby looked at her face for a moment then scooted back onto the seat and sat with his hands folded in his lap until the oxen finally came to a stop. He had such an angelic expression on his face that Charisse's lips twisted in sardonic amusement. "It's a little late for that now," she said. "The damage has already been done."

He managed to look contrite for all of ten seconds. "Can Franklin and I go walk with Pa now?"

"You better leave Franklin here. I don't think your father is ready to forgive him yet." She glanced at Luke, who was calming the young oxen. "I guess it would be all right for you to go with him, though. Just don't spook the oxen and stay away from the wheels."

"Don't worry," he said, scrambling over the side. "My Pa will watch out for me."

"What are you doing?" Luke demanded, glaring back at Charisse.

Charisse smiled sweetly. "It's your turn to entertain him."

"I thought that was what I hired you for."

"You hired me to take care of your son and see to his needs. Right now, he needs to stretch his legs and work off some of that excess energy."

Luke looked down at Toby's hopeful face for a moment, then sighed and glanced back at Charisse. "All right, I guess he can walk with me till we stop for the night." He picked his hat up off the ground and jammed it back on his head. "Let's get moving before the wagons behind us have to stop."

Resisting the urge to stick her tongue out at his back, Charisse lifted the reins and gave the oxen the signal to go. As the wagon started again, she couldn't help wondering if the creaking and groaning came from the wheels or from her own poor, tortured body. Franklin whined from his place under the seat.

"I know, boy," she told him. "I feel the same way." With a weary sigh, she shifted her weight, trying to get comfortable on the hard seat. All she managed to do was move the discomfort to a different spot, one equally tired and sore.

The countryside rolled by, mile after dusty mile, until it all blended together in mind-numbing monotony. She'd been so worried about the dangers of the trail, she'd put her derringer in her satchel and stored it behind the seat within easy reach.

Little had she known the worst danger would be expiring from boredom. Charisse suspected the time would come when she yearned for the sight of the neat farms and small hamlets they passed, but right now she was too tired to appreciate it.

By the time they reached their camping spot for the night, she wasn't sure she'd be able to climb down from the wagon. With a deep sigh, she wrapped the reins around the brake lever and began her weary descent.

About halfway to the ground, strong hands grasped her around the waist and lifted her the rest of the way down as Luke's deep voice flowed around her. "Tired?"

"Heaven's no," she said sarcastically. "I'm fresh as a daisy. Aren't you?"

"Let's hope the wagon master was right when he said it only takes a couple of weeks on the trail to train young oxen," he muttered.

Charisse hid a smile. Oh, the temptation to remind him whose idea the oxen were and say, 'I told you so.' "Where's Toby?"

"Pestering a rabbit he saw when we drove up. I came to get the bucket so I can send him to the creek for water."

Charisse frowned. "By himself? What if he falls in?""

Then he'll get wet. It isn't much more than knee deep. Maybe we'll get lucky, and he'll tire himself out," Luke said, heading for the back of the wagon.

Charisse caught sight of her charge rapidly dodging between a man and the yoke of oxen he was trying to lead. "I wouldn't count on it," she said, lifting Franklin down from the wagon. He stretched, gave a huge yawn, then trotted off to join Toby.

By the time Luke found the bucket and rejoined her, Toby was running full speed around a large boulder. With no warning, he suddenly took a running leap at the rock and clambered over the top like a monkey before sliding down the other side and landing in a heap at the bottom. A heartbeat later he was on his feet racing toward something else that had grabbed his attention with Franklin at his heels.

Luke watched in silence for a moment, then cleared his throat. "Maybe I'd better go to the creek with him this first time."

"I think it might be for the best, at least until he knows what to do."

"By the way, I threw a couple of chunks of firewood in the back of the wagon this morning. It's right next to the box of kindling," he said over his shoulder as he walked away. "That should be plenty to get the fire going. Toby and I will look for more fuel down by the creek."

With her heart sinking, Charisse watched him leave. Get the fire going? How in the heck am I supposed to do that? She'd never even lit a cook stove. The Prairie Traveler had gone on at length about all the different ways of starting a fire even in inclement weather. Unfortunately, she'd been unable to locate the book since the accident. She looked around at her fellow travelers. Most of the men were either leading their teams down to the creek, or securing them in the makeshift corral formed by the circle of wagons. Several of the women were already lighting their fires and preparing to cook dinner. Charisse wondered uneasily if she was the only one who didn't know what she was doing.

She watched as the woman in the next camp coaxed a small flame out of a pile of kindling. In no time at all, a good strong fire was burning. That didn't look too difficult, Charisse thought as she fed Petey. It will be easy as pie, she told herself. No problem at all. She retrieved the wood from the back of the wagon and carried it to an open space near the front. It's simply a matter of getting the kindling burning first, and then piling on the larger wood chunks.

Just when Charisse was ready to kick the whole mess clear across the camp, a thin wisp of smoke began to rise from the kindling. She stared at it in disbelief for several seconds before dropping down to blow gently on the tiny glowing ember. Gradually it grew until a flame appeared and licked at the wood with a rapidly increasing appetite.

Charisse cautiously laid one of the larger pieces of wood next to the flame. It flickered ominously for a long tense moment, then caught and held. With a sigh of relief, Charisse rose to her feet and went to the wagon to retrieve her pan of beans. They had been sitting under the wagon seat all day soaking in a pot of water, just as The Prairie Traveler suggested.

It wasn't until she knelt to put the pan on the fire that she realized there was nothing to set it on. She balanced it on her leg as she cast about her for something to use as a support. A flat rock lay slightly behind her. That should do nicely, she thought. The pot wobbled a bit, but she managed to steady it with one hand while she retrieved the rock with the other. As she turned back to the fire, she suddenly found herself nose to nose with a large green frog. With a startled yelp, she jerked away and lost her hold on the handle.

"Isn't he great, Mama?" Toby said proudly. "I found him by the creek." His words were punctuated by a loud hiss as the pot of beans toppled into the fire.

"Oh Toby," Charisse murmured in dismay as she stared down at the smoldering remnants of her fire.

"This is all the wood I could find." Luke dumped a broken tree branch on the ground near the wagon. "Don't you think you'd better get the fire going?"

"It doesn't seem to want to burn," she said sarcastically.

Luke looked at the soggy pile of wood, then back to her face. "The wood's wet."

"No kidding."

"Why didn't you use the fire ring?"

"What?"

"The fire ring." Luke pointed to a ring of soot darkened rocks slightly to the right of the wagon. "It was probably left by the wagon train that stopped here last night. I've always found it a whole lot easier to start a fire in one than out on the ground. The rocks keep the wind from blowing your flame out."

"I don't suppose you thought to tell me all this before," she said.

Luke shrugged. "It never occurred to me I needed to. I figured you'd know all about starting fires from your book."

"The Prairie Traveler didn't mention fire rings."

"What a surprise." Luke didn't even try to keep the smug self-satisfaction out of his voice. "By the way, I think you should know your dog is about to eat what's left of our supper."

She swung around in time to see Franklin sniffing at the pot of beans less than an arm's length from Luke, who made no move to stop him. Charisse bit her lip and counted slowly to ten, then twenty under her breath. Keeping her temper curbed was something she had learned the hard way. There was no way she was going to let Luke McCabe shatter her hard-won control.

"Toby," she said in a deceptively calm voice. "Why don't you take Franklin and go play inside the ring of wagons where I can see you?"

"Sure thing, Mama. Do you want to keep my frog?"

She could see Luke's smirk out of the corner of her eye and had a sudden desire to turn the tables on him. "I appreciate the offer, Toby, but I really don't have any place to put him while I'm cooking supper. Perhaps your father..."

"Good idea. Here, Pa, don't squeeze him too tight."

A moment later, Toby and Franklin disappeared around the far end of the wagon.

"Just remember, stay where I can see you," Charisse called.

Luke stared down at the large, damp frog in his hand. "What the devil am I supposed to do with this?"

"You might want to get him in some water." Charisse allowed herself a slight smile as she bent to pick up the kettle. "He looks like he's starting to dry out."

As she straightened, she suddenly found herself wrapped in a pair of muscular arms and pressed against a very masculine body. She froze.

"Do you know what my family motto is?" purred a deep voice in her ear.

He rubbed his cheek against hers in a gentle caress, and Charisse's alarm melted away. "N-no."

"Never walk away from a challenge." His breath, soft against her neck, sent shock waves of sensation skittering along her already taut nerves. "Unless I much mistake the matter, you issued me a challenge."

"No, I—"

"It does leave me in a bit of a quandary though," that sinfully sexy voice continued as though she hadn't spoken. "I don't quite know what to do with a challenge from a woman, especially one that's posing as my wife."

The word "wife" sent another shock reverberating through her body and made her suddenly aware of every delicious masculine contour pressed against her.

"Luke—"

"Tell you what," he whispered as his lips brushed her ear. "I'll start the fire; you take care of the frog."

A heartbeat later the frog was in Charisse's hand and Luke was gone. Anger and humiliation burned in her face as the full impact of his chicanery hit her. He'd known exactly how his unexpected embrace would affect her and had used it shamelessly.

"You... You..." A dozen blistering epithets tumbled around in her mind, each one more biting than the last. She whirled around, intending to give full rein to her fury.

There he was, hunkered down next to the fire ring, carefully arranging the kindling as though he hadn't a care in the world. As she stood there, fairly bursting to give him a piece of her mind, a small flame appeared in his cupped hand. It licked at the wood for a moment or two then caught and held.

"Better get that frog in some water," he said, without looking up. "Wouldn't want him to dry out."

Gritting her teeth and telling herself it was worth it to get a fire going, Charisse turned toward the creek.

Luke grinned as he watched her go. It would be a miracle if she didn't choke on her own irritation. All because he'd followed an impulse to tease and managed to get the best of her in the process. Who would have thought Charisse Jones could be so unsettled by a little physical contact? She'd stiffened like a poker the minute he'd put his arms around her.

His smile faded as the memory of her pressed against him resurfaced with a vengeance. For some reason, he hadn't expected her to feel quite so... feminine. Nor had he expected to find himself fighting the urge to trace the length of her neck with kisses and explore the sensual delights hidden beneath the whalebone corset and thick layer of petticoats. Suddenly, the trail to Oregon seemed very long and fraught with dangers he hadn't even considered.

CHAPTER 6

Toby poked the beans on his plate. "How come some of these are hard?"

"For the same reason some are scorched," Luke muttered. He picked a charred lump from the beans on his spoon and flicked it into the fire. "I expect cooking over a campfire takes a bit of getting used to."

Charisse nodded. Now was probably not the time to admit her cooking skills were nonexistent with or without a campfire. How in the heck was she supposed to know she had to stir the darn beans while they were cooking? You'd think a cookbook would mention something that important. She didn't even have to look at Luke to know how he felt about their first meal on the trail.

"Where's the sugar?" he asked, staring down into his tin cup.

"Sugar?"

"Pa's partial to sugar in his coffee," Toby said.

"Oh, I'm afraid it's still packed." Charisse said. "Do you want me to get it?"

"No." Luke sighed and lifted the cup to his lips.

"Look, Pa, we've got company," Toby said eagerly, pointing to a man approaching from the west.

"You the McCabes?"

Luke gave the man a friendly smile. "I'm Luke McCabe."

It was impossible to tell if the man smiled back. His mouth was all but invisible beneath the bushy handlebar moustache. Charisse was so focused on the large knife he wore on his belt that she hardly heard his words. "The captain's called a meeting in half an hour."

Luke nodded. "We'll be there."

Without another word, the man turned and walked away.

Charisse shuddered. "Talkative sort, isn't he?"

"Probably didn't have time for friendly conversation." Luke grimaced and fished a chunk of something out of his mouth. "He said what he needed to say."

"He didn't even tell us what the meeting was about or where it was going to be held."

Luke gave up the pretense of trying to eat and scraped the remainder of his supper into the fire. "It's probably so everyone can get acquainted, and it shouldn't be too hard to figure out where it is. This isn't a very big camp, after all."

"Will those other boys we saw down by the creek be there?" Toby asked, bouncing up and down.

"I imagine so," Luke said.

"You should'a seen them, Mama. They look just alike. Pa and me thought we were seeing bubbles."

Luke chuckled. "He means seeing double. There's a set of identical twins who look about nine or ten. Toby, why don't you get your chores done so we can go to the meeting?"

"All right, Pa," he said, jumping to his feet. His half-eaten supper lay forgotten on the rock next to where he was sitting. Franklin ran over and sniffed at the beans, then turned away with a disgruntled expression on his face.

Charisse swallowed a sigh as she bent to pick up the abandoned plate. "What chores?"

"I gave him the job of pulling the bed rolls out of the wagon. It should keep him busy until it's time to go." Luke stood and stretched. "I'm sort of looking forward to meeting our neighbors."

"I'm glad someone is," Charisse murmured. Meeting the other women of the wagon train was about the last thing she wanted to do. "You know, I'm really tired. Maybe I'll skip the meeting and clean up around here instead."

Luke wasn't fooled for a moment. "You aren't going to be shunned, Charisse. Those days are behind you."

"Are you sure of that?"

"Positive. As far as anyone knows we're a happily married couple. They won't have any reason to think otherwise."

"I don't enjoy socializing."

"Fine. After tonight, you won't have to."

She stared at him for a long moment then nodded with a noticeable lack of enthusiasm and finished gathering the plates.

Luke watched her as she pulled the dishpan out of the wagon and filled it. Though Charisse obviously didn't have a very clear idea of how to wash dishes in such primitive conditions, this afternoon's little interlude made the notion of helping her muddle through seem less than prudent. Just thinking about the impromptu embrace sent the blood pounding through his veins. A case of sexual frustration was the last thing he needed right now. After a long moment, he went to help Toby with the bedding.

Toby stood at the back of the wagon frowning helplessly at the piles of supplies. He gave his father a frightened glance. "I...I can't find the bed rolls, Pa," he said with a hint of tears in his voice. "Please don't be mad."

Luke felt a pang as he realized Toby expected to be punished for his failure to locate the bedding. In spite of the inconvenience and possible danger, Luke was very glad he had removed Toby from his grandparents' home. Luke squeezed his son's shoulder comfortingly.

"I'm sure they're buried in here somewhere. Don't worry, we'll dig them out." Luke glanced at the heavy dark clouds overhead. "It looks like we could get some rain tonight. Maybe we'd better put up the tent, too."

"Tent?" Toby frowned. "I don't member a tent, Pa."

"I don't either, but surely...." Luke began rummaging around in the back of the wagon. "Do you remember a big piece of canvas like the one we have stretched over the top of the wagon when you helped Charisse go through the supplies?"

Toby looked doubtful. "I'm not sure."

They located the bedrolls quickly, but no tent. After several minutes of fruitless search, and a few descriptive phrases that would have raised Charisse's eyebrows had she heard them, Luke gave up. Charisse was finishing up the last of the dishes as he came around the front of the wagon. "All right," he said. "I give up. Where did you hide the tent?"

Charisse looked up in surprise. "Tent?"

"Yes, tent. You know, a shelter to keep the rain off our heads and the wild animals out of our bedrolls. I can't seem to find it."

Charisse looked stricken. "That's because there isn't one."

"Don't tell me, it's another of those things The Prairie Traveler forgot to mention," he said in disgust.

"Not exactly."

"What do you mean not exactly? Either the damn book said you'd need a tent or it didn't."

Charisse jaw tightened as she scrubbed harder on the pot. "It said to take an extra square of canvas in case of bad weather, but I figured I'd sleep in the wagon."

"Sleep in the... Lord, woman, have you looked back there? There isn't room enough for Toby to sleep! We'd have to unload half the wagon to make room for all three of us."

She stood and carried the pot past him to the wagon. "I know, but I didn't realize everything was going to fit so tight. I never thought about needing to buy the extra canvas after I saw how full the wagon was."

"Where the hell do you suggest we sleep?"

Charisse glared up at him. "Since when is it my job to solve all the problems around here?"

"You're the one with the book." He glowered back.

"Oh, as if you'd listen to any advice from The Prairie Traveler. You're the know-it-all. Why don't you come up with something?" If she were eight inches taller they'd be nose to nose. She didn't seem aware of his superior height, or the advantage it gave him.

"C...could we all sleep under the wagon?" asked a small frightened voice.

As one, Charisse and Luke glanced down at Toby, who stared up at them with a worried expression on his face. Their gazes lifted again and locked as a silent message passed between them. No matter what their differences, they'd call a truce for Toby's sake.

"You know, that's not a bad idea," Luke said. "We wouldn't have to set it up at night and take it down in the morning like a tent."

Charisse smiled. "Now that you mention it, I believe that's where my driver was going to sleep. I don't know why I didn't think of it myself."

"Come on, Pa." Toby tugged on Luke's sleeve. "Take a look."

Luke glanced at Charisse again. Her glare said clearer than words—the truce was for Toby's sake and didn't extend to him. Luke shrugged and hunkered down to peer under the wagon bed. "I don't know, son. This wagon is pretty narrow. There's no way all three of us will fit under it."

"Sure we will, Pa. You sleep here," Toby said, pointing to the right side of the wagon. "Charisse can sleep over there, and I'll sleep in the middle. We'll be as cozy as fleas on a dog."

"That's what I'm afraid of," Luke muttered to himself. "All right, let's go get the pallets."

By the time they'd located the pallets and carried them around to the side of the wagon, Charisse was tying Franklin to the back. Half expecting her to come up with another excuse to wiggle out of going to the meeting, Luke plucked her shawl from the wagon seat and draped it around her shoulders.

"Time to go."

"I suppose," she said with a resigned sigh. "Come along, Toby. We don't want to keep our neighbors waiting."

As much as he hated forcing Charisse into an uncomfortable situation, Luke needed her by his side tonight when he met Joshua Simms for the first time. Though he'd been careful trailing Simms, it was possible he'd been seen. It was imperative everyone's first impression be of a family man with a wife and child. Hopefully, Simms would think any fleeting recognition was a coincidence and never give it another thought.

As Luke had predicted, the meeting was easy to find. A dozen or so people were already gathered around a fire on the far side of camp. As they drew near, Toby tugged on his father's hand. "Pa, look, there's the twins, and they have a little brother!"

Luke had no trouble spotting the twins and their family on the fringes of the crowd as though they themselves had just arrived. Their father was easily the tallest man there. He topped Luke's own six feet by several inches, as did his older son who was only an inch or two shorter. The child who had drawn Toby's attention grabbed his father's hand and pointed to the McCabes.

The man looked down to listen to what his son was saying, then turned his head toward the newcomers. A wide, welcoming grin spread across his face. "Well, howdy folks." There was a hint of the deep South in his voice as he stuck out a beefy palm. "The name's John Jessup."

"Luke McCabe," Luke said, gripping the other man's hand. "This is my wife Charisse and our son Toby."

"Ma'am." John Jessup tipped his hat. His grin widened. "I'm mighty glad to see you. I was beginning to think I was the only one with young'uns on this train."

"I'm Morgan," said the youngest boy. Except for a patch of white blond hair peeking out from under his hat and light blue eyes, he looked very much like the darker-haired twins. The eldest brother appeared to be an exact copy of John Jessup. "And those are my brothers, Will, Matt, and Andy. Matt and Andy are twins. Do you want to see my snake?"

Toby's eyes grew round. "You have a snake? I had a frog, but it got away. Can we go see your snake?"

"Oh, I don't think—" Charisse began.

"Our rig's just over there," John said, pointing to the next wagon. "I'll send the twins along to keep them out of mischief."

Luke's profession called for an instant assessment of any situation, and a stranger offering to take his son anywhere constituted a situation. Still, as he sized up the man before him, gut instinct said John Jessup was what he seemed. A covert scan of the area revealed nothing in the way of a threat. Jessup could still be one of Simms' cohorts, but his son's offer was genuine and completely innocent. Luke relaxed.

"If your Toby is anything like my Morgan," Jessup said, "it might not be a bad idea to get them out from underfoot."

Luke chuckled. "Especially since ours seem to be the only children here. We wouldn't want to overwhelm anyone our first night out."

"Thanks, Pa," Toby yelled over his shoulder as he, Morgan and the twins raced off toward the wagon.

Charisse stiffened. "Toby..."

Luke glanced down at her in surprise. Her expression reminded him of a drowning woman going down for the third time as she stared after the boys. Without Toby for moral support, her resolution was wavering, and she looked ready to bolt. He gave her shoulder a squeeze, then dropped his hand to the middle of her back. "Come on," he said with a reassuring smile. "It will be over before you know it."

Joshua Simms hadn't arrived yet, but the rest of the company had. As they moved through the small gathering, Luke smiled, introduced them both, shook hands, and took mental notes on everyone there.

Pierre Jeveraux, the captain of the wagon train, was the first to greet them. "Mr. McCabe," he said, gripping Luke's hand and shaking it enthusiastically. "So glad you decided to throw in with us at the last minute. And this lovely creature must be your wife."

Luke nodded. "Yes, this is Charisse. Sweetheart," he said, pulling her forward slightly, "I'd like you to meet Pierre Jeveraux, captain of this wagon train, and our savior. I'd about given up hope of finding a train with room."

"I am delighted to meet you, Mrs. McCabe." The darkly

handsome Frenchman took her hand and bent over as though to kiss it.

Luke's eyes narrowed. He had liked the man when they'd met, yet now he seemed a bit too much, too handsome, too charming, spending too much time trying to impress Charisse. Not that she was interested.

"Captain," she said, extricating her fingers from his grip before his lips made contact.

He beamed at her. "Please, call me Pierre. I'm not a real captain, you know."

Charisse gave him a slightly nervous smile and started to step away. Luke caught her other hand and squeezed it reassuringly.

"We won't take up any more of your time," Luke said pleasantly. "Come along, dear. Let's go meet the rest of our neighbors."

And an interesting group they were. The swarthy Swindell brothers were friendly but looked more like professional gamblers than the store keepers they professed to be. Their wives didn't exactly fit the storekeeper image either. Even restrained in a respectable bun, Sadie's hair was an improbable brassy blonde, and Violet's voluptuous figure looked somewhat out of place in the simple cotton dress.

Henry Duncan and his sister Eliza, on the other hand, looked exactly like store keepers. What they didn't look like was siblings. Henry was short and bespectacled with thinning blonde hair, a sweet smile and an unhealthy pallor to his skin. Eliza was an inch or two taller and several stone heavier. Where Henry was slight, almost frail, Eliza was large and robust, with ordinary brown hair pulled back into a severe knot at the back of her head, and snapping hazel eyes. Her bosom was fully as impressive as Violet Swindell's, but where Violet gave off an air of blatant sensuality, Eliza Duncan made Luke think of his primary school teacher. Here was a woman you didn't want to cross.

Then there was Mrs. Mantella and her simple son, Robbie.

For the life of him, Luke couldn't figure out why anyone as old and crippled as Mrs. Mantella would venture into the Wild West with only her dimwitted son. Yet, here they were—Mrs. Mantella, dressed entirely in black and seated on her chair in the middle of the group like a wizened black crow. Her hulking son Robbie stood next to her, surveying the crowd with guileless blue eyes, never uttering a word. When Luke spoke to him and held out his hand to shake, Robbie blinked in confusion and shrank back from the proffered hand. Luke had the odd impression the young man was close to panic as he looked at his mother for guidance.

"Never mind Robbie," she said with a cackle and a wave of her hand. "He ain't much of a talker, and he don't take well to strangers. I expect he'll loosen up as time goes on."

Luke was very aware of Charisse' stiffening even more as they came to the next group, five men headed to the California gold fields together. George Bartell, with his handlebar moustache and mean eyes, looked like someone you might expect to see on a wanted poster. Except for height and hair color, James Cassex, Calvin Dempsey, Tom Nugent, and Jack Snyder were practically interchangeable. All were scruffy and unshaven, the type of rough men that drifted from job to job, working as cowboys, building railroad tracks, or panning for gold as the opportunity presented itself. Aware of Charisse's unease, Luke gave each a perfunctory hand shake and moved on.

Joshua Simms and his pretty young wife finally arrived, and the introductions began all over again. Simms was remarkable only because he was so very unremarkable. Of average height and build with medium brown hair and hazel eyes, he'd have passed completely unnoticed in a crowd. His wife, Caroline, however, was another matter entirely. With a wealth of lustrous dark hair, brown velvet eyes and a slightly dusky complexion, there was an earthy beauty about her that was hard to ignore.

Luke watched closely for any sign the Simms' already

knew any of their companions. Not so much as a flicker of an eyelash was out of place. Either Simms was working alone, or he and his wife were damn good actors.

Since they were standing on the perimeter of the group, Luke and Charisse were among the last to be introduced. Charisse returned Caroline's shy smile with a small one of her own. It was the most she had relaxed since their arrival. As he watched, Luke suddenly realized that if the two women became friends, he'd have far better access to the Simms' wagon.

Once the introductions had all been made, Pierre Jeveraux reminded them all of the rules of the wagon train, and told them what they could expect over the next few days and weeks. A few people asked questions. Then the meeting broke up and everybody went back to their wagons. Toby, Morgan, and the twins came racing out when they saw Luke and Charisse. All four children jabbered a mile a minute, fast friends already. They stopped long enough to get permission to go see Franklin and Petey, then dashed off again.

"Looks like Toby found some friends," Charisse said with a smile. "That's bound to make the trip more fun for him."

"How about you?"

Charisse raised a brow questioningly. "Me?"

"I think you should further your friendship with Caroline Simms."

"What friendship? I barely spoke to the woman."

"I know, but she seemed nice."

"Pretty, too."

Luke shrugged. "I suppose. What's that got to do with anything?"

"What indeed?" Charisse gave him an enigmatic glance, then closed her mouth in an unyielding line.

Luke resisted the urge to sigh. If that wasn't just like a woman. They all twisted a man's words around and found hidden meanings where none existed. Though he didn't have a clue what he'd done wrong, he had enough experience to know nothing he said at this point would do anything but make matters worse. Maybe he'd get lucky and the two women would decide to be friends on their own. They were close to the same age, after all. Surely the rigors of the trail would draw them together.

In the meantime, he had his work cut out for him. He couldn't help but wonder if he'd stumbled into a nest of rattlesnakes. All through the meeting, the conviction had grown that this was anything but a typical wagon train. Just the fact that it was so small and there were so few children was highly suspicious. Nearly as odd were the half a dozen single men who seemed to be traveling with only a pack horse and no wagon. Granted, many people traveled that way, especially when they were heading for the gold fields of California. Still, there seemed to be a rather large number of them for such a small train.

In fact, with the exception of the Jessup family, there didn't seem to be a normal group of people in the entire bunch. Any or all of these people might be accomplices of Joshua Simms. Even the wagon master, Pierre Jeveraux, wasn't above suspicion. He'd made too big a show of kissing Charisse's hand, in Luke's opinion.

Luke resigned himself to long nights of covert investigation over the next few weeks.

CHAPTER 7

Charisse gave Luke a wary glance as they crossed the wagon circle. His expression made her distinctly uneasy; it had been dark and brooding most of the way back from the meeting. In her experience, men had a tendency to take their temper out on whoever happened to be handy. She wasn't afraid of him precisely; she was just too tired to deal with a confrontation right now.

When they finally arrived at the wagon, the four children and Franklin were involved in a raucous game of tag. "Looks like everybody's having a good time," she said cautiously.

Luke's face cleared as if by magic, the forbidding frown replaced by a sunny smile. "At least we don't have to worry about Toby being too rambunctious for them."

"No, I imagine the Jessups can handle anything he comes up with," Charisse said. "They all seem pretty well matched."

"True enough. Even Franklin's having fun. Well," he said, shifting his attention away from the children. "I'd best see to getting our beds ready."

"Fine. I need to locate a few things in the wagon."

Luke nodded. "All right, which part do you want me to open up for you?"

"I'm not really sure. Things got kind of mixed up after the wreck. I guess the back would be the best place to start."

"What exactly are you looking for? Maybe I've seen it."

"Oh, nothing in particular. I just wanted to find a few things we'll be needing." Charisse wasn't about to admit she'd lost *The Prairie Traveler*. Luke would probably laugh himself silly.

"While you're looking, see if you can locate the sugar,"

Luke said as he unlashed the ropes that tied the canvas down over the load. "I hate drinking coffee without it."

"All right." She moved to the back of the wagon, lifted the lid off the first box and started to dig. Thirty minutes later the light was fading and frustration was setting in. She'd found Toby's ball, Franklin's sleeping blanket, her lap desk, and even a bottle of whiskey she'd brought along for medicinal purposes, but there was no sign of Luke's sugar or her book. She scanned the piles of boxes and barrels filling the wagon. Even if she had all night, it would be nearly impossible to look in every one.

"What's the matter?" Luke's deep voice startled her out of her contemplation.

"Nothing really." She sighed. "I guess I just never thought what it would be like to live out of the back of a wagon for six months. It's rather daunting."

"I expect we'll get used to it." Luke seemed ill at ease as he took off his hat and ran his fingers through his hair. "It'll be dark soon."

"Yes, I suppose it will."

Luke shifted from one foot to the other. "It's time I took the Jessup children back to their wagon."

"They probably know the way," Charisse said, giving him a puzzled glance.

"I thought...well, Toby and I..."

Charisse frowned. What on earth ailed the man? He was blushing, for heaven's sake. "Is there something wrong?"

"No...I just...Oh, hell." Luke jammed his hat back on his head. "How much time do you need?"

"For what?"

"To get ready for bed."

It was Charisse's turn to blush. "Oh, I hadn't thought...that is...um... would half an hour be all right?"

"Fine," Luke said. "We'll be back in half an hour."

Charisse was touched by his kindness. It hadn't even occurred to her she might have some trouble attending to her dressing and undressing with two males around.

Her smile faded. If she was going to have any privacy to take off her clothes, she was going to have to clear a space in the wagon. With a resigned sigh, she began pulling boxes out and piling them on the ground. It took a long time to clear a space big enough to stand in. By the time she lugged her satchel back from the front of the wagon and clambered into the cleared space, she was breathing hard. She frowned as she reached up and pulled the piece of canvas down. It didn't quite cover the opening, but it was going to have to do.

Charisse's breathing gradually slowed as she removed her dress and began working the hooks on the front of her corset loose. When the last of the hooks gave way and she was able to slip the corset away from her body, she gave a final sigh of relief. With a grimace, she rubbed the tender spots where the stays had cut into her. Tomorrow she'd try padding those spots and see if it helped.

She pulled the pins from her hair and let it fall down her back in a soft blanket. Charisse had always loved the feel of her hair against her skin. The long silken strands caressed the bare skin softly as she tipped her head back and ran her fingers along her scalp.

"Mama, Mama, where are you?"

Charisse jumped in startled surprise as Toby's voice sounded right outside the wagon. There was an underlying urgency in his speech that went straight to the pit of her stomach. Had something happened? With her heart jerking in panic, she wrapped the canvas flap around her chest and held it against her body with her left arm as she leaned out of the back of the wagon. "I'm right here, Toby," she said. "What's the matter?"

"Franklin almost caught a rabbit..." His voice trailed off and his eyes widened in shock. "How come you aren't wearing any clothes?"

Luke stalked around the back of the wagon. "Toby, I thought I told you to leave Charisse alo—"

If Toby's expression was shocked, Luke's was

thunderstruck. His Adam's apple bobbed up and down a couple of times, but no sound came out. He seemed incapable of speech.

As he stared at her in open-mouthed silence, Charisse became very conscious of standing there in only her shift and drawers. "I…I was getting ready for bed. I'll be finished in a few minutes."

"Won't you get cold sleeping like that?" Toby asked curiously.

Toby's ingenuous question seemed to snap Luke out of his stupor. A dull red blush climbed his face. "I'm…. uh… I mean, we're sorry. We didn't intend… Come on, Toby. Let's give Charisse some privacy."

"But Pa, I wanted to tell her about Franklin."

"You can tell her later," Luke said severely, as he dragged his son around the side of the wagon.

Charisse watched them go, her heart slowing to its normal rhythm as he stalked away. Somehow, seeing the self-possessed Luke McCabe so discomfited reduced her own embarrassment. With a small smile, she lowered the canvas and finished undressing.

As she slipped the cotton nightgown over her head, Charisse suddenly realized she didn't have a clue where her brush was. Normally she'd give her hair a hundred strokes before bed, but tonight she was far too tired to worry about it. Instead, she pulled her hair into a single thick braid and tied it off.

Thankful for the concealing folds of her blue chintz robe, Charisse pulled it on and belted it about her waist. The thought of sleeping outside was a little alarming, but she supposed she'd adjust. It was just one more thing she had never considered when she decided to make the trip out west. She paused for a moment then opened her satchel, removed the derringer, and tucked it into the pocket of her robe. She felt a little silly for being so nervous, but the weight of the gun was comforting against her leg as she covered Petey's cage for the night. The canary gave a sleepy chirp, and Charisse smiled. Riding in the back of the wagon didn't seem to have done him any harm.

With a yawn, she picked up Toby's nightshirt and stepped down from the wagon. "Toby," she called, hoping he and his father hadn't gone too far away.

Just as she was wondering if they were out of earshot, Toby and Franklin came tearing around the side of the wagon. "Here I am, Mama. I was helping Pa get some wood for the morning, but I thought I heard you call me."

"You did. It's high time you got ready for bed. We'll be getting up early and we have another long day ahead of us tomorrow."

Toby looked at the nightshirt in her hand then up at her face. "I wanted to tell you about Franklin and the rabbit."

"And I can't wait to hear about it. Now, why don't you hop up into the wagon and tell me what Franklin did while you're changing?"

She was rewarded with a heartwarming grin. Toby was still chattering excitedly when he climbed out of the wagon dressed in his nightshirt and ready for bed.

Charisse smiled to herself as he bounced around the corner of the wagon. "You sleep here next to me," he said, crawling into his bedroll as Franklin investigated the other two, "and Pa will sleep over there. We'll be as cozy as three caterpillars in a cocoon."

Charisse hoped he was right. She had never slept on the ground before, but her bed looked surprisingly inviting. As tired as she was, she thought she could probably fall asleep on a boulder if she had to. Apparently approving of Charisse's bed, Franklin gave Toby a friendly lick and sniffed at Luke's blankets. A low growl sounded in his throat, and Charisse's heart sank. He'd had the same reaction to Preston. Usually, she appreciated his protectiveness, but it was going to be very awkward if he decided to take exception to Luke sleeping this close to her. "Come on, Franklin," she said, "I'll fix your bed at the back of the wagon."

"Isn't Franklin going to sleep with us?" Toby asked.

"No, I think we'd better tie him up. He'll do a better job watching the camp that way. Franklin, come here!"

The dog ignored her, his full attention fixed on Luke's blankets. "Oh, for pity sake, Franklin, it's just Luke. You like him fine during the day." Charisse smiled ruefully as she moved to the rear of the wagon. He was the friendliest dog in the world unless he thought one of his people was threatened.

Toby was sound asleep by the time Charisse had spread Franklin's sleeping blanket and gathered the rope. The dog lay tight up against him as though shielding him from the man who would occupy the bed. Again, he refused to come when she called him.

"Honestly, Franklin I can't imagine what's gotten into you," she said, reaching under the wagon and tying the rope around his neck. Franklin whined but crawled out and followed her reluctantly. He barked as she tied him to the back of the wagon.

"Hush!" she said sharply. It was a command left over from their lives with Preston when he'd threatened to get rid of the dog if she couldn't keep it quiet. Franklin obeyed but looked miserably unhappy. "Look, if it makes you feel any better, I promise Luke will stay on his side of the wagon," Charisse said, ruffling his ears.

Charisse shook her head. She really had to get over this habit of talking to her animals as if they were people. She moved around to her bed and took one last peek at Franklin. He was settled on his blanket, his nose as close to Luke's bed roll as he could get.

Glancing around to make sure she didn't have an audience, Charisse removed her robe, and quickly slid into bed. Settling herself on the hard ground, she thought longingly of the nice soft mattress she'd left behind at the hotel and wondered how long it would be before she slept in a bed again.

In spite of the discomfort, Charisse's eyes had already

drifted shut when Luke arrived a few minutes later. Thinking she should tell him he could use the space she'd cleared in the wagon, she opened her eyes then blinked in surprise. He sat on the other side of the wagon dressed in only his undershirt and his trousers. How had he managed to get out of his clothes so fast?

The buttons at the top of his undershirt were open, giving her enticing glimpses of his broad muscular chest as he tugged his boot off. Even during the early days of her marriage, Preston had undressed behind a screen and come to bed decently clad in a nightshirt. Charisse, who had never given her husband's body a second thought, found herself intensely curious about Luke McCabe's. With a grunt of satisfaction, Luke pulled off the second boot then stood and unbuttoned his pants.

With a sudden start, Charisse realized what she was doing and closed her eyes in mortification. How could she lay there and watch him get undressed that way? It was indecent and vulgar. Charisse lay there listening to his movements, telling herself it was only the artist in her, and hoping the light of the full moon wouldn't reveal the blush staining her cheeks.

Why had it never occurred to her that there were bound to be many moments like this and the one in the back of the wagon? She and Luke McCabe would be living together with little or no privacy for the next six months. The thought filled her with conflicting emotions.

"Shit!"

Charisse eyes popped in in startled surprise at the unexpected curse. Luke crouched next to his bed, apparently frozen in place as a strange buzzing noise filled the air. "What's wrong?"

"Don't move," he said in a low, urgent voice.

She followed the line of his gaze and nearly choked, biting back the scream that rose involuntarily to her throat. Suddenly, Franklin's strange actions made sense. A rattlesnake lay coiled at the far end of the blanket, its tail vibrating menacingly, and its head tracking Luke's every move.

It took Charisse several seconds to realize why Luke hadn't gone for the gun lying next to his pile of clothing. He couldn't move without the snake striking. Slowly, so as not to draw the snake's attention to herself and Toby, Charisse reached over and pulled the derringer out of her pocket.

What if she missed? She wasn't exactly what you'd call a dead shot. Maybe she should forget the gun and throw her robe over the top of the snake. That would give Luke time to go for his gun. But if it didn't work the snake would strike in the direction it perceived as a threat, right at Toby. The thoughts flipped through Charisse's mind at lightning speed as she took aim. Somehow drawing a bead on the snake's head wasn't quite the same as aiming at bottles and paper targets. Forcing herself to keep her eyes open and her hand steady, she took a deep breath and squeezed the trigger.

The snake jerked violently, its body heaving away from her as the .38 caliber ball found its mark. Luke grabbed the still thrashing snake by the tail and hurled it away into the darkness.

Charisse dropped the derringer from suddenly nerveless fingers and covered her face with her hands.

CHAPTER 8

"Hair the color of polished mahogany and changeable eyes." The words whispered through the night. They were familiar, but for the moment Charisse couldn't recall where she'd heard them. Then it didn't matter anymore as an arm encircled her waist and a masculine hand grasped hers in a firm but gentle grip. With a surge of music, they swept out onto the floor in the intricate steps of a waltz.

On and on they danced, twirling around an invisible room bathed in the silvery light of a full moon. His face was in shadow, but her body somehow recognized his touch; every nerve responding with a delicate hum of anticipation. As the music came to a halt he gazed down at her for a moment, then began feathering light kisses along her brow.

Charisse closed her eyes and gave herself over to the pleasure. She could feel the warm dampness of his breath as his mouth traced a path down the side of her face. The dampness grew steadily more intense until the kiss became a lick.

She awoke with a jerk. "Franklin, stop that!" she said, pushing his head away.

Halted in the middle of licking her face, Franklin gazed at his mistress with a wounded expression as though he'd been falsely accused.

"Don't try that innocent look with me, mister. You know very well I don't like to be licked."

Franklin sat back on his haunches and gave her his best doggie smile.

"Actually, I told him to wake you," Luke said with a grin. "I didn't really expect him to do it, though."

Charisse glanced at the horizon where a slight trace of pink was beginning to show. She groaned and threw her arm over her eyes. "I just got to sleep."

"Didn't sleep well?"

"I don't feel like I slept a wink all night," she groused. It was true, she had spent a good portion of the night tossing and turning on the hard ground. Even when she had drifted off, her sleep had been so disturbed by dreams she hadn't slept long. Most of them had been terrifying, filled with snakes, blood, and barking dogs.

Luke nodded. "Even without all the excitement we had last night, sleeping on the ground takes some getting used to. I started the fire for breakfast, so if you want to wake Toby, I'll go get some more water."

Charisse's eyes narrowed resentfully as he turned and walked away. It appeared the events of the night before hadn't bothered him much. He looked rested and ready to go. Unless she was mistaken, he'd even shaved.

Her face softened as she turned to Toby. Sometime during the night he'd cuddled into her warmth and lay snuggled close to her side. "Time to wake up, sweetheart," she said, gently touching his shoulder.

He woke as he had every other morning with a yawn and a sunny smile. "Morning, Mama. Where's Pa?"

"He went to get water. He'll probably round up the oxen as well. We've got to be ready to go an hour after daybreak."

Toby rolled out from under the wagon and scrambled to his feet. "Come on, Franklin, let's go help Pa."

"Not so fast, young man. You need to get dressed before you go gallivanting across camp."

"Oh, Mama, Morgan might already be down there, and I want to tell him about the snake."

"Then I suggest you put your clothes on in a hurry."

Without another word, Toby turned and ran to the back of the wagon. At least he knew better than to waste time arguing, Charisse thought. From what she heard of Toby's grandmother, he'd probably learned at an early age that it was useless.

With a groan, Charisse threw back the blanket and rose stiffly to her feet. Yesterday she'd thought she couldn't possibly hurt any worse. Now she realized how wrong she'd been. There wasn't a part of her that wasn't stiff and sore. Even the bottoms of her feet ached.

By the time she'd hobbled to the back of the wagon, Toby had finished dressing and took off after his father with Franklin at his heels. Charisse chided herself for resenting the easy way they moved. Climbing into the back of the wagon was agony as a whole different set of muscles screamed in protest. At least it gave her something to think about besides the night before, not that it did much good.

Charisse still couldn't believe the way she'd fallen apart. By the time the rest of the wagon train had arrived to see what all the shooting was about, she'd been holding onto Toby for dear life and sobbing in Luke's arms. That was probably why Luke was so darn cheerful this morning. The three of them had looked like a perfect family, huddled together that way. Now nobody would ever think to question whether they were really married.

Her corset was more uncomfortable than usual, but the pads she fashioned out of handkerchiefs and inserted where the stays jabbed into her seemed to do the job. She frowned at the pile of petticoats waiting to be donned. Even without her hoops, it looked like a mountain. Perhaps a few less... Ten minutes later, she emerged from the wagon, wearing about half the usual number. She might be slightly less fashionable, but she was also several pounds lighter and considerably more comfortable.

Charisse eyed the cheerfully crackling campfire with misgivings. Surely cornmeal mush wouldn't be too hard to make. Wishing for The Prairie Traveler, she set about fixing breakfast.

"Mrs. McCabe?"

Charisse looked up from her bubbling pot of mush in surprise. The Jessup twins stood before her, with their hats in hands and hopeful looks on their faces. "Good morning," she said pleasantly.

"Morning," they chimed in unison. Then they exchanged a nervous glance and took a deep breath.

"Pa said we had to ask first—" said one.

"Since by rights it belongs to you," the other continued.

"But we figured you wouldn't know what else to do with it—"

"So you wouldn't care that we haven't ever done anything like this by ourselves before-"

"And Pa will be checking to make sure we do it right!"

"So, is it all right with you?"

Bewildered, Charisse looked back and forth between them. Two identical pairs of brown eyes stared expectantly back at her. "What exactly is it you're asking?"

They exchanged another look. "We want to try tanning the skin," said one of them while the other pulled his hand out from behind his back.

Charisse gave a startled scream and fell backwards. The snake she had shot the night before dangled from the boy's hand.

"Where did you get that horrible thing?" she gasped.

"Pa found it on the way back from your wagon last night."

"It was still alive, so he killed it—"

"And we went out and found it this morning—"

"'Cause we figured you'd want the rattles—"

"But then we decided we shouldn't waste a good skin like that..."

"We thought it would make a nice hat band for you—"

"On account of the hole won't matter so much."

For the first time, Charisse noticed a bloodied bullet hole about a third of the way down the snake's body. She hadn't shot the creature in the head after all. In fact, she'd very nearly missed it all together. She shuddered. "What in heaven's name made your father think I'd want it?"

"Pa didn't. He told us to ask your husband since he didn't

figure you'd be interested —"

"But when we found Mr. McCabe he said we'd better ask you —"

"In case you already had plans for it."

Charisse's eyes narrowed. "Oh, he did, did he?"

"Yep, just now —"

"Down by the creek."

"And he thought I'd want a snake-skin hat band?" she asked.

They both nodded, their faces set in identical hopeful expressions.

"Actually," she said, "I don't need a hat band, but I could use a couple of strong backs for an hour or so. Would you be willing to trade me some work for the skin?"

"You mean we could keep it?"

Charisse nodded. "Most definitely. Are you interested?"

The twins exchanged a delighted glance. "Sure, what do you want us to do?"

"I've misplaced some things in my wagon and need help moving the boxes around. Mr. ...my husband doesn't have time."

"When do you want us to come?"

"Hmm." Charisse looked thoughtful. "How about when we stop at noon? We'll have an hour or so then. If it's not enough time maybe we can finish up this evening or tomorrow."

The twins each gave her a blinding smile. "We'll be back."

"Just as soon as we stop to noon-up."

Charisse smiled as she watched them run across the wagon circle. They were quite a pair. She wondered if they always finished each other's sentences. Then she thought of Luke sending them to her. Honestly, the man's sense of humor was going to be a sore trial. She hadn't seen such a terrible tease since... well... since long before her marriage.

Luke couldn't help grinning as the Jessup twins left his wagon at a dead run. Even from where he stood on the creek bank, he could see their boyish excitement. Oh, wouldn't he have loved to be a fly on the canvas when they'd presented Charisse with her trophy! He couldn't help but admire the way she'd handled herself last night, though. His heart had almost stopped when that derringer went off. One minute she was staring at the snake in wide-eyed terror, and the next she was blasting away at it like some kind of avenging angel.

"Hey, Pa, can I go help Morgan water the horses?" Toby ran up with Morgan right beside him.

"You don't know the first thing about watering horses," Luke pointed out.

"I could learn," Toby said eagerly. "Morgan knows all about it."

Morgan nodded. "Pa says Will is too busy so I have to help the twins. They're really tame."

Luke raised an eyebrow. "The twins?"

"No, Pa, the horses," Toby said.

Luke looked down at the two eager faces. "All right, go ahead, but don't get into the creek yourself. Char—uh… your mama won't be pleased if you come in wet."

"Right, Pa, I'll remember. Thanks!" He turned to Morgan with an eager look on his face. "Maybe my mama will show us how to shoot her little pistol later. You should have seen the look on Pa's face when she hit that snake…"

Luke shook his head as the two returned to the creek and Morgan's father. To Toby, the near brush with death had been a great adventure. He glanced upstream and saw Caroline Simms dip a bucket of water out of the creek. A glimmer of an idea fluttered through his mind. Not only did she look like she could use some help, it was the perfect opportunity to get closer to her husband.

"Here, let me give you a hand with that," Luke said, moving to her side. He removed the empty bucket from her hand.

"Oh!" she gave him a startled look. "That really isn't necessary."

He smiled as he filled the bucket. "Maybe not, but my wife would have my hide if I didn't lend a helping hand to a neighbor."

Her face relaxed. "How is your wife this morning?"

"Still a little jumpy. Snakes always do that to her."

"I'm sure I wouldn't have done half so well." Caroline gave him a shy smile. "You'll give her my best, won't you?"

"Maybe you can stop by and tell her yourself."

"Oh, no." Caroline Simms looked terrified at the thought. "I'm sure I wouldn't have time." She reached for her bucket. "Thanks for your help."

"Don't mention it. Why don't I carry these for you? I was going that way anyhow," Luke lied. "I need to talk to your husband."

"Oh? About what?"

"I was wondering if he'd be willing to part with some canvas."

Caroline looked suddenly frightened. "I don't think—"

Luke shrugged. "Maybe not, but I don't figure it will hurt to ask. In the meantime, I can pack this water back to camp for you." He removed the other pail from her hand and started up the hill toward camp. She had little choice but to follow.

Simms was nowhere to be seen when they arrived at the wagon. Luke set the buckets down next to the fire as Caroline hurried to the back of the wagon. "Joshua?"

"Where the hell have you been?" he roared.

Caroline winced. "I…I went to get water."

Simms emerged from the wagon, his face set in angry lines. "I haven't had my breakfast yet, and it's damn near time to hitch up the…" His voice trailed off as he caught sight of Luke.

"Mr. McCabe needs a moment of your time, Joshua." Caroline gave Luke a nervous little smile. "He was kind enough to carry my buckets since he was coming to see you anyway."

"Morning, Simms," Luke said with a cheerful smile.

Joshua's eyes narrowed suspiciously. "McCabe."

"I suspect you came better prepared for this trip than most."

If possible, Joshua Simms' eyes narrowed even further. "What makes you say that?"

"You're the only one of us who didn't have to unload half your wagon to make camp last night." Luke grinned. "I swear, my wife went through every box we have and still hasn't found the sugar."

"If it's sugar you want—"

"No, no." Luke gave a deprecating wave of his hand. "I'm sure she'll find it eventually. What I really need is a piece of canvas."

Simms raised his eyebrows. "Canvas?"

"Yep, seems we got away without a tent. We slept under the wagon last night but I don't suppose that will work all the way to Oregon."

"Sorry, I don't have any extra."

Luke frowned. "I can pay cash money."

"Is that so?" Sims gave him a shrewd look. "Tell me, Mr. McCabe, do you play poker?"

Luke shrugged. "Some, why?"

"Last night after the meeting, me and some of the others were talking of getting a game going. Interested?"

"I might be. Evenings on the trail are bound to get pretty boring."

"Drop by tonight, then. We'll deal you in."

Bullseye! Luke had to fight to keep his expression bland. It was the break he'd been looking for. "I'll do that."

"Sorry I couldn't help out with the tent."

"Well, I expect I'll find one somewhere. Tonight then." He tipped his hat to Caroline. "Mrs. Simms."

As he walked away, Luke resisted the urge to whistle. Unless he missed his guess, he'd hit the jackpot. Simms' excitement when he thought he had a sucker on the line was apparent. If Luke played his cards right he'd be spending a great deal of time with Joshua Simms and his friends. All he had to do was lose often enough to keep them interested and win enough to keep it believable. Who knew what he'd find out?

Luke was still smiling to himself when he walked into his own camp a few minutes later.

Charisse looked up from the fire where the coffee pot bubbled. "Well?"

"Well, what?"

"Where's Toby?"

"He's helping Morgan water the horses."

"He's what?" Charisse's face blanched. "You left two seven-year-olds alone down at the creek with a dozen animals ten times their size?"

"No, of course not. John Jessup was with them."

"That's certainly a relief." She glanced at his empty hands. "Where's the water? What did you do with my buckets?"

Luke blinked. He'd forgotten all about the buckets he had taken down to fill. "I...uh... must have left them down at the creek."

"I suppose you have some good reason for leaving your son and my buckets at the creek instead of bringing them back where they belong?"

"I gave Caroline Simms a hand carrying her water."

There was a long moment of silence, then Charisse looked back at the coffee pot. "I see."

Luke felt a guilty flush rise in his face. "She looked about done in, and I..."

"I found the sugar," she said calmly, as she picked up a stick and placed it carefully in the flames.

"...just gave her a hand, so..." he blinked in surprise. "What did you say?"

"I found the sugar. It was behind a box of books." She looked up at him. "Do you want a cup of coffee?"

"Uh...sure, but don't you want the water first?"

"Yes, that would be nice if you don't mind. I have enough

for breakfast but not enough to clean up."

He turned to go, feeling oddly disoriented. For a moment, he'd felt like an errant husband scrambling to appease an angry wife. It was exactly the kind of thing that would have sent Elizabeth straight through the ceiling and barred him from her bed for at least a week. Charisse had been justifiably worried about Toby but didn't seem to care that her "husband" had been with another woman. And why should she? They weren't married; they weren't even lovers. Luke couldn't help wondering if he was in danger of falling for his own charade.

It wasn't until Luke had filled the two buckets and started back up the hill that an odd thought flitted through his mind. As he watched his son sprint from the Jessup wagon to his own, he realized why Charisse's reaction had been such a jolt. In the same situation, Elizabeth would have been so focused on what she'd consider infidelity, she wouldn't have had a moment to spare for Toby. It was an image of Elizabeth he'd never considered before, and one he wasn't particularly comfortable with.

Moments later the whole thing was forgotten when Toby ran toward him, his small face radiant with pleasure from his adventure with Morgan Jessup. As always, Luke felt his heart expand and fill with the wonder of the love he felt for his child. No matter how many things he'd done wrong in his life, Toby was something he'd done right. Even though having his son along on this mission wasn't what he would have chosen, Luke found he couldn't regret the impulse that made him bring the boy along.

Toby's excited chatter continued all through the breakfast of burnt cornmeal mush and greasy bacon. Watching Charisse respond to his son's incessant prattle gave Luke a warm glow. As he tried to choke down the disgusting mess, he told himself Toby's happiness was far more important than good cooking. At last his plate was empty, and he reached for his cup of coffee with a relieved sigh. He'd saved it until the end so he could enjoy it.

"Don't forget the sugar," Charisse said with a smile as she handed him the container.

"Not to worry," he said, returning her smile, "I've been looking forward to this all morning. I can't tell you how much I've missed it." He added two full teaspoons of sugar and began to stir.

"Then why did you wait until the end of breakfast?"

"I wanted to give it time to cool," he lied. Charisse would be devastated if she knew he'd held off so the wretched meal wouldn't ruin his pleasure. He savored the rich coffee smell wafting upward to his nostrils in the steam.

Charisse began gathering the dirty dishes. "How soon will we be leaving?"

Luke lay down the spoon and lifted the cup to his mouth. "About three quarters of an hour, I suspect." He smiled in anticipation and took a large mouthful of coffee. Even if the food was inedible, and the oxen undrivable, he'd survive if he had his coffee. The next instant he spat the mouthful clear across the fire.

"What in the—?" Luke grabbed the container of sugar, shook a little out on his hand and tasted it. "Shit."

"Luke!" Charisse glanced at Toby then gave Luke a warning look. "What on earth is the matter?"

He glared at her across the fire. "Somebody," he said in a menacing voice, "put salt in the sugar bowl!"

CHAPTER 9

"Hey, look at all these books." Matt Jessup elbowed his brother and pointed at the box he'd pulled out of the wagon.

"Ah heck, that ain't nothing," Toby bragged. "She's got boxes and boxes of them, don't you, Mama?"

"That isn't anything,'" she corrected, "And yes, I have many books. All three of these boxes are filled with them."

Andy gazed up at her with wide-eyed wonder. "Have you read them all?"

"Most of them."

"We've never read a book," Matt admitted.

"Nope," added Andy. "Don't know how."

Toby looked back and forth between the twins with a pleased expression. "You don't know how to read?"

Matt shook his head."Ma taught Will—"

"But she died before Matt and me were old enough—"

"And Pa doesn't have time."

"My mama could teach you." Toby said proudly. "Couldn't you?"

"I suppose so—"

Matt's eyes brightened. "Can we start tomorrow?"

"Well—"

"I want to come, too," Morgan put in. "I'm almost as old as Matt and Andy."

The image of Annabelle bent over a book—honey-blonde hair pulling loose from her blue bow and spilling across the page—brought a sudden hard knot to Charisse's throat. The last child she had taught to read was dead.

"Please, Mrs. McCabe. We'll all work real hard."

Charisse was jolted back to the present by Matt's voice and

three pairs of eyes gazing expectantly up at her. The knot loosened infinitesimally. Maybe it wouldn't be so bad. They were very different from Annabelle, after all. "All right, we'll give it a try."

"Can we start now?" Morgan wanted to know.

"No, not today. It's going to take us some time to find the books we need."

"Maybe we can start tonight."

"I don't think we'll have time," Toby said. "We've got chores to do, and after supper I have to go to bed."

Charisse looked pensive. "That's true. I suppose we can do it during the noon rest. That is, if you want to."

"We do!" the three Jessups yelled in unison. Their shining eyes and bright smiles gave Charisse a warm feeling, like a sunbeam straight to her heart. Perhaps teaching these four boys would even help put the ghosts to rest.

"What treasures have you uncovered today?" Luke's deep voice pushed all other thoughts from her head. They'd been on the trail for over a week, and he still had the power to startle her. For such a large man, his movements were remarkably quiet.

"Mrs. McCabe is going to teach us how to read," Morgan told him proudly.

Luke raised his eyebrows. "Is that so?"

Charisse shrugged. "They got excited when they saw the books. I don't suppose it will hurt to take half an hour or so during the noon rest. Maybe it will help keep them out of mischief."

"I'll believe that when I see it," Luke said, ruffling his son's hair. "By the way, I brought you something, Charisse."

"Oh?"

"Caroline Simms sent this over." Smiling, he reached into his pocket and pulled out a brown cone-shaped object. "She sent us some sugar."

"That doesn't look like sugar to me, Pa," said Toby.

Morgan looked at him in surprise. "'Course it is. What else

would sugar look like?"

"Ours is white, or it used to be. That's how it got mixed in with the salt."

"Only rich people use white sugar," said Matt.

"Are we rich, Pa?" Toby wanted to know.

"Not hardly."

"Then how come we use white sugar?"

"Because your father is particular about his sugar," Charisse said. "Franklin, get away from the bacon. You know better than that." Franklin gave a guilty start, then lay down and started to lick his front paw as if that was what he'd had in mind all along.

Charisse found Luke staring at her with an oddly speculative look, as though seeing her for the first time. It never even occurred to her to buy the cheaper sugar. "Well" she said, hoping to distract him. "We won't have to worry about getting this mixed up with salt."

He shrugged. "I don't intend to overturn the wagon again, so I don't suppose we need to worry much about it anyway."

It was impossible to know who had accidently poured salt into the sugar, but Charisse suspected Luke blamed her.

"I'm surprised Mrs. Simms had any to spare."

"Says she has plenty."

"I'll bet she does," Charisse muttered under her breath as he turned away.

"You've got about half an hour before you need to have this loaded back up," Luke said cheerfully. "In the meantime, I told Simms I'd help him fill his water barrel." He grabbed the bucket and walked off whistling.

Charisse glared after him, fighting the urge to throw the sugar cone at his head. Luke actually expected her to believe his friendship was with Joshua Simms and not the oh-so-pretty Caroline. Ever since he'd taken to spending so much time at the Simms' wagon, Luke had been dropping little hints about the way Caroline Simms handled all the domestic chores on the trail. Honestly, Luke made the woman sound like an absolute paragon.

"What's wrong, Mama?"

Charisse glanced down and found Toby's anxious gaze on her. She forced her face to relax into a smile.

"Not a thing. Come on, we'd better get a move on if we're going to check these boxes of books."

Fifteen minutes later they packed the last of the books back into the crate. As soon as they realized the men were hitching up the oxen and preparing to hit the trail again, the Jessups went back to their wagon. Charisse sighed in defeat. Over the last week they had checked every square inch of the wagon, and *The Prairie Traveler* still hadn't turned up.

"Are you mad, Mama?" Toby asked.

She gave him a reassuring smile. "No, I'm just disappointed we couldn't find my book."

"Why not use one of those?" He pointed to the closest box. "There's lots of books in there."

"I'm looking for a specific book." Charisse smoothed his hair back off his forehead. "Don't worry, it will turn up. In the meantime, we can get ready for our reading lessons with the Jessups."

Toby stubbed his toe in the dirt. "Pa said I wouldn't have to go to school."

"Reading for half an hour a day could hardly be called 'school.'"

"But we'll still have to read, won't we?"

"Yes."

Toby gave a deep sigh and plopped down on the wagon tongue. "I was afraid you were going to say that."

"Why?"

"'Cause I can't learn to read."

"Well, of course you can. Why would you think you couldn't?"

"I don't have enough brains."

Charisse frowned. "Where ever did you get that idea?"

"My teacher said I was stupid and couldn't learn."

"Maybe she didn't know the right way to teach you."

"She made me sit in the corner and wear a dunce cap. She told all the other kids I was stupid, and they laughed at me."

Charisse's jaw tightened. "The woman was obviously unenlightened."

"Grandmother said it was true, too."

Charisse took him by the arm and squatted down until she was eye to eye with him. "Toby, have I ever lied to you?"

He shook his head. "No."

"And do you trust me to always tell the truth?"

"Yes."

"Then listen to me." Charisse stared earnestly into his blue eyes. "When I first met you I thought to myself, this is a very intelligent young man. Nothing has happened since then to change my mind."

"Really?"

"Really."

Toby was silent for a long moment while he digested this. "What does 'telligent' mean?"

"It means you're smart. I'm sure I'll have you reading in no time."

Toby looked hopeful. "You will?"

"Yes, I promise. Now, run and help your father. He's ready to hitch up the oxen."

Toby jumped up and gave her a quick hug. "You're the best mama in the whole world," he said, then dashed off to help Luke, who was leading the oxen up from the creek. Charisse watched him go, her heart swelling with emotion. *The best mama in the whole world.* Oh, if only she were. Annabelle would still be alive, and Charisse wouldn't be trekking clear across the country to start a new life.

With a sigh, she turned away and walked around to the far side of the wagon, only to come face to face with a very large horse. It was hard to say who was more alarmed, Charisse or the horse. She plastered herself against the side of the wagon as the animal shied away from her.

"Whoa there, Adonis." The rider's voice seemed to have a soothing effect on the horse. Both it and the pack horse trailing behind settled immediately. The man smiled down at her. "Sorry if he startled you, ma'am. Adonis doesn't always have the best manners."

Charisse stared up at the horse in surprise. With an overly long nose, white eyes, and a hide some color between brown and gray, it had to be the ugliest horse she had ever seen. "Adonis?"

The man's smile widened to a grin as he reached down and patted the horse's neck. "The first time I ever saw this critter, I could tell he'd be an attention getter so I bought him straight out. I knew the ladies wouldn't be able to resist such a fine-looking animal." He gave her an audacious wink. "Seems to be working too."

It was so completely ridiculous that a gurgle of laughter rose to Charisse's lips. "And I suppose you had a good reason for naming him after the most handsome Greek who ever lived?"

The man shrugged. "It's as good a name as any. Besides, Adonis hasn't ever taken a gander at himself in the mirror. As far as he knows, he's a right handsome fellow."

Charisse raised an eyebrow. "And I think his owner has a lively sense of humor."

"I've been accused of that before," he admitted. "The name is Ben Baxter, by the way."

"I'm Charisse J... McCabe."

She could have sworn she saw a spark of surprise in the man's eyes, but it was gone in an instant as he tipped his hat. "Glad to meet you, ma'am."

"And I'm Luke McCabe," came a deep voice from behind her.

Ben glanced at Luke then back at her. "I don't suppose that's your brother?"

Charisse's lips twitched as she shook her head.

"I was afraid of that." He gave her a rueful smile, then

transferred his smile to Luke and held out his hand. "Ben Baxter."

Luke stepped forward, and the men shook hands. "What brings you out this way?" Luke asked.

"Heading to Oregon, like the rest of you," Ben said with a wide smile.

"Where's your wagon?"

Ben jerked a thumb over his shoulder at the pack-horse. "I travel light. I was hoping to find a wagon train I could sign on with, though. It's a mighty long trip by yourself."

"Ever done any scouting?"

"Some. Why, do you need one?"

Luke shrugged. "Don't know for sure, but there doesn't seem to be anyone here who knows anything about the trail." He pointed to a wagon on the opposite side of the circle. "You'll probably find the captain over there."

Ben nodded. "Thanks. I'll go see what the man has to say." He tipped his hat to Charisse. "It was a pleasure meeting you, ma'am."

"Yes, you too," Charisse said with a smile. "Perhaps we'll see you again if you decide to travel with the train."

"You can count on it," he said with another disarming grin. Then with a glance at Luke, he nudged Adonis with his heels and rode away.

"What was that all about?" Luke wanted to know.

Charisse shrugged. "It wasn't about anything. I startled his horse when I came around the side of the wagon. Did you get Mrs. Simms' water barrel filled?" she asked sweetly.

"Sure did."

"Then do you suppose you could do ours too? It's nearly empty."

Luke looked surprised. He apparently hadn't given his own barrel a thought. "I…uh… I came back to get the bucket."

"Better hurry," Charisse said. "Everyone is hitching up the teams."

"Right. Come on, Toby, let's go get Mama her water."

As Charisse watched them walk away, she told herself it hadn't been a lie. They did need water. The barrel was closer to half-full than empty, and *The Prairie Traveler* had been very definite about keeping the water barrel full whenever possible. But she had an uncomfortable feeling that her words may have been prompted more by jealousy than actual need. With a sigh, she picked up the cone of sugar and went to put it away.

The afternoon was a repeat of every other one, filled with dust, sweat, and jouncing around on the wagon seat. By the time they stopped for the night, it was all Charisse could do to tie the reins to the brake lever. If Luke hadn't been there to lift her down, she wasn't sure she could have managed by herself. In spite of the extra padding, her corset stays had rubbed her raw. Unfortunately, there was nothing she could do about it until bedtime.

Luke started the fire for her, then went off to take care of the animals. Supper wasn't quite the disaster it usually was. The beans weren't burnt this time, but they had little flavor. Though Charisse found them about as tasty as eating a bale of straw, her two dinner companions seemed oblivious. Toby ate quickly, asked to be excused, and then ran off to play with Morgan until bedtime. Luke had sugar for his coffee and that seemed to satisfy him.

Charisse was packing the freshly washed dishes in the grub box and Luke was sitting by the campfire savoring his coffee when Toby and Franklin bounded back into camp with Ben Baxter.

"Evening folks," Ben said with a cheerful smile. "I found these two wandering around. He said his name was McCabe so I figured they belonged to you, and you'd want them home this close to dark."

"We weren't wandering," Toby said earnestly. "We were chasing after a rabbit. It was a baby, and I thought we could take it to Oregon with us."

"Somehow, I don't think Franklin and a rabbit would get along very well," Luke said. "Besides, I think we have enough animals already."

"Franklin likes rabbits, Pa."

Luke's lips twisted with wry humor. "I'm sure he does."

Charisse gave Ben a welcoming smile. "Thank you for bringing Toby home, Mr. Baxter. I was beginning to wonder if I should send his father out after him."

"Glad to oblige. He's quite a boy."

Charisse smiled even wider and gave Toby a hug. "We think so. I take it you'll be traveling with us to Oregon?"

"It looks that way. I signed on as a scout for the train. May do some hunting later on, too."

"Would you like a bite to eat?" Charisse asked. "We have plenty left over, and it won't keep until morning."

Ben shook his head regretfully. "Wish I could, but the captain put me on guard duty tonight. I have the first watch as soon as it gets dark."

"Maybe some other time then."

"I'll take you up on that, ma'am." He glanced at the setting sun. "Guess I'd best be on my way."

"Thanks again for bringing Toby and Franklin home," Charisse said.

"I reckon it's part of the job." He touched his hat brim. "Good night, folks."

"Good night." As Charisse watched him walk away, she couldn't help thinking what a handsome man he was. That heart-stopping smile of his was enough to turn a girl's head. It was a good thing she was a grown woman and immune to such things.

"Looks like our new scout made a big impression on you," Luke said dryly.

"What? Oh!" Charisse blushed to the roots of her hair as she realized she was staring after Ben Baxter like a moonstruck calf. "I was just…I…"

"Never mind," he said, tossing the dregs of his coffee into the fire. "It's none of my business. I think I'll go tell my son goodnight."

Charisse's embarrassment turned to self-righteous anger as she went back to her dishes. So what if Luke caught her looking at a handsome man? It wasn't like they were really married. Her appreciation of Ben Baxter was no different than Luke's preoccupation with Caroline Simms.

"Will you tuck me in, Pa?" Toby's voice broke into her thoughts.

"Just as soon as Franklin gets done checking the bedrolls for snakes," Luke said. "He looks like he's doing a pretty thorough job of it."

"Franklin's a really smart dog, Pa."

Luke chuckled. "I'll say. Looks like he found his bed for the night."

"But that's Mama's bed. Where will she sleep?"

"Oh, I wouldn't worry. I expect he'll move when Mama comes to bed. Under the covers now, son."

"Was my real Mama like Charisse?" Toby asked.

Charisse found herself leaning forward to hear how Luke would answer his son's question.

"No, not really," he said, after a slight pause. "Your Mama would never have made this trip to Oregon with us."

"I don't member her much."

"No, I don't suppose you do." Luke sighed as though the weight of the world rested on his shoulders. "You were only two when she died. I wish you could have known her better."

"It's all right, Pa," Toby said. "I have Charisse now. We can keep her forever, then I'll always have a mama."

There was a dull thump and sharp curse as Luke bumped his head on the bottom of the wagon, and Charisse winced. This was a difficulty neither of them had thought about. Once they got to Oregon, Toby and Luke would go on with their lives just as Charisse would. Poor Toby would again be motherless.

"Charisse probably won't want to stay with us," Luke said. "She has her own plans."

"You said she wouldn't want to go to Oregon, either."

"That was different. Anyway, we're still a long way from

Oregon. Things might change before we get there."

"What kinds of things?"

"Oh, I don't know. Maybe Charisse will fall in love with somebody and decide to get married."

"Hey, Pa, what if you married Charisse?"

Uh oh. Time to step in. Charisse hung the rag over the edge of the dishpan to dry and rose to her feet. "Toby McCabe," she said in an ominous voice, as she walked around the side of the wagon. "What are you still doing awake?"

"I was talking to Pa."

She bent down and peered under the wagon. "Well, it's time you quit. Your Pa has things to do, and you need your rest. Tomorrow is another long day. You don't want to be late meeting Morgan to help water the horses, do you?"

"No!"

"Then you better go to sleep." She transferred her gaze to Luke, who was hunkered down next to his son. "As for you, it's time you finished your chores for the night."

Luke gave her a lopsided grin and a semi-salute. "Yes, ma'am. I'll hop right to it." Then he rose to his feet and sauntered toward the camp kitchen at the back of the wagon.

"Are you coming to bed, Mama?"

"In a little while. I still have a few things to do. In the meantime, you're safe with Franklin."

"He's sleeping on your bed."

"I see that. He'll have to move. Goodnight, Toby."

Toby gave a yawn. "Goodnight, Mama."

"Goodnight. I'll see you in the morning."

Luke was waiting for her by the deserted dishpan. "He's never asked me about his mother before," he said in a low voice.

"It's natural he'd wonder about her."

"I know, but I didn't expect it right now. I didn't know what to tell him."

"The right words will come to you."

He sighed. "I suppose. It's going to be damn tough to

answer some of his questions, though."

"How did she die?" Charisse asked gently.

"That's the part that's going to be tough," he said, his voice raw with pain. "She took her own life rather than be married to me." Without even looking Charisse's way, he plucked his hat off the wagon seat and put it on. "I think I'll take a walk over to the Simms' wagon and see if there's a poker game going."

Charisse watched Luke disappear into the night. God surely had a sense of humor to throw two such emotionally scarred people together. She hoped He was enjoying his little joke, because she sure didn't feel like laughing.

CHAPTER 10

Dappled patterns of light and dark danced eerily across the ground as the night breeze rustled through the leaves in the grove. Luke stood in the shadow of a large tree and observed Ben Baxter on the other side of a small clearing. With his hat pulled over his eyes, and his back against a tree, the guard appeared to be sound asleep.

Luke bent over and picked up a small stone. Taking careful aim, he threw it across the clearing and smiled as it landed with a satisfying thunk on the far side of the sleeping guard. In the blink of an eye, Ben's revolver was out of its holster and pointed straight at Luke.

"Nice try." He raised his hat and gave Luke a menacing stare. "Now put your hands up and come out where I can see you. I'm a little jumpy, so you might want to make it nice and slow."

Luke did as he was told. "You sure have a funny way of showing that jumpy streak," he said, sauntering out into the clearing. "I could have sworn you were sound asleep."

"Things aren't always the way they look. What are you doing out here this time of night, McCabe?"

"Just taking a walk. Mind if I put my hands down?"

Ben shrugged. "That depends. See anybody else?"

"Nary a soul. Pretty late for folks from the wagon train to be out wandering around. Everyone's all tucked in nice and safe."

"You sure about that?"

"Positive. Kind of hard for someone to hide with the full moon lighting everything up like the middle of the day."

"Then what the hell took you so long?" Ben asked, twirling

the pistol around his finger and sticking it back in the holster. "I've been expecting you for the last three hours."

"A poker game."

"You stood me up for a poker game?"

"Actually, I was infiltrating the enemy camp," Luke said. "Dangerous business, too. I lost more money than I planned. So how was New Orleans?"

"About like you figured. I spent the better part of two weeks fighting mosquitoes, snakes and chiggers, while I rounded up a gang of penny-ante criminals."

"What about the nightlife in the big city? Didn't you say it would make up for the aggravation?"

Ben made a rude noise. "Let's just say, the next time we flip a coin for an assignment, I'm taking the boring one."

"No Cajun Queen, then?" Luke said with a grin.

"Oh, there was a Cajun Queen, all right. She was the ringleader of the gang. Ugly as a yellow-tailed alligator and twice as mean."

Luke chuckled. "But you charmed her with your handsome face and witty conversation."

"Charmed her, hell. I was lucky to escape with my manhood intact. Turns out she was a voodoo priestess with a strong dislike for nosey strangers. She made some pretty nasty threats when I arrested her."

"Withered body parts?"

"Among other things. She also said I was going to be sent straight into the bowels of hell."

Luke pursed his lips and looked thoughtful. "Sounds like one of McNesby's jobs."

"That's what I figured. Turned out to be right, too. Didn't even have time to unpack before he and Pinkerton sent me to save your hide. Care to brief me on your investigation?"

"So far all I've been able to find out is that Simms' seem to use an inordinate amount of water. Their water barrel empties twice as fast as ours."

"Now that's an important detail," Ben said with a grin.

"And that took you what, a week to find out?"

"Closer to two." Luke sighed. "If I hadn't seen him burning that ledger, I'd think we were off on a wild goose chase."

"Any other suspects?"

"Just about everybody."

Ben gave him a wry smile. "Just what I like. A case that starts out confusing and quickly becomes complicated."

"This is that, all right." Luke sat on a boulder and crossed his arms. "I think Jesse and Frank Swindell are the most likely to be Simms' accomplices."

"Why?"

"For one thing, they're the only men who never go near Simms. And they have three wagons for the four of them."

"What are they carrying that needs three wagons?"

Luke shrugged. "You've got me. The women drive the one with all their household goods, and the two men drive the other two whose contents are covered with thick tarps."

"Interesting."

"I thought so."

"Any idea what we're dealing with here?"

Luke shook his head. "I don't really know yet, but I have my suspicions."

Ben listened intently while Luke described what he had deduced from the scanty evidence he'd found so far in the investigation. He gave a low whistle when Luke finished. "Rebellion, do you think?"

"It's possible. Simms has ties to some of the most vocal secessionists in the South, but I can't quite figure out why we're on a wagon train to Oregon."

"It does seem strange, doesn't it?" Ben looked thoughtful. "Where does the woman come into it?"

"Woman? Do you mean Caroline Simms?"

"No, I mean your *wife*," Ben said with a grin. "I about fell off my horse when she introduced herself. Last I knew, you were single."

"I still am."

"Then how do you explain traveling across the country with a beautiful woman who introduces herself to strangers as Charisse McCabe?"

"Charisse is part of my cover. Besides, we have a mutually beneficial business relationship."

Ben grinned. "I'm sure you do. Though I have to admit, I'm kind of surprised. You've never been much in the petticoat line."

"She takes care of Toby."

Ben laughed outright at that. "A nanny? Who are you kidding? That woman looks about as much like a nanny as I look like a nursemaid."

"I didn't hire her for her looks," Luke said. "I hired her because she can handle Toby, something no other woman has ever been able to do."

"I've got to tell you, I wasn't best pleased to find my godson in the middle of a nest of vipers like this. It's a good thing he doesn't remember me or the whole jig would have been up. What's he doing here, anyway?"

"I told you I was going to see him when you left for New Orleans."

"I thought you were going to drop in for a visit. What the hell were you thinking, bringing him along?"

"It was a spur-of-the-moment decision, and probably not a very good one. When I got to my in-laws' place, I found him locked in his room on a diet of bread and water. I thought his grandparents were being a bit overzealous in their punishment." Luke sighed. "Elizabeth's father and I... had words. I wound up breaking down the door, scooping up my son and most of his clothes, then stomping out of the house. We were on the train to Missouri before it dawned on me it wasn't the brightest thing I'd ever done."

"Been having second thoughts ever since, huh?"

Luke's expression hardened. "Not after the first night, I haven't. Toby told me his grandfather had taken a switch to him, but I didn't realize how bad it was until I put him to bed.

He still had bruises all over him from a beating he'd gotten almost a week before."

Ben frowned. "What in God's name had he done to deserve that?"

"You know, I never asked. I can't think of anything a seven-year-old could do that would warrant that kind of punishment."

"No, neither can I. So where did you find Charisse?"

"Actually, Toby found her. They met by accident one day and liked each other on sight. When we ran into her later that same evening, Toby took it upon himself to offer her the job."

"And you let him?" Ben asked in surprise.

Luke shrugged. "I didn't expect her to accept. Who would have thought a woman who looks like Charisse Jones would be going to Oregon?"

"Good question. Almost seems a little too convenient, doesn't it?"

"I'm way ahead of you. Her story checks out, at least as far as I was able to trace it before we left. She'd been in Independence long before McNesby's nephew blew the whistle. My gut feeling tells me she's just what she says she is."

"And what is that?" Ben asked.

"A woman running from the shame of divorce, hoping to start a new life in Oregon Territory."

Ben's eyes widened. "Divorce?"

Luke nodded. "That's one of the things that makes me believe her. What woman would set herself up for that kind of humiliation if it wasn't true? Calling herself a widow would be far more acceptable."

"That's for sure."

"Anyway, I set McNesby on it. If Charisse Jones has anything to hide, he'll ferret it out."

"And find a way to get the information to you in record time," Ben said with a grin. "Still, as your partner, I'd better drop by for supper now and then. Just to help you keep an eye on her, of course."

Luke made a rude noise. "That would be considered dangerous duty, my friend. Charisse Jones doesn't know one end of a frying pan from another. I don't know where she spent her life, but it sure wasn't anywhere near a kitchen."

"Maybe she just doesn't know how to cook over an open fire."

"Or maybe she's always had someone who bought groceries and cooked for her. You should have seen the look on her face today when Caroline Simms sent over a cone of sugar. It was like she had never thought of buying sugar that way."

"You think she was born with a silver spoon in her mouth?"

Luke shrugged. "I don't think it's out of the realm of possibility. At any rate, she's been a godsend where Toby is concerned, and I will be forever grateful for that, whoever she is."

"Not too hurtful on the eye either," Ben put in.

Luke was surprised by the deep twist of apprehension Ben's words caused. Benjamin Baxter had been his partner and best friend for many years. Luke trusted the man with his life, and yet Ben's frank admiration of Charisse bothered him for some reason. Perhaps it was the many women Luke had seen come and go in the other man's life. Ben had fancied himself in love with a few, but not one of them had really captured his heart.

"Charisse has had a pretty rough time of it," Luke said. "She doesn't need any more pain."

Ben looked surprised. "What makes you think I'd hurt her?"

"I don't think you'd do it intentionally. Anyway," Luke said, thinking it was high time they changed the subject. "I'm damn glad you're here. There is no way I could cover everything by myself."

Ben shrugged. "You don't think I'd let you have all the fun, do you?"

"Speaking of that, I hope you brought plenty of money

along."

"Some, why?"

"Because your poker skills are better than mine when it comes to playing with people like Simms and his gang."

Ben raised an eyebrow. "I take it you want me to out-cheat the cheaters."

"Exactly."

The two men spent the next half an hour planning strategy and deciding which of the signals they'd developed over the years fit the situation. By the time they were finished, the clouds had thickened until they partially obscured the moon.

"I don't suppose you brought any extra canvas with you," Luke said with a rueful look at the sky.

"My pack cover, but I was planning on using it for a tent. Why?"

"Because that's the one thing Charisse forgot to bring." He sighed deeply. "We're sleeping under the wagon, but our luck won't hold forever. Sooner or later it's going to rain, and if I don't locate a tent of some kind, we're going to get very wet."

"Maybe sooner than later. Those clouds look like rain to me."

"I hope not." Luke stood up and stretched. "It's time I went to bed. Dawn comes early."

"My relief guard should be here pretty soon, anyway. I'll see what I can find out tomorrow and try to get myself dealt into the poker game."

"Good. I'll kind of lay low for a day in case anybody is suspicious." Luke glanced back toward camp. All was quiet. Even the glow of the fires had disappeared in the darkness. "I'm glad you're here to watch my back. This mess would make me nervous in the best of circumstances, but with my son and Charisse along…"

"With the two of us, we ought to be able to keep them safe."

"I surely hope so," Luke said. "Because if anything happens to either one of them, I'll never forgive myself."

Charisse awoke with a start. Confusion and the last wisps of sleep were still swirling through her mind when Franklin rose from his place at Toby's feet and went to investigate. A moment later, she heard Luke's low-voiced greeting to the dog and relaxed.

She didn't have any idea what time it was; she'd been drifting in and out of sleep since she'd gone to bed. It was late, though, and the poker game was long over. The murmur of male voices had faded into the night hours ago. Where had he been? The image of Caroline Simms popped into her head, and Charisse found herself gritting her teeth.

With a concentrated effort, she forced her jaw to relax. It was none of her business what Luke did with the lovely young Mrs. Simms in the dark of the night. Her only concern was what could happen if Mr. Simms found out. The ensuing fight would be devastating to Toby and could even result in someone getting hurt or killed.

Charisse could tell herself all night her only concern was how all this would affect Toby, but deep in her heart she knew it wasn't true. The emotion causing her stomach to churn and her throat to thicken didn't feel like worry. It felt like jealousy.

Certain her feelings would show, Charisse closed her eyes so he'd think she was asleep. A few moments later, Franklin sniffed at her legs before turning around three times and settling on Toby's blanket again. The rustle of fabric as Luke shed his clothing and crawled into bed reminded her of the masculine chest she'd glimpsed so briefly the first night on the trail. There was a deep sigh, and then silence.

Gradually, Charisse drifted into sleep once again. With Luke finally tucked into his bedroll, her little family was all safe and accounted for. For the first time all night, she relaxed and fell into a deep sleep. Even the wind whipping around the wagon and the distant sound of thunder didn't penetrate her exhausted slumber. It wasn't until the first rain drops hit her face that she jerked awake.

With a gasp, she rolled to her side so her whole body was under the wagon and found herself almost nose to nose with Luke. With the clouds covering the moon, it was so dark she could barely see him, but she knew he was there. His warm breath on her cheek brought every nerve to tingling awareness.

"It's raining," she said.

"I noticed." He reached down to get something from the foot of his bedroll. "I had a feeling it might, so I grabbed this before I came to bed."

"What is it?"

"My rain slicker." He spread the oilskin coat over the three of them. "It isn't much, but it's better than nothing."

"I'm sorry I forgot the tent," she murmured. "It was stupid."

"It's as much my fault as yours. I should have been paying attention when we repacked the wagon. I knew you didn't have any experience packing for this kind of trip."

"And you do?"

"Not exactly, but I have spent a lot of time sleeping out under the stars. If I'd been thinking, I'd have brought my own tent."

Charisse blinked. It had never occurred to her that Luke hadn't been prepared to make the trek to Oregon. Now the realization hit her with all the subtlety of a cannon shell. "Why didn't you?" she asked.

"I hadn't really planned on leaving Independence."

"You didn't know you were going to Oregon?"

His teeth flashed in the darkness as he smiled. "I guess you could say I suddenly caught Oregon fever."

"No one heads for Oregon on a whim."

"I did. I tend to be a bit impulsive at times. As you pointed out when we first met, I'm rather like my son that way."

"You decided to completely change your life around on an impulse? That's the craziest thing I ever heard."

"That's why Toby and I need you, sweet Charisse." He

reached out and ran a finger down the side of her cheek. "Without you to keep us in line, who knows where we'd wind up. Now, close your eyes and go back to sleep. Morning will be here before you know it."

For once Charisse was speechless. There seemed to be no response to such a statement. She lay in the darkness listening to Luke's breathing deepen as he fell asleep, but it was a long time until sleep claimed her once more.

CHAPTER 11

"I'm sick to death of dust," Charisse said, shaking out her shawl.

Luke slapped his hat against his leg, sending a cloud of dust into the air. "Just proves our luck is holding."

"How do you figure that?"

"We've only had one rain storm, and we were on a little knob that night, so the water ran away from us instead of underneath the pallets. Even then our wagon never got stuck in the mud."

Charisse blinked. "That's true. We're about the only ones who didn't have trouble."

"Yep, and that's because you didn't fill your wagon with a lot of useless family treasures. I still can't believe Miss Duncan brought along her piano."

"I felt sorry for her when she had to leave it behind on the trail. It really was a beautiful piece," Charisse said. Her heart had gone out to the other woman, who stood by her precious piano and cried for a good ten minutes before her brother could get her calmed down and back into their much lighter wagon.

"I'm sure you had beautiful things too, but you were smart enough not to bring them along. Where did my son get to?"

"He went to find Morgan and the twins."

"All right then. I guess I'll go help get the Simms wagon on the trail again."

"You do that," she muttered as he walked away. At least he'd said she was smart. She made a face as she went to answer the call of nature. Good thing he didn't know the truth. Everything she owned was in the wagon. All of her family heirlooms were still in the ostentatious house Preston had built with her inheritance, and everything precious to her lay buried in a beautiful little churchyard nearby.

On her way back, an odd little sound brought her out of her dark thoughts with a jerk. It seemed to have come from a small thicket. As she tried to peer through the branches into the interior, the sound came again, a small sniffling gasp. One of the children was crying.

"Toby? Morgan?" Charisse parted the branches and made her way through the brush to a tiny clearing in the center. "What's the matter…Oh!" Charisse stopped in surprise. Caroline Simms sat in the center of the thicket trying to stifle her sobs.

"I'm sorry," Charisse said, starting to back out. Then Caroline looked up at her and all thought of leaving flew out of Charisse's mind. The whole right side of Caroline's face was red with faint purpling beginning to show under the skin. Her lip was split and swollen.

"Good heavens! What happened to you?"

Caroline looked away. "I fell," she said, fumbling for her handkerchief. "So clumsy of me…"

Charisse put her hand on the other woman's arm. "It's all right," she said quietly. "I don't need to know. Wait here. I'll be right back." She gave a furtive look around as she left the thicket and hurried back to the wagon, grabbed a clean rag which she dipped into the water barrel, and hastened back to Caroline Simms.

"Here," she said, handing her the wet rag. "This will make it feel better."

Caroline looked up at her for a long moment then took the rag and laid it on her face. "Thanks."

"Sure." Charisse sat on the log next to her and studied the willow branches in front of her. "You know, I used to fall down and run into things quite a lot, too."

Caroline looked startled. "You did?"

"Oh, yes. The first time I'd only been married a month or so, and I forgot my place at an important dinner." She gave

Caroline a rueful smile. "My parents were liberal thinkers and had encouraged me to speak my mind. Preston wasn't impressed."

"Preston?"

"My husband."

Caroline frowned. "I thought his name was Luke."

"I meant my first husband," Charisse said, mentally kicking herself for the slip. "Luke has never laid a hand on me. The point is, some men take out their frustrations on anyone who's handy."

"I broke the wagon wheel," Caroline said. "I didn't see the rock until the wheel went over it and broke."

Charisse shrugged. "There were six wagons in front of you. If they all made it through, why would you think it would be any different for you?"

There was silence between the two women for a long moment. When Caroline spoke, her words were a complete surprise. "Did you love him?"

"Who?"

"Your first husband."

"Preston?" Charisse frowned thoughtfully. "In the beginning, I think I did, but he killed it long before the end. Being alone was hard at first, but there's not a day goes by that I don't thank God Preston is no longer a part of my life."

"And then you met Mr. McCabe," Caroline said softly.

Charisse smiled. "I think it's safe to say there isn't anybody less like Preston than Luke McCabe."

Caroline dabbed at the cut on her lip. "This really was my fault though. I should have been paying closer attention."

"The worst of it was that Preston always somehow made me feel like it was my fault; that I deserved his abuse. It wasn't until he was out of my life that I realized it was his problem, not mine." She looked at the other woman. "It isn't yours, either. So what if you didn't see the rock? The same thing could have happened to any of us. It was an accident, plain and simple."

"But the whole wagon train had to stop."

Charisse shrugged. "Who cares? If you want to know the truth, I was kind of grateful. It was high time we stopped to give the animals a rest." She sighed. "And me too. My corset is killing me."

"The wagon seat isn't particularly easy to sit on all day, is it?"

Charisse snorted. "I've seen rough-cut tree stumps more comfortable. I thought it would get better with time, but it hasn't."

"Mrs. McCabe…" the name came distantly on the wind.

Both women looked toward the sound. "It's one of the Jessup twins," Charisse said. "They probably want to continue their lessons. I've been teaching them to read during the noon stops."

Caroline gave her a wistful look. "That sounds like fun."

Charisse smiled. "With Toby and all three of the younger Jessups, I'm not sure *fun* describes it." She gave Caroline a sidelong glance. "Are you going to be all right?"

"Oh… yes, of course." She handed the rag back.

"No," Charisse shook her head. "I don't need it right now." She paused. "If you ever need a place to go, or someone to cover for you…"

Their gazes met and held as a wealth of understanding passed between them. Finally, Caroline nodded. "Thanks."

Charisse returned the nod and left the protection of the willows.

"There she is!" Toby and Franklin came bounding up with happy grins on their faces. "I found a trick Franklin can do. What were you doing in those bushes, anyway?"

"Toby, a gentleman never asks a lady why she is in a particular place at a particular time," she said, guiding him back toward the wagon train. "Now, what about this new trick of Franklin's?"

"I told him to find you, and he did. He's a really smart dog."

"Mmm. Part tracker, no doubt. I guess you and the Jessups are ready for your reading lesson." She had to bite back a smile at Toby's look of consternation. Apparently he'd forgotten why he was looking for her.

"You know," he said. "I might have to miss it today."

"Oh, why is that?"

"The wheel on the Simms' wagon broke so Pa and the other men will probably need my help fixing it."

"I doubt that," she said. "I expect they have it well in hand."

"Oh." His face fell again.

Charisse smiled and put her arm around his shoulder. "You're coming along fine, Toby. I know you thought you'd be reading by now, but it takes a long time to learn."

"Morgan reads better than I do. So do Matt and Andy, and we all started at the same time."

Charisse shrugged. "Everybody learns differently. You'll catch up."

"The letters all sound the same, and the words always get tangled up in my mind so I can't keep them straight."

"Hmm," Charisse looked down at him thoughtfully. "Maybe we need to work on that."

It was easy to tell Toby wasn't crazy about the idea, but it was soon forgotten as they neared the wagons and were suddenly surrounded by excited Jessups. Matt, Andy and Morgan were all talking at once.

"Mr. Baxter was out scouting this morning," Matt said excitedly.

"—and he says the first big river crossing is up ahead," Andy added.

"A wagon train had just crossed when he got there—"

"—and a man met the elephant!"

Charisse blinked in confusion. "Met an elephant? Out here on the trail? I think Mr. Baxter is pulling your leg."

"Meeting the elephant is what they say when they mean someone died," Will Jessup said, as he joined his younger brothers.

Charisse's hand went to her mouth. "Someone died?"

Morgan nodded. "He drownded on account of his wagon tipped over."

"That's horrible!"

"That's why Mr. Baxter and my Pa are going on ahead while the rest of us fix the Simms' wagon. They're going to help out," Will said.

"And learn the best way to get us across, I hope," Charisse said.

"I think so." Will glanced at his siblings. "Pa wanted to know if you could keep an eye on the young'uns for him."

"Certainly. We were just getting ready to do our reading lesson for the day."

Will looked relieved. "Thank you, ma'am. He was afraid they'd get underfoot and cause trouble."

"What if the wagon train starts again before he gets back?" Charisse asked.

"I reckon me and the boys can drive our rig if you'll keep Morgan."

"How come I can't help drive?" Morgan asked.

"You ain't old enough, that's why."

"Toby and I will be glad of Morgan's company," Charisse put in hastily. She could tell by the belligerent set of Morgan's jaw that an argument was brewing.

Will smiled with relief. "Thanks." He put his hat on his head and turned to go. "Oh, I almost forgot. Luke wanted to know if you could send your book back with me."

"Which book is that?"

Will looked pensive for a moment. "It's your Oregon Trail Guide. He called it The Wagon Traveler, or Prairie Guide... I don't remember for sure."

Charisse blinked. "*The Prairie Traveler*?"

"That's it. He said it tells all about fixing wagon wheels and fording rivers."

"I'm not sure where it is off hand."

"Darn, he figured it would help since nobody really knows how to fix the wheel." Will shrugged and put his hat back on. "Reckon we'll have to figure it out ourselves, then. By the way, Luke said not to worry about lunch today. He'll grab something later."

"All right. Thank you." Charisse frowned as she herded Toby and the younger Jessups to her wagon. *How the heck does Luke know* The Prairie Traveler *explains how to fix wheels? For that matter, since when does he believe what it has to say?*

Charisse decided she had more important things to worry about. Namely keeping four boys occupied long enough for the men to complete their task. Charisse settled the three Jessups on crates beside the wagon, and they were soon bent over their slates copying words. She and Toby sat several yards away.

"We're going to try something new today," she told Toby as she opened a bottle of ink and set it on her lap desk. She took out a piece of paper and dipped her pen into the ink. " 'A' has two sounds. The first one is 'aaa', like 'aaa….pple,'" she said, sketching an apple on the page. "What else can you think of that has "aaa" in it?"

Toby stared down at the page for a moment. "Aaa….pple," he said softly. His brow furrowed with concentration as he continued to repeat the sound.

He looked away from the page, and Charisse's heart sank. It wasn't going to work after all, and Toby would see it as one more failure. She bit her lip as he looked around still mumbling to himself.

Toby's gaze passed over the ground at his feet then swung back. He swept up his hat and gave Charisse a hopeful look. "Hat?"

"Yes! Hat has an "aaa" in it. H-A-T," she spelled out as she wrote the word under the picture of the apple.

Toby looked at the word curiously. "Hat. That sounds kind of like cat."

"Yes, it does." She wrote the word 'cat,' then glanced at him and wrote 'mat.' "What about this one?"

Toby studied the word for a moment then looked up at her. "Mat?" he said uncertainly.

"Exactly! And how about these?"

"Fat, rat?" he read as fast as she scribbled words on the page. "Sat, bat, pat, tat."

"Yes!" Charisse cried, giving him a big hug. "Oh, Toby, you got it!"

A huge grin split his face. "Do some more!"

"All right. R-A-N is 'ran,' so what is C-A-N?"

"Can," Toby said promptly, with barely a glance at the page.

Charisse happened to look up and saw Caroline emerge from the thicket. Caroline returned her tentative wave then turned back toward her wagon. Charisse marveled at the change in her thinking. Before her encounter with Caroline Simms, the news Luke wasn't coming "home" for lunch would have infuriated her. It still stung a bit, but now she found herself glad Caroline would have a champion to protect her.

With a small smile, she turned her attention back to Toby. Before long, he was making long lists of rhyming words and reading them with great enthusiasm as the Jessups cheered him on.

"What do you mean you don't know where it is?"

Charisse started. The deep voice was the first indication she had that Luke was there. "What are you trying to do, scare me to death?" Charisse glared up at him. "Didn't your mother teach you sneaking up behind people was rude?"

Luke ignored her complaint "Look, we really need that book."

"Well, I'm sorry," she said irritably, as she turned back to her students. "I haven't a clue where it is, but you're welcome to search the wagon."

"What happened to it?"

"If I knew that, I'd know where it was, wouldn't I?"

"I put it back where it belonged last night. Did you move it?"

Charisse looked up at him in surprise. "You had the book last night?"

"I knew we were coming to the river, so I decided to see what the book had to say about it." He sighed. "All right, all right, you win. I'll admit it. The Prairie Traveler wasn't written by a two-bit greenhorn who'd never been west of the Mississippi. I was wrong, and you were right. Now, can I have the damn book?"

"Uh…sure, but you'll have to get it yourself. I'm busy."

It was hard not to flinch under his look of disbelief, but Charisse managed to keep her expression calm as she turned her attention back to Toby. Though she focused on the list of words Toby was writing, Charisse was very aware of Luke standing there staring at her for the longest time. She was about to sneak a look at him, when she felt his arms go around her from behind.

"Are you flirting with me, lady wife?" His deep, sexy whisper raised gooseflesh all across her skin.

"No, I—" She gasped as his teeth nipped her earlobe, and his left arm tightened, holding her immobile while he reached for the drawer in the bottom of her lap desk.

"Yep," he said, sliding the drawer open. "Right where I left it."

Charisse's jaw dropped as he removed *The Prairie Traveler* and closed the drawer.

"Thanks," he said. There was a butterfly touch on her hair before he released her abruptly. "I'll bring it back when we're finished."

Charisse sat there stunned; unsure which shocked her more, the fact her book had been right under her nose the whole time, or the certainty that Luke McCabe had dropped a kiss on top of her head.

CHAPTER 12

"Mr. Baxter says the river is right over that hill," Toby told Charisse. "Can Franklin and I go take a look?"

A feeling of dread seized Charisse. "No, I think you'd better stay here with the wagon."

"Aw, how come?"

"Because I don't want you to get lost," she said. "If it's right over the hill, we should be there long before dark. You'll see it soon enough."

Toby looked disappointed. "Can I go find Morgan, then?"

Charisse hesitated, unwilling to let him out of her sight but unable to think of a good reason to keep him with her. "I suppose, but stay with the wagon train," she called as he took off like a shot. She knew she was being overly protective, but she couldn't help it. They had passed a child-sized grave early this morning, and the image wouldn't leave her.

Luke looked over his shoulder as his son streaked by with Franklin hot on his heels. "Something wrong?" he called over the creak of the yokes and the rumble of the wagon.

"No, he's going to find Morgan."

Luke nodded and turned back to his oxen. Their training was coming along nicely. In a week or so Luke thought he'd be able to take over the job of driving, leaving her free to ride in the wagon or walk alongside. Charisse sighed and shifted uncomfortably. It couldn't happen soon enough. Riding on the wagon seat all day, every day, hadn't improved much in the week they'd been on the trail. Her backside still hurt all day long, and she had developed sores where her corset stays dug into her.

When they'd first started out, the ever-changing landscape

of hills, rocks, trees and the occasional animal kept her entertained. The trees and rocks soon disappeared, replaced by the prairie she'd heard so much about. The prairie grasslands were interesting when the wagon train had first come to them— a vast sea of grass undulating in the wind as far as the eye could see in every direction. There were herds of antelope and deer, and once, in the distance, a dark line of buffalo stretched from horizon to horizon. But there was a monotonous sameness about the prairie and its inhabitants that soon dulled the senses.

Most days the distraction of watching Luke guide the oxen was enough to keep the worst of the boredom at bay, but today he was just another source of irritation. The fact he'd known where *The Prairie Traveler* had been the whole time was like a burr under the saddle since she had a sneaking suspicion he'd known she was looking for it. He claimed he'd found it when they were cleaning up after the wagon wreck and figured her lap desk was the logical place to put it. It made sense, but he seemed a little too cheerful about the whole incident for it to be totally innocent.

"Afternoon, Mrs. McCabe," Ben Baxter's voice broke into her thoughts.

"Hello." Charisse smiled. She barely knew the man, but somehow she always felt better when he was around.

"Captain says to tell everyone we'll be staying an extra day at the river."

"Oh? Why is that?"

"The animals need rest, and it's going to take a while to caulk the wagons."

Charisse blinked. "What are you going to do that for?"

"So we can float them across."

"You mean like a boat?"

"Pretty much. The last train tried to ford, but the water was too deep. That's what caused the trouble."

She gave him a doubtful look. "And floating the wagons across will be safer?"

"According to Luke's book, it will be."

"His book? You mean *The Prairie Traveler?*"

"Yep. That's a right handy book he's got there. Tells you everything from fixing wagon wheels to crossing rivers. He says nobody should be allowed out on the trail without a copy."

"Oh, he does, does he?" Charisse's eyes narrowed as she glared at the back of Luke's head. "Imagine that."

"Anyway, the captain said to pass the word we'll be stopped for a day. Figured that would please you ladies."

Charisse gave Ben a blank look. "Why is that?"

"So you can bathe and do laundry, of course."

"Oh, of course." *How in the world did one do laundry in the river?* Charisse wondered. Not that she knew how one did it the normal way. She had paid someone else to do it for her until the money got low, then she washed things out in the wash bowl in her room at the hotel. Now she'd not only have to do her own, but Luke's and Toby's as well.

"Damn!" Ben's sharp exclamation brought her sick musing to an end.

"What's wrong?"

"I'm afraid Adonis is coming up lame."

Charisse glanced at the horse and saw that he was indeed limping. "Will he be all right?"

"I hope so." Ben pulled back on the reins and swung down off the horse. He was lifting the injured foot as the wagon rolled on, and he passed out of sight.

"What was that all about?" Luke wanted to know.

"His horse may be going lame."

"No, I mean before that."

"We're stopping by the river."

Luke nodded. "That's what I figured." He turned back to his oxen. "Say, is that Toby up ahead?"

Charisse followed his line of sight, and her mouth fell open in surprise. Toby and Morgan were rolling around on the ground in the throes of an intense battle. As she watched, Will Jessup pulled the two combatants apart by their shirts. Though they were too far away to hear what was being said, Morgan and Toby were yelling and swinging at each other.

"Luke, don't you think one of us had better go see what's going on?"

Luke eyed the altercation for a moment. "I suppose so. It looks like more than young Jessup can handle."

Charisse tied the reins to the brake lever and scrambled down from the wagon. "This needs a woman's touch. You keep the wagon moving, and I'll take care of this."

Luke grinned. "A woman's touch?"

"You men think fighting is the way to solve everything. I'm sure Will never even thought of the best way to handle it."

"And that would be...?"

Charisse ignored Luke's raised eyebrow as she walked past him. "Finding out what caused the fight in the first place."

"Give 'em hell!" she heard him call as she hurried toward the small group. *Leave it to Luke to find this all humorous*, she thought with a flash of irritation. Then all else was forgotten as she got her first good look at Toby and the blood streaming from his nose.

"What in heaven's name is going on here?" she asked, pulling her handkerchief out of her sleeve and handing it to Toby.

"He called me a name," Morgan said.

Toby shook his head. "Did not!"

"Did so!" Morgan kicked him with a small foot.

"Stop that!" Will pulled Morgan farther away.

"Toby, stand still," Charisse said sharply, as she pinched the bridge of his nose.

"Ow, that hurts," he complained.

"It will stop the bleeding. What did you say that got Morgan so upset?"

"All I said was, 'You're a girl!'"

"Oh, Toby, that's not—"

"Is that what this is all about?" Will gave his little brother a shake. "Morgan, you've got to stop being so all-fired sensitive about that."

"Sensitive about…Oh, my." Charisse had been so focused on Toby's nose she hadn't taken a good look at his adversary. Now, she was hard put to keep her mouth from falling open in shock. Morgan's hat had been knocked off, revealing two flaxen braids that hung halfway to her waist.

"I'm real sorry about this, Mrs. McCabe," Will said. "For some dumb reason Morgan wants people to think she's a boy."

Morgan glared. "Girls are sissies! I can beat any boy out there."

Charisse glanced at Toby, who still held her blood-soaked handkerchief to his nose. "I'm sure that's true, but I don't think Toby meant to hurt your feelings."

"Huh-uh." Toby shook his head. "I was just surprised. You ain't nothin' like a girl."

"Toby," Charisse began, but Morgan's hopeful expression stopped her.

"Really?"

Toby nodded. "Really. I've been in lots of fights, but nobody ever gave me a bloody nose before."

"They haven't?"

"Nope, this is my first."

Morgan gave him a suspicious look. "So you won't make fun of me?"

Toby shook his head.

"All right," she said, "Then I guess we're still friends."

"Bestest friends?" Toby asked.

"Bestest best," Morgan agreed, and held up her pinkie.

Toby glanced up at Charisse. "You can let go of my nose now."

"Oh, right." Charisse slowly released the pressure, and took the handkerchief from him. "I guess it's stopped."

Toby linked pinkies with Morgan. "Bestest best friends forever," they recited together, then grinned.

"Come on," Toby said. "I'll race you to the river."

"Hold on." Charisse grabbed his shoulder. "You're not

going anywhere but back to the wagon with me."

"But, Mama, the river's right over the hill."

"So you've told me, and I'm sure it will still be there this afternoon. I think you need to ride in the wagon for a while to make sure your nose has stopped bleeding. Besides, you have blood all over your shirt."

"Oh, Mama…"

"Morgan's not going anywhere, either," Will said, with a fierce look at his sister. "Pa's going to have something to say about this."

"Oh, Will, you know what Pa said about me fighting," Morgan whined.

"You should have thought about that before you started throwing punches."

"Gosh," Toby said as he watched Will drag Morgan away. "What do you think will happen to her?"

"I expect her father will give her a good talking to."

"I can't believe she's a girl!"

"I imagine Morgan will be happier if you don't think about it," Charisse pointed out as they walked back to the wagon.

"Why does she want to keep it a secret?"

"I don't know, but—"

"Women keep secrets just to drive men crazy," Luke said with a grin, as they approached their wagon.

Charisse glared at him. "You couldn't possibly know what we were talking about."

"Didn't need to. I heard Toby say *she* and *secret*. That's all I needed to know."

"Do all women keep secrets, Pa?" Toby asked.

"Every one I ever knew did."

"Perhaps you just knew secretive women," Charisse said.

Toby looked up at her. "Do you have secrets, Mama?"

"Of course, she does," Luke said before she had a chance to answer. "She has more secrets than the rest of them put together, don't you, Charisse?"

"I'm sure I don't know what you're talking about. My life

is an open book," she said, with a toss of her head.

"A book of puzzles, maybe."

"Humph!" Charisse didn't bother to answer. She knew there was no reasoning with him when he was in a teasing mood. "Come along Toby. Let's get you cleaned up."

Luke's chuckle followed her all the way to the back of the wagon.

They reached the river by early afternoon. The instant Luke told the oxen to "whoa," Toby was on the ground, sprinting toward the Jessup's wagon with Franklin at his heels.

"Stay out of the water!" Charisse called after him. "Much good as that will do," she muttered as Toby disappeared.

"Don't worry," Luke told her. "I heard John Jessup tell the twins to keep an eye on the youngsters once we got to the river."

"That's like sending the fox to watch the chickens."

"You're probably right about that."

With a deep sigh, Charisse wound the reins around the brake lever and stood.

"Tired?" Luke asked as he reached up to help her down.

"A little, but not as bad as usual. I'm looking forward to stopping for a day." Her breath caught in her throat as his hands tightened around her waist and plucked her from the wagon seat. She'd never get used to the effortless way he swung her to the ground as though she weighed little more than a child. Next to his muscular bulk she always felt small, delicate even. It was a novel experience. She'd lost count of the times Preston had called her "robust." He'd made it sound vulgar, somehow. Try as she might, Charisse had never even come close to the delicately-bred, languishing female he wanted.

"Let me get the oxen picketed, and I'll get your washboard out."

"There's no hurry," Charisse told him. The longer she

could put off doing the laundry, the better.

"All right then, I'll go down and see if they need any help setting up the crossing," he said. "Let me know when you're ready, and I'll pack all the laundry down to the river."

"How about the twelfth of never?" Charisse muttered as she watched him set off across camp. With another deep sigh, she turned back to the wagon. It was too early to start supper; might as well figure out the clothesline. The coil of thin rope was easy to find, but she was still standing there wondering what to do next when she saw Ben Baxter striding across the enclosure toward her.

"What do we have here?" he asked, eyeing the rope. "Planning on hogtying those menfolk of yours?"

Charisse gave an unladylike snort. "As if either one would slow down long enough to allow such a thing. Actually, this is supposed to be my clothesline if I can figure out how to string it up without any trees."

Ben glanced around. "I see your point. Hmm." He eyed the wagon for a moment, then took the rope from her hands. "How about if we string it along the side of the wagon?"

Charisse blinked. "I hadn't thought of that." She watched as he tied one end of the rope to the struts beneath the wagon seat. "How is Adonis?" she asked. "Has he really gone lame?"

"No, he had a cactus spine in his foot, but I managed to get it out before it became too deeply imbedded. He'll be right as rain tomorrow."

"That's good." She smiled as he tied the other end of the rope to the tailgate of the wagon. "I'd have never thought of that. I don't know how to thank you, Mr. Baxter."

"You can start by calling me Ben."

"Only if you'll call me Charisse."

"It's a deal," he said, sticking out his palm.

Charisse hesitated for a moment then put her hand in his. His clasp was warm and strong and the twinkle in his eye impossible to resist. Before she knew it, she was grinning like a fool and fighting the girlish giggle that threatened to escape her lips.

"What's this?"

The deep voice sent Charisse's pleasure crashing to the ground. Luke. She started to pull her hand away, but Ben's grip tightened.

"I was just telling your wife there was no reason for us to stay on formal terms."

"Is that so?"

"Yep. Friendship has its compensations, after all." He raised her hand to his lips and kissed the back of it. "I plan to flirt outrageously with her every chance I get."

"Doesn't the fact she's a married woman put a hitch in your plans?" Luke asked.

"No, why should it? A husband just means she won't take me seriously. Much safer for me in the long run."

Charisse laughed. "You're incorrigible."

"I do try." Ben sighed. "But, I suppose we'll have to stop now that the husband has returned."

"If you know what's good for you." Luke frowned. "What is it you want, anyway?"

"Nothing. I was on my way down to the river and saw your wife struggling so I stopped to help." Ben gave Charisse an audacious wink and dropped her hand. "Guess it's time I was on my way."

"Just what I was thinking," Luke said.

Ben grinned, tipped his hat to Charisse and walked away.

"Luke!" she said, as soon as Ben was out of earshot.

"What?"

"That was rude!"

Luke shrugged. "What did he help you with?"

"He rigged a clothesline for me," she said.

"I would have done that. Why didn't you ask?"

"I never thought about it." Charisse's eyes narrowed. "What are you doing back here anyway? I thought you were going down to the river."

"What?" Luke pulled his gaze away from the retreating

figure of Ben Baxter. "Oh. The other women are planning to go to the river to bathe. Mrs. Simms said they'd meet you at the first bend above the ford in half an hour or so."

"Mrs. Simms! Where did you see her?"

"I stopped to see her husband."

"What for?"

"To tell him it was his night for guard duty."Luke frowned at the small grove of trees where Ben had disappeared. "You seem to be pretty cozy with Baxter."

"I hardly know the man."

"Exactly, and you have no idea what he's capable of. You'd do well to give him a wide berth."

Charisse raised an eyebrow. "Let's see. He brought Toby home the other night and today he put up a clothesline. Which of those do you think is a threat to me?"

"I'm not talking about that, and you know it."

"Oh, really? Maybe if you told me what you're referring to…"

"I'm referring to the way I keep finding him here every time I turn around. How long do you think people are going to believe we're married if you're constantly flirting with another man?"

"Flirting!" Charisse's eyes flashed. "How dare you accuse me of flirting? Ben Baxter has spoken to me a grand total of four times and never once has he ever been anything other than a complete gentleman." She glared at him. "Unlike others I could name."

"I'm thinking of how it must look."

"In case you've forgotten, neither of us owes the other a darn thing. I can spend every waking moment with Ben Baxter if I choose to, and it's none of your business! If it comes to that, you've spent much more time with Caroline Simms than I have with Ben Baxter. I've never said a word about it, because I didn't figure it had anything to do with me."

"There is nothing between Caroline Simms and me!"

She gave him a sweet smile. "Exactly. Now don't you need

to be getting down to the ford?"

For an endless moment Luke stared at her. "Damned contrary females," he muttered, as he turned and stalked off in the same direction Ben had taken.

Charisse watched him go with a very feminine smile on her face. Mr. Luke McCabe had just been given a taste of his own medicine, and he hadn't liked it one bit.

CHAPTER 13

"Mrs. McCabe?"

Charisse glanced up from her open trunk. "I'm in here."

John Jessup's head appeared in the opening at the back of the wagon. "You busy?"

"Why, good afternoon, Mr. Jessup," she said.

"Call me, John. My youngun's talk about you so much, I feel like we're old friends."

"John it is, then," Charisse said with a smile. "And I'm Charisse. So, what brings you here this afternoon?"

"I wanted to apologize for my Morgan. Don't rightly know what gets into that girl sometimes."

"No need for an apology. Toby has a bad habit of opening his mouth before he thinks. He wasn't very diplomatic, I'm afraid."

"Don't know why she's so doggone prickly about it, anyway." He sighed. "Morgan's never had anybody but me and the boys. Her mother died a few hours after she was born. I expect that's got something to do with it."

Charisse felt a pang of pity. "Oh, John."

He took off his hat, and ran his fingers through his hair. "Emma wasn't one to let her condition stop her. I kept tellin' her to take it easy, but she just laughed and called me an old mother hen. Don't know what caused the baby to come early or why it was harder than the others. I sent Will after the doctor, but she was gone before they got back."

Charisse's heart went out to him. How well she understood the pain etched into the man's face and the guilt that haunted his soul because he hadn't been able to save the one he loved.

"It was hard to lose Emma that way," he said. "Thought

we'd lose Morgan too. She was such a tiny thing, not much bigger than my hand, but she has her mama's strength of will, and she's a fighter." The ghost of a smile crossed his face. "She wasn't one you could put off to the side and forget, either. Her beller was bigger than she was."

"That must have been hard. The twins couldn't have been very old."

"Nope. They were walking good and into everything." He shook his head. "Near thought I'd go crazy for a while, but Will and me got through it."

"You've done an amazing job, raising them all by yourself."

He gave her a rueful smile. "Except that Morgan's more boy than girl. Some folks might say I haven't done right by her. Emma might even be one of them."

"No," Charisse said softly. "She'd be proud of all your children and the fine job you've done with them. As for Morgan, I expect she'll outgrow it. She's not the first little girl to dress in britches, and I doubt she'll be the last."

"No, but most little girls got a woman around to show them the right way to go." He shook his head. "I know as much about being female as Franklin does about flying like a bird."

Charisse chuckled. "I suppose so. Still, Morgan will probably show an interest when she's a little older. I'm sure there will be women in Oregon who will be more than happy to take her under their wing." Especially if Morgan's father is part of the package, Charisse thought. There were many women who would find his bluff good humor and soft southern drawl irresistible.

"Thing is, Morgan doesn't take to most women." He smiled. "Except for you, of course. All my young'uns think you're about the best part of this adventure."

"I'm glad, because I like them too." Charisse paused. "You know, the women are getting together in a little while. We're going to the river to bathe. How about if I take Morgan?"

John looked doubtful. "I wouldn't mind, but Morgan isn't

real fond of bathing. Don't know as you'll be able to convince her to go along."

"Maybe not, but it might help her start to see herself as female."

"It might at that." John shrugged. "If anyone can get her to do that, it'd be you. You've got a real way with young'uns, Mrs. McCabe, and that's a fact." He returned his hat to his head and pushed away from the back of the wagon. "Reckon it's time I got back to the river. We're building a ford so we can float the wagons across."

"Thank you for stopping by," she said. "I'll pick Morgan up in fifteen minutes or so."

"I'll tell her you're coming."

Charisse turned back to the open trunk with a sigh. "Now, if I can find something to wear, we'll be all set," she muttered. There was little left of her once extensive wardrobe. Most of it had been sold to help finance the trip to Oregon. Not that any of it would have been appropriate here, anyway. Silks, satins and heavy brocades had no place on the trail—or in the wilderness of Oregon, for that matter.

Pushing aside the memories, Charisse concentrated on what was left. She needed something to wear to the river, something decent but easily removed. Her dressing gown was a possibility, of course, but she had no desire to parade through camp in the middle of the day in her nightclothes. Near the bottom of the trunk, she found a green gingham Mother Hubbard dress left over from her pregnancy thirteen years before.

As she pulled out the simple dress, she smiled in satisfaction. High fashion styles came and went, but the dependable Mother Hubbard stayed the same. Charisse pursed her lips as she shook out the folds. She couldn't remember exactly why it had survived the great wardrobe purge. Most likely because it was plain and of little value. Of course, it could have had something to do with Preston's profound hatred of the garment. He called it a creation of the lower class and forbid her to wear it in public.

It only took a few moments to strip out of her dress, corset, and petticoats. As they pooled around her feet, Charisse couldn't help but marvel at the way her life had changed in the few short weeks since she'd met Luke McCabe. A mere month ago she would have considered it scandalous to go about with less than half a dozen petticoats. The rigors of the trail had given her a whole new perspective. She was down to three and figured on reducing that number as soon as her days weren't spent on the hard wagon seat where the extra padding was welcome.

Charisse slipped the Mother Hubbard over her head and tied the inside piece around her breasts. As with all Mother Hubbards, it fell from her shoulders straight to the floor, its shapeless style effectively hiding the female form beneath.

With a delightful sense of freedom, she climbed from the back of the wagon. The sight of the clothesline made her stop. Why not air out her corset while she was bathing? Her dress and petticoats she'd wash tomorrow, but this was the only chance she'd get to freshen the corset. She glanced around the camp to make sure no one was watching, then reached back into the wagon to retrieve her clothing. It only took a few minutes to hang it over the clothesline. She was a little embarrassed to leave her underwear hanging out that way for everyone to see, but there was no help for it.

With a shrug, she gathered her soap and towel and made her way to the Jessup's wagon. She found Morgan sitting on the wagon tongue staring glumly at the ground. "Good heavens, what's the matter?"

"Pa says I have to take a bath." Morgan kicked at a small beetle near her foot. "It ain't fair. None of the boys have to."

"It isn't fair," Charisse corrected, "and I guess it's my fault. I led your father to believe we were going to bathe, which isn't strictly true."

Morgan looked up in surprise. "It's not?"

"No. You have to have a proper tub and hot water to take

a bath, you know. What we're doing is more like swimming."

Morgan brightened. "It is?"

"Certainly, but don't tell the boys. They'll all want to do it too, and I don't think any of the men will be able to take time away from building the ford to keep an eye on them."

"So, it's only the women that get to go swimming?" Morgan looked distinctly pleased.

Charisse smiled. "That's right."

Excitement lit the little girl's face. "What are we waiting for? She bounced off the wagon tongue and grabbed Charisse's hand. A moment later she was dragging Charisse along as she raced toward the water.

"You don't have to run," Charisse said with a chuckle.

"I want to see the river. Pa wouldn't let me go by myself."

"It isn't going anywhere." Charisse might as well have saved her breath because Morgan continued to pull her along at a good clip.

As they neared the river, though, the sound of feminine voices drifted to them over the ripple of the water, and Morgan suddenly slowed her headlong flight. Nothing was said, but Charisse understood how the little girl felt. She wasn't exactly eager to arrive herself. Though these women knew nothing of her divorce, it had been a long time since she'd been accepted by decent folks.

"What do you think they'll say?" Morgan asked in a small voice.

"Say?"

"About me being there. None of them knows I'm a girl." She looked up at Charisse with a woeful expression.

"I don't suppose they will say much of anything. Most of them probably haven't noticed you." She smiled. "Besides, you're with me."

She was rewarded with a relieved grin. "And they wouldn't dare say anything against you."

Charisse wished she were as certain as Morgan. There was little chance any of the ladies knew of her shame, but she couldn't help but feel nervous.

"Mrs. McCabe?" A soft voice behind her made Charisse glance back over her shoulder.

"Mrs. Simms, I'm so glad you came!"

Caroline gave her an uncertain smile. "Please, call me Caroline."

"Only if you'll call me Charisse. I don't know if you've met Morgan Jessup yet. She decided to come swimming with the rest of the women." She winked at Morgan.

Morgan nodded eagerly and grinned at Caroline. "We told the boys we're bathing though, so we wouldn't have them following us down here."

A flicker of surprise crossed Caroline's face as she glanced at Morgan, but it was gone in an instant. "No, we wouldn't want that."

She was rewarded with a bright smile from Morgan and returned it with a rather hesitant one of her own. Charisse felt a pang of pity. How dismal and joyless Caroline's life must be. She watched as Caroline gave the small group at the river an uncertain look and suddenly realized Caroline was as uneasy as she and Morgan. What a trio of nervous Nellies they were, and the other two were looking to her for guidance. What a joke that was! Yet, somehow, knowing they were depending on her gave her a boost of courage. "Well, ladies," she said cheerfully, "shall we join the others?"

"Guess we might as well get it over with," Caroline said.

Charisse gave her an encouraging smile then turned with a show of confidence she was far from feeling, and walked down the trail to the tiny beach where the other women were staring at the river.

"I don't know, it looks awfully swift," Mrs. Duncan said. "And that poor man from the other wagon train did drown."

"Yes," said Sadie Swindell, "but my husband told me he got tangled up in the wagon somehow and was pulled under out in the middle where the current is strongest. If we stay close to the bank —"

"Good afternoon." They all turned toward the new voice in surprise. Mrs. Mantella sat above them on the riverbank safely ensconced in her special chair. Her son had evidently carried her, chair an all, down to the river. Charisse was reminded strongly of a queen on her throne as the muscular young man helped Mrs. Mantella alight.

"There's a good boy, Robbie," she said, with a pat to his cheek. "You go find the men. I'll send someone when I'm finished."

"The men?" he looked confused.

"Yes, dear. Follow the river that way, and you'll find them."

"But you said —"

"Robbie!" Mrs. Mantella's voice was sharp. "Do as I say." She turned away as though her son's compliance was a foregone conclusion. He stared after her for a minute as she shuffled toward the bank. Finally, he turned and trudged down river with a bewildered look on his face. Charisse couldn't help feeling a little sorry for him, then reminded herself she had no experience with the feeble-minded. Perhaps harsh words were all he understood.

"You there," Mrs. Mantella said, gesturing toward Caroline, "What are you waiting for? Can't you see I need a hand?"

Caroline started, then scrambled up the bank.

All eyes were on them as Caroline helped the elderly lady down the trail to the river. Watching the tiny little bird of a woman totter down the trail was nerve-wracking, and Charisse knew she wasn't the only one to breathe a sigh of relief when the trip was over.

"Thank you," Mrs. Mantella said brusquely as Caroline moved away.

Suddenly, Charisse felt Morgan's hand slip into her own and the little girl's body push close to her side. She glanced down and was surprised to see her watching Mrs. Mantella with a troubled frown.

"Is she a witch?" Morgan whispered.

"Good heavens, no. Whatever gave you that idea?"

"She looks like one."

Charisse thought of her conversation with John Jessup and wondered if Mrs. Mantella was the first elderly woman Morgan had ever been around. "Mrs. Mantella isn't a witch. She's just old." Charisse gave the little girl a reassuring smile. "Come on. Let's get ready."

In the end, Morgan seemed to forget all about Mrs. Mantella as she splashed joyfully with Charisse. If the other women noticed Morgan's underthings were more in the male style than female, none of them mentioned it, and the little girl soon relaxed enough to let Charisse wash her hair.

For herself, Charisse found bathing in the open, dressed only in her shift and drawers, a bit daunting. The water was cold and not nearly as clear as she would have liked. Still, the thought of being clean again was well worth the discomfort, and she emerged from the river refreshed and very glad she had come.

When all the women were dressed, Mrs. Mantella imperiously commanded Caroline to fetch Robbie for her. Incensed by the woman's audacity, Charisse had just opened her mouth to give the autocratic Mrs. Mantella a piece of her mind when she caught Caroline's eye. The other woman gave her a warning look and a slight shake of her head. Charisse said nothing, but watched with a jaundiced eye as Caroline did the old woman's bidding.

Robbie arrived a short time later, helped his mother to her chair and strapped her in. Then he put his arms through the special straps, heaved the whole apparatus up onto his back and set out toward their wagon with a careful, long-legged stride. Charisse wasn't the only one to watch in amazement. Robbie Mantella was the strongest man any of them had ever seen. The topic occupied the rest of the women of the wagon train for a good five minutes while they finished their ablutions.

Charisse and Morgan sat on the bank, allowing their hair

to dry. One by one the women returned to their wagons, but Charisse was reluctant to leave the grassy hillside and the warm sunshine.

Relaxed and content, Morgan lay on the ground watching Charisse brush her hair with open curiosity. "How come you keep brushing it instead of letting it dry?"

"Brushing makes it soft and shiny. I give it one hundred strokes every night."

"Every night? Doesn't it hurt?"

"No, it feels kind of nice. Doesn't your father brush your hair?"

"He used to until the boys broke my mother's hairbrush." Morgan pulled a stem of grass and stuck it in her mouth. "They tried to brush the mud out of a horse's tail with it. Pa tanned their backsides good for that one."

"And Pa never got around to buying a new hairbrush?"

"Nope." Morgan rolled to her back and gazed up at the sky. "I was pretty little then so my hair was short and a comb worked just as well."

Charisse watched the little girl studying the clouds for a long moment then patted her leg. "Come here, Morgan. Let's brush your hair."

With Morgan settled on the ground before her, Charisse gently pulled the brush through the soft mass. "You have beautiful hair, Morgan. It's such an unusual color."

"Papa says it's like Mama's, and Will says it's exactly the same color as a palomino's mane and tail."

"I think it's called 'flaxen,'" Charisse said with a wry smile. "Anyway, it's very pretty."

"Do you think so?"

"I do. If your father said it's like your mother's, it probably won't get any darker. Someday it will make you a beautiful woman."

Morgan sighed and settled herself more comfortably as Charisse continued brushing. The rhythmic stroking of the brush and the warm sunshine nearly put both of them to sleep.

At last Charisse glanced at the sun dipping slowly toward the western horizon. "Goodness, it's almost time to start supper. Your father will be wondering what happened to us."

"I'll tell him we were busy doing woman things." Morgan reached up and felt her hair. "It's so soft!"

Charisse set the brush down and quickly braided Morgan's hair. "That's what brushing does. Would you like me to teach you how to take care of it?"

"Would you?"

"I'd love to, but right now, we'd best get back to the wagons."

As soon as Charisse tied off the last braid, Morgan helped Charisse gather the soap and towel, chattering happily the whole time. When they arrived at the Jessup wagon Morgan turned to Charisse and gave her an impulsive hug. "Thank you, Mrs. McCabe. This was the best day ever!"

"I'm glad. I enjoyed it, too." As Charisse hugged her back she felt the cold band of ice around her heart loosen another notch. "Run along now. I'll see you later."

With a smile on her face, Charisse stood watching her go. Six months ago, she wouldn't have believed it possible, but with the help of Toby, and now Morgan, she was starting to heal. Perhaps it was time to take that first step, the one she had been dreading with every fiber of her body for two years. Perhaps it was time to start letting go.

With a determined set to her jaw, Charisse climbed into the wagon and opened the lid of her trunk. It only took a few minutes to find what she was looking for. The box was at the very bottom, tucked carefully under the last of her grandmother's quilts and a large leather-bound book.

Charisse closed her trunk, set the box on the top, and ran her hand across the polished wooden surface, then opened it before she lost her courage. Inside rested a lifetime of memories. She removed a tissue wrapped package, then stared down at it for a long moment, knowing what lay inside but afraid to look. At last she took a deep breath and folded back the paper. The child-sized hair brush and mirror looked the same as they had when Charisse, sobbing with grief, had put them away.

She blinked back tears as she picked up the silver-backed brush. Annabelle hadn't been much more than four when Charisse had bought the set for her. Every night they sat on the edge of Annabelle's bed, and Charisse brushed her daughter's hair. Then, with Annabelle tucked into bed, Charisse would settle in the rocker and read aloud. It always ended with a "happily ever after" and a goodnight hug and kiss.

Charisse lay the brush aside, picked up the mirror and smiled as she ran her fingers over the polished surface. Annabelle had called it her magic mirror and said it made her look like an enchanted princess.

or the first time, the memory of their nightly ritual brought Charisse a warm glow instead of overwhelming pain. Somehow, she thought Annabelle would approve of giving her brush and mirror to Morgan Jessup instead of hiding them away in the bottom of a dark trunk.

"I'll be damned. Will you look at that?" The masculine voice outside the wagon made Charisse jump. She glanced up and saw four silhouettes on the canvas.

There was a low whistle of surprise. "I've heard of things like that happening, but I never really believed it."

"Actually, it's pretty common. I guess they do it for the salt."

"Yep, an ox is just a big cow, and you know how they love salt. Can't say I envy you explaining this to the missus, though, McCabe."

She heard Luke sigh. "No, I don't think she's going to be very happy about it."

What in the world? Charisse made her way out of the wagon and rounded the corner. Luke and three other men stood next to the wagon staring at something on her makeshift clothesline. "What's going on?"

All four gave a guilty start. "Uh...afternoon, Mrs.

McCabe," John Jessup said, doffing his hat. "Me and Will was just on our way back to our wagon. See you tomorrow, Luke."

"Me too," said a man Charisse knew vaguely. He blushed a bright red and hurried away after the Jessups.

Charisse stared after them in surprise.

"I'm sorry, Charisse," Luke said. "I didn't know the oxen would do this."

"Will you quit shilly-shallying, and tell me what you're talking about?" she said irritably.

Luke pointed to the clothesline. "Near as I can tell, Polly and Lightning are responsible."

"For what— Oh, my goodness!" Charisse's hands flew to her mouth in shock as she gazed at the tattered bits of cloth and whalebone hanging from her clothesline. While she'd been bathing and lazing about in the sunshine, the oxen had eaten her corset!

CHAPTER 14

"There's got to be an easier way to do this!" Charisse muttered as she knelt next to the wash tub and tried to get the stains out of Toby's shirt. Though she had watched the other women closely she couldn't seem to get a rhythm going. Just when she thought she had it, her hand slipped off the washboard, and she nearly plunged headfirst into the tub of suds.

Caroline watched her efforts quizzically. "If I didn't know better, I'd think you'd never used a washboard before."

Charisse sat back and sighed. "It's that obvious, is it?"

"Only because I was watching. Besides, you're not the only one. The Swindell ladies aren't doing much better." She nodded over her shoulder to Violet and Sadie Swindell. Sadie was wet from shoulder to waist and Violet's bright red hair hung around her face in untidy strings.

"At least they seem to know what they're doing."

"You should have seen them before Miss. Duncan showed them how. Here look, you're not using enough pressure on the washboard." Caroline took Toby's shirt from Charisse's hand. "First you rub soap on the spot and scrub the sides together over it. Then you use the washboard like this." She demonstrated as she spoke, her elbows working up and down like pistons and her forearm muscles straining. "See, you have to press down hard. Here, now you try it."

Charisse took the shirt back and tried again. Caroline shook her head. "You're not pressing hard enough. You have to put some power behind it. Think of someone you'd like to give a good drubbing to and pretend that's who you have in your hands. It works like a charm."

A sudden image of Preston appeared in Charisse's mind,

and she set to work with a vengeance. The improvement was apparent almost immediately. Caroline nodded approvingly, and it wasn't long before the pile of laundry had been washed. With Caroline's guidance, Charisse soon had it rinsed in the river and ready to hang, though she hadn't been able to wring it out very well. She stood staring down at it with a satisfied feeling of accomplishment. Her laundry might not be quite as clean as the other women's, and it was certainly wetter, but Charisse felt better than she had in months.

"Mama, come quick!"

Charisse's head jerked up, and her heart caught in her throat as Toby and Franklin raced toward her. "What is it?" she said in alarm.

"They're taking a wagon apart to build a ferry! Can I ride in it when they get it finished?"

"No, you may not."

"Rats!"

"You'll probably cross on the ferry tomorrow, but you're not stepping one foot on it until they've taken it across several times, and we're sure it's safe." She ruffled his hair. "Don't worry, by the time we get the whole wagon train across the river, you'll have your fill of it. In the meantime, you can help me hang these clothes."

"Aw, Mama. Do I have to?"

"No, and I don't have to fix supper either, but I don't suppose you or your father would be too happy if I didn't. Think how nice it will be to have clean clothes."

Toby gave her a look that clearly said what he thought of having clean clothes to wear, but he started helping her pile them into the empty washtub without any further complaint.

"Uh oh."

Charisse glanced at Eliza Duncan, who was dumping the last of the hot water from the tub they'd set on the fire. "What's the matter?"

"We didn't get everything out," she said, picking up a man's steaming undershirt with the broom handle they'd used for stirring. "Anybody recognize it?"

"Oh, dear." Charisse suddenly realized she hadn't washed Luke's undershirt. "I think it's mine," she said, scanning the contents of her laundry pile.

Miss. Duncan eyed it critically before handing it over. "It's seems to be all right."

"Thank goodness. Luke would have a fit if I ruined his undershirt!" Charisse gingerly took the stick, wondering what the heck she was supposed to do now. The shirt was way too hot to wring out. Besides, it hadn't been washed yet, and she'd already dumped her water.

"Here," said Violet Swindell. "I still have my water. You can use it if you like."

"Thanks." Charisse dumped the shirt in the tub and used her newly acquired skills on the washboard. She couldn't help but smile as the conversation ebbed and flowed around her. These women accepted each other at face value, no questions asked. They had been on the trail less than a fortnight, and already she was happier than she'd been since Annabelle's death.

With Toby's help, Charisse lugged the clean clothes back to the wagon. Luke had switched the clothesline to the other side so the oxen wouldn't make another meal of their clothing. In very little time, she and Toby had the clothes on the line and were on their way to the river.

As they drew nearer, sounds of hammering and men's voices rose above the rush of the water. Charisse walked upstream a little way and found a place for her and Toby where the high grassy bank fell away to the river below where the men were working. "This looks like a good spot," she said. "We can see everything that goes on but we won't be in the way."

They had just sat down when Will Jessup stepped away from the group of men with a scowl on his face and pointed toward the trail. Moments later a belligerent Morgan appeared. Though Charisse couldn't hear what was being said, it was plain that Will wanted Morgan away from the activity.

Charisse cupped her hands around her mouth and called.

At the sound of her name, Morgan looked up and a sunny smile broke out on her face. A second later she was flying up the trail toward them and soon settled in beside her friends, perfectly content to watch the action from afar, now that Toby was there.

Charisse smiled at the animated conversation between the two of them as she focused on the activity below. The men had emptied one of the wagons, removed the wheels and set the box upside down on the canvas top.

"Look, Mama. Mr. Baxter is crossing the river," Toby said, pointing far upstream on the opposite bank where Ben was waist deep and leading his horse into the water. As they watched, he urged Adonis in deeper and deeper until the animal started swimming. Baxter grabbed Adonis's tail and allowed the horse to tow him across. They drifted downstream with the current and finally struck the bottom less than a hundred feet from where Charisse sat with the children.

"Well, isn't that clever!" Charisse said. She had an impression of long muscular legs and a bare masculine chest as man and horse climbed out on land. Ben had stripped to his drawers, probably to keep his clothing dry when he crossed. Charisse quickly averted her eyes, praying he hadn't seen her watching him.

"Hey, there's Pa," Morgan said. "And the twins are with him."

"I'll bet they're going to water the horses," Toby said. "Can we go see if they need help, Mama?"

"I don't know —"

"It's all right, Mrs. McCabe," Morgan put in. "If Pa doesn't want us there we'll come right back."

"I suppose it's all right then, as long as you promise to come back if he tells you to."

The two were off like a shot, and Charisse was left alone on the bank. Mindful of Ben Baxter dressing a few yards upstream, she kept her gaze fixed on the men working on the ferry. They were busy pulling the canvas top up around the wagon bed and attaching it to the sides. What in the world were they up to?

"We do seem to keep running into each other, don't we?"

"Oh!" Charisse started and turned. Ben Baxter stood next to her on the bank. He was fully dressed and completely dry. "I…I didn't know you were there." She gestured toward the men below. "I was watching them and wondering what they're doing."

He moved to the edge of the bank for a better look. "Looks like they decided to make a boat. Luke's book said the best way was to turn a wagon bed upside down and fill it with empty water barrels to make it float. When I left, they were trying to locate the barrels. Must not have found enough."

"I thought you were going to help build the ford."

"I was, but Captain Jeveraux sent me across the river to scout."

"Oh?" As Charisse looked up at him her eyes strayed to the back of his saddle where the wet drawers were tied. She looked quickly away, hoping she wouldn't blush. She knew she hadn't been successful by the quizzical way he looked at her. "Did you…um… find anything of interest?" she asked.

He took his hat off and ran his fingers through his hair. "The other wagon train is only about fifteen miles ahead. They have a lot of sickness, and they're hoping the slower pace will give folks time to recover."

"I see."

"Is something wrong?" he asked.

"Wrong? Heaven's no, why would you think that?"

"You seem sort of…. jumpy, I guess."

"I was just, uh… wondering if you saw anything else."

"Well, I did see some Indians."

"Indians!" Charisse squeaked in alarm. "How far away are they?"

"At the speed we've been traveling, I'd say we'll pass their camp a day or two after we cross the river, but they —" With a sharp cry he disappeared from sight. Adonis gave a terrified snort, jerked back on the reins, and took off across the prairie.

Charisse sat frozen for several seconds, too stunned to move, then scrambled to her feet and rushed toward the spot where the bank had crumbled beneath his feet. "Ben!" she cried, peering over the edge. "Ben, are you all right?"

Below she could see him floundering in the muddy water of the river, and he was being swept downstream at a rapid rate. "Help!" she yelled, running toward the men at the ford. "Help!"

As they looked up at her, she realized she had pulled their attention away from the river, and Ben was going to go right by them without anyone knowing the difference. "Man overboard!" she yelled and pointed toward the water. By then Ben had righted himself and managed to swim into the shallower water near shore. He rose to his feet and waded out, wet and bedraggled.

Charisse hurried down the trail to the water's edge where the other men had stopped work to watch his struggles.

"There are easier ways to wash your clothes, Baxter," said one with a deep chuckle.

"That's right. I reckon a good-looking fella like you could'a sweet-talked the ladies into doin' it for you."

Joshua Simms spit on the ground. "Or maybe you were takin' a swim. Seems a might odd since you were so careful to keep your clothes dry when you forded your horse."

Ben walked past them all in stony silence as the whole crowd laughed at his expense.

Luke gave Charisse a quizzical look. "Man overboard?"

"It was all I could think of," she said. "He could have drowned!"

"Baxter was never in any danger," he said. "The current is farther out and it's only two feet deep here. That's why we're building the ford here."

Luke's grin told her she'd over-reacted. Flushed with embarrassment, and with the men's laughter ringing in her ears, she beat a strategic retreat in Ben's wake.

"A-are you all right?" Charisse asked hesitantly as she caught up with him.

His expression softened a trifle. "I should have known better than to stand on a bank that's been undercut by the stream." He gave her a rueful smile. "I wouldn't recommend swimming in your clothes, though. They tend to drag you down."

"I'm glad they didn't pull you under."

"If the water had been deeper they might have." He sat on a rock at the top of the hill and pulled off his right boot. "You didn't happen to notice which way my horse went, did you?" he asked as he dumped the water out.

"Toward the wagons, I think. Maybe someone caught him for you."

"Maybe." He poured the water from his other boot. With a grimace, he pulled them back on and stood. "I hope you'll excuse me, Mrs. McCabe. I need to go find Adonis and change clothes."

"Of course, I... oh, wait. There's your hat." She hurried over to the bank where she'd been sitting, scooped up his hat, and took it to him. "You must have dropped it when you fell."

"Well, at least that's dry." He plopped it on his head. "As usual, it's been a pleasure, Mrs. McCabe."

"A pleasure! How can you say that?"

He gave her one of his heart-stopping grins. "With you around, a man never knows what might happen next." He tipped his hat and moved off toward the wagons.

Charisse thought she might be sick.

It was sometime after midnight that Charisse woke with a start. At first, she didn't know what had awakened her. Then she realized Luke was getting out of bed. She was about to ask what was wrong when he glanced over his shoulder at her. The movement seemed furtive, somehow. Telling herself he just wanted to make sure he hadn't disturbed her, she closed her eyes to a crack and held her tongue. He slipped into his pants, then quietly picked up his shirt and boots before creeping off into the darkness.

Charisse opened her eyes and watched until he was out of sight. *He could be going to answer the call of nature*, she told herself, but when he still hadn't returned fifteen minutes later, she knew he wasn't coming back. She told herself it didn't matter, but deep inside she knew it did—it mattered a great deal.

CHAPTER 15

"Do we have everything caulked?" Luke asked, studying the inside walls of the wagon.

"I think so." Charisse dropped her dauber back into her bucket. "Everything is covered with pine tar, including Toby. I'm glad you thought of sending him out to gather firewood before he completely ruined everything he had on." She eyed Luke's tar-covered chest. "I'm afraid your undershirt is a lost cause. It's a good thing you took your vest and shirt off first."

"Guess I'd better change before we start reloading."

"Your other undershirt is in the top of my trunk with the rest of your clean clothes."

Charisse was thoughtful as she untied her soiled apron. For the first time, she pondered the inconsistency of the McCabe clothing. Toby had an entire wardrobe from play clothes and underwear to his Sunday best. Most of it was new by the look of it. Luke, on the other hand, had only the clothes on his back and a single change. It was more what she would expect a man to take for a week away from home rather than starting a whole new life. It didn't make sense. Luke was not particularly impulsive, and yet, by his own admission, he'd thrown a change of clothes in a saddle bag and set out for Oregon on a whim.

"What the hell?"

The loud exclamation brought Charisse's head around with a jerk. "What's the matter?" she asked as she stepped from the wagon. "Oh, my!"

The arms of Luke's undershirt ended a good two inches above his wrists and a wide strip of skin peeked out between its bottom and the top of his pants. The rest was molded to his body, clearly defining the well-developed muscles beneath. "It must have shrunk in the wash."

"Really?" he said with heavy sarcasm.

"I left it in the boiling water too long. I'm sorry. It was an accident, all right? I never claimed to be a laundress."

"Or a cook?"

"No, and while we're at it, I'm not great at scrubbing floors either." She wadded up her apron and threw it at him. "Next time do your own laundry!" With that, she turned and stomped off. Dratted man, anyway. It wasn't like she was actually his wife!

Charisse was almost to the river before she slowed. After her divorce, she'd decided to never again be the meek little mouse that bowed to some man's every whim. Going on the offensive with Luke had worked rather better than she'd expected. She'd left him speechless. Anyway, she refused to feel guilty. So, Luke's shirt was a little tight. It would stretch… maybe.

If the truth be known, she thought he looked darned good in it! Her one peek at his manly chest the night of the rattlesnake attack had left its mark. The image popped into her head quite frequently, but what she'd seen this morning was oh, so much better. She permitted herself a small smile. Yes indeed, the sight of Luke in that undershirt was going to stay with her a good long time.

She stopped at the top of the hill where the road dipped down to the river. Chaos reigned below with men and animals all moving in different directions. The biggest source of confusion seemed to be Jessup's small herd of horses as they milled around near the river. As she watched, John swung Morgan up on the first horse and picked up a lead rope. When he led them up the shore, Charisse realized the horses were all tied together, each attached to the one in front by a short rope. The twins brought up the end of the procession holding onto the ropes of the last two and making sure they stayed in line.

John stopped at a place about ten yards upstream and

yelled something across the river. About twenty yards downstream, on the other side, Will and Ben Baxter picked up a rope and waved a hand. John walked into the river leading the first horse. As Will and Ben pulled on the rope, Charisse saw it was attached to John's rope and the horse Morgan was riding. John waded into the river until he was about thigh deep, let go of the horse he was leading and patted his daughter on the leg as she went by.

Charisse's heart jumped to her throat as she realized Morgan was expected to ride across by herself, but she soon saw there was little danger. The small girl clung to the broad back of the horse like a lichen to a rock, encouraging it and keeping its nose pointed in the right direction. The other horses followed behind like so many trained dogs. Ben and Will kept the rope taut and the horses moving.

"I'm sorry I yelled at you, Charisse."

Luke's deep voice drew her attention away from the river. She glanced at him with raised eyebrows. "Which time?"

"Just now." He looked so contrite she was hard put not to laugh. She hadn't planned on staying away this long, but had gotten so involved in watching the horses she'd forgotten all about Luke and their supposed fight.

"Look, Charisse, about the undershirt; I may have overreacted a little."

"A little?"

"All right, a lot. Anyway, I'm sorry." He extended his hand palm up. "Friends?"

Charisse looked at his hand and pretended to consider for a long moment, then nodded. "Friends." She put her hand in his and allowed him to pull her to her feet. "This has more to do with you needing help to reload the wagon than a guilty conscience, doesn't it?"

"It might have occurred to me." He gave her a sheepish grin. "Besides, you didn't throw a fit yesterday like you could have. I guess if you can get along without a corset, I can get along without an undershirt."

The thought of them both without their underthings suddenly struck Charisse with the subtlety of an earthquake. Skin to skin and heart to heart—it was an image that wouldn't go away. Without a word, she started back toward the wagon, praying Luke wouldn't notice the blush staining her cheeks.

Any constraint between them was soon forgotten in the rush to repack the wagon. Toby returned, and they put him to work, too. They were loaded in record time and lined up with the rest of the wagons ready to cross the river. Luke left to help the other men herd the cows and horses across. Charisse had her hands full keeping Toby and Franklin out of the way.

When it was their turn, Luke arrived to hitch the oxen up to pull the wagon down to the ford.

"You and Toby will be crossing on the ferry," he said.

"What? I thought someone had to be in the wagon in case it leaks!"

"Will Jessup is going to do it."

Charisse was incensed. "Why? Don't you think I can do my job?"

"Yes, I think you can do your job. In fact, that's exactly what I need you to do." He hooked the last harness tug to the wagon, then leaned on the wagon box. "You are the only one who can control Toby. How long do you think you could keep him on the wagon seat if you also have to watch the inside of the wagon?"

"Oh," she said. "I see your point."

"Besides," he said, "I'll feel better with both of you on the ferry where it's safe."

"Since you put it that way—"

Luke grinned. "Good, because I told John Jessup you probably wouldn't mind watching out for Morgan and the twins too."

Everyone had been told to pick items that needed to go across on the ferry in case the wagon box leaked. It wasn't long before Charisse was in the ferry with four children, a dog, a canary, five boxes of books, and Mrs. Mantella. The men on the other side of the river were about to begin the arduous task of pulling the small boat across when Luke signaled them to wait and deposited a large crate in the ferry.

"Granny's dishes," he said. "If they get broken in the crossing, I'd rather have you responsible for them than me."

"Good thinking!" Charisse said with a smile. "Thank you."

His eyes twinkled. "I'm always on the lookout for things that will save my hide." He reached down and ruffled Toby's hair. "Remember to mind your mama, and I'll see you on the other side, son."

The gesture touched her heart and warmth welled up inside her as she watched him walk away. Slowly, her smile faded. What in the world was she thinking? In a little less than two months she and Luke McCabe would part company. It was going to be hard enough to say good-bye to Toby. The last thing she needed was to develop tender feelings for his father.

Other than Mrs. Mantella's visible disapproval of traveling with Franklin, and the children's desire to hang over the edge of the boat, the trip across was uneventful. Still, Charisse breathed a sigh of relief when the small craft reached the other side. She unloaded her charges, and then sat down to watch the wagons as they came across.

It was interesting at first, but soon became monotonous. Toby and the Jessups went off to check the horses. Charisse carried her boxes to the wagon, then went for a walk down by the river.

"Mrs. McCabe. Charisse."

Charisse glanced back over her shoulder, and saw Ben walking toward her. "Ben," she said with real pleasure. "I see you're none the worse for wear after your ordeal yesterday."

"Nope. We Baxters bounce back pretty fast."

"That's good. I was afraid you'd—Uh oh."

"What's the matter?"

"Simms' wagon," she said, pointing back upstream to the ford. "I think it's stuck."

"Stuck?" He turned to look. "I think you're right."

"How is that possible?" she asked. "The wagons are floating on the water."

"Not that one." He pointed to where the water lapped the side of the wagon almost to the canvas. "Look how much lower it's sitting in the water. I think its wheels are on the bottom of the river and stuck in the mud."

Charisse frowned as Caroline stood and started rocking the wagon from side to side. "It looks like she's trying to dislodge the wheels."

That won't work. All it will do is make the wagon more susceptible to the current.

They'll have to pull it from... Jesus!" Charisse wasn't sure if he was praying or swearing as they watched the wagon teeter unsteadily for an impossibly long moment then begin to topple.

The sound of Caroline's scream as she pitched sideways into the water galvanized Ben into motion. "Don't let her out of your sight," he yelled to Charisse as he stripped off his shirt and raced toward the river. At the water's edge, he stopped long enough to jerk off his boots and shed his pants. He waded out until the water was about mid-thigh, then dove in and struck out toward the middle with long, sure strokes.

Caroline was nowhere to be seen. Charisse held her breath as she scanned the turbulent waters, desperately looking for some sign of her friend. This wasn't like Ben's dunking yesterday. He'd been out of the current, in the shallow water along the shore. Caroline had gone in where the water swirled and eddied with the power of a runaway freight train. Just when she was beginning to lose hope, Caroline's head popped above the surface about fifty feet upstream.

"There she is!" Charisse yelled, as Caroline disappeared again. There was no way of knowing if Ben heard her above the roar of the river. Caroline reappeared, then went under again. It was as though some mighty invisible force were dragging her down.

"Hang on!" Charisse shouted as Caroline came abreast of her. "Help is coming!" She picked up her skirts and ran along the bank, keeping pace with Caroline. Her friend seemed to struggle less each time her head cleared the water.

Charisse finally spared a glance for Ben. It took a moment to locate him, swimming steadily toward an interception point downstream. At first she thought it wasn't going to work, that Caroline would be swept by too far out in the channel for him to reach. Then the current changed, and the river carried her closer to the shore. It took a moment for Charisse to realize Ben had been banking on it.

Caroline was still more than an arm's length away when the current brought them within a few feet of each other. Ben threw himself forward to make a grab for Caroline just as she was pulled under again, and they both disappeared from sight. For a heart-stopping minute Charisse thought he'd missed, and her hands flew to her mouth as she searched the roiling water for some sign of them. Just when she'd about given up hope, they resurfaced.

Ben only had a tenuous hold on Caroline's clothing and the current threatened to pull her out of his grasp. Fighting the irresistible force of the water, Ben slowly pulled her closer until he had her in his arms and secured against his body. For a moment, Charisse thought all was well. Then, with dawning horror, she realized Ben didn't have the strength to get them to shore.

She searched the bank in front of her looking for something, anything she could use to get Caroline and Ben out of the river. There was nothing. A feeling of helplessness welled up inside. She was going to watch her friends drown and there wasn't a thing she could do about it. A stitch was starting to develop in her side, but she kept running, determined not to give up until she dropped from exhaustion.

Her breath coming in hard painful gasps, Charisse knew her endurance was nearly at an end when she heard hoof beats behind her. Before she even had time to wonder who it was, Adonis streaked by with Luke bent low over his neck.

he pair thundered down the bank another hundred yards

until they reached a place where the river curved toward the land, forming a bend that thrust the bank out into the channel. They skidded to a stop so quickly that Adonis was nearly thrown onto his back haunches. In the blink of an eye, Luke was off and running toward the river.

Luke secured one end of the rope around his waist and formed the other into a lasso. Just before Caroline, Ben and Charisse reached the bend, Luke twirled the rope around his head and sent it sailing out over the water, just missing Ben's outstretched hand. Charisse could barely keep up with Luke as he ran down the bank and threw the second loop. This one fell wide and was carried downstream by the current. As they rounded the bend, it was plain to see that Ben and Caroline would soon be out of reach of the rope. Luke formed a third loop and threw it.

"Oh, no!" Charisse cried when it hit the water upstream out of Ben's reach. "No, no, no!" Then, miraculously, the rope floated almost straight to Ben who grabbed it and looped it around himself and Caroline. Charisse realized the rope had landed upstream just where Luke had intended it to. Luke braced himself on the bank, and the rope pulled taut. The jerk when Ben and Caroline hit the end nearly pulled him off his feet, and Charisse knew even with Ben's help Luke was going to have a tough time getting them out of the river.

"Get the horse!" Luke yelled.

Charisse stumbled up the slight incline with her breath still coming in painful gasps and her heart feeling as though it might burst from her chest. Though Adonis was a bit skittish, she managed to gather the reins and lead the horse down to the river's edge.

"Help get the rope on him," Luke yelled.

The relentless flow continuously jerked Ben and Caroline back and forth, threatening to wrench them away from their rescuers. Luke and Charisse struggled against the might of the river. It took both of them pulling with all their strength to get the rope tied around the saddle horn. Then Luke gave Adonis the signal to back, and Charisse prayed.

Slowly, inexorably, Ben and Caroline moved toward the bank of the river. At last, Ben staggered to his feet and carried Caroline to the shore where he dumped her into Luke's arms and collapsed on the sand.

Luke lay Caroline down next to Ben, and Charisse bent over her limp form. "Luke, she's not breathing!"

"Damn!" Ben pushed himself to his hands and knees, wavered for a moment then crawled over to Caroline. "I know what to do," he said, rolling her to her stomach. He gently turned her face to the side, then straddled her hips and began alternately pushing against her back and pulling her arms. "Come on, sweetheart. I'm not going to let you die on me now, not after what we just went through."

On the fourth push, Caroline suddenly heaved and water gushed out of her mouth. "That's it," Ben said. "Get it all out."

Caroline took a ragged breath and started coughing. Ben helped her sit up then supported her as the spasms wracked her body. He pulled her into his arms and rested her head against his chest when she was finished. She sat there for several seconds, then began to cry great gulping sobs. Ben patted her back and spoke soft encouragement until the storm passed.

"Oh, thank God!" Violet and Sadie Swindell arrived with a crowd of other people from the wagon train close behind. "We were afraid you wouldn't get to them in time."

Charisse helped drape blankets about Caroline and Ben. Then she followed closely as both were transported back to the wagon train where Mrs. Mantella insisted on putting Caroline in her own bed since the Simms' wagon had some drying out to do. Joshua Simms arrived, and expressed concern about his wife's condition, though Charisse felt it was too little, too late.

"Here are your clothes, Mr. Baxter," called Toby as he and Morgan came running up from the river.

"Thanks," he said, wincing as he reached out his hands.

"Are you all right?" Charisse asked.

"As well as can be expected. Thanks for your help out there today."

"What help? All I did was run along the river like a chicken with her head cut off."

"That's how I knew where Mrs. Simms was, and that's how Luke managed to find us. Without you, at least one of us would have died." He grinned suddenly. "You know, if I didn't know better I'd think you didn't want to talk to me. It seems like something happens to me every time I try."

He left to change clothes, oblivious to Charisse's stricken look.

CHAPTER 16

"I'm beginning to think Jeveraux has it in for you." Luke sauntered over to a large rock and sat down. "This is the third time this week you've pulled guard duty."

Ben shrugged. "Doesn't like getting beat at poker, I'm guessing."

"Still, I'd have thought he'd let you have one night off since you are the hero of the day."

"Some hero. We wouldn't have gotten out without you."

"Thanks to my good luck charm. I was only able to find you because Charisse was running alongside. Without her…" Luke shook his head.

"How did you get across the river so fast? The last I knew you were driving wagons down to the ford."

"I was. It seemed like a good way to check out Swindell's and Simms' wagons without anybody getting suspicious."

"And?"

"I find it strange that as protective as the Swindells are of their two extra wagons, they didn't bother to caulk them."

"Did they unload them?"

"They took about two dozen boxes out of one, but didn't touch the other."

Ben raised an eyebrow. "What was in the boxes?"

"Haven't a clue," Luke said. "But if I had to guess from the way they handled them, I'd say nitro glycerin."

"What?"

Luke shrugged. "They were very careful to only stack the boxes two high, and padded them with blankets. Even more interesting is that both Jesse and Frank traveled across the river with the load, then went back to drive the wagons across."

"Does seem a bit overprotective, doesn't it?" Ben frowned. "What about Simms?"

"Simms' wagon was the last. We ferried their supplies over first, and I came over with them."

"Good thinking. Find anything?"

"Nope. Nothing the least bit unusual. In fact, I think they're the only family who brought less than Charisse."

"That's strange," Ben said thoughtfully. "Especially since it looked to me like the wagon was too darn heavy to float."

"Looked that way to me too, but when I looked in the back of that wagon before the crossing, it was empty. They had taken everything out."

"False bottom, do you think?"

"I'd be willing to bet on it." Luke frowned. "Something else struck me as odd."

"What's that?"

"While you were risking your life to save his wife, Simms was risking his to save an empty wagon."

Ben raised an eyebrow. "What?"

"The minute that wagon started to tip, he was in the water trying to steady it. I swear he never even spared a glance for Caroline when she went into the water. In fact, he seemed angry she hadn't managed to rock the wheels loose like he told her to."

"That son of a bitch told her to stand up like that?" Ben eyes narrowed. "He doesn't deserve a sweet little thing like her."

"Nope, and it's going to be a pure pleasure to watch Mr. Joshua Simms fall."

Ben frowned. "So how exactly did he manage to save his wagon?"

"No idea. I'm pretty sure it didn't tip over, but I don't know how they got it unstuck. I was too busy running to find that piece of lightening you call a horse so I could save your backside. All I know is that when we came back, the wagon was safely on this side of the river and half reloaded again."

"I'd sure be interested to take a closer look at it."

Luke nodded. "Me too. Trouble is Simms never seems to leave it. Caroline does most of the chores. I'm sure you'll think of something, though."

"Me! Since when am I the problem solver?"

Luke grinned. "Since McNesby sent you to back me up."

"Jinx! Jinx! Jinx!" the crowd taunted Charisse as she walked the tightrope stretched across the river. Caroline Simms walked in front, carefully balancing a basket of laundry on her hip. Suddenly she seemed to stumble. For a long moment she teetered, then fell headlong into the roiling water below. Before Charisse's horrified eyes, she was swallowed up by the flood. A second later Ben Baxter pitched into the water. He stared up at her with accusing eyes before he too disappeared.

"It's all your fault!" yelled a condemning voice. "You're a jinx." Charisse turned and looked up into angry brown eyes. Preston. She backed away as he advanced on her, shaking his finger. "They're all going to die because of you. Toby, Luke, all of them."

Charisse jerked awake and blinked at the bright stars above her head. A whimper of denial rose to her lips, and she stifled it with the back of her hand. It wasn't true, never had been, though what happened today had badly shaken her confidence.

A slight noise on the other side of the wagon drew her attention, and she clutched her blankets to her chest in sudden fear. "Wh-who's there?"

Luke's face suddenly appeared as he hunkered down next to the wagon. "It's me, Charisse. I'm sorry I woke you."

"You didn't. I had a nightmare and…" She frowned. "What are you doing up this time of night?"

"I went to visit the bushes."

"Oh." She knew he was lying. Nobody got completely dressed for a five-minute trip to answer the call of nature.

"Are you all right?" he asked with concern. "You seem kind

of shaky."

"I'm fine. It was just the nightmare."

He took off his coat and tossed it to the end of his bed. "After what you went through today it's not surprising. That was a damn close call. Lucky thing you were there."

Charisse's eyes popped open. "What?"

"I said it was lucky. If you and Baxter hadn't been there, nobody would have been close enough to get to Mrs. Simms."

"Oh."

"And," he grunted as he pulled off a boot. "Without you, we would have lost them both."

He pulled off his other boot. "It's nearly impossible to locate somebody in the water if you don't keep track of them. I'd have never found them without your help. If not for you, we'd be having a funeral tomorrow."

"Ben said almost exactly the same thing."

"Because it's true." He pulled his blankets back and crawled into bed. "In my book, you're as big a hero as Ben Baxter. Now, go back to sleep. We're starting out extra early in the morning."

Charisse knew he was right, but sleep didn't come immediately. She lay looking at the stars, wondering where he'd been and trying to sort it all out. The only thing she knew for sure was that Luke's words had warmed a part of her she'd thought frozen forever.

It was still dark the next morning when Luke rousted her from her nice warm bed. As usual, he looked rested and ready to go. It irritated her because she knew darn well he'd had even less sleep than she'd had.

Charisse's humor was restored somewhat when she climbed up to her place on the wagon seat shortly after dawn. A smile split her face as she settled herself and picked up the reins. For the first time since they'd left Independence, she could drive without her corset stays poking into her. The thought of how horrified Preston would be if he could see her now cheered her up even more.

The next few days passed much as the others had, and Charisse began to wonder if the monotony of the trail would turn out to be the most difficult hardship of all. One day moved into the next with such unchanging sameness, she began to feel as though they hadn't made any progress at all.

Nearly a week after crossing the river, huge thunderheads began to build in the west in the late afternoon. By the time they stopped for the night, the clouds had turned black, and gale force winds bore down on them. Charisse and Toby huddled inside their wagon, terrified by the howling storm and wondering what was coming next, while Luke and the other men tried to secure the camp.

Predictably, Will Jessup brought Morgan by, then hurried off to help his father and brothers with the horses. Though Toby and Morgan were frightened by the storm, they were both incensed that they weren't allowed to help with the animals. Charisse wrapped them in blankets and sat down on her trunk, one child on either side of her. "We're the lucky ones, you know," she said.

Toby looked skeptical. "We are?"

"Of course, we are. Will and the twins are out there getting blown around in that terrible wind." She gave a dramatic shiver. "And it's probably going to rain on them too. Meanwhile, we're safe and dry in here."

Both children looked at the canvas cover above their heads that snapped and popped in the wind, disbelief clearly evident on their faces. They needed something to distract them. Then she had it. "You know what," she said. "I have a book I've been wanting to share with the two of you. Hop up and I'll get it out of my trunk."

Charisse could feel Toby and Morgan trying to peer around her back as she opened her trunk. She made a great show of digging clear to the bottom and carefully lifting the book out.

"This book was given to me by my mother when I was a

little girl. Her grandmother gave it to her."

Toby and Morgan stared at the book in wide-eyed fascination. "What is it?" Toby whispered.

"It's a book of fairy tales." Charisse reseated herself on the trunk and patted the top. "Come take a look."

Morgan reached out and touched the cover reverently. "What are fairy tales?"

Toby plunked himself down on the other side and scooted closer for a better look. "They're stories, huh, Mama?"

"Yes, they are, but they're special stories about dragons and witches and fairies and all kinds of magical things."

"Will you read us one?"

"Of course. That's why I got it out." She opened the book and started paging through it. "Which one shall it be?"

The storm howling outside was nearly forgotten as Toby and Morgan studied the pictures. "I like this one about the lady with the glass shoe," said Morgan.

"No, I want the one about the dragon."

They were halfway through the book before they hit on one they both wanted. Charisse winced inwardly. Hansel and Gretel. It was a gruesome tale, one she wouldn't have chosen herself. Still, she had promised, and they were ignoring the wind for the moment, at least. At the end they both sat back with a satisfied smile. "That was a really good story," said Morgan.

"Do wicked witches really eat children?" Toby wanted to know.

Charisse smiled. "There are no such things as witches. Even if there were, I'm sure it wouldn't be allowed. People care too much about their children to let someone hurt them."

"There's a witch on this wagon train," said Morgan. "Charisse and I saw her when we went to the river to bathe."

"Mrs. Mantella is not a witch," said Charisse, determined to stop that nonsense once and for all. "She's just an old woman."

"Then why is she so scary looking?"

"She probably wears black because she's in mourning for her husband. She looks the way she does because she's old."

"Pa says my grandmother is an old witch," Toby put in, "but she doesn't look anything like Mrs. Mantella."

"Your father was just upset with your grandmother. He didn't think she was really a witch, Toby. I hope you didn't repeat that."

Toby shook his head. "Nah, I haven't seen her since then." He sighed gustily. "And I probably won't on account'a 'cause she said good riddance to me. She didn't know how her sweet Elizabeth had produced such a little hellion. Elizabeth was my mama. Grandmother said I was the death of her."

Charisse suddenly found herself very much in agreement with Luke's assessment of his mother-in-law. "That's probably why your father called her an old witch. What she said to you was mean and not true. I'm sure your mother loved you very much."

"That's what Pa said. Anyway, I don't miss Grandmother or Grandfather, and I'm having a great 'venture so it's all right. I'm glad my Pa took me away."

Took him away? Charisse frowned as an odd frisson of unease trickled down her spine. *Did Luke fight with his in-laws, then snatch Toby up in a fit of anger and spirit him away?*

Morgan looked confused. "I thought Charisse was your Mama."

"She's my pretend Mama," Toby said. "My real Mama died when I was little."

Charisse winced. All they needed was to have it spread around the camp that she and Luke were only pretending to be married. "I'm your stepmother," she corrected him, "not pretend."

Morgan's eyes widened. "You mean like Hansel and Gretel had?"

"No, and I don't think most stepmothers are bad like that. The stories in this book are make-believe. None of the things in them are true."

"Will you read us another one?" Morgan asked.

"All right, choose one." If she hadn't quite convinced Morgan that Mrs. Mantella wasn't a witch, at least she'd squelched the "pretend mama" idea.

"This is the one," Morgan said, pointing to a picture of a woman in a tower.

"Rapunzel?" Charisse smiled. It had been one of Annabelle's favorites. At least the witch in this one wasn't quite as bad.

The story was an instant success with both children. Toby liked the prince with his dashing ways and vowed to grow up just like him. Morgan was more taken with Rapunzel, most particularly her hair.

"It's like mine, isn't it, Charisse?"

Charisse smiled. Annabelle had always said the same thing. "Yes, I think it is, though hers was a little darker."

"And a lot longer." Morgan took her hat off and touched her braid. "Maybe I'll let mine grow long like that."

Toby looked interested. "Will you let me climb it, like the prince?"

"Heck no! That would hurt. Besides it'll take a long time for it to grow that much. You'd be a man by then."

"Well then, how would I get you out of the tower?"

"You'd have to bring a ladder."

"On a horse?"

Charisse chuckled. "I don't think you'll have to worry about it. I doubt there are many towers in Oregon." She reached out and touched Morgan's hair. "That reminds me. I have something for you."

"For me?"

"Yes, I thought of it the other day when we washed your hair at the river. Here, Toby, hold the book while I get my box." Charisse rose and retrieved the wooden box from the crate where she'd set it, waiting for just the right moment to give Morgan the brush and mirror set. Both children were all agog as she settled herself on the trunk and opened the box. She carefully unwrapped the tissue paper and took out the brush and mirror.

Morgan's eyes widened and her mouth formed a perfect O as she stared at them. "Can I touch them?"

"Of course. They're yours."

"Mine?" Morgan looked up at her in utter disbelief. "Are you sure?"

Before Charisse could change her mind, she thrust them into the little girl's hands and looked back at the box, unable, for a moment, to stand the pain.

"Oooh!" With a soft sigh of incredulous joy, Morgan stroked the raised design on the back of the mirror with reverence. "Is it a fairy?"

A smile trembled on Charisse's lips and the lump dissolved in her throat. "Yes, and her name is Bella. At least it was, I suppose you can call her anything you want."

Toby leaned across Charisse's lap for a closer look. "Were they yours when you were little, like the book?"

"No, th-they belonged to my daughter, Annabelle."

"What happened to her?"

Charisse stared down at her tightly clenched hands and willed the tears not to fall. "She got very sick and died."

Toby put his hand on top of hers. "Like our mamas?"

Charisse nodded. "Yes, like your mothers."

Morgan's hand joined Charisse's and Toby's. "I'll bet she's with my mama and Toby's right now. I'll bet they're taking care of her the way you're taking care of us."

Charisse looked at them and smiled mistily. "I'll bet you're right. You know, Annabelle would have loved you two. She always wanted a little brother and sister."

"What did she look like?" Toby wanted to know.

"Would you like to see a picture?"

They both nodded eagerly. Charisse reached behind her trunk and pulled out her sketch pad. It was surprisingly easy to open. For the first time since the funeral, Charisse looked into her daughter's face and smiled. "I did this when she was about five," she said.

"She had pretty hair," said Morgan.

Charisse nodded. "She liked to wear it in curls with lots of ribbons and bows. Would you like to see more pictures of her?"

"Yes, please."

As she paged through her sketchbook with Toby and Morgan, Charisse once again felt the magnetism of her art. Though it was not something Preston approved of, drawing had been a secret passion of hers. She'd taken guilty pleasure in it whenever she got the chance. Maybe it was time she started drawing again.

"You know what?" Morgan said suddenly. "I know what to call the fairy on my mirror."

"Oh, what's that?"

"I'll call her Annabelle!"

Charisse smiled. "I think Annabelle would be very pleased."

Toby reached across Charisse's lap and touched the mirror. "I wish I had long hair."

"Don't be silly, Toby. You'd hate sitting still every morning while I brushed and braided it." Charisse opened the box again. "I have something for you, too. Let me see… here it is." She pulled out an emerald green bag held shut with a gold drawstring cord. "These were my father's when he was a boy. He gave them to me when I was a little girl, and I gave them to Annabelle because she loved them so."

Toby eagerly opened the bag and gasped with delight. "Marbles! Grandmother took mine away 'cause she said I didn't take care of them."

"You're older now, and I'm sure you'll take care of these," Charisse said. "They're very special to me, you know, and I wouldn't give them to you if I didn't think you'd be careful with them."

"Oh, I'll take the bestest care of these marbles. Can I look at them?"

"We'll need to put them in something… Ah, the very

thing." She emptied the few remaining items from the box and laid them on a nearby crate. "There. We'll pour them in here. That way you won't have to worry about losing any."

Toby and Morgan scooted off the trunk and settled on the tiny piece of empty floor space with the box between them. Charisse watched them explore the marbles for a few minutes, then, on a whim, opened her sketchpad to draw, and another piece of her heart fell back into place.

Charisse lay on her side, listening to the rain pounding the ground around the wagon. At least the storm had kept Luke home tonight. She stared at the crisp hairs on the back of his neck and wondered how he could sleep. If they lay on their sides, the wagon protected them from the worst of the storm, but she was still damp and uncomfortable.

The memory of the time spent with the children lay soft and warm in her heart. She'd been almost sorry when John Jessup arrived to claim his daughter. Charisse's mind wandered to Toby's surprising revelations. His reference to Luke taking him away puzzled her. Had he been living with his grandparents? In retrospect, she realized the few stories he'd told of himself with his father had all been recent, as though they had spent little time together in his younger years.

Then it clicked into place. The spur-of-the-moment trip to Oregon, Toby coming with everything and Luke with nothing. It all made a horrible kind of sense. They were running. She didn't know why Toby's grandparents had been in charge of the boy, but Luke had taken him away. Perhaps Luke wasn't even his father.

A sudden chill ran through her, and her stomach tightened in sick reaction. There was a name for things like that. It was called kidnapping, and Charisse was up to her neck in it.

CHAPTER 17

"**M**r. Baxter said we'll be reaching Fort Laramie tomorrow or the day after," Charisse said.

Luke nodded. "That's what I heard."

"Do you think we'll have time to do any trading?"

"Probably. I think the plan is to spend a couple of days there before we move on. Why, did you need something?"

"No. I was just wondering." Charisse lifted her skirt and stepped gingerly over a puddle. "One thing I do know is that I'm sick of mud!"

Luke grinned. "Seems to me you were saying the same thing about the dust two weeks ago."

"That was before it rained for three days straight. I'll never complain about dust again."

"At least it isn't raining now."

Charisse glanced at the leaden sky. "It isn't time to go to bed yet, either."

"At least our luck is still holding."

Charisse gave him a dumfounded look. "How do you figure that?"

"We still have enough dry wood to start the fire." He pulled half a dozen sticks of wood out of the back of the wagon and carried them over to the fire pit.

"The ground's wet."

"Then we'll start it in the frying pan like your book says."

"I suppose you want me to dig it out for you."

"You read my mind."

"Do you want the Lucifer matches too?"

"Yes, thanks." Luke put several pieces of wood in the fire ring, then hunkered down and started whittling thin slivers off another chunk.

"You know," Charisse said, as she brought the frying pan and matches to him, "This is the last of the wood, and I haven't seen any trees for the last few days."

"*The Prairie Traveler* said that would happen. It also said what to use instead."

Charisse made a face. "I know, buffalo chips. Somehow I find the idea of gathering buffalo dung and cooking with it less than appealing."

"At least it will give Toby and the Jessup children something to keep them out of mischief as we travel."

"Why are you always so darn positive?" Charisse asked irritably. "Nothing ever seems to affect you."

"I figure everything has a good side and a bad side," Luke said, as he arranged the kindling in the pan and lit the match, "I choose to see the good." He glanced up at her. "Is there some reason you're such a cynic?"

Charisse shrugged. "I don't know. I guess it's gotten to be a habit."

"Preston again?"

"Preston?" Charisse was about to deny it, then thought of all the times he'd berated her for petty little inconveniences and blamed her when things didn't turn out the way he wanted. Memories of a dozen arguments flashed through her mind as she watched Luke carefully transfer his fledgling fire to the wood in the fire ring. "Yes," she said slowly. "I suppose he did have something to do with it. The truth is, I wasn't a very good wife."

"Why, because you're smart and can think for yourself? Or was it because he wasn't able to control you? Is that why he ended your marriage?"

"N-no. He put up with that…sort of." Charisse crossed her arms over her chest and rubbed her elbows. "He divorced me because I did something unforgivable."

"You slept with another man?"

Her mouth fell open in shock. "No! Whatever made you

think that?"

Luke stood. "Because I can't think of anything else that would make a man walk away from a woman like you."

"What do you mean, 'a woman like me?'"

He regarded her quizzically. "You truly don't know, do you?"

"Know what?"

"That you're beautiful." He reached over and cupped the side of her face with his hand. "You, Miss Jones, are the kind of woman men fantasize about."

She stared up at him in astonishment. "I am?"

"Absolutely." His voice was a deep, sexy rumble as he ran the pad of his thumb across her lips. "They wonder if your mouth is as kissable as it looks, and if your skin is as soft." He eased her bonnet back and ran his fingertips against her hair. "Every man who sees this incredible hair of yours wonders how long it is, and how it would feel to make love to you with it curling around him."

Her eyes darkened to a soft, muted green "D-do you?"

"All the time," he whispered as he lowered his head and tasted her. "Definitely kissable," he murmured, then delicately touched the corner of her mouth with another kiss.

Charisse's breath left her with a soft sound somewhere between a whimper and a sigh as she settled against his chest. He smiled and took possession of her lips. At first it was soft and sweet, like the first rain of spring or the delicate inner petals of a rose. Then he tightened his arms around her and everything changed.

A curious melting sensation flowed over Charisse, and she lifted her arms to encircle his waist. This was no perfunctory touching of the lips like the kisses she was used to. It was full-bodied and demanding. Something warm and wonderful uncoiled inside as the kiss deepened, and she dissolved in his arms.

Then, without warning, a hunger like nothing she'd ever known began to grow inside her. Like the tiny flame in the fire ring, it caught and held, growing brighter and hotter by the second.

"Mama, is it all right if—hey!"

At the sound of Toby's voice, they broke apart and stared at each other.

"Pa, how come you were kissing Mama?" Toby wanted to know.

Morgan punched him in the arm. "'Cause that's what mamas and papas do, silly."

"Is it, Mama?" Toby wanted to know.

"Uh…" Charisse could feel herself blushing as she struggled to find an answer.

"It is if they're lucky," Luke said with a soft smile. Then he dropped another kiss on Charisse's forehead and turned away. "Come on, Toby, let's get this wagon unloaded so we have a place to sleep." He strode to the back of the wagon and began unloading boxes and crates. On the second night of rain, Luke had decided the supplies would fare better under the wagon than they would. All the unpacking and repacking added an hour on both ends of the day, but at least they could sleep. Morgan and Toby rushed to the back of the wagon, but Charisse just stood there and stared after them with a bemused look on her face.

Sleep didn't come easily to Charisse that night, even though they were warm and dry in the wagon. She kept remembering Luke's kiss and her reaction to it. Granted, it was the first kiss she'd had in several years, but it was more than that. Even at the beginning of her marriage, when she still fancied herself in love with Preston, she'd never felt the way she did with Luke.

Of course, Preston had never kissed her the way Luke had, either. Even in bed, his kisses had been very proper, almost chaste. It was probably a good thing, too. The one time she'd reacted to him had earned her a severe reprimand and a lecture on proper behavior for the people of their class. He would definitely not have approved of the way she'd melted in Luke's arms. Preston had performed his marital duty, as he termed it, though Charisse had always suspected he didn't find it particularly pleasant, at least not with her.

Somehow, she didn't think Luke would consider it a duty.

She was shocked awake several hours later by the sound of gunshots and frantic bellowing of frightened cattle. "You two stay here," Luke said as he pulled on his pants and boots.

"What's wrong?" Charisse asked.

"I don't know. Secure this flap as soon as I leave." With that, he grabbed his rifle and was gone.

Charisse did as he asked, feeling stupid the whole time. As though tying down a canvas flap was the same as barring a door. She crawled to the front of the wagon and peered out. She could see Luke in the dim light striding across the camp with Franklin at his heels. For a moment, she considered calling Franklin back, then decided against it as the two disappeared into the darkness. Franklin could be intimidating if one of his people was threatened, and he considered Luke one of his people.

Toby sat up and rubbed his eyes. "Mama, what's wrong?"

"I'm not sure. I think there's something after the cattle."

"Where's Pa?"

"He went to help."

"Oh, all right." He lay down and went back to sleep.

Charisse smiled to herself, then looked back outside. Lights appeared all over camp as people lit lanterns and candles. She could see a vast confusion of movement in the shadows beyond the glow of the lights. The main activity seemed to be beyond the perimeter of camp, which didn't make sense. The whole point of circling the wagons was to keep the stock contained. What were the cattle doing outside the circle? The occasional bark of a dog made her wince. Luke would not be pleased if Franklin was causing trouble.

A sudden noise right next to the wagon drew her attention.

There was something moving out there. Even though it was probably only one of the oxen, Charisse quietly pulled her derringer out of its hiding place and set the extra powder and balls nearby on her trunk. She was about to call out when a raspy whisper right next to the wagon froze the words in her throat.

"Are you sure this is McCabe's wagon?"

Charisse couldn't make out the words in the low-voiced reply, but there was something sinister in the tone.

"What are we looking for, exactly?"

Charisse thought she heard the word suspicious, but she wasn't sure. Then all thought of what they might be saying went out of her head as the point of a knife suddenly cut through the canvas at the back of the wagon.

The little derringer in her hand was no match for a man with a knife in close quarters. Surprise was the only chance she had. Aiming at a spot about a foot above the knife, Charisse took a deep breath and pulled the trigger.

The explosion of black powder was loud within the closed confines of the wagon, but not so loud it covered the yelp of surprise outside.

"Mama?" Toby sat up in alarm.

Charisse didn't even pause in her hurried efforts to reload. "Stay down," she ordered. She shoved the bullet down the barrel and seated it with the ramrod before crawling the few feet to the back of the wagon. Flattening herself on the floor, she reached up and undid the flap. That's when it occurred to her she had no idea what to do next.

If they were still out there, she was no better off than before. It was possible she'd wounded one, of course, but chances were good he was still alive. Besides, there was no way she'd hit them both. She considered calling for help, but wasn't sure Luke could hear her from here. He was the only one she could trust. Anyone else answering her call might well be the very ones who had tried to get in.

She was still considering what to do when she heard

running footsteps outside the wagon. With her heart thundering in her chest she cocked the little derringer, knelt on the floor of the wagon and slowly lifted the corner of the canopy to peek out.

"Charisse!"

Charisse screamed, whirled, and fired at the man at the front of the wagon before his identity registered. Luckily, the shot went wild, whizzing by Luke's head into the darkness beyond.

"What the hell?"

"Luke! Thank God!" The derringer dropped from nerveless fingers as Charisse rose to her feet.

"Somebody was trying to get into the wagon," Toby said. "Mama shot him with her little gun."

"I thought you were asleep, Toby," she said.

"I was only pretending, but I stayed down like you said."

"I knew I could count on you, Toby." Her knees were wobbly and there was a quaver in her voice as Luke climbed inside.

"Shh," he said, as he folded his arms around her. "You're safe."

"They were looking for something," she murmured against his shoulder, "but I don't know what."

"What do you mean?"

"I heard them outside the wagon." Charisse burrowed deeper into his comforting embrace as she told him of the whispered conversation.

"Did you recognize either of the voices?"

"Not really, though they both seemed familiar. It could have been anyone. I'm so glad you came when you did." She shuddered. "I could have shot an innocent person."

"You almost did," said a voice from the back of the wagon.

"Mr. Baxter, is that a hole in your hat?" Toby asked.

"Looks that way." Ben stood at the back of the wagon fingering a large hole in the crown of his hat. "Your Mama is a crack shot with that little pistol of hers."

Charisse felt the blood drain from her face. "You?"

"He's not your mysterious visitor." Luke said, with a shake of his head. "He was with me the whole time."

"Right behind him when you fired your pistol, in fact. In this case, that was definitely not the place to be." Ben shrugged and put his hat back on. "No sign of anybody, but I did find this." He held up a wicked-looking knife. "Ought to be somebody that recognizes it."

Luke nodded. "It's a Bowie knife. They're not all that common anymore."

"George Bartell," Charisse said suddenly. "He wears a knife like that on his belt. I noticed it the first night when he stopped to tell us about the meeting."

"What happened?" Eliza Duncan's face appeared next to Ben's, her eyes large and frightened.

"Nothing." Luke gave Charisse a warning squeeze. "My wife was a little jumpy, and her derringer went off accidentally."

"Oh no, is everyone all right?"

"We're all fine."

As other members of the wagon train gathered outside, Luke repeated his assurances that it had all been an accident. Charisse couldn't help but wonder why no one questioned his glib explanation. Surely someone had noticed there were two shots rather than one, and would realize she'd had to reload between.

Perhaps it was because everyone was focused on the question of how the stock had managed to escape the confines of the ringed wagons and how far they had scattered into the night. Within ten minutes, the women had returned to the wagons and the men to the task of rounding up the missing animals.

"Come on, Franklin," Luke said as he started to walk away.

"You're taking him?"

Luke looked surprised. "Yes, unless you'll feel safer with him here."

"I don't want him to get in the way."

"In the way?" Luke laughed. "I see you don't know about Franklin's hidden talents."

"Hidden talents?"

"He's a natural herd dog. Without him, we'll be hunting animals until dawn." Luke leaned down and scratched the dog behind the ears. "Yep, old Franklin is full of surprises— just like his mistress." He winked and blew her a kiss, then turned and walked away.

Charisse was left wondering exactly what about her surprised Luke. Their kiss loomed large in her mind, and she wondered if that was what he meant. She went over it and over it but found no answer. It wasn't until Luke and Franklin returned that she realized how successfully Luke had distracted her from worrying about the attack. She narrowed her eyes, wondering if that had been his intention all along.

They were just getting settled for what was left of the night, when a cry of alarm once more echoed through the camp. Ignoring Luke's terse, "Wait here," Charisse threw on her robe and followed him across camp toward the group gathered on the other side.

Snatches of conversation came to her as they approached.

"…was on guard tonight."

"…must have caught them filthy savages in the act."

"I thought the Indians were friendlies."

"No such thing as a friendly Injun!"

Charisse was jostled by the crowd as she tried to see what they were all looking at. Finally, she managed to push her way through. A man lay on the ground, staring sightlessly up at the dark sky above him. There was a look of shock on his face as though death had taken him by surprise. It was George Bartell, and there was an arrow sticking out of his chest.

"Luke—"

"Shh," he said, wrapping his arms around her as though to comfort her.

"But isn't he—"

"It's all right, sweetheart. They're gone now." He pulled her roughly against his chest. "Play it dumb," he whispered against her hair. "Don't let on you know anything." He shook his head apologetically. "I need to get her back to the wagon," he said to the group at large. "She's overwrought."

There were a few murmurs of sympathy as he led her away, but it was clear they were forgotten the second they left the group.

"Overwrought?" she hissed, jerking away from him. "I'll show you overwrought."

Luke grabbed her arm and pulled her back to his side. "Shut up or you'll get us both killed!" He whispered as he put his arm around her and held her in a tight grip. "No, darling," he said out loud. "I'm sure the Indians are long gone. They were probably after the cattle."

"What do you mean, I'll get us both killed?" she demanded in an undertone. "I thought the Indians were gone."

"There never were any Indians.

"What?" Charisse stopped walking and looked up at him in disbelief.

"Keep walking, damn it!"

She fell into step beside him again. "That arrow looked pretty real to me."

"Oh, it was real all right, but that's not what killed him."

"How do you know that?"

"If he'd been alive when that arrow went into him there'd have been more blood."

Charisse blinked. Now that she thought about it, he was right; Bartell had bled very little. "Then how did he die?"

"I can't be sure without examining the body," he said carefully.

"But...?"

"There were bruises on his throat. I think someone broke his neck."

CHAPTER 18

"Ashes to ashes and dust to dust..." Pierre Jeveraux's voice droned on in the early morning sunshine.

Charisse couldn't help thinking what an odd funeral it was. There was no casket and no minister, only a raw hole in the earth and a rugged Frenchman who knew a few of the appropriate words. Even mourners were curiously lacking. Charisse scanned the faces of those circling the mound of dirt, searching in vain for some sign of sorrow or regret at his passing. George Bartell had been a member of their company for over a month but seemed to have made no friends. And yet, Charisse knew he had connected with at least one other person. She had heard them talking outside her wagon just last night.

Because Bartell had no family on the train, Eliza Duncan had volunteered for the grisly task of laying him out. Everyone, including Luke, had been shocked when Charisse stepped forward and offered to help. It hadn't been pleasant, but she'd had ulterior motives. Now she knew for sure George had been one of her midnight visitors. Not only had the knife been missing from the sheath on his belt, but there was also a hole in his shirt, and a slight graze on his arm beneath it. Eliza hadn't appeared to notice the hole or the slight smattering of blood on the sleeve of the shirt, but Charisse was certain it had been caused by her pistol.

She turned her attention back to the grave at her feet and wondered for the hundredth time what Luke's part was in all this. Not only had he not revealed the true nature of Bartell's death to the others, he'd never mentioned Charisse's suspicion that the man had been snooping around their wagon, apparently bent on mischief, less than an hour before he died.

Both seemed like details the other members of the wagon train had a right to know. When she'd made a suggestion along those lines, he'd brushed her off, pretending he didn't have any idea what she was talking about.

"—and may God have mercy on his soul," Jeveraux finished, then gave a deep sigh and glanced at the sun before putting his hat on his head. "Well, guess it's time we hit the trail."

Charisse and the other members of the wagon train silently followed him back to the wagons and began hitching up their teams.

"Mama, can I go with Morgan this morning?" Toby asked. "Will's going to show us how to find buffalo chips."

"I suppose so, but don't get out of sight."

"All right. Come on, Franklin."

Charisse watched the pair run full tilt toward Jessup's wagon. "Maybe gathering buffalo chips will wear off some of that excess energy."

"There's always that chance," Luke said with a grin. "But I'm betting they'll figure out some way to get into mischief with them."

A short time later, the oxen were hitched up and the wagon train started forward again. "I don't know if I can do this," Charisse said as she picked up the reins. "It seems like sacrilege for every wagon to drive over the grave."

"It's the only way to keep scavengers from digging up the body," Luke reminded her.

"I know, but that doesn't make it any easier to do."

Luke glanced at the oxen and then back at her. "I'll drive," he said, climbing up to the seat.

"But who will guide the oxen?"

"Hopefully I will. I think they're ready." He took the reins from her hands. "I was planning on testing them soon anyway. Giddyap!" He gave the signal to go as he slapped the backs of the oxen with the reins. The animals seemed confused for a moment, then the wagon in front of them began to roll. The lead oxen followed after a moment's hesitation. After a few experimental "gees" and "haws" to make sure the animals would follow directions, Luke pronounced himself satisfied.

"Well, good," Charisse said. "Then you can start doing the job I hired you for."

Luke raised an eyebrow. "I thought I hired you."

"You did, and I've been performing my duties since the first day. But if you'll remember, I hired you to drive my wagon, which you've only done twice. Once, I might add, with spectacularly disastrous results."

"Caused by those damn mules of yours and your dog."

"True," she admitted. "Which is why I haven't said anything until now."

"And now?"

"And now you'll do the driving." She gave him a beautific smile. "I quit!"

"I suppose you plan on sitting there telling me how to do it."

"Nope, I'll be getting down the next time we stop. I'd rather walk."

He grinned. "Even if it means collecting buffalo chips?"

She made a face. "Yes, even that, and you'll find out why after you've sat on this darn seat for an hour or so."

"In that case, I guess I'd better enjoy your company while I can."

"I've wanted to talk to you about last night anyway."

A shutter seemed to come down in his eyes, and the smile slipped from his face. "The less said about last night, the better."

"Why?"

"Because we don't know what's going on, that's why."

"Don't you think we should tell somebody what Bartell was up to?"

"We don't know what he was up to. Nor do we know who we can trust and who we can't. If we talk to the wrong person, we could wind up the same way Bartell did."

"There must be somebody you can trust. How about John Jessup?"

Luke shrugged. "He has enough on his mind with four kids and a herd of horses to get to Oregon. Even if I was willing to saddle him with my problems—which I'm not—he wouldn't have time to do anything about it."

"Well, how about Ben Baxter, then? He doesn't even have a wagon to worry about."

"Baxter again. What is it with you and him?"

Charisse gave him a blank look. "What do you mean?"

Luke glared at her. "I mean every time I turn around you're carrying on with him."

"I've never carried on with anybody," she said indignantly, "and certainly not with Ben Baxter."

"Oh no? Then why is he always around you?"

"How would I know? I don't invite him, if that's what you mean."

"So you say. It seems odd to me that wherever you are, sooner or later he shows up. How do you explain that?"

"Why don't you ask him?" she snapped.

"Personally, I'd rather not talk to him at all. I really don't understand what you see in the man."

"I don't see anything in Ben. Why are you so obsessed with him, anyway?"

"I'm just trying to warn you for your own protection," Luke said. "Oh, I'll grant you he has a certain amount of charm, but I wouldn't trust him if I were you."

"Whatever gave you that idea?"

He gave her an almost pitying look. "As far as he knows, you're a married woman. A decent man would be keeping his distance. Mark my words, it's only a matter of time before he makes his move and tries to talk you into a clandestine affair."

"And you think I'd accept?"

Luke shrugged. "He's a handsome man."

Charisse gritted her teeth. "Oooh, there's no talking to you, is there? I think you'd better stop this wagon and let me down before I do or say something I'll regret."

"If you say so. Whoa there, Polly. Whoa, Lightning." The oxen obediently stopped and Luke gave her an innocent look. "I'll give you a hand down if you'll give me a minute to tie off the reins."

"Don't bother," she said through clenched teeth. "I can get down fine without your assistance."

Her wrath carried her clear through her descent from the wagon. It wasn't until he'd given the oxen the command to go and pulled away that she realized how skillfully she'd been manipulated. Luke had distracted her from her questions as adeptly as he'd distracted her when he'd driven over Bartell's grave without her noticing. She was no closer to the answers than before. There was one thing she was sure of, though. Luke McCabe knew a lot more than he was telling.

Maybe it was time to discover what was going on for herself. First on her list was to find out where Luke went every night. For the next several nights she tried to stay awake. But after walking the full twelve to fifteen miles they traveled every day, she was asleep every night almost before her head hit the pillow.

Tonight's the night, she vowed one morning. *I'll stay awake and follow him tonight if I have to sleep on a rock!* She stayed close to the wagons all day instead of wandering out on the prairie to look for buffalo chips. They were much harder to find along the trail, of course, but she wouldn't be so tired at the end of the day. She might even ride in the wagon part of the afternoon to help conserve her energy. Charisse smiled to herself as she thought of what Luke's reaction would be. It might even be fun to goad him a little.

"Where's Toby?" Luke asked.

Charisse glanced up at Luke on the wagon seat as she walked past. "Gathering buffalo chips like the rest of us." She dumped her bucket into the basket that hung next to the seat. "Why?"

"Baxter just got back in from scouting, and said he spotted

the remains of an Indian camp not too far ahead."

"Oh, no!"

"Now, don't panic. Baxter said it looked like they had been gone a week or more. Jeveraux told him to pass the word to pull everybody in close to the wagons just to be safe."

"I'll go find the children."

Luke nodded. "Good idea."

Charisse put her bucket in the back, then stepped away from the wagons and dust-filled air around them so she could see better. Far off in the distance she could see two small figures. She hurried back to the wagon. "They're over there," she said, pointing. "I'm going after them."

"Keep your eyes open."

She nodded. "I will."

Charisse realized it was the Jessup twins—not Toby and Morgan—long before she reached them. Though she scanned the prairie continually, there was no sign of the younger pair. She was nearly frantic by the time she got to Matt and Andy. "Do you know where Toby and Morgan are?"

"Right over the hill," Andy said, pointing to the south.

"Yeah, they keep sending Franklin over—"

"And we send him back."

"See, you can hear him now."

Charisse realized she could hear Franklin's familiar bark on the wind, though it seemed a long way off. "Why did you let them get so far away?" she demanded.

"They're not far—"

" —It just sounds that way because of the hill."

Charisse frowned at them. "I can't believe you let them out of your sight! What were you thinking?"

"It was Toby's idea."

"He wanted to see if Franklin would come find us—"

" —even if he couldn't see us—"

" —and he did every time—"

" —'cause he's a really smart dog."

"Toby and Morgan are seven years old!" Charisse scolded.

"They're too young to be wandering off by themselves like that."

They hung their heads. "Yes, ma'am," they said in unison.

"Do you want us to get them for you?" Matt asked.

"No, the captain called everybody in. You two go back to the wagons. I'll go get Toby and Morgan." She gave them a severe look. "From now on I expect you to do a better job of watching them."

"We'll never let them out of our sight—"

"—or let them wander off again."

"Good. Now scoot. Your Pa and Luke will be wondering where we all are."

"We'll tell Luke you're on your way." Matt said earnestly. Then he grinned at his brother and started running. "Race you back," he called over his shoulder.

Andy was right behind him. "Last one there is a buffalo chip!" he called.

Charisse shook her head as she watched them go. They were a pair. She felt a twinge of conscience as she walked up the hill. If she hadn't been so focused on trying to outsmart Luke, she'd have realized the children had strayed before they got so far from the wagons. It was a lesson she wouldn't forget in the future.

She saw Toby and Morgan the instant she crested the hill. They were walking along the bottom of a small valley. Even from where she was, Charisse could tell a large buffalo herd had passed this way. The grass was trampled in a wide swath, and the ground was no doubt dotted with buffalo chips. After scouring the prairie for enough to build a fire the last few days, Toby and Morgan probably felt like they'd stumbled on to a treasure trove. Charisse cupped her hands around her mouth and called, but the wind threw her words back at her. With a sigh, she started picking her way down the hillside.

She was about halfway there when half a dozen riders appeared on the other side of the valley. One minute the hilltop was empty, the next they were there. Charisse shaded her eyes to see who it might be, and her heart seemed to jerk in her chest. Even from this distance she could see their half-naked bodies and long flowing hair. Indians!

Though she was out in the open, a small patch of willows blocked their view of the children. As she stood frozen, the Indians began streaming down the hill, coming toward her impossibly fast. She'd been spotted, but if she could lead the Indians away, maybe Toby and Morgan could escape.

"Indians!" she yelled. "Run and hide!"

The children stood like statues for a long moment, then scrambled for the brush. Charisse watched them disappear, then turned and started running back toward the top of the hill. With any kind of luck, the horsemen wouldn't see the children, and she could lead them away.

A stitch developed in her side and her breaths were coming in hard gasps, but she kept going, expecting to feel an arrow in her back at any moment. She was almost to the top of the hill when the first man caught up with her.

Out of the corner of her eye she saw a horse, dodged away from it and nearly crashed into one in front of her. A scream tore from her throat, but was choked off almost immediately by her lack of air. The Indian nearest her vaulted off his horse in one smooth motion and grabbed her arm. Charisse tried to kick him and jerk free, but he was too strong. He managed to get an arm around her waist and lift her off the ground where her flailing did little good.

Suddenly, Franklin flew out of the sagebrush, barking and snapping. Gone was Charisse's slightly lazy pet and Toby's erstwhile companion. In his place was a ferocious protector bent on saving his mistress or dying in the process. Her captor let out a howl as Franklin fastened his teeth on the man's leg, and Charisse saw him go for his knife.

"Franklin, down!" she yelled. Instantly, Franklin let go and dropped to the ground. The downward swipe of the blade barely missed him, but he seemed oblivious to it as he stared at his mistress, awaiting her next command.

"Go find Luke," she gasped out.

Franklin cocked his head to one side, as though to ask if she knew what she was doing.

"Franklin, go find Luke!" Her voice was firm this time, and Franklin was on his feet, dodging through the sagebrush, racing for the top of the hill. Charisse closed her eyes in relief as he disappeared over the top. It was a long shot, but it was the only hope they had.

"Mama!" The single terrified word hung in the air like a death knell.

Charisse's eyes popped open and she uttered a cry of horror. Down the hill Toby and Morgan struggled with the other four Indians. As she watched, one of them yanked Toby up on his horse. Toby fought like a cornered coyote and managed to squirm out of the man's hands. He fell to the ground and lay there like a broken doll, unmoving and still.

"NOOO!" The anguished cry ripped from Charisse's throat. A sudden sharp pain on the back of her head sent her into blessed oblivion.

CHAPTER 19

"Ohhhh," Charisse groaned as she opened her eyes to persistent swaying. She was on her belly, draped over the front of a horse, her hands were tied together with a leather thong. All she could see were the brown and white markings on the horse's legs and a small patch of moving ground. A headache pounded behind her eyes, and her stomach rolled in protest to the abuse it was taking.

She turned her head and spoke to the man's leg next to her. "I need to get up," she said. There was no response, so she braced her elbows against the horse and raised her head. "No, really, I need to get up."

All she got for her pains was a sharp reprimand and an impatient hand pushing her back down. It was too much for her poor tortured stomach. She vomited, first on the horse and then on the man's leg. Before the third round erupted, he jerked her upright by her hair.

"I can't help it," she said, and emptied what was left in her stomach on his thigh.

She didn't have to understand the language to know he was cursing at her.

"I did tell you," Charisse said, knowing full well he didn't understand her. She pushed herself up on her elbows once more. "Now let me up."

He started to push her down, then seemed to think better of it. The horse stopped and strong arms scooped her up. Charisse wasn't quite sure how he managed it, but he flipped her around and settled her in front of him straddling the horse.

With her wrists still tied together, there was no hope of escape, but at least the nausea was gone. The rest of the horsemen were behind them, so she couldn't see where the children were or how they were faring. "Toby?"

"Are you all right, Mama?" Toby's voice was tearful and frightened. "I thought you died."

"I'm fine. I just fainted. How about you and Morgan?"

He sniffed. "We're all right. Mama, what are they going to do with us?"

"I don't know, sweetheart."

The man behind her spoke sharply and gave her hair a yank. He apparently didn't want them talking. Charisse lapsed into silence. At least they were all still together.

As they rode along, Charisse couldn't decide what was worse: the smell of her vomit and the horrid taste in her mouth, the itchy horsehair rubbing on the insides of her legs, or the chafing of the leather thong on her wrists. She was in the process of shifting slightly to relieve the strain on her legs when something exploded out of the ground at the horse's feet. The horse reared in fear, and Charisse screamed as she tried to grab hold of its mane. Her fingers clawed uselessly at empty air and she flew backward off the horse. She landed on the ground with a solid thunk, but something had broken her fall. It took only a moment to realize, what—or rather, *who*—it was.

Charisse rolled to the side and looked back at the man she'd landed on. The dark eyes looked distinctly menacing as he glared at her. She dropped her gaze, her eyes widening as she took in twin scars, an inch wide and six inches long, that ran parallel to each other just above the well-defined muscles of his chest. The pain must have been agonizing. What sort of accident could produce such horrendous results? Suddenly, the man froze, his eyes widening as he abruptly became aware of something over her right shoulder. With one swift motion, he reached for his knife, and came up empty. It had apparently been knocked from its sheath when he fell.

As he searched the ground for his knife, Charisse turned to see what had called his attention. A snarling badger crouched less than six feet from her, and looked about as friendly as the man she'd been riding with. Its tiny ears were flat against its head, and long, sharp teeth showed beneath its curled lip.

Deciding she'd rather take her chances with her human enemy, she scrambled away from the badger as the knife went singing over her head. It struck the badger right between the eyes, and he dropped like a rock just as Charisse crashed into her captor and knocked him over again.

"I'm sorry," she said, backing away. "I really didn't mean to do that."

He winced as he started to get up, and Charisse saw his right hip had landed against a prickly pear cactus. Numerous spines stuck out of his fringed leggings and the bare skin above.

"Oh dear." Charisse's hand went to her mouth. "That must hurt," she said. "Here, let me — " With some thought of helping, she reached toward the injured hip only to have her hand knocked aside.

The man rose to his feet and limped over to his horse, picking out the worst of the spines as he went. The sound of the other Indians' laughter filled the air, but he ignored them.

Charisse looked for Toby and Morgan and found them almost immediately; each perched on the front of a horse with a young brave behind them. Other than dirty, tear-streaked faces, neither looked the worse for wear, and Charisse smiled encouragingly at them.

As she scanned the faces of the other Indians, she was surprised to see they all looked quite young. Only the one who held her captive appeared to be over the age of fifteen, and she didn't figure him to be much more than twenty. He suddenly returned with a long rawhide rope, which he tied securely around her bound hands. Then he limped back to his horse and mounted, though not without difficulty. Once he was settled, he pulled on the rope and gestured that she was to follow.

Charisse blinked. Surely he didn't expect her to walk to wherever they were going. But apparently, he did. Not once did he look back after he kicked his horse and they started out. It was difficult to keep up, though Charisse figured the man on the horse wouldn't much care if she fell and he had to drag her.

In some ways walking was better than riding. At least she didn't have to smell the vomit anymore, and she didn't have the horsehair irritating the insides of her thighs. Better yet, she had only to look over her shoulder to see the children, who seemed to be frightened but otherwise fine. Still, she felt like cheering when they topped a hill in the late afternoon, and she saw an Indian camp spread out below them. Twenty or so tipis were scattered in a rough circle near the banks of a creek. Smoke rose into the air from a dozen campfires and Charisse could see a rough corral containing a herd of horses off to one side of the encampment.

The arrival of the riders and their captives caused quite a stir. Women and children ran alongside the horses, chattering like a bunch of magpies. Charisse expected open hostility, but these people seemed more curious than angry, reaching out to touch her as she passed. The group she was with rode through the center of camp and stopped in front of a large tipi with pictures of the sun and a buffalo painted on the side. The delicious smell of roasting meat wafted up from the cooking fire, and Charisse's stomach growled in response.

The young man leading Charisse dismounted and went inside. She could see the angry red welts above his hip where the cactus had penetrated the skin, as well as other scrapes and cuts she hadn't noticed before. Charisse fought a surge of remorse. She hadn't actually inflicted any of his wounds, and he *had* kidnapped them. He deserved what he got.

All thoughts of her captor fled from her mind a second later when Toby and Morgan were brought to her side. Even with the bonds still on her hands, she managed to give them each a hug and whisper encouraging words to them. They were still hugging each other and celebrating their reunion when the flap of the tipi opened, and her captor returned with three other men.

The first two were elderly with gray hair and wizened skin. The third, Charisse guessed, was about Luke's age. His powerful body and proud demeanor marked him instantly as a leader. Two scars, almost identical to those her captor sported, marred the perfection of his chest. Charisse stared at them in shock. No accident then, but a purposeful injury. What sort of savages were these people? Fearing she would offend him by staring, Charisse pulled her gaze away and tried to concentrate on what was happening.

An aura of power surrounded the three men, who were listening intently to Charisse's kidnapper. There seemed to be a disagreement of some kind going on. Then the young man yanked Charisse's bonnet down and pointed to her hair. The three older men exchanged a look, and heated discussion followed. The two elderly men returned to the tipi, apparently leaving the decision up to the powerful man Charisse had decided was the chief.

The chief stared at the children for several seconds, then switched his attention back to her. Though she was quaking inside, she raised her chin slightly and looked him square in the eye. Finally, he shrugged and said something that appeared to cause the young brave a great deal of consternation. When the younger man started to speak, the chief raised his hand in a take-it-or-leave it kind of gesture, and followed the elders into the tipi.

Toby and Morgan were led away by two of the women, and their panicked cries filled the air.

"Mama!"

"Charisse!"

Charisse struggled to follow, but the young man yanked her rope tight. If his look had been hostile before, now it was positively murderous. Without a word, he turned and strode through camp with her running to keep up.

She kept glancing over her shoulder trying to locate the children. Her toe caught on something, and she tripped, sprawling full length on the ground. He paused only long enough to jerk her to her feet and snap an angry order. She didn't have to know the language to understand his meaning.

Charisse fought tears of pain and anguish as she stumbled along behind him, frantic with worry about Toby and Morgan, terrified for them all. Separated from the children and surrounded by an entire village, she couldn't even consider escape. Better to bide her time, lulling them into thinking she'd given up hope.

To Charisse's immense relief, they finally stopped at a smaller tipi on the edge of the village. A girl of about seventeen or eighteen knelt by a fire, stirring a pot suspended over the flames. She smiled when she saw them coming and rose to her feet. Charisse was shocked to see she was heavily pregnant. Watching the two exchange a tender greeting and noticing the possessive way the young man caressed the woman's belly, Charisse realized this must be his wife. The woman listened intently as he talked. She glanced first at his injured hip, then at Charisse, and finally back to his face. Charisse could imagine the tale he was telling of his abuse at the hands of the evil white woman. When he finished at last, his wife asked a question which seemed to startle him.

When he didn't answer, the young woman looked at Charisse and frowned as though concentrating. "You...talk...Anglish?" she asked haltingly.

"English? Yes," Charisse said, nodding eagerly. "Yes, I speak English. Do you?"

The young woman smiled and shook her head, then turned back to her husband. She gave him a look and pointed back the way they had come.

He appeared torn, as though he wasn't quite sure what he should do. An argument ensued with the woman insisting he go back for some reason. The darkling looks he kept giving Charisse told her she was somehow involved, but she had no clue how.

Finally, he threw up his hands in surrender. As he turned to go, the woman touched his arm and pointed to Charisse's bonds. He frowned so fiercely his eyebrows nearly touched as he shook his head no. When she insisted, he gave her what appeared to be a lecture. At last, she waved him on his way and watched him go with a shake of her head.

Then she smiled at Charisse, pointed to herself and said something that sounded like, "Tissawa".

"Tissawa?" Charisse frowned as she tried to comprehend the other woman's meaning. "Tissawa...oh, it's your name?" Charisse asked. She pointed at her. "Tissawa?"

Tissawa beamed at her as she nodded.

"Charisse," Charisse said, pointing at herself.

"Reese?" Tissawa asked.

"Close enough," Charisse said, knowing her pronunciation of Tissawa's name was equally wrong.

Tissawa gestured for her to follow. They both ducked through the tipi opening. It was surprisingly roomy inside, and Charisse looked around curiously. Baskets containing the family's possessions and piles of furs were scattered about the interior. A fire ring dominated the center directly beneath the opening at the top. Smoke-darkened leather near the apex showed what the purpose of the hole was. There were two flaps at the top that allowed daylight to filter down. The sides of the covering all around the bottom of the tipi were rolled up about ten inches to allow the air flow. A noticeable breeze came in and was drawn up through the smoke hole. Charisse thought the whole setup rather ingenious.

As she stood gazing up at the smoke hole, her hostess returned with a sharp knife. Charisse eyed it warily, but the woman smiled encouragingly at her and indicated she should hold out her hands. With a quick flick of the knife, Tissawa cut Charisse's bonds.

"Oh, thank you," she said, rubbing her wrists. How surprising! Tissawa was acting as though Charisse was an honored guest rather than a captive. It was not at all what she had expected from Indians, especially not after the way she'd been treated by Tissawa's husband.

Tissawa smiled again and handed her a small cup full of water.

Charisse drank gratefully, and the woman refilled it for her. When she had drunk her fill, Tissawa handed her another small container that appeared to be filled with some kind of grease. Charisse looked at it and then back at her hostess. Tissawa pointed to the grease and rubbed her wrists.

"For my sores?" Charisse cautiously sniffed the concoction and resisted the urge to wrinkle her nose at the unpleasant odor. The last thing she wanted to do was put it on her open sores, but she dared not offend the one friend she seemed to have here. Gingerly, she dipped a finger in and dabbed a little on her wrist. The relief was almost instantaneous, and Charisse blinked in surprise. "This is wonderful," she said, smearing it on her wounds. "Thank you."

The two women exchanged a smile. Then Tissawa sighed and rubbed her belly. Charisse watched, remembering what it was like to be so near her time and wishing there were some way she could help.

A sudden noise at the back of the tipi called Tissawa's attention and brought another smile to her face. She walked to a pile of furs, bent over and picked up a small child.

"Oh my," said Charisse. "You have another baby."

"Chonqo," Tissawa said proudly.

"Hello, Chonqo." Charisse tickled the little one under the chin and got a giggle in return.

Tissawa balanced Chonqo on her hip and went back outside to check her cooking pot. Charisse watched the younger woman struggle to balance the toddler and her own swollen body as she reached for the spoon she'd been stirring with.

"Here," Charisse said, holding her arms out for the baby. "I can take Chonqo for you."

Tissawa looked at her, apparently weighing the pros and cons of trusting a complete stranger. Finally, she nodded and handed him over.

Charisse settled with the youngster on a nearby chunk of wood, and vowed Tissawa would never regret the generous impulse to help a strange white woman.

Chonqo wanted down almost immediately and was soon running around, bringing small sticks and pebbles to Charisse. Tissawa watched with a fond eye as she stirred her pot.

When Tissawa's husband returned with another woman, he glared at Charisse. It was plain to see he wasn't pleased to find his captive untied. Tissawa listened to his harangue politely, then turned to the other woman.

"Reese," she said, pointing to Charisse, and then continued on in her own language.

The other woman nodded, then picked up Chonqo and came to sit down by Charisse as the other two went inside. "I am Sarah," she said.

Charisse was surprised. "Sarah? You're white?"

Sarah shook her head. "My father was of your people. He was—how you say?—one who catches beaver?"

"A trapper?"

She nodded, "Yes. He take Indian wife, but when he die my mother come back to her people."

"Sarah, do you know where my children are? Are they safe?"

She nodded again. "We hold children sacred. Yours are in no danger."

"I want to be with them."

"It is not possible." She gave the tipi behind them a meaningful look. "You are still White Otter's..." She paused, searching for the word.

"Prisoner?"

"Yes, prisoner and slave."

"Slave!"

"It is the way of my people. If no one comes to pay, you will work for White Otter."

"What do you mean if no one comes to pay? No one knows I'm here!"

"They know. Three suns ago two men come to the elders and ask them to take a white woman from the wagon train. The elders refused. They not want to anger the blue coats."

"They asked them to kidnap a white woman? What on earth for?"

Sarah shook her head. "No, not a white woman. They want you."

"Me?" Charisse was taken aback. "That makes no sense. Are you sure?"

"They say woman have hair with hidden fire and eyes that change."

"But that's ridiculous! That description could fit any number of people."

Sarah shrugged. "Maybe, but White Otter think you the one."

"I thought the elders said no."

"White Otter not think sometimes. He take the boys out hunting and find you. Think maybe white man will pay with the guns he promised, so he take you." She grinned. "And now his wife has to pull cactus spines from his hide. Maybe White Otter learn lesson."

"The white men offered rifles to take this woman?"

"That is what they say. Rifles better than blue coats have. The young men want."

"What were they supposed to do with the white woman once they had her?"

Sarah shrugged again. "They not care. Make slave, kill, not matter as long as she is gone from wagon train."

"But why?"

"Not know. White men—how you say?—loco. Cougar Tail say not worth trouble with blue coats."

"Cougar Tail, is that the chief?"

"Yes," Sarah smiled. "My husband. He not happy you here."

"No, I could see that. His decision, whatever it was, made White Otter very angry."

Sarah chuckled. "Yes, White Otter angry. Cougar Tail say he bring you here, he have to take you into his lodge."

"No wonder he acted like he had a burr under his tail. He probably thinks I'm about the worst thing that ever happened to him."

"He say you will burn his lodge or cause his horses to die."

Charisse was startled. "What?"

Sarah grinned. "White Otter likes to tell big stories. He say you white witch and bring bad luck."

Charisse flinched inwardly.

CHAPTER 20

"Would you like some more stew?" Charisse pointed to White Otter's bowl and then to the stew pot. He grunted and handed her his bowl. Charisse refilled it and handed it back. It had been an odd meal. Sarah had impressed upon Charisse how important it was to keep White Otter happy. Charisse knew she should do her best to comply, but it went against the grain to turn herself into a slave without a fight

For his part, it was apparent White Otter didn't want her here and would have cheerfully dropped her over a cliff. Left to their own devices, Charisse and White Otter would certainly have had a major confrontation. But Tissawa was between them, and neither of them wanted to upset her. So, Charisse had taken care of Chonqo until Tissawa was ready to nurse him, then finished cooking the meal. She'd served White Otter first as Sarah had told her she must.

"I hope you know, I'm doing this for your wife," she said as she handed White Otter his bowl of stew. "I couldn't care less what you want. I don't much like bullies, but I want my children back and for Tissawa to be happy." She smiled to herself. This is kind of fun. I'm glad he doesn't speak English.

He said something in his own tongue, and indicated she should now serve Tissawa.

"I'd be glad to, Your Royal Highness." She dished up the stew and carried it over to Tissawa, who had finished feeding Chonqo. Charisse set the bowl down and held out her arms. "Do you want me to take Chonqo while you eat?"

Tissawa smiled and handed over the child. The rest of the meal passed in peace, but Charisse was constantly aware of the way White Otter watched her and his son as though he didn't trust her. "Serves you right," she muttered. "Maybe this will teach you not to grab innocent white women and children."

White Otter glared at her and made a sharp demand in his own tongue. Charisse didn't need Tissawa putting her hand on her mouth indicating silence to know what he'd said.

When everyone was finished eating, White Otter disappeared into the night, and Tissawa indicated Charisse could now eat. Afterward, she gathered wood, helped Tissawa bank the fire, and put Chonqo to bed. Then Tissawa pointed to a buffalo robe on the far side of the tipi. "Sleep," she said and mimed sleeping.

"That's where I'm to sleep?" Charisse asked.

Tissawa nodded.

"I want to see my children first," Charisse said, pointing first to herself and then to Chonqo.

Tissawa shook her head and pointed to the buffalo robe. They argued back and forth until Charisse finally gave in and walked toward her bed. "All right, but I'm going to see them first thing tomorrow morning even if I get punished for doing it."

Tissawa smiled and nodded before saying something Charisse thought was probably "Good night," and then moving to her own bed.

With a deep sigh, Charisse lay down on the buffalo robe and found it surprisingly soft. She suspected it would be extremely warm if she were to use it for a blanket. A refreshing breeze blew in through the gap left between the rolled-up bottom of the tipi and the ground. It was the most comfortable bed she'd had since leaving Independence.

Charisse found herself fighting sleep as she tried to figure out a way to get the three of them away from Cougar Tail's camp and back where they belonged. There was little hope of rescue from the wagon train. Even if Franklin had understood her command and gone to Luke, how would he convince the man to follow him back to the spot where they'd been abducted? Even then, there would be no way to find out where they went. Franklin might have proved his worth herding cows, but he wasn't a tracker.

No, she would have to do this herself. They wouldn't be able to sneak away. Even if they stole some horses, there was no way she could get them back to the wagon train without help. She wouldn't even know which direction to go. The one skill she had that these people might respond to was her ability to barter. They were traders, weren't they?

The question was, what could she trade? She didn't have any of the guns they wanted, and she didn't see any of them trading three slaves for one small derringer. Would they be tempted by what she had hidden in the box of Granny's dishes? Somehow, she didn't think so.

Charisse was still trying to puzzle it out when White Otter returned. She closed her eyes to give him privacy as he got ready for bed. The soft murmurs he exchanged with Tissawa made Charisse smile. She didn't much care for the man herself, but the love between White Otter and his wife was special. As she lay there and listened to their whispered conversation, Charisse vowed she would never again marry without that kind of bond with her mate. She fell asleep, and dreamed of Luke McCabe.

Charisse was jerked from sleep by a rough hand shaking her shoulder.

"Wha... huh?" she blinked her eyes and tried to focus on the dark figure bending over her.

"You help Tissawa?"

"Tissawa... what—?"

"Baby come. You help."

White Otter's words penetrated her sleep-fogged mind. "The baby? Of course, I'll help." She scrambled from her bed and hurried across the tipi. Tissawa gripped a lodge pole with one hand and pressed her belly with the other as her face contorted with pain.

"You need to lie down—"

"No," White Otter shook his head. "I get Sarah. You take Tissawa."

"Take her where?"

"Baby not come here," he said. "Great Spirit help in other place. Understand?"

Charisse frowned. "You mean your women have their babies in a special place, and you want me to take Tissawa there?"

White Otter looked relieved. "You take?"

"Yes, of course. You go get Sarah and make it fast. I've never done this before."

White Otter nodded and ducked through the entrance as Charisse turned her full attention to Tissawa. The other woman's face relaxed as her contraction passed. She sighed with relief and pointed toward the doorway.

Charisse nodded. "If you're ready, let's go."

It wasn't until they were outside that Charisse suddenly realized White Otter had spoken to her in her own language! "Oh my Lord, he speaks English!"

Tissawa stopped suddenly as another contraction hit, and the shocking discovery was pushed from Charisse's mind and forgotten. They managed to reach their destination, a small tipi, before the next contraction rippled through Tissawa's body. They paused at the entrance and Tissawa gripped Charisse's hand as the pain flowed through her.

Sarah arrived about midway through the contraction. She put her hand on the young woman's belly as though judging the intensity, then nodded in satisfaction and said something in an encouraging tone. As soon as the pain had passed, Sarah helped Tissawa into the birthing lodge, then turned to Charisse.

"Where is Chonqo?"

"Oh, my goodness. I forgot all about him. He was still asleep when we left." Charisse didn't even wait for Sarah to enter the birthing lodge. She lifted her skirt and ran back to White Otter's tipi as fast as she could. Her panic didn't disappear until she found Chonqo still sleeping peacefully. With a sigh of relief, she pulled her buffalo robe over next to his bed so she would know instantly if the youngster woke up and wanted his parents. For now, her main focus was keeping Chonqo safe.

Charisse lay down and closed her eyes, only to groan as she suddenly remembered White Otter's ability to speak English. Her behavior at supper came back in vivid detail. No wonder he'd glared at her. She had insulted him, called him names and impugned his honor. Probably the only thing that kept her from receiving some sort of punishment was that White Otter hadn't wanted to upset his wife. And this was the man she needed to convince to let her and the children go? *There is about as much chance of that as me sprouting wings and flying us all back to the wagon train,* she thought miserably.

Try as she might, sleep would not come. As she lay there inventing and rejecting plans, the blackness outside began to give way to the gray of morning. Charisse was just beginning to consider getting up when she heard an odd thundering noise outside and voices yelling.

Charisse leapt to her feet, grabbed the sleeping child and ran for the entrance. As soon as she cleared the door way, she gasped in dismay. A herd of horses streamed through camp, knocking over cooking pots, scattering wood piles, flattening meat-drying racks and leaving a swath of destruction as they came. Men of the village ran out of their lodges trying to stop the leaders. They succeeded only in turning them in another direction.

"Oh, no!" Charisse gasped as she realized the herd were coming her way. It was impossible to tell if their flight would come close enough to put them in danger, but she wasn't taking any chances. Clasping Chonqo tightly, she ran toward the relative safety of the other side of the camp. The sight of her spooked the horses even further and they veered to the right, straight toward White Otter's lodge.

"Uh oh." Charisse watched the structure rock, sway, and

then finally collapse as the horses surged past on either side. She started back across and was almost run down by three men on horseback who were chasing the herd. The dust was still settling when White Otter arrived. Charisse stopped where she was. The look on his face as he stared at the wreckage of his home was enough to send her running in the opposite direction.

She was looking for a place to hide from his wrath, when he started frantically searching the ruins calling his son's name.

"He's safe." Charisse called out, but White Otter didn't react. She wasn't sure if he hadn't heard, or if he was ignoring her. "White Otter," she said, moving closer. "I have Chonqo!"

White Otter's head jerked up, and an expression of profound relief crossed his face when he saw his son safe in Charisse's arms. He was reaching for the toddler when someone called his name.

Cougar Tail strode toward them. The anger on his face brought to mind every terrifying tale Charisse had ever heard about Indians on the warpath. Toby and Morgan were on either side of him, each gripped by the elbow and running to keep up with his long-legged strides.

Charisse thrust Chonqo into his father's arms and ran to meet them.

"Mama!" Toby cried.

Cougar Tail shoved the children at her and stalked over to White Otter. They appeared to be discussing Charisse and the children, but she paid them little attention.

"Are you all right?" she asked, hugging Toby and Morgan.

Toby nodded. "We tried to steal the horses, but they runned the wrong way."

"You what?"

"They sent us both out to do chores this morning," Morgan explained. "Only we found each other."

"And then we saw all the horses in a corral. We decided if we stole some we could find you and get away," Toby said. "We caught three for us to ride, only then Morgan said if we let all the other horses go, the Indians couldn't chase us."

Morgan frowned. "Except when we let them out they didn't run away like they were supposed to."

"So, we threw rocks at them."

"But they went the wrong way," Charisse murmured. "No wonder Cougar Tail is mad."

"What do you think he'll do to us?" Toby asked.

"I don't know. None of us are too popular right now." She looked toward the two men. Cougar Tail was doing most of the talking, and White Otter didn't look at all pleased. He tried to protest at one point, but Cougar Tail cut him off with a sharp gesture of his hand. A few minutes later, the older man finished his tirade and turned to go.

Charisse pulled the children close and set her jaw belligerently. He was going to have to fight her to take them this time, and she wouldn't give up easily. But Cougar Tail never even looked their way as he strode past. Charisse blinked in surprise. She glanced back at White Otter, who looked angry enough to chew cactus spines.

"Uh oh. I think Cougar Tail told White Otter he has to keep all three of us," she said. "He doesn't look too happy."

"I'm hungry, Mama. When do we get breakfast?"

"Shh, never mind. I'm sure they'll feed us later." Charisse didn't like the look on White Otter's face as he stalked across the camp toward them. When he reached them, he looked back and forth between Morgan and Toby for a moment, then pushed Chonqo into Morgan's arms. He grabbed Charisse by the elbow and dragged her back to his ruined tipi with Toby and Morgan trailing behind. Once there, he dug through the wreckage until he found a rawhide rope which he used to bind Charisse's and Toby's hands. Once he had bound them together, he led them over to a tree and tied the end of the rope too high for Charisse to reach. Then he turned to go, gesturing for Morgan to follow.

"You can't leave us here like this," Charisse protested. "And you're not taking Morgan anywhere!"

White Otter whirled around and cuffed her across the mouth. "Woman not talk!" His eyes blazed as he glared at her, daring her to challenge his authority again.

Charisse hadn't lived with Preston for the better part of twelve years without learning when to keep her mouth shut. She dropped her gaze and swallowed the retort that came to her lips.

Apparently convinced he'd subdued her, White Otter turned on his heel once more and gestured for Morgan to follow.

The little girl turned tearful eyes toward Charisse. "The baby is too heavy," she whispered. "I'm going to drop him."

"He can walk," Charisse said quietly. "Put him down and hold his hand. Only hurry. White Otter has no patience left."

Morgan set Chonqo on his feet and took his hand. She cast Charisse one more helpless look, then hurried to catch up with White Otter.

Toby gazed after them with a worried look on his face. "Where is he taking her?"

"I don't know, but I don't think he'll hurt her."

"He hit you!"

"But I talked back to him, and Morgan won't do that. Besides, he really didn't hit me hard. It could have been much worse."

"We're tied up," Toby pointed out.

"I know, but he could have tied us to the tree so we couldn't move. As it is, we can sit down if we want."

"Mama, I'm scared."

"Me too, but at least we're together." Charisse sat on the ground and leaned back against the tree. "Come here."

He sat next to her, cuddling up as close as he could. "Mama," he said in a small voice. "You're going to be mad at me."

Charisse looked down at him in surprise. "Why would I be mad at you?"

"I did something bad."

"White Otter and Cougar Tail may think letting the horses out was bad, but I'm rather impressed the two of you thought of it. The plan might have worked, too, if the horses had run the other way."

Toby shook his head. "It wasn't that. I broke a promise."

"Sometimes we have to. I'm sure whomever you promised will forgive you."

Toby shook his head miserably. "I don't think so. It was a really important promise." He sighed. "When they caught us and put us on their horses yesterday, I thought of Hansel and Gretel and how they left a trail so they could find their way back."

Charisse smiled. "So, you left biscuit crumbs from your lunch?"

"No, the birds would eat crumbs like they did Hansel's!" He lifted his hands to wipe away a tear. "I used Annabelle's marbles. I dropped one then counted to thirty and dropped another one."

"Why, Toby! How very clever of you! I would have never thought of that."

"But I promised you I'd take good care of them, and now they're all gone."

"Oh, Toby, they're just marbles. You tried to save us, and it may even work. I sent Franklin after your father. If he finds the place we were captured, they'll be able to follow your trail!" She knew the chance was still very slight, but it made her feel better to say it.

"Then you're not mad at me?"

"Of course not. That was a very smart thing you did." She lifted her arms. "Come sit here. It will make us both feel better." He crawled on to her lap, and leaned against her chest as she brought her arms down around him. "There," she said, resting her bound wrists on his shoulder. "That's much nicer."

It wasn't very comfortable, and Charisse knew they wouldn't be able to stay that way for long, but for the moment, holding him in her arms was enough. They sat there, absorbing strength from each other, taking comfort in their closeness.

Charisse's legs were starting to go to sleep, and the muscles in her shoulders were beginning to ache when she saw Morgan, Sarah and several other women walking toward them. "Toby, I think we'd better get up," she murmured.

By the time they all arrived, Charisse and Toby were standing by the tree waiting for them.

Morgan ran to them and hugged Charisse tightly. "I was afraid they wouldn't bring me back," she said.

"So was I, sweetheart," she said, trying to ignore the frank appraisals she was getting from the other women. There was a great deal of discussion and laughter. Sarah gave Charisse and Toby each a piece of jerky.

"I'm sorry there is not more," she said apologetically. "But White Otter is very angry."

"I know. I'm surprised he let you feed us at all." Charisse frowned at the other women. "Is it a common practice for your people to come and laugh at the prisoners?"

"They do not laugh at you. They laugh at White Otter. All want to see the white woman who has beaten one of the mightiest warriors in the village."

"Oh, no, I didn't do anything like that." She glanced at the flattened tipi. "Not on purpose, anyway."

Sarah waved her hand. "Cougar Tail says it is good for his son to see things can't always be his way. It will make him great chief someday."

"His son? You mean White Otter is Cougar Tail's son?" Charisse paused then closed her eyes. "Of course he is, and he's yours too. That's why he can speak English."

"Yes, he speaks but not like to." Sarah gave her another apologetic look. "I promise him I not untie you like Tissawa."

"Oh, my goodness! I never even asked about her? Did she have her baby? Is everything all right?"

Sarah nodded as she tied Morgan to the rope with Charisse and Toby. "She have fine daughter. We come to fix lodge so she can come home."

Charisse looked at the other women who were carefully piling Tissawa's and White Otter's personal belongings off to the side. "You're going to do it? Is White Otter so mad he won't even come near me?"

Sarah chuckled. "No, we put up lodge because is woman's work."

"Oh." Charisse and the children sat in the shade of the tree and watched as the women reassembled the tipi. It was surprisingly simple; the whole process was finished in far less time than it took Charisse and Luke to reload their wagon each morning. "That was downright amazing!" she told Sarah as the other woman brought them some water. "I wish I had one of these."

Sarah gave her an odd look. "Why you want lodge? You not have cabin?"

"No, not right now I don't, but I don't want one to live in. I just want a small one to sleep in at night. It's exactly what we need on the trail!" With a pang, she realized she might never see the trail or Luke again. The hopelessness of her situation suddenly crashed in on her, and she had to fight tears. She pushed them back fiercely, reminding herself she had the children back. For now, nothing else mattered.

The women left, and other than some sort of commotion at the other end of the camp about an hour later, the village might have been deserted. Charisse tried to keep the children entertained with stories, but she was beginning to run dry when she saw White Otter coming toward them. His expression was almost smug.

"Uh oh," she said, scrambling to her feet. "What now?"

But as he untied their bonds, she realized the look on his face was triumphant rather than angry. He gestured for them to follow and set off for the other end of the village. If she didn't know better, Charisse would have said there was jubilation in his step.

As they drew nearer to Cougar Tail's lodge, Charisse saw he had visitors. One was extremely tall and the other —

"It's Pa and Mr. Jessup!" Toby shouted excitedly.

"Pa!" yelled Morgan and broke into a run. John Jessup met her halfway and swung her up into his arms. Luke wasn't far behind, and suddenly Charisse and Toby were in his embrace, and she was sobbing against his chest. "Oh, Luke, you found us! I was so scared!"

He tightened his arms around them. "Shh, it's all right. You're safe now. They were willing to make a trade."

Now she understood White Otter's look. He'd gotten his ransom, and they were off his hands for good. Franklin was barking at her feet. Charisse hunkered down to scratch him behind the ears and receive his joyous licks of welcome.

"I think it's time we left before these good people change their minds," John said.

In moments, they were mounted and on their way, with Charisse in front of Luke on his horse and Toby riding double with Morgan. Charisse looked behind in surprise. Besides the three horses they were riding, John Jessup was leading a string of three more. "Where did those horses come from?"

"They're John's. He brought them along to trade."

"How many did you have to pay them?"

"Two. They said it was to make up for the damage Morgan and Toby caused."

Charisse nodded. "You got off cheap. The stampede they started could have wrecked the whole village." She frowned as she caught sight of a hide rolled and tied to one of the horses. "What's that?"

"A tipi cover."

"Oh, Luke, how wonderful. Now we'll have a tent to sleep in. You're so clever."

He shrugged. "It wasn't my idea. The interpreter seemed to think you wanted it."

Charisse smiled. "Sarah. Bless her heart. How much did you have to pay for it?"

"That's the strange part. I didn't pay anything for it."

"What?"

"The man named White Otter gave it to me in exchange for a promise."

"Oh, Luke, you didn't promise him guns, did you?"

"Of course not. What kind of an idiot do you take me for?" He grinned. "I gather you two didn't get along very well?"

"That's kind of an understatement. Why, what did he tell you?"

"He said I was a brave man to have you for a wife, and then offered to trade me a tipi cover for a promise."

"Luke, for heaven's sake; what did you promise him?"

"That I would take you away with me and make sure you never found your way back to his camp."

CHAPTER 21

"I know there aren't any trees, but I still wish I could get poles for the tipi," Charisse said as she drove the last stake in the ground. "If you could have seen how fast those women put that big one up and how cool it was to sleep in."

Luke stepped back to look at the shelter they had just erected. "This worked fine last night." Charisse's tipi cover was stretched over a frame that came out from the side of the wagon. They had nearly twice as much room as they'd had under the wagon, were protected from the weather, and it was open so the cooling night breeze could blow over them.

Charisse nodded. "That's true, and I'll be satisfied with it until we can get tipi poles.

"All right, I promise we'll look for some as soon as we get to the mountains," Luke said with a grin. "How about I lay out the beds while you finish supper?"

"Fair enough," she said, and handed him the hatchet she'd been using to pound stakes.

Charisse started toward the front of the wagon, then stopped. "Luke," she said hesitantly, "I never did thank you properly for coming to get us."

"What did you expect me to do? I couldn't very well let them take my son, could I?"

"No, but that doesn't make what you did any less heroic. When I think about you and John riding into that camp alone, I get cold chills."

"They were friendly Indians."

"But you didn't know that. Besides, I didn't think you'd be able to find us."

"Thank your dog and Toby's marble trail. If it hadn't been

for them, we'd probably still be looking." Luke grinned suddenly. "Of course, if we'd waited another day White Otter probably would have come looking for us, especially if he made you cook for him."

"Very funny." She wrinkled her nose at him. Then she frowned. "Did you give any more thought to the white men paying Indians to kidnap white women?"

"I suspect you may be right about White Otter mistaking you for someone else. We're going to play it safe, though. Jeveraux sent out the order that nobody gets more than a hundred yards from the wagons when we're moving."

Charisse nodded. "That's what I told the children, even if there aren't any buffalo chips close to the trail. Do you have guard duty tonight?"

"I don't think so. Jeveraux will send someone to let me know if I do. Why?"

Charisse shrugged. "I was just wondering." In reality, she wanted to know if she should follow him if he decided to sneak off again tonight.

"Evening folks." Ben's cheerful voice brought her musings to a halt and a smile to her face.

"Mr. Baxter," she said, "What brings you our way this evening?"

"Just coming to pay my respects." He gave her his disarming smile. "Come now, I thought we'd moved beyond Mr. Baxter and Mrs. McCabe."

Charisse smiled back. "You're right, Ben, we have. Do you have time for a cup of coffee?"

"You bet." He swung a leg over the wagon tongue and sat down. "You don't look any the worse for wear after your adventure with the Indians."

"No, but we were very lucky. For the most part, they were nice to us. I think they want to stay friendly with whites. Still, it's not something I care to go through again."

"I heard Toby's version of it this afternoon and have been waiting ever since to hear the tale from your own lovely lips. It sounded as if you were quite the heroine."

Charisse blushed as she brought him his cup of coffee. "I don't know as I'd go that far. In fact, I rather think they let us go because we were more trouble than we were worth."

Ben raised his eyebrows. "That makes me even more anxious to hear your story."

"It was actually a string of odd coincidences, and none of them very impressive." She smiled. "First I fainted, and then I threw up all over my captor and his horse." Ben listened with rapt attention as Charisse told her story, laughing in some places and praising her quick thinking in others. By the time she'd finished, Toby had returned, supper was ready, and Ben accepted her invitation to stay.

Luke joined them as soon as the bedrolls were laid out, but never said a word. He glared at Ben as though the other man might decide to walk off with all their valuables. Through it all, Ben remained oblivious to Luke's dark looks, chatting with Charisse and Toby, paying her lavish compliments on her cooking and generally making himself agreeable. He even helped her wash the dishes. The more pleasant Ben was, the more Luke glowered. By the time their guest left, Charisse was more than ready to do battle with her pseudo-husband.

"Toby, why don't you go see if Morgan and the twins need help watering the horses," Charisse said.

"You mean I don't have to get ready for bed?"

"Not just yet."

"Yippee!" he yelled, then took off at a high run with Franklin at his heels.

"Be back before dark," she yelled after him.

Luke watched them go. "Something tells me you're going to regret that."

"Maybe so, but I didn't think he needed to see us fight."

He raised an eyebrow. "Oh, are we about to fight?"

Charisse crossed her arms and scowled at him. "I don't appreciate the way you treated our guest."

"What do you mean? I didn't say a word to him."

"No, you didn't. Not even when he asked you a direct question. I couldn't believe you could be so incredibly rude!"

"I don't care for the man."

"That was certainly evident. I happen to like him and enjoy his company!"

Luke snorted. "That's pretty evident, too. Frankly, I don't trust him as far as I could throw him."

"Why not?" Charisse asked in surprise. "What has he ever done that makes you think you can't trust him?"

"You ask me that after I sat here and watched him flirt with you the better part of an hour?"

"What are you talking about?"

"A man who would flirt with a woman in front of her own husband is one who would do about anything. You can't trust him!"

"Oh, for pity sake, we weren't flirting, and even if we had been, so what? I'm not your wife."

"No, but he doesn't know that," Luke pointed out. "It's lucky for him we're not really married. Because if we were, I'd teach Ben Baxter a lesson he wouldn't be forgetting for a while."

Charisse made a disgusted noise. "I suppose that means you'd go after him with your fists."

"Damn right I would!" Luke stood up and dumped the dregs of his coffee in the fire. "I'm going to go find my son. We'll be back in about fifteen minutes. Best be quick about it if you want any privacy."

"Oooo!" Charisse stamped her foot and gritted her teeth as she watched him walk away. He couldn't possibly want to hit Ben Baxter as badly as she wanted to hit Luke McCabe!

She feigned sleep when Luke returned with Toby and Franklin half an hour later. They seemed to take an inordinate amount of time getting ready for bed and settling in. It was hard not to react when a warm little body cuddled up next to her, but the kiss on her cheek and the whispered, "Good night, Mama," just about did her in.

Luke's soft chuckle told Charisse her ruse had been less

than successful, but she refused to give him the satisfaction of proving him right by opening her eyes. Though it had been a long day and she was tired, her seething sense of mistreatment kept her awake.

Still, Charisse had never been one to hold on to a grudge, and gradually she began to relax. She was on the verge of sleep when a soft sound suddenly jerked her awake. Luke was getting up. Peeking out from under half closed eyelids, she watched him quickly slip into his clothes, then check to make sure she was asleep before putting on his boots. He was definitely not making a late-night visit to the bushes.

Shortly after he left the shelter, Charisse was up and into her shoes and dressing gown. Franklin gazed up at her questioningly, then rose from his place at the foot of Toby's bed and stretched. "No, Franklin, stay," she whispered. "Watch Toby."

Franklin looked at her for a moment then turned three times and sank back onto his bed with his nose inches from Toby's feet.

"Good dog," she whispered and gave his ears a quick scratch before following Luke into the darkness. At first, she thought he was going to the Simms wagon, but he skirted it and set off for a patch of willows down by the river.

He was meeting Caroline! The knowledge was like a knife in her chest. A wise woman would turn back now and save herself the indignity of catching her man cheating on her. Charisse set her jaw and quickened her pace to keep up with his long-legged strides. Luke McCabe wasn't her man, she reminded herself, but her life was affected by what he did. She had a right—no, a responsibility—to find out what he was up to.

The glow of a cigarette showed someone was walking up ahead. Charisse frowned. She couldn't tell who it was from this distance, but it was definitely a man. How strange. The man stopped on the bank of the river and glanced at the sky, turning his profile to Charisse. She gasped in shock. It was Ben Baxter!

Had Luke followed him here to start a fight?

Charisse stepped up her pace. Who would have thought Luke would have such a jealous streak, especially when there was absolutely nothing between her and Ben? She had to stop the fight before it started. She was about to make her presence known when Ben spoke.

"Took you long enough. I was about ready to give up and go to bed."

Luke shrugged. "I had to wait until Charisse went to sleep. It took longer than usual tonight."

Charisse blinked in astonishment. They had planned to meet? What on earth for? She frowned. Certainly not to fight, neither of them sounded angry. Knowing she'd never get a straight answer by asking, she stepped into the shadow of the willow thicket.

Ben took a final drag off his cigarette and dropped it to the ground, "Ah," he said as he ground it out under his boot. "Finally decided to romance your *wife*, I take it."

"Not hardly. Thanks to you, we had a fight. Seems like you used to get me in trouble with Elizabeth, too."

"What can I say? Women love me."

Luke chuckled. "So you keep telling me." He sobered. "What did you think of Charisse's story?"

"I think you've blown your cover. Someone wanted you out of the way until we left Fort Laramie. At the very least, they suspect you aren't what you say you are."

Luke nodded. "That's what I was thinking, too. Did you see anything?"

Ben shook his head. "Nope, everything was quiet. Of course, something could have taken place away from the wagon train. I couldn't watch everyone at once."

"Somebody went through the wagon while I was gone," Luke said.

"Did they find anything?"

"Nothing to find. I know better than to leave incriminating evidence lying around."

"Didn't figure you had. Still, they suspect, and that puts a crimp in things."

"I know," Luke said with a sigh. "I'll have to play my cards close to my chest. I don't think anyone has figured you out, though."

"The way you keep giving me the evil eye every time I get within ten feet of Charisse has helped keep me in the clear."

"That's what I'm hoping. It's got Charisse convinced, anyway."

"Really?"

Luke nodded. "She thought I was going to beat the crap out of you tonight."

Ben snorted. "You might try."

"Seems to me, the last time we boxed I won."

Ben shrugged. "I was recovering from influenza."

"Sure, you were. What about the time before that?"

"Hangover, and if you'll recall, I won the time before that."

"That's not the way I remember it. Your brother got in on that one and..."

As the two moved down the river bank out of the range of her hearing, Charisse sagged against the willow bushes. Was there ever a greater fool than she? Far from hating Ben Baxter, Luke considered him a close friend and the two of them went back a long way.

Worse yet, both of them were using her to cover whatever nefarious scheme they had. Her kidnapping and probably the knife-wielding George Bartell were all part of it, whatever it was. Sick at heart, Charisse made her way back to the wagon.

Franklin tried to lick her face when she crawled back into bed, but she pushed him away, too miserable to share her pain even with Franklin. She lay there next to Toby trying to make sense of it, but everything kept going around and around in her head. None of it fit together.

The only thing she knew for sure was that Luke McCabe had known perfectly well who Ben Baxter was the day he arrived. No wonder Ben had looked so surprised when she introduced herself as Mrs. McCabe.

Charisse lay there reliving the whole trip, recalling small incidents that had meant nothing at the time, but now took on a whole new meaning. In spite of it all, the images that kept haunting her were a few tender touches and one blazing kiss. Luke had said himself they had been merely to give the illusion of a happy marriage. Her head told her it was so, but her heart steadfastly refused to believe it.

CHAPTER 22

"Evenin', McCabe," Ben said as he sat down on a boulder next to Luke and pulled out his tobacco pouch.

Luke raised an eyebrow. "You're late, Baxter. You were supposed to relieve me two hours ago."

"I was busy," Ben lowered his voice. "Are we alone?"

"Haven't seen anybody around. You?"

"Everyone's in bed as far as I could tell. You know," Ben said conversationally as he rolled a cigarette, "if it hadn't been for the Indians grabbing Charisse and the kids last week, I'd be wondering if you misinterpreted what you saw back in Independence."

Luke gave him a wry look. "Trust me, that thought has crossed my mind. I don't suppose you found something tonight."

"Maybe." He stuck the cigarette in his mouth and lit it. "I was several minutes early tonight and saw Simms studying some kind of document. I only caught a glimpse before he rolled it up and stuck it in the wagon, but I'm almost sure it was a map."

"A map of what?" Luke asked.

"I couldn't tell, but I think we need to find out."

"Definitely. Maybe it will finally shed some light on this mess. How do we find it?"

"I have a general idea where it is," Ben said. "After the game, I circled back because I figured Simms would put it in a more secure place the first chance he got."

"And did he?"

"Yep. As soon as the coast was clear, he pulled it out and knelt by the side of the wagon. I couldn't tell exactly what he was doing, but when he stood up a few minutes later, his hands were empty. I'm pretty sure he hid the map under the wagon somewhere."

"I'm tempted to try and retrieve it now."

Ben shook his head. "I don't think it's any accident that his sleeping tent is on that side of the wagon. I'll keep them distracted tomorrow night during the poker game, and you can look."

"All right. I wish we had a few more men so we could keep track of Simms and all his bully boys twenty-four hours a day. Fort Laramie is still within riding distance. One of them could easily sneak away and ride back to the fort or rendezvous with someone halfway."

Ben nodded, "We're getting close to Platte River Station too. Dammit! It's been way over a month and we aren't a bit closer to figuring out what's going on than we were at the beginning!"

"Let's hope I can find something tomorrow night," Luke said. "We're about due for a break in this case."

Instead of planning his raid on Simms' wagon as he drove the oxen down the trail the next day, Luke found himself trying to come up with a way to thaw Charisse's reserve. Unfortunately, nothing had occurred to him by the end of the day.

"Jeveraux says we'll reach the Platte River Station tomorrow or the day after," Luke said as he washed his hands for supper. "I hear there's a small trading post there."

"Oh?" Charisse didn't even look up from the pot she was stirring.

"I thought you might be interested since you didn't have time to do any trading at Fort Laramie."

She shrugged. "Maybe."

Silence fell between them again, and Luke watched her go about her daily chores with a sense of defeat. It had been the same since their "fight" the week before. Charisse had closed up against him, speaking to him only when necessary. She didn't even respond to his teasing anymore. He'd think it was her anger at his interference in her budding romance, but she wasn't talking to Ben either. In fact, about the only adult she was talking to was Caroline Simms, and that was odd in itself. After a fortnight of pokering up every time the woman's name was mentioned, Caroline had suddenly become Charisse's best friend. If not for Joshua Simms, who viewed the friendship with a jaundiced eye, the two women would spend all spare their time together.

"Mama, look what Morgan and I found!" Toby came tearing into camp with Franklin at his heels and a bouquet of wilted wild flowers clutched in his hands.

Charisse smiled the first real smile Luke had seen on her face all day. The only thing that hadn't changed was her attitude toward the children. She was still warm and responsive to them. He felt a pang as he watched Charisse give Toby a hug of thanks for the flowers and wondered if he was jealous of his own son.

Luke swallowed a sigh and turned away. The plan for him to steal the map during the nightly poker game was risky at best, but they hadn't been able to come up with anything else. Despite the danger, Luke felt the familiar tingle of anticipation. This was the part of his job he enjoyed the most: meeting the enemy head on and coming out on top.

Meanwhile, there was supper and bedtime to get through. Luke touched the folded paper in his pocket and glanced at Charisse. It was time to tell her of its contents. He'd been waiting for the right moment, but it didn't look as though that was ever going to happen. Not with her current mood.

The meal passed the way half a dozen before it had. Toby kept up a steady stream of chatter. Luke was achingly aware of Charisse sitting on the other side of the campfire, her silence like a wall around her. He thought wistfully of other nights they'd shared. Though the conversation usually centered around the day or Toby and often bordered on the mundane, Luke and Charisse had developed a deep sense of camaraderie, something that had been sadly lacking in his marriage. Between Elizabeth's busy social schedule and his preoccupation with his job, there never seemed to be time for more than a brief exchange of pleasantries. Luke had talked more to Charisse in a month than he had to his wife in the two years before her death. He wondered if Charisse missed it as much as he did.

At last, supper was eaten and the remains cleared away. Luke tucked Toby into bed for the night, then walked back to the fire and stood for a moment, watching Charisse wash the dishes. "We need to talk," he said finally.

Her expression was guarded as she looked up at him. Luke waited for a long moment, but she didn't speak.

He swallowed a sigh and tried again. "There are things I need to tell you, just in case."

"In case of what?"

Luke shrugged. "A lot of things can happen on the trail." He handed her the packet of papers from his inside pocket. "It's best to be prepared."

She gave him a blank look. "What's this?"

"My will."

"Your what?"

"My last will and testament."

Charisse eyed the packet of papers in her hand as though it was a nest of poisonous spiders. "Why are you giving it to me?"

"Because it concerns you."

She looked up in surprise. "It does?"

"I made you my executor and Toby's guardian."

She blinked. "Wouldn't it be better to appoint someone in your family?"

Luke shook his head. "There's no family left. Toby is all I have." He gave her a direct look. "I realize it's a lot to ask, and if you'd rather not..." He let his voice trail off with just the right amount of doubt.

"No, no, of course I don't mind," she said. "It's just that I'm sure there must be someone better suited."

He made a rude noise. "And who would that be? So far,

you're the only person who has ever been able to keep him under control. Besides, you couldn't love him more if he was your own flesh and blood, and he feels the same about you."

"Surely there's someone in your wife's family…"

"Not who gives a damn about Toby. Besides, they've all washed their hands of both of us."

"Luke, is there something you're not telling me?"

"Not that I can think of. Anyway, it's all lined out in my will. There isn't a great fortune, but it's enough to give Toby a decent home."

"Why did you suddenly decide it was time to write your will?"

"I guess it was all the graves we've been passing, and the news from the other wagon trains that got me thinking. Any of us could meet the elephant out here." Luke sighed. "If something happens to me, Toby will be all alone in the world. If I know he'll be with you, I can rest easy again."

Charisse was quiet for a long moment then nodded. "If you're sure…"

"Never been more sure of anything in my life. Besides, it's only a precaution. Chances are, I'll live to a ripe old age and die in my bed."

She looked at the papers in her hand. "I suppose we should put these somewhere safe then."

"How about the lap desk?"

"Good idea." She handed them to him and turned back to her dishes.

He was halfway to the back of the wagon when she spoke again. "Luke?"

"Yes?"

"I… Thank you."

He frowned. "For what?"

"For trusting me."

He turned and looked at her in surprise. "Why wouldn't I?"

"Oh, you know, the divorce and everything."

Luke snorted. "From everything I've heard, Preston is the one who can't be trusted. You've never given me any reason to doubt you."

She gave him a wistful look, and it looked for a moment like she was going to say something more. Then she gave a slight shake of her head and turned away.

Luke's heart sank. He'd thought she was going to tell him what was bothering her, but she'd shut down as surely as the slamming of a door. He didn't know any more than he had before. Even more of a mystery was why it bothered him so much.

The tiny sliver of moon provided little light, but the inky darkness suited Luke fine as he waited patiently in the shadow of Simm's wagon. Caroline had blown out the light half an hour ago, and the poker game was proceeding as usual on the other side of the wagon. He heard Ben's slurred voice and smiled. If he hadn't seen Ben drink many a man under the table and still act dead sober, he'd have thought his partner was well on his way to passing out. Apparently, the other players thought so too. The stakes were even higher than usual, and everyone's attention was focused on the game.

It had been a long time since he'd heard anything but silence from inside the tent. Though he had no way of knowing for sure, it was a pretty good bet that Caroline was asleep. The time had finally come for action. Luke crept forward in the darkness, careful not to make a sound.

With deft fingers, he explored the underside of the wagon looking for an abnormality that would indicate a hidey-hole. Nothing. Luke sat back on his heels and studied the wagon. Ben said it had only taken Simms a few seconds to stow the document. It had to be there somewhere, relatively easy to access. His eyes traced the length of the wagon searching for any clue, the slightest irregularity or flaw. Everything looked perfectly normal. Suddenly, his gaze snapped back to the water barrels attached to the side. In his mind's eye, he relived a dozen trips to fill those barrels, almost twice as often as he filled his own. Either Caroline Simms was using a hell of a lot of water, or the barrels were not quite what they seemed.

With a surge of excitement, he hunkered down next to the barrel and felt along the underside. A small imperfection gave under the pressure of his fingers, and a section of the barrel slid open to reveal a false bottom. Exultation flowed through him as he reached cautiously into the hole. His fingers closed on a roll of paper. At last, something tangible.

Luke tucked the paper inside his coat and listened to the men on the other side of the wagon. Good, the poker game was still going strong. He should have plenty of time to see what was on the paper and return it to its hiding place without anyone being the wiser.

Like a creature of the night, he melted into the darkness. Briefly cursing the same lack of moonlight that pleased him earlier, he made his way to his own wagon, hoping to find light enough to see what was on the paper.

All was quiet in the camp as he stirred the embers of the fire and sat on the small three-legged stool. With a feeling of anticipation, he withdrew the document and opened it. A blast of jubilation thundered through him. It was indeed a map. At last, something they could build their case on! But as he studied the map his smile faded, and his joy was replaced by a sense of dawning horror. McNesby's intuition had been correct. The clerk in Independence had stumbled onto something important, but this was far worse than any of them had anticipated.

Luke spent a few more minutes memorizing details, then rerolled the map and covered the fire. His trip back Simms' wagon was uneventful. In fact, it didn't look as though any of the poker players had moved. He'd just slipped the map back into its hiding place and closed the secret door when he caught a whisper of sound behind him.

Pivoting on the balls of his feet, Luke had the momentary impression of a man looming above him before a huge pair of hands locked around his throat. From his crouched position, Luke launched himself forward and threw his full weight against his attacker. They both crashed to the ground and rolled away from the wagon, each trying to do as much damage to his opponent as possible. Luke managed to get in a few punches, but they seemed to have little effect. There was a woman's scream, then a starburst of pain exploded in his head — and everything went black.

CHAPTER 23

"What the hell?" Joshua was on his feet and moving before the words left his mouth. It was impossible to miss the crashing and banging on the other side of the wagon.

Damn, Luke's in trouble. "What's going on?" Ben asked in his best drunken slur. He lurched to his feet and staggered after his host. "Sounds like there's a lady in distress," he mumbled. He might as well have saved his breath. No one even looked up from their cards as he followed Simms around the wagon.

"Oh, Ben, do be careful," Caroline whispered, peering out of her sleeping tent.

He looked into her fear-filled eyes and felt his heart turn over in his chest. Ben didn't mess with married women. It was a hard and fast rule he never broke. But there was something about Caroline's tremulous smile that turned him inside out. It had been that way since he'd saved her life, as though the act had somehow forged a bond between them. He gave her a slight, reassuring smile of his own, then staggered around the tent to a scene of confusion.

Boxes and barrels were scattered about, and Luke lay in a crumpled heap in the middle of them, a dark puddle of blood pooling under his head. Joshua Simms knelt next to the wagon, apparently more concerned with his hidey hole than the man who lay like a corpse in the wreckage.

Two long strides brought Ben to Luke's side. Kneeling in the dirt next to his friend's body, he breathed a sigh of relief when he felt the strong beat of a pulse under his fingers. A quick survey of the damage showed it to be less than it had first appeared. The blood seemed to be coming from a broken nose, painful but not life-threatening. Of more concern was the egg-sized lump behind his ear and the swelling on his jaw. Someone had beat the hell out of Luke McCabe, no small feat. Finding out who and why would have to wait until Luke woke up.

In the meantime, Ben had to make it all look as innocent as possible. Hoping he wasn't making things worse, he slipped a flask of whiskey out of his pocket. With a glance over his shoulder to make sure Simms was still occupied, he sprinkled liberal amounts of the potent brew over Luke's clothing, and slid a small roll of money into his vest pocket. It wasn't great, but it was the best he could think of on the spur of the moment. He prayed it would be enough as he rehid the flask in his coat.

"What's going on here?"

Ben squinted up at Joshua Simms. "I dunno," he said. "Looks like McCabe wasn't watching where he was going and tripped over your supplies." He stood up and swayed slightly on his feet. "Can't figure what he was doin' here this time of night, though. That missus of his keeps a pretty tight rein on him."

"Looks like he got away from her. Smells like he's been drinking." Joshua bent over and plucked the money from Luke's pocket. "Reckon he was headed over to the poker game."

Ben leaned over and took a sniff. "I don't smell nothin'."

Simms laughed as he tucked the money into his own pocket. "Don't reckon you do. The question is, what do we do with him?"

"Take him back to his wife?" Ben said, giving Simms a bleary squint.

Simms looked pensive for a moment, then nodded. "Guess so."

"Want me to do it?"

Simms laughed again. "Sure, go ahead."

Ben heard him mutter, "This should be interesting," under his breath. Mentally cursing Simms' warped sense of humor, Ben bent over and attempted to lift Luke from the ground. Packing Luke McCabe was going to be tough enough without having to maintain his drunken appearance. Luke was no featherweight and Ben had a bit of a struggle hoisting the limp body onto his shoulder. The stagger in his step wasn't all faked, as he lumbered toward Luke's wagon. He had to stop three times to catch his breath before he reached his destination.

I need a lighter partner, Ben thought, easing Luke to the ground. He rolled his shoulders in relief before approaching the sleeping shelter. A low, threatening growl sounded from the darkness and stopped him in his tracks. "Franklin, it's me."

Franklin moved out of the shadow, his lip curled back over his teeth menacingly. His hair bristled over his back, and Ben wondered how he had ever thought the animal friendly.

"Charisse," he called, "Charisse wake up."

"Wh…what? Who's there?"

"It's Ben Baxter. Call off your dog."

He could hear the rustle of bedding over Franklin's growls. Then a match flared in the darkness and a lantern sprang to life. Charisse stepped out holding the light high. "What do you want?" she asked, in a tone that wasn't much friendlier than her dog's growls.

"Luke's been hurt," he said, wondering when she had become so cautious.

"Oh, no! Where is he?"

"Right here." He pointed over his shoulder. "I brought him home."

The words were barely out of his mouth before she brushed by him to kneel at Luke's side. "Dear God, there's so much blood!" she said, trying to wipe it away with the hem of her night gown. "Don't let him die, God, please. I couldn't bear it—"

"Charisse." Ben touched her shoulder. "It's only a broken nose."

"What?"

"The blood, it's all from his nose. I think it's broken."

Charisse wiped her eyes and looked closer at Luke's battered face. "I…I think you're right," she said after a moment.

"Could you get me some water please? There's some in the coffee pot by the fire ring."

By the time Ben returned, Charisse was examining Luke for other injuries. She gave Ben a distracted smile as she accepted the pot of water. "Do you know what happened to him?"

"Not really."

"There's a big lump behind his ear and look at these marks on his neck." She pointed to a couple of wide red bands that ran across his throat. "What do you think caused this?"

Ben hunkered down for a closer look. Cold chills chased their way down his spine as he stared at the marks. It looked like the imprints of two very large thumbs, as though someone had tried to choke Luke. "Don't know what would cause something like that. What do you think?"

Charisse shook her head. "I've never seen anything like it before," she said, gently sponging the blood from Luke's face. "You were right about the blood. It does seem to have all come from his nose." She glanced up at him. "Is that all his too?"

"All what?"

"Your shirt."

For the first time, Ben looked down and realized he was covered in blood too. "Yes, it's all Luke's. Whoever did this to him was long gone by the time I got there."

"Ben," she said quietly, after a moment, "what's going on with you two?"

"Going on? You mean with Luke?" Ben shook his head. "You've got it all wrong, Charisse. I didn't do this. I know he's got it in his head that I was flirting with you, but I didn't—"

"I know you're friends," she said quietly, "and that the whole flirting charade was to hide that fact."

Ben kept his face carefully blank. "Where did you get an idea like that?"

"I overheard you after we left Fort Laramie."

"I don't know what you thought you heard, but—"

"You've known each other a long time." She looked up at him. "He even knows your brother."

Damn! They were well and truly caught. There was only one thing to do in a situation like this— lie. "I don't have a brother."

She gave him a disgusted look. "I don't care what you and Luke are to each other, and I don't care about the past you share. I just want to know what you're up to and how it relates to me."

He sighed. His gut told him to trust her, but he'd learned long ago that trust often came with a huge price. "Look, Charisse—"

"What the hell happened?" Luke groaned and opened his eyes.

Ben was never more glad of anything in his life. "We were hoping maybe you could tell us."

"The last I remember was someone sneaking up behind me." He squinted up at Charisse. "Where am I?"

"Lying on the ground next to our camp. Mr. Baxter brought you home unconscious and covered with blood." She glared up at Ben. "You both smell like the inside of a saloon, but since the closest one is probably several hundred miles behind us, I'd venture a guess you were playing poker with Joshua Simms and his cronies."

"I wasn't playing poker, and I wasn't drinking," Luke said as he sat up.

"Then how do you explain the way you smell?"

"I accidentally spilled whiskey on him," Ben said quickly. "It happened when I picked him up."

Charisse rose to her feet and glared at both of them. "Fine, don't tell me. I couldn't care less what you do with your spare time, or who you do it with. What I am concerned with is how it pertains to me and to Toby. I'll give you until tomorrow morning to tell me what's going on. If you haven't told me by then, I'm going to Pierre Jeveraux with my suspicions."

Ben frowned. "What suspicions?"

"That Luke kidnapped Toby from his grandparents' protection, and that he's running from the law." With another glare, she picked up the pot of water. "Here, let me help you wash off the whiskey smell." With that, she dumped the remainder of the water on Luke's head and marched off to the wagon.

"Whew," Ben said as he watched her blow out the lamp and disappear into the darkness. "The lady has quite a temper."

"You haven't seen the half of it." Luke winced as he felt behind his ear. "Damn. What happened?"

Ben glanced around to make sure they were alone and lowered his voice. "I'm not sure. We were playing poker when all hell broke loose on the other side of the wagon. By the time I got there, you were out cold and Simms was checking his hiding place." He crossed his arms and studied his friend. "The idea was to find out what Simms was hiding without attracting attention."

Luke stood and shook his head to clear it. "I found it all right, and had it tucked back in its hidey hole. I was about to leave when somebody sneaked up behind me and koshed me over the head."

"Did you see who it was?"

"No, other than he was big, damn big! I suspect it was the same man who killed Bartell. The first thing he did was go for my neck." Luke frowned. "The only one I can think of who's big enough is John Jessup."

"You think Jessup's in with Simms?"

Luke shook his head. "Not really. What kind of fool would bring his family along on a dangerous mission like this?"

Ben grinned. "I can think of one, and he even took on a fake wife to complete his cover." He sobered. "Those kids of Jessup's do spend an awful lot of time with Charisse and Toby."

"I know, but it doesn't feel right."

"I have to agree with you there," Ben admitted. "Still, it wouldn't be the first time the villain turned out to be someone completely unexpected. Did you get a chance to look at the map before you got caught, or was it all for nothing?"

"I saw it all right, and it's not good. It was a plan for

secession."

"Secession! I know the Southern states have been unhappy, but— "

"It's not just the Southern states."

"What?"

Luke sighed. "It appears that's only half of the plan. The map also showed the New Mexico and Utah territories as well."

"You mean the land we got after the War with Mexico?"

Luke nodded. "Everything but California. Could be the inhabitants aren't happy with American rule and would rather be part of Mexico again, or start a whole new country. It looked as if the plan is for a rebellion to start in the Mexican territory and the Southern states to secede at the same time."

Ben gave a low whistle. "Civil war on two fronts."

"Exactly. Divide and conquer. The United States would be hard put to carry on two wars at the same time."

"And if the army forts were under supplied…"

"The rebellion would have a far better chance of succeeding."

"So where does the trek west come into this? Simms could have continued to falsify the records in Independence without risking his neck coming west."

Luke shook his head again. "I don't know. I'd be willing to bet it has to do with whatever he has hidden in that wagon of his."

"Find anything tonight?"

"Just the map, and it was hidden under the water barrel."

"That would explain why he was afraid of the wagon tipping over in the river. It would have destroyed the map."

"But it doesn't explain why the wagon didn't float. The box of the wagon was solid from the outside. It must have a false floor like we thought."

"We've got to figure out a way to find out what's in that wagon." Ben looked pensive. "Do you think whoever attacked you saw you with the map?"

"Not unless they waited until I had it stowed away before

they made their move."

"So, you may still be in the clear."

"They'll know I was snooping around, but not that I'd seen the map."

"They suspect you anyway, and this will confirm their suspicions. Still, we really aren't any worse off than before."

Luke looked toward the wagon and frowned. "Speak for yourself. I still have to face Charisse." He sniffed his shirt. "Whew! No wonder she was so mad. How did I get whiskey all over me?"

Ben shrugged. "Just sprinkled a little of my private stock on you is all. It was to convince Simms you were just a wandering drunk. He seemed to think you were on the way to the poker game. Even relieved you of your cash. I guess he figured he'd have had it off you if you'd actually joined the play anyway."

"Cash? I didn't have any money on me."

"I know. I planted that too, and I fully expect you to pay me back." He glanced toward the darkened wagon. "What are you going to do about Charisse?"

"I don't know." Luke rubbed his face. "Tell her as much of the truth as possible."

Ben frowned. "I don't think she's part of all this, but you can't be sure until we hear from McNesby."

"I know, but damn it, Ben, my gut tells me to trust her."

Ben was silent for a long moment. "Are you falling in love with her?" he asked quietly.

"Falling in love?" Luke gave him an incredulous look. "With Charisse? No, of course not!"

Ben crossed his arms and raised his eyebrows.

Luke sighed. "All right...maybe...I don't know. I may not be sure what I feel for Charisse Jones, but I do know enough not to let it jeopardize the mission."

"So, what are you going to tell her?"

Luke glanced at the darkened wagon again. "I don't know, but I won't reveal our mission."

"It wouldn't be the first time love blinded a man."

"Ben, the problem with my marriage was that when I was on a job, I was totally focused on it. I'm still that way. There's no room for Charisse Jones or anyone else."

"Good, stay focused this time, and we'll be fine."

"Guess I'd better go face the music." He gave Ben a rueful smile. "Too bad you can't go with me."

Ben grinned. "I don't have that kind of courage."

"Not sure I do either," Luke said with a grimace.

"Good luck," Ben said as his friend walked away, then turned toward his own camp. As he passed the Simms wagon, an image of Caroline's sweet smile flitted through his mind. *Focus on the job,* Baxter, focus on the job. He wondered if he'd be able to follow his own advice.

CHAPTER 24

Charisse's rage lasted all the way to the wagon and through the process of changing into a clean nightgown. Then, unable to face the thought of going back to bed while she was still so stirred up, she sat on her trunk, unbraided her hair and began to brush it. Giving it one hundred strokes had been a nightly routine for as long as she could remember. She'd given it up early on in the trip along with her corset and petticoats, one more casualty chalked up to the rigors of the trail.

She could hear Luke and Ben talking, but the murmur of voices was too low for her to make out their words. The familiar feel of the silver-backed brush gliding through her hair did little to soothe her anger. Which was fine with her, she didn't want to be calm when she faced Luke. Suddenly, without warning, there were tears streaming down her face. The image of Luke covered in blood and her blind panic were still fresh in her mind. Angrily, she dashed them away with the back of her hand. He didn't deserve her tears, the lying snake!

"Charisse, are you in there?"

The sound of Luke's voice right outside the wagon made her jump. "Yes, I'm here."

"Is it all right if I come in?"

Charisse hastily dabbed at her eyes to erase any lingering traces of tears. "I can't stop you. It's half your wagon."

She thought she heard him sigh, then his outline blocked the entrance and the wagon rocked a little as he pulled himself up into it.

"Damn, it's dark in here. Mind if I light the lantern?"

"Suit yourself." She heard him fumbling around in the dark. Then a match flared and illuminated the interior of the wagon.

"There, that's better," he said as he lit the wick and replaced the lantern glass. "What were you doing sitting here in the dark, anyhow?"

"My nightgown was covered with blood, and I needed to change. I didn't want to put on a show." She shrugged. "Plus, I was hoping you'd decide to talk to me, and I don't want to wake Toby."

"No, neither do I." He set the lantern on the floor and took a seat on the flour barrel facing her.

Silence fell and they sat staring at each other. "I hardly know where to begin," he said at last."

"How about why you stole Toby from his grandparents?"

Luke gave her a wry smile. "I think of it more as liberating him from his grandparents." Charisse raised her eyebrows but said nothing.

"I don't think they were all that sorry to see him go, if you want to know the truth. Maybe if he'd been more like his mother..." He sighed again. "I probably shouldn't have married Elizabeth in the first place. Her father was the local banker, and her family was the richest in town. Elizabeth was the darling of the community; we all fancied ourselves in love with her. I'm not sure why she picked me. I've always wondered if it was because her father didn't approve."

Charisse blinked. "Why on earth would she do a silly thing like that?"

Luke shrugged. "To assert her independence, maybe. I realize now she was spoiled and a little too used to getting her way. At the time, I thought myself the luckiest man in the world. We were happy for a while, I suppose, but we really had very little in common, and it wasn't long before we began drifting apart."

"You both discovered you hadn't married the person you thought you had," Charisse said almost to herself. How well she knew that story.

"Exactly. I started spending less and less time at home, but she never seemed to care. I grieved when she died, but I think it was more because I felt I'd failed her. I think we had stopped loving each other long ago." He fell silent, staring into the past.

"And her parents blamed you," Charisse said quietly.

"Not really. Elizabeth had always had periods of... melancholy. It wasn't the first time she had tried to kill herself, but it grew worse after Toby was born. Her parents were devastated, of course, and saw Toby as the one tangible piece of their daughter they had left. They couldn't bear to let him go. Besides, he was just a baby, and I..." He made a helpless gesture with his hand.

"So, you left him with them."

He nodded. "I went to see him every chance I got, but I see now it wasn't enough. As he grew older I began to suspect things were not...perfect, but I never doubted their love for him." He rubbed his hand over his face. "Unfortunately, he took after me rather than his mother. Elizabeth's parents are..."

"Not the kind that enjoy rambunctious little boys, perhaps?"

Luke smiled. "Precisely. I didn't realize how bad it had become until my last visit."

As Charisse listened to him tell of his father-in-law's mistreatment of Toby, she put it together with what she had already heard from the boy himself. It all fit—grandparents who didn't have the first idea how to handle a child as lively as Toby and who, on some level, might even have blamed him for their beloved daughter's death.

"Taking Toby out of that house probably wasn't the best thought-out plan I ever had, but I don't regret it, and I didn't kidnap him."

"No, it was definitely the right thing to do," Charisse agreed, "but why go all the way to Oregon Territory?"

Luke shrugged. "Why not? Aren't you going there to make a fresh start?"

"Well, yes, but—"

"Just because you're running from your past doesn't mean

everyone else is too."

Charisse's mouth fell open in shock. "You think that's what I'm doing?"

"Isn't it?"

Her blistering denial died in her throat. He was right, of course—running was exactly what she was doing. Suddenly, the shame of her divorce threatened to overwhelm her again. She looked down at her hands.

"You're right. I had no reason to judge you that way. I'm sorry."

"Charisse—"

"You've always given me the benefit of the doubt and accepted me at face value. You've even over looked my…." She paused. "My shortcomings."

"Charisse." He crooked his finger under her chin and gently raised her face. "I wasn't criticizing. Your so-called shortcomings aren't any worse than anyone else's on this wagon train. None of us really knows what we're doing."

She gave a ghost of a smile. "Then you don't mind burnt beans and crusty mush anymore?"

"They've sort of grown on me. I'll probably crave them once this is all over." He ran his thumb over her cheek. "You've been crying."

Charisse shrugged. "Nerves. I think I was reacting to all the blood."

"And the uncertainty of all this." He caressed the side of her face with the backs of his fingers.

She fought the melting feeling brought on by his touch. "Please, Luke, can't you tell me what's going on?"

Luke sighed."It's not mine to tell, but I promise you I won't let anything hurt you or Toby."

"Is it illegal or immoral?"

"Nope. I'm one of the good guys."

"Is that right?" she said with a slight smile.

Luke raised his hand. "Trust me."

Her smile faded. "Trust—that's what it all comes down to,

isn't it?"

"And do you trust me, sweet Charisse?" he asked softly as he knelt in front of her.

Charisse fought to hold onto her misgivings, but his guileless gaze cut right through her better sense. "I suppose I do," she said at last. "Preston always said I was too darn trusting."

"But we both know he's a complete idiot." Luke picked up a lock of her hair and watched it curl around his hand. "Only a fool would let someone like you get away."

The warm melting sensation spread through her body. "Preston didn't exactly let me get away," she murmured. "He made me leave."

"My point exactly." He stroked the length of her hair where it hung over her shoulder. "God, you have beautiful hair."

"I've been told it's my best feature."

"Hmm. I'm not so sure I agree." His voice was a deep rumble as he leaned closer. "A man could lose himself in your eyes, and your ears were made to whisper sweet nothings into." The warmth of his breath brushed her ear.

Charisse shivered, but it had nothing to do with being cold.

"Your neck," he continued, "is as graceful as a swan's."

She closed her eyes as his lips traced a path down the sensitive skin of her throat.

"But your mouth is enough to drive a man crazy all by itself." His lips whispered along hers, igniting a fire deep within her. "Ever since the first time, I've wanted to kiss you again. His voice was a barely-audible whisper that twisted the pit of her stomach and sent shafts of heat lower yet.

The touch of his mouth on hers sent Charisse into a head spin. He pulled her into his arms and her hands slid up his chest, tracing the hard contours beneath his damp shirt. The kiss deepened, and Charisse whimpered.

"We can do without this." Luke blew out the lamp and pulled her tighter into his arms. They kissed open-mouthed, hungrily, as though they couldn't get enough of each other.

Unfamiliar yearnings swirled through Charisse with an intensity that left her breathless. It was wild, wicked, and wonderful.

A gasp of surprise turned to a moan when his hands slipped inside her nightgown to caress her naked skin. She hadn't even been aware of the buttons parting beneath his fingers. Then he was kissing her again, and she forgot everything but his mouth and his hands as they stoked the seething fires within her.

"Mama?" Charisse and Luke jerked apart at the sound of Toby's small, frightened voice. They stared at each other for a long moment, their breath coming hard and their hearts pounding. Then, the plaintive voice came again.

"Mama, where are you?"

"I—I'm right here in the wagon, sweetheart. I'll be out in a minute."

"Oh, hell," Luke whispered as he watched her try to do up her nightgown with shaking fingers. After a moment, he gently pushed her hands aside and made short work of the buttons. With a grateful look, she pulled her hair over her shoulder and quickly began to plait it.

"What are you doing?" Toby wanted to know.

"Just brushing my hair." She hurriedly tied off her braid and stood up. Luke took her hand and rubbed it against his cheek before kissing it and smiling up at her. She gave him a wobbly smile in return, then pushed past him and scrambled down from the wagon.

By rights she should have been thankful for Toby's abysmal timing. It wasn't hard to figure out where it would have ended, and it was a line neither she nor Luke was ready to cross. But a tiny treacherous part of her heart was anything but grateful.

It wasn't until hours later she realized how successfully Luke had distracted her. She still didn't have a clue what he and Ben Baxter were up to.

CHAPTER 25

"Well, I must say, Platte River Station is something of a disappointment." Eliza Duncan stood with her hands on her hips, looking down on the small community below. It consisted mostly of tents, with a few rough cabins scattered through the encampment. The women had gathered together as they waited for Pierre Jeveraux and Ben Baxter to return. They had gone to make contact with the soldiers at the Platte River Station in order to make arrangements for the train's crossing.

"It looks like more of an army depot than an actual trading post," Charisse agreed. "I was looking forward to doing some shopping since I missed out at Fort Laramie."

"I doubt they have anything there you want to buy."

"They say this is the first year the army's even been here," Caroline said. "Before it was just a ferry built by the Mormons. The army is here now to stop disruptions of army supply trains and to protect travelers from the Indians."

The other women looked at her in surprise. Caroline rarely spoke and never volunteered information. She shrugged. "I heard my husband talking about it."

"Where the army is, there are men, and men have appetites to feed." Violet Swindell said with a speculative look at the camp below.

Sadie gave her a quelling glance. "What Violet means is there's bound to be some kind of a trading post."

"Yes, that's what I meant, all right. I think I'll go find Jesse and see what he thinks about…" Violet flashed her sister-in-law an unrepentant grin. "…trading."

Charisse wondered about the by-play between the Swindell ladies for a moment, then sighed and stretched her back. Whatever it meant, it had nothing to do with her. "I wouldn't mind stopping for a day, trading post or not," she said.

"Oh, look! Here comes that nice Mr. Baxter," Eliza said. "Perhaps he knows something."

The women watched Adonis make his way up the hill to where they stood. They could see Ben's grin from a long way off, and it hadn't dimmed a bit by the time he'd reached them. "Ladies," he said, doffing his hat.

"What did you find out?" Caroline asked. "Are we spending an extra day here?"

"No, there isn't enough graze for us to stay. The army needs it for their stock."

"Darn," Charisse said. "I was looking forward to a day of rest and maybe a touch of civilization."

"They did say we could stay the rest of today. We just have to leave before nightfall," Ben said. "You have the better part of today to enjoy Platte River Station, such as it is."

"I don't suppose there are any bathing facilities like there were at Fort Laramie," Eliza said wistfully.

Ben shook his head. "No, but there'll be time to do laundry."

"That's a real cause for celebration," Charisse muttered.

He flashed her a grin. "I knew you'd think so. What would it take to convince you to take pity on a poor bachelor and throw his laundry in with yours?"

"You'd be better served to use your charm on Caroline. She knows what she's doing, and you'd be more likely to get wearable clothes out of the deal."

Charisse was surprised by the twin looks of consternation that crossed both of her friends' faces.

"I—I'd be happy to do it for you," Caroline said hesitantly. "But I don't have any place to hang them to dry."

More like she's afraid to hang them where her husband can see them and get mad, Charisse thought. What had she been thinking to suggest it, even playfully? "Maybe Eliza could—"

"No." Caroline looked up at Ben with a shy smile. "I can do it, I just need a place to hang them."

"You can throw them in with ours, Ben," Charisse put in quickly. "I owe you for rigging my clothesline anyway."

"That's all right. I was only jokin—" he began.

"Nonsense!" Eliza said briskly. "We'll all share the work. You've earned it, Mr. Baxter. However," she said, giving him a fierce look. "We'll thank you not to say anything to the other bachelors on the train. Otherwise, we might be expected to do their laundry as well."

Yes, ma'am," he said meekly.

Charisse watched Ben and Caroline for a moment more, then turned away. Perhaps she'd imagined the emotionally-charged exchange, fraught with hidden meaning and romantic tension. *What Luke and I almost did two nights ago is coloring everything I see.*

What she had experienced with Luke had been new and exciting. His hands and lips had created feelings she'd never even suspected existed. Just thinking about it started a strange tingle which, if she were honest with herself, was rather wonderful. The problem was, she couldn't think about anything else. And the more she thought about it, the more she wondered what else she'd been missing— what Luke could have shown her if they hadn't been interrupted. It went around and around in her head until she felt like she'd go crazy.

At least she would have something to distract her. Thanks to Ben, there was laundry to be done. Drat the man, anyway!

Simms was easy to track down. The interminable poker game was going full tilt beside the wagon, and Luke was relieved to see it was the same old group: Simms, Dempsey, Cassex, Snyder and Nugent. Had any of the soldiers from the fort been involved, he would have felt obligated to join the game. As it was, he passed by with nothing more than a wave. Ben could check it out when he was finished with the scouting mission Jeveraux had sent him on. Personally, Luke wouldn't care if he never played another hand of poker as long as he lived.

The Platte River Station proved to be as small and uninteresting as Ben had predicted. There were plenty of strangers, but most were soldiers. Theirs was the only wagon train since immigrants were encouraged to move on. The few civilians seemed to be connected to the army in some capacity. It didn't rule any out as accomplices, of course, but he could watch Simms from his own wagon and easily see who came and went.

He smiled to himself as he crossed the parade ground toward the wagon and Charisse. Their encounter two nights ago had changed everything. Seduction had been the last thing on his mind when he'd climbed into that wagon. But the sight of her in the lantern light with her hair curling softly around her was more than a mortal man could resist. He'd felt as if the air had been sucked from his lungs. Somehow, he'd gotten through his confession when all he could think of was kissing her. And when he'd finally given in to temptation, it had been more incredible than he had ever imagined. Who would have thought the prim and proper Charisse Jones would react with such enthusiasm?

What had happened between them was unexpected and ill-advised, but he couldn't bring himself to regret it. She'd been shy at breakfast and had blushed adorably when he'd bid her good morning. There hadn't been time to explore the change in their relationship then, but now the whole afternoon lay before them.

Luke's pleasant thoughts came to an abrupt halt as he saw his son on the other side of the parade ground with Morgan Jessup and Franklin. The children had stopped to talk to an unfamiliar man. Even from this distance Luke could see Franklin bristle. That was odd. Franklin liked everybody unless he thought someone was a threat to one of his people. As Luke moved toward them, Franklin sank to the ground and laid his head on his paws, but continued to stare at the stranger with watchful eyes.

Luke frowned. Something didn't feel right. Why would a stranger approach two children, and why had the normally-friendly Franklin felt threatened? By the time he reached them, the children were in an animated conversation with the man.

"Pa," Toby said when he caught sight of him, "Mr. Jackson showed us a trick with Franklin!"

"Is that right?"

The man smiled and held out his hand. "Sam Jackson, at your service, sir. And I take it these two fine boys are yours?"

"One is," Luke said. As he shook hands, he was startled to feel what he was sure were blisters on the man's otherwise soft palm. "I hope they haven't been bothering you."

"Quite the contrary. They've been telling me about your trip. It sounds like you've met with your share of excitement on the trail."

"Some." Luke studied the other man. Jackson was of average height and slender with brown hair and a fair complexion. There was nothing particularly threatening about him. In fact, the remnants of what looked like a bad sunburn and a rash of mosquito bites made him look rather pathetic.

"I couldn't help but notice your dog," Jackson commented. "I don't think I've ever seen one like him before."

"He's a wet corky," Toby volunteered. "He belongs to my mama, and he's really smart."

"Your mother?" Jackson looked surprised. "I see."

"Actually, he's a Welsh Corgi," Luke said with a smile. How well he remembered his own puzzlement over the name. "According to my wife, they hale from England, which is probably why you've never seen one before."

"Franklin minds him real good, Pa," Toby put in. "He snapped his fingers and Franklin laid right down."

"I have a way with dogs," Jackson said.

Not so you could tell, Luke thought as he glanced down at Franklin. The dog lay perfectly still, but continued to watch

Jackson with a wary eye. That in itself was odd. Franklin was usually making up to strangers within a few minutes of discovering they meant his people no harm. This one he didn't appear to like at all. "So, what brings you all the way out here by yourself?"

"I'm a peddler, by profession."

"Kind of a long way from civilization, aren't you? I'd think customers would be a little sparse out here."

"On the contrary, this country is wide open. Folks are starting to miss all the things they left behind." He nodded toward the rudimentary sign over the sutler's store which was housed in a tent. "The farther west I go, the less competition I have."

"You're going to Oregon, then?"

He shrugged. "Maybe, or maybe I'll turn south and go to California. I haven't decided yet. I expect there is more money to be made in the gold fields than in Oregon."

"You're not traveling with a wagon train?"

"I was, but decided to stay on here for a while and rest up. Too much sickness in the train I was with. I hear your train has been lucky that way."

"True. We haven't had any sickness to speak of. Just a few fevers and chills here and there." Was that it? Was he angling to join them? Could he be another of Simms' accomplices?

"I hope it continues to hold for you. I'm going to wait here awhile longer, myself. Well, it was nice talking to you." Jackson tipped his hat and walked away.

Luke's eyes narrowed with speculation as he watched him go. "How exactly did you meet Mr. Jackson, Toby?"

Franklin growled at him.

"We thought it was real strange," Morgan put in, "'cause Franklin likes everybody. But then Mr. Jackson snapped his fingers, and Franklin laid right down."

"Why, Pa, is something wrong?" Toby asked.

"No, I just wondered," Luke said. Though he kept a sharp look out for Mr. Jackson, the man never went anywhere near their wagon train. Given his profession, that was odd. One would think a peddler would be interested in potential customers. Luke had done all the investigating he could do without raising suspicions. It looked like Ben would be making a trip back to the army camp tonight to see what he could find out about the peddler.

"Everything packed and ready to go?" Luke called from the front of the wagon.

"Just about." Charisse finished draping the half-dry laundry over boxes and crates before setting the birdcage on the floor of the wagon. Petey gave a chirp, and she smiled at him. He was the only one who would be happy about this late afternoon move. The sway of the wagon caused him to sing with joyous abandon. The oxen had grown used to it, and she was able to leave his cage uncovered during the day.

"Need some help?"

Charisse turned at the nearness of Luke's voice and found him smiling up at her. Just looking at that smile of his sent a wave of heat straight through her. Lord above! She had to get this insanity under control before she did something crazy. "No, I just finished. Do you know how far we're going to travel before we camp?"

"Only a few miles. Baxter already found us a spot close to the river where we can set up camp." He put his hands on either side of her waist and lifted her down. "Did you find anything you wanted at the trading post?"

Charisse gave him a mysterious smile as she stepped away. "It was more a matter of me having what they wanted."

Luke raised his eyebrows. "What's that supposed to mean?"

"Let's just say I made a tidy little profit off of some of Granny's dishes."

Luke frowned and followed her around to the front of the wagon. "You sold some of your grandmother's dishes at an army post?"

"In a manner of speaking. Say, is that Violet Swindell over there in that crowd of soldiers?"

Luke glanced toward the rowdy group. "Looks like it. Don't change the subject."

"What subject?" Charisse gave him an innocent look. "I'm a little worried about Violet. I don't know as I trust that group."

"I expect Violet can take care of herself."

Charisse frowned, her attention now completely focused on the other woman. "Maybe, but that bunch looks sort of dangerous to me, and it looks like they're getting ugly."

"All right," Luke said with a sigh. "I'll go break it up."

Charisse smiled as she watched him walk away. Now they were even— she didn't know what he and Ben were up to and he didn't know about Granny's dishes. Her smile faded. She had a feeling there was no comparison between the two.

CHAPTER 26

"About time you got back," Luke greeted Ben with a sense of relief. It was well past midnight, several hours after he had expected his partner's return. "It's almost time for Jessup to relieve me. I was beginning to think I'd have to go looking for you as soon as I got off guard duty."

"What, you don't want to take a nice moonlight ride?"

"I need my beauty sleep."

Ben grinned. "Here I figured you'd spent the whole afternoon lying around, catching up on your sleep."

Luke snorted. "You seem to forget we moved camp while you were gone." He watched as Ben swung down from the saddle. "I did find out one interesting piece of news, though. I think we can cross the Swindell brothers off our list."

"Oh? I thought we had decided they were hiding something."

"They are. Their profession."

"And what's that, robbery, kidnapping, smuggling?"

"Nothing so mundane, I'm afraid. They're saloon keepers."

"What?"

"Yep, they're planning on joining another wagon train at Fort Bridger and heading south toward California. They figure there's a fortune to be made there."

"What about all those heavy boxes they were so all-fired concerned about?"

"Irish whiskey and Kentucky bourbon. They have a fortune invested in it." Luke grinned. "They gave me a sample of the whiskey, and I have to say—it's some of the best I've ever tasted."

"What about the extra wagons?" Ben asked as he started to

brush Adonis.

"One is carrying a solid cherry bar and a roulette wheel. The other has a matching piano."

"A piano! Wait a minute — how can that be? Miss Duncan's piano didn't make it two hundred miles."

"For one thing, it's made to fit the bottom of the wagon. For another, there's very little else in there but padding. They knew it was going to be a long hard, trip so they made sure everything was shipshape before they left. That's why they didn't unload the wagons to caulk them. They didn't have to. It was all done before they left home."

Ben frowned. "They showed you what was in their wagons?"

"Sure did. Seemed quite proud of it all. To tell the truth, I think they've been dying to show it off, especially that piano. Sadie says there's a company that specializes in building wagon-box pianos. Theirs is one of the first."

"I'll be damned. Why all the secrecy?"

"It was Sadie's idea. She thought the good women of the wagon train would be scandalized to be traveling with them." Luke shrugged. "She may have been right, too."

"How did all this come about?" Ben asked. "Their revelation seems awfully convenient to me."

"They didn't seek me out, if that's what you're thinking. Charisse saw Violet surrounded by a group of shady-looking soldiers and sent me to the rescue."

"And you discovered she didn't want to be rescued?"

"Exactly. Violet was arranging a little party for this evening. She had every one of those soldiers eating out of her hand, while she mentally counted up their available cash. I suspect she sent me to talk to her husband rather than lose her momentum for what promised to be a profitable venture. Jesse was more than happy to discuss their dreams for the future.'

Ben sighed. "Good. I didn't think we'd ever be able to cross anyone off our surveillance list. If we don't get a break pretty soon, we'll have to have McNesby send reinforcements."

What did you find out at Platte River Station?"

"No one there has heard of Sam Jackson, and there hasn't been a peddler go through for at least a month, let alone one who has been there for a week or more."

"I suspected as much when he didn't approach the women. No peddler would ignore a group of prime customers like that." Luke sighed. "I don't suppose you had any luck with the description, either."

"There was one man who might have seen him, but he thought Jackson was with our wagon train, because he showed up and left about the same time we did."

"Which means he's following us," Luke said. "I hate it when I'm right like that."

"Me too." Ben shrugged. "At least we finally have some idea who Simms' contact is."

"Now all we have to do is figure out what they're up to and stop them before they can start a civil war."

Ben looked thoughtful. "Why do you suppose he tipped his hand by talking to Toby and Morgan? We wouldn't even have known he was here if he hadn't."

"I'm not so sure that was intentional," Luke said. "From the sounds of things, Franklin started it by growling at the man. I can't quite figure that out, either. He's one of the friendliest dogs I've ever seen."

"Not necessarily. The night I brought you home, he made me pretty nervous," Ben admitted. "Thought he was going to take a chunk out of me. Maybe he thought Jackson was threatening the children."

"It's possible."

"Could Jackson have been causing all our odd little accidents along the trail?"

Luke shrugged. "Maybe, though judging by the man's looks, I'd say that's probably pretty far-fetched. He looked like a greenhorn."

"Could be a disguise."

"Pretty hard to fake a sunburn and blistered palms." Luke

rubbed his face. "Why is it every time we get a break in this case, it just seems to complicate matters?"

"You got me."

Charisse lifted the edge of her apron to wipe the dust and perspiration from her brow. It was their turn to bring up the rear of the wagon train, and she had been walking in a cloud of dust all day. Her mouth was gritty and her throat parched. Just one more endless day in a parade of endless days. For the first time in two years, her drawing pad was calling her with a nearly irresistible force. She wanted to get back to the portrait she'd started several days ago when the children had been occupied helping with the horses at the noon stop. Time had hung heavy on her hands, and Charisse had sat down to draw. She hadn't even been surprised when the picture of Luke had begun to appear beneath her fingers. What had surprised her was the form the drawing was taking. It was Luke McCabe all right, but it was a Luke she didn't know— except, perhaps, in her wilder dreams.

The tousled hair and slumberous eyes, she had seen time and again when they were sleeping under the wagon and woke up nose to nose. But then she'd added a sensual half-smile and the well-defined muscles of his chest and arms. It was the look of a man bent on seduction, one who fully expected a woman to fall into his arms and into his bed.

And that was the whole problem. Falling into Luke's bed was exactly what Charisse wanted. It wasn't smart, she wasn't even sure it was sane, but try as she might, she couldn't get it out of her head. It was an odd mixture of curiosity and lust created the night they had kissed with such abandon. The more she thought about it, the more she wanted to see what else she'd been missing.

She couldn't even rationalize it by saying she was blinded by love. She wasn't. Luke might be her dream, but there could be no love where there was no trust. Who knew how many times he'd lied to her? Even when she'd asked him point-blank what was going on, he'd been evasive and distracted her.

There was no question of loving Luke McCabe, but that didn't necessarily preclude making love with him. For the last year and a half, Charisse had been treated like a woman of loose morals. She had already paid the price; why not reap the benefits? Everyone thought they were already married, so they wouldn't even have to be particularly discreet except where Toby was concerned.

For the last three days, she had done little else but think about it. The more she thought about it, the more she liked the idea. Still, thinking it and doing it were two entirely different things. The truth was, no matter how much she wanted to flout society's conventions, Charisse Jones was not the immoral being the world had branded her. *Unless I find some courage somewhere, I'm doomed to walk down this dusty trail, yearning for my sketchpad and mooning like a lovesick school girl,* she thought irritably as she trudged on.

The sight of Ben loping toward them was a welcome diversion, until he got close enough for her to see his expression and hear what he'd been yelling all the way down the line of wagons. The stark terror on his face had her heart pounding in her throat even before he yelled, "Prairie fire!" to Luke, then wheeled Adonis and raced off toward the front of the wagon train.

Charisse lifted her skirts and ran to the front of the wagon as it rolled to a stop. Luke sat there shading his eyes with his hand as he looked off to the south.

"Son of a—Charisse, take the reins." He tied the reins around the brake lever and vaulted to the ground.

Charisse accepted a boost up to the seat. By the time she'd settled herself and unwrapped the reins, Luke was sprinting toward the front of the wagon train. For the first time, she looked toward the south. A black cloud boiled up along the horizon. Smoke? Charisse felt the bottom fall out of her stomach. If it truly was a fire, they were in big trouble—the smoke stretched several miles in either direction. There was no way they could outrun it!

"Toby!" she yelled frantically. "Toby, where are you?"

"We're right here, Mama."

Charisse turned and saw Toby and Morgan gathering buffalo chips about twenty feet from the wagon. "Thank heavens! Come here, and bring Franklin with you!"

By the time she had the two of them and Franklin safely stowed in the wagon, the rest of the wagon train had stopped. The men were gathered in a knot, their collective gaze riveted on the southern skyline, clearly at a loss. A sudden thought popped into Charisse's head: The Prairie Traveler!

It only took a minute to locate the book and flip it open. Her finger shaking, she ran through the table of contents, desperately looking for some solution to their dilemma. She found what she was looking for in Chapter Five between "Making Fires" and "Jerking Meat."

Knowing there was not a moment to lose, Charisse clambered down from the back of the wagon and hurried toward the men. By the time she reached them, she was out of breath.

"Luke," she cried, waving the book. She handed it to him and pointed out the pertinent paragraph.

Luke scanned the words quickly. "Of course. Fight fire with fire." He gave her a swift smile. "Good work, Charisse. We may get out of this yet."

CHAPTER 27

In the few minutes it took for Luke to share The Prairie Traveler with the rest of the men, the fire had move closer, and there was no longer any question what it was. Charisse stared, hypnotized by the size of it. Black clouds of smoke boiled up from the prairie, bringing death and destruction as it raced toward them.

Pierre Jeveraux began barking orders. "Baxter, you and I will mark out the circle. The rest of you men go get your shovels and get back here as fast as you can. Mrs. McCabe, would you gather the rest of the women and explain what's happening?"

"What do you want us to do to help?"

He looked momentarily at a loss, as though the thought of the women being able to help had never occurred to him. "Uh, well, if you could just keep them calm..."

"All right," Charisse said, trying to hide her disgust. You'd think that over the last month and a half Mr. Jeveraux would have realized how tough and resourceful these women were. If he thought they were going to stand around wringing their hands while their men fought the prairie fire, he had another think coming!

It didn't take long to gather all the women. They looked at the oncoming fire with fear in their eyes, but none started wailing as Pierre Jeveraux seemed to expect.

Mrs. Mantella hobbled forward, pushing women out of the way with her cane. "What's the plan?"

"My husband said we're going to fight fire with fire," Charisse said. "They're going to burn the grass off an area big enough to put the wagons on for a start. Then they're going to make a fire line. They won't be able to stop that fire by themselves. We'll all have to pitch in if we want to live to see tomorrow."

Caroline nodded. "What do we need to do?"

"We won't unhitch the oxen yet, but we can round up all the rest of the livestock. We'll need all the blankets we can find to beat out flames, and we should get the water barrels ready."

The livestock were skittish, spooked by the approaching fire, but Franklin was more than a match for them. It wasn't long before all the animals stood corralled and the children set to guard with Franklin's able help. By then, the men had marked a large circle with a trench and were now burning the grass within.

The women beat out the fire with blankets any time it threatened to get out of control. By the time the circle was cleared, the flames of the prairie fire were visible in the distance. The sight intensified the sense of urgency. The wagons were transferred to the burned-out circle, and the oxen unhitched in record time. John and Will Jessup added their horses to the rest and herded all the animals into the center of the wagon ring. Charisse put Toby and Morgan in her wagon with instructions to "stay put— or else." John Jessup and the twins stayed to keep the increasingly frantic animals under control.

Franklin refused to leave them for the relative safety of the wagon. Charisse gave up trying to coax him away and hurried to catch up with Will Jessup, who was going to join the rest of the men.

Smoke surrounded them, blown ahead by the wind, choking and blinding. Ben Baxter and several others had already started burning a fire line outward away from the wagons, burning all the grass, destroying the fuel before the fire could reach it. The job was next to impossible with the wind blowing the flames back toward the wagons instead of outward. Then Caroline Simms was there next to him beating out the errant flames with a blanket. Charisse barely had time to register the fact before Will Jessup was there too, and Luke.

Grabbing a blanket, Charisse joined the line next to Luke. Her world became a constant battle, pushing the small line of flames ever outward, coaxing it toward the oncoming fire and away from the wagons. It could have been a few minutes or a lifetime—Charisse had lost all reference to time—before Luke grabbed her elbow urgently.

"Time to retreat!" he yelled.

Charisse looked up for the first time and gasped. The fire was almost upon them, a hissing, crackling inferno that towered above them with terrifying power. The heat of the fire scorched her skin as she stared at it, mesmerized by the monster devouring everything in its path.

"Charisse, come on!" Luke yelled above the deafening roar as he yanked on her arm again. She snapped out of her daze, hiked up her skirts and ran back to the wagons.

Within moments a ten-foot wall of flame surrounded them. She could feel the heat and the smoke stung her eyes, but the fire line held.

"Sparks on the canvas," Luke yelled, scrambling up the front of the wagon "We need water."

Charisse grabbed one of the buckets she'd left near the wagon. "Toby, Morgan," she yelled. "Out of the wagon!"

Two heads appeared in the front of the wagon.

"Hurry, the canvas is on fire!" She panted as she lifted the bucket to Luke's waiting hands.

Morgan scrambled out, then turned back toward Toby who disappeared back into the wagon and reappeared with the bird cage, which he handed to Morgan before joining her on the ground.

"Under the wagon," Luke ordered as he put out the fire and doused the canvas with water. "But be ready to run to the center of the circle if I tell you to."

There was a mad scramble to follow his directions as Charisse handed up another bucket. The fire raged on, the roar of it all but drowning out the frightened bawling of the cattle and whinnying of the horses.

And then it was gone—racing off across the grasslands, leaving the circle of wagons behind on the smoking prairie. Charisse wiped her forehead with the back of her arm and glanced around the circle. John Jessup and his three sons worked to contain the milling cattle and horses, apparently oblivious to the many smoldering holes in their wagon cover. Franklin ran back and forth between Matt and Andy, barking and helping to keep the animals contained.

Everyone else seemed focused on the wagons that held all their worldly possessions. Most were snuffing small fires started by flying sparks. Mrs. Mantella's dimwitted son, Robbie, was wetting the cover of their wagon while his mother stood on the ground below, directing his efforts and wringing her hands.

Charisse smiled, giddy with relief. By some miracle, they seemed to have come through the conflagration more or less in one piece. Maybe Luke was right— Lady Luck had been following them after all.

"Petey!"

From his perch at the top of the wagon, Luke saw a flash of yellow streak off toward the burned out prairie, with Toby in hot pursuit. A feeling of dread ran through him as he glanced toward the prairie. The worst of the fire had moved on, but there were hot spots everywhere, places that still had enough fuel to burn. Toby was heading right for the biggest one.

"Toby, no!"

Luke relaxed as he watched Charisse catch up with Toby and stooped down to give him a quick hug before delivering what appeared to be a lecture. It never ceased to amaze him how he'd lucked out in finding her. Toby had blossomed under her guidance. Truth be told, she had a positive effect on him, too. In spite of the difficulties of his ongoing investigation, Charisse had brightened a trip that might have been intolerable otherwise.

The smile suddenly slipped from his face. A tiny plume of smoke appeared at the hem of Charisse's dress. He straightened, hoping his imagination was playing tricks on him. It wasn't. The grass hummock next to her had flared and set her skirt afire.

"Charisse!" he yelled, scrambling down from the wagon. He grabbed what was left of a bucket of water and sprinted toward her.

Charisse turned at the sound of his voice, a questioning look of surprise on her face, unaware of the smoke curling up over her shoulder.

Luke felt as if his feet were made of lead as he raced toward her. He knew the smoldering cloth could burst into flame at any moment, and he had only seconds to save her from horrible injury or death.

"What is it?" she asked as he reached her.

He didn't even bother to answer as he emptied the bucket on the back of her dress. Her gasp of shocked surprise had barely cleared her lips before he swept her off her feet, and carried her back across the burn line where he knew there were no sparks or embers.

"Pa, what's wrong?" Toby cried.

"Charisse got too close to the fire," Luke said, setting Charisse on her feet. "Are you all right?" he asked as he turned her around to look at the charred remnant of her hem.

"I-I think so." She looked over her shoulder and shivered, though Luke suspected it had more to do with her close call than the water.

"I'm sorry, Mama," Toby cried. "If I hadn't let Petey get away…"

"Shhh. It wasn't your fault. I must not have gotten his cage door shut tight."

Luke recognized the quiver in her voice and saw a tremor in the hand that patted Toby's back. With a groan, he gathered the two of them into his arms, gently pressing her face sideways into his shoulder as she continued to hold his son. The three of them stood that way for a long time, a family gaining strength from each other.

Toby was the first to move away. With the natural buoyancy of youth, the crisis was forgotten as new urgencies pressed upon him. "Gosh, oh fish hooks. I forgot all about Matt and Andy taking Franklin. I better go check on him, and Morgan too." With that, he was off on a new adventure. Charisse called after him, but it was no use. He was already out of earshot.

Luke pulled her more fully into his embrace. "He's all right, sweetheart. John will keep a close eye on him."

"I-I know, but—" Her hand trembled against his chest as he gazed down at her. Kissing her seemed the most natural thing in the world right then.

At the first tentative touch of her tongue against his, he was lost. When her arms crept up around his neck, and her body pressed against his, it was all he could do not to sweep her off her feet and carry her away to a private spot where he could make sweet love to her.

Luke was the one to end it, knowing if he didn't, they'd wind up making a spectacle of themselves. Even then it was a very near thing as her eyes, luminous with arousal, opened to gaze up at him.

Luke swallowed hard, thinking seriously about throwing caution to the wind.

"Luke—" she began.

Without warning, Luke felt something whiz by his ear. A heartbeat later, Charisse slumped in his arms, blood welling from a wound on the side of her head. "Oh hell!" He scooped her up in his arms and ran for the wagons, dodging left and right, trying to make himself an impossible target.

Stupid, stupid, stupid! How could he have forgotten the investigation even for one moment? These were desperate people, people who wouldn't hesitate to kill someone they saw as a threat. He and Ben had been lulled into thinking their ruse had worked, that Simms and his crew remained unaware Luke had seen the map. Now, because of their laxness, Charisse had been shot— with a bullet meant for him!

CHAPTER 28

"How is she?" Ben stood at the back of the wagon watching Charisse with a

worried frown.

Luke sighed. "I don't know. It's only a flesh wound, but it's been over an hour and she still hasn't opened her eyes." He gave his partner a fierce look. "I hope you caught the bastard that did this."

"He was long gone by the time I got there. You were right about him hiding in the rocks, though. Apparently panicked when he saw me coming. He took off so fast he forgot this." Ben held up a ramrod. "He must have headed off across the unburned prairie. I tried to track him, but there was no way to tell where he left the outcropping."

"Damn!"

"I was able to follow his tracks back through the soot to where he came from, though."

"The wagon train?"

Ben shook his head. "I don't think so. It appears our friend is the same one who started the prairie fire. The burned area went right up to the edge of his camp fire."

"That doesn't make sense," Luke said. "Why would one of Simms' men start a prairie fire that threatened whatever Simms has hidden in the wagon?"

"I don't know, unless he didn't set the fire on purpose."

"What do you mean?"

"I couldn't tell if he lit it deliberately, or if it was an accident. Can't figure out why he picked now to take a pot shot at you either. Seems like there would have been better opportunities— at night when you're on guard duty or off by yourself somewhere. For that matter, he could have done it when you were out there on the fire line." Ben shrugged. At least he won't be shooting anyone else until he finds another ram rod."

"Baxter, what are you doing here?" Pierre Jeveraux's voice sounded impatient.

"I stopped to see how Mrs. McCabe is doing," Ben said. "Didn't figure an extra couple of minutes would make much difference."

Jeveraux's face appeared in the opening at the back of the wagon. His concerned expression seemed genuine enough, though it was impossible to know for sure. "How is she?" he asked.

"About the same." Luke sponged her face again. At this point he didn't trust anybody but Ben. The rest were all suspects.

"Strange how that rock exploded," Jeveraux said, shaking his head. "I've seen it happen in a campfire, of course, but I didn't realize a prairie fire could get that hot."

"I'm not precisely sure that is what happened," Luke admitted, "but I can't think of what else it would be."

Jeveraux looked at Ben. "Were you able to find a place to camp?"

Ben nodded. "About three miles down the trail. We should be there in plenty of time to get settled."

"I'm sorry, Luke, we can't stay here any longer. We need to find a place with graze for the animals before dark." Jeveraux frowned at Charisse. "Maybe one of the other women could sit with her…"

"I sent Toby after Sadie Swindell," Luke said. "If she can't do it, I'll ask one of the others."

"Good. We'll move out in half an hour, then. Baxter, help spread the word, will you?"

"Sure thing, Captain."

Luke paid no attention when the other two men left. He knew Ben was surprised he hadn't sent for Caroline Simms.

Ben was blind where Caroline was concerned, and trusted her in spite of her husband. Truth was, Luke was inclined to trust her too, but he wasn't going to take a chance with Charisse's life when she was comatose and unable to fight back. If he didn't exactly trust the Swindells, at least he knew they weren't connected with whatever Simms was into and hadn't shot Charisse. He'd seen all four of them scurrying around like ants trying to keep their wagons safe during the fire, and again when he'd brought Charisse in. They simply wouldn't have had time to get to the rocks, shoot Charisse, and get back to the wagons.

Worry curled through him like the tendrils of a poisonous vine. His jaw hardened. No matter how long it took, he'd find the person responsible — and make him pay.

A confusing collage of images flashed behind Charisse's closed eyes: the prairie fire, Toby chasing Petey out onto the burned-over prairie, a knee-melting kiss from Luke. She lay as still as possible, willing her head to stop pounding and her queasy stomach to settle.

With a sudden jerk and the jingle of harnesses, her world began to rock to and fro. She was in a moving wagon. A sharp, sweet sound filled the air next to her. Petey! Charisse's eyes popped open. There he was, sitting on his swing, singing his heart out. "You're back," she murmured.

"And you're awake!"

She turned toward the voice and blinked in surprise. Sadie Swindell sat next to the bed holding a pair of knitting needles and a half-knitted sock. "Where am I?" Charisse asked, glancing around the unfamiliar wagon.

"One of our wagons," Sadie said cheerfully. "Luke didn't like it much, but there wasn't enough room in your wagon for a bed."

"But why?"

"Don't you remember?"

Charisse shook her head then winced. "Ouch." She lifted

her hand and encountered a bandage. "Good heavens, what happened? The last thing I remember was my dress catching fire and Luke putting it out. Did I fall and hit my head?"

"No, they figure a rock exploded, and a piece hit you."

"A rock exploded?"

"Yeah, you know, from the fire. Sometimes rocks will explode when they get too hot." Sadie looked thoughtful. "Anyway, something hit you and knocked you colder than a wedge."

"You talking to yourself back there, Sadie?" Violet called from the front of the wagon.

"Nope, Mrs. McCabe is awake."

"Thank God for that. Maybe Luke will settle down now."

Sadie smiled at Charisse's look of confusion. "We were beginning to worry you weren't ever going to wake up. Your husband's been... difficult."

"How long have I been asleep?"

Sadie picked up her knitting. "Two days."

"Two days!"

"Two and a half, actually."

Charisse glanced at Petey. "How did Toby manage to catch my bird?"

"He didn't. The bird came back to your wagon not too long after you were hurt. All your son did was open the cage door — Petey went right in." Sadie chuckled. "I expect he didn't like the wide-open spaces as much as he thought he would. Can't say as I blame him. Not a tree or grass for miles."

Charisse made a face. "He didn't pick the best place to leave his cage, did he?"

"Nope. Are you hungry?"

"A little."

"Good." Sadie put her knitting down and picked up a teakettle. "Mrs. Simms made you some broth from dried beef." She poured some of the brown liquid into a mug. "She's made it every morning since you were hurt, and then helped Luke pour it down you — morning, noon and night."

"They forced it down me?" Charisse was vaguely appalled by the image.

Sadie handed her the cup. "Kept you from starving. Here, it's probably warm. Heaven knows it hasn't had a chance to cool off much. The weather's hot enough to boil water."

Charisse took a sip from the cup. "This is delicious!"

"That's because Mrs. Simms made it," Sadie said with a chuckle. "If it had been left up to Violet and me, Luke would still have to pour it down your throat. We ain't much good when it comes to cooking."

"Neither am I," Charisse admitted. "Truth is, I'm worse than not much good. I'm downright lousy at it."

"That explains why Luke and Toby didn't seem to mind the supper we fed them last night," Sadie said. "I wouldn't worry too much about it, though. That man is so crazy in love with you, he's been driving us all loony!"

Charisse blinked in surprise. "What do you mean?"

"Well, for one thing, he acted like poor Mrs. Simms was trying to poison you when she showed up with broth the first night. Even made her drink some before he'd give it to you."

"What on earth did he do that for?"

"Who knows? I think the fact they couldn't figure out exactly what happened to you sort of had him off balance."

Charisse was dumfounded. "I've never known him to be rude before."

"He probably never worried about you dying before," Sadie pointed out. "Anyway, Mrs. Simms drinks half a cup every time she brings it over to show him it's safe, and then stays to help feed you."

"It seems I am beholden to all of you."

"That's what neighbors are for. Besides, you've always been nice to Violet and me."

Charisse frowned. "Why wouldn't I be nice to you?"

"See, that's what I mean. You treat us like you do everyone else," Sadie said with a mysterious smile. Charisse was left to wonder why Sadie and Violet should be treated any differently.

Charisse was still puzzled when she fell asleep, but not as puzzled as she was by Luke's odd behavior. Her last thought as she drifted into oblivion was to wonder what in heaven's name the man was thinking.

"Mama?" Toby's loud whisper roused Charisse several hours later. "Mama, are you awake?"

"Hmmm?" She blinked opened her eyes and smiled up into the anxious face that hovered over hers. "Toby," she said, reaching up to touch his cheek.

"Are you better?" he asked worriedly.

"I think so." Other than a slight headache, she felt as though she had wakened from a long restful nap. She sat up and stretched. "In fact, I feel good enough to get up."

Toby started to cry. "Oh, Mama!" he said and threw himself into her arms.

"Don't cry," she said, hugging him. "I'm fine."

"I was afraid you weren't going to wake up," he sobbed. "Pa said we'd have to leave it in God's hands. Only God took my first mama, and I thought you were going to die, too."

She hugged him tighter. "Well, I didn't, and I'm not going to."

"Promise you won't ever leave."

"Oh, Toby…"

"Promise!" His hug became frantic.

"Sweetheart. You know I can't make that promise."

"You'll go away just like my real mama."

"Toby." She lifted his chin with the crook of her finger. "Look at me."

He raised his tear-filled gaze to her face.

"We've always known this wasn't forever," she said softly.

"I know, but—"

"Shh…" She put her finger on his lips. "I promise I'll stay with you as long as I can, but you'll always have me here," she touched his forehead, "and here." She laid her hand on his heart. "And I'll always have you."

"You mean like Annabelle?"

"Exactly like Annabelle. There isn't a day I don't think about her, and I still love her very much."

"But I want you to stay with Pa and me."

"I know, but that isn't going to happen." She wiped the tears from his face. "Maybe you and your Pa will settle close to me, and we can see each other every day."

He brightened perceptibly. "Maybe you can still take care of me when Pa's gone on his job."

"I wouldn't be surprised."

He gave her another hard hug. "I'm going to go tell Pa right away." With that, he pulled out of her arms, jumped out of the wagon and disappeared.

The sound of his voice calling Franklin as he ran to find Luke carried back to her on the late afternoon breeze. Charisse swallowed against the knot in her throat and blinked back tears. The little boy was firmly entrenched in her heart. *And it's not just Toby you love*, said an insidious little voice in her head. *You love Luke just as much as you do his son*. Oh Lord, it was true. She'd fallen in love with Luke! That was why she couldn't face the thought of his death, even if it meant having Toby forever. *The question is, how am I going to live without them?*

Charisse looked at the canary sitting peacefully on his perch. "Well, Petey, looks like Luke and I didn't anticipate quite all of the problems that might come up. I can't imagine how we're going to fix this one."

"Oh, I don't know," Sadie said from behind her. "Things have a way of working themselves out."

Charisse started and looked over her shoulder. Sadie Swindell had moved her chair toward the front of the wagon to make room for the little stool Toby had been using. She sat there slightly behind Charisse, calmly mending a shirt.

With a horrible sinking sensation in the pit of her stomach, Charisse felt her face drain then flush. "I... I didn't realize you were here."

Sadie smiled slightly. "Obviously. I probably should have let you know, but I didn't want to interrupt."

"It isn't what it looks like. Luke needed someone to look after Toby, and I needed a driver."

"You don't owe me or anybody else an explanation." Sadie arranged the pillows behind Charisse and eased her back against them.

"What you must think of me..."

"I think you're one of the kindest women I know. Look at the way you handle that poor motherless child. Ain't anyone wouldn't think he was yours from the day he was born, and I don't think he's the easiest child to manage." She gave Charisse a wry look. "I don't expect his Pa is either. Most women would be at wit's end by now, but you have them both wrapped around your little finger. What you are is a wonder, Mrs. McCabe."

"Please, call me Charisse." She looked down at her hands as Sadie pulled her chair forward and settled back into it. "I don't really have any right to the 'Mrs.' anyway."

Sadie made a dismissive motion of her hand as she picked up her sewing. "Neither do Violet or I, for that matter."

"You're not...?"

"Nope. Jesse and Frank decided to head for the gold fields and convinced us to go along. Violet and I pretend to be married to them so folks don't get all riled up. Besides, this wagon train is full of people pretending to be something they ain't."

"What do you mean?"

"Mrs. Mantella ain't near as crippled and helpless as she likes to pretend." She peeped up at Charisse and grinned. "And if Eliza and Henry Duncan are brother and sister, I'll eat my hat."

Charisse's mouth fell open in shock. "What?"

"Let's just say, I've heard some mighty strange noises coming from their tent in the middle of the night, if you know what I mean." She looked speculative for a moment. "Really wouldn't have figured him for the lusty type — nor her to be a moaner — but you just never know about folks."

"Oh my."

"Everyone has their secrets, and I reckon you and Luke are the least of it."

Charisse was still digesting Sadie's startling revelations when Jesse Swindell appeared at the back of the wagon. He looked pleasantly surprised to see Charisse awake. "Well, Mrs. McCabe, good to see you back with us."

"It's good to be back. Thank you all for your help."

"Think nothing of it. You and Luke would have done the same for us. Mind if I take Sadie for a few minutes?"

"Heaven's no. I'm ready to go back to my own wagon anyway."

"I'll let Luke know. He'll be mighty glad."

"Do you need some help getting dressed?" Sadie asked, as she got to her feet.

"Oh, no, I can manage," Charisse said. "Thanks for all your help."

"Don't mention it."

Charisse had a wave of dizziness when she stood, but it passed quickly and she was able put on her clothes. She sat down and bent over to put on her shoes, then collapsed on the bed. *Whew, not completely recovered after all,* she thought, willing her stomach to settle and her head to stop pounding.

As she lay with her arm over her eyes, she thought about Sadie's revelations. *A wagon train of secrets! Who would have thought?* Would Oregon be the same, or would the people there somehow discover her past and think her a woman of loose morals and despise her like the good folks in St. Louis had?

Suddenly she didn't care. She was through living her life to please other people. One thing her brush with death had taught her was to live for the moment. It was time to grab what she wanted out of life and consequences be damned! Right now, that meant finding a way to finish what she and Luke had started, to fully experience all the wondrous things his caresses had promised. She wasn't quite sure how, but in the very near future, she was going to seduce Luke McCabe!

CHAPTER 29

"Please can I go, Mama? It's the 'tunity of a lifetime."

"You mean 'opportunity,'" Charisse corrected with the hint of a smile.

"That's right," said Matt Jessup earnestly. "It's our chance—"

"—To go down in history," Andy put in. "A hundred years from now—"

"—People will know we were at Independence Rock."

"Are you sure they'll care?"

Will Jessup grinned at her. "Maybe not, but you've got to admit there is something kind of exciting about the idea."

"I suppose." Charisse gazed at the huge granite outcropping towering above them and tried to imagine hordes of people standing around staring at the thousands of names scrawled across the smooth, weathered surface. "I guess it isn't every day you get to sign a rock that looks like a gigantic turtle."

"Please, Mama, please?" Toby's voice took on a wheedling tone.

"I'll watch them real close, Mrs. McCabe," Will told her.

As she looked into five pairs of pleading eyes, it struck her out of the blue that all of them had put her firmly in the role of mother, and the thought warmed her heart. "All right," she conceded, "as long as you're all careful."

Before the words were out of her mouth, the young people cheered and took off. "Watch out for snakes!" Charisse called after them.

"Off to carve their names into the rock, I suppose."

Charisse turned in surprise to find Mrs. Mantella right

behind her. "They are indeed."

"Damn foolishness, if you ask me." She leaned on her cane and stared after the youngsters. "Glad to see you have more sense."

For an irrational moment, Charisse thought about calling for the children to wait for her. With an effort, she shook off her vague feeling of distaste. "I'm rather old for that sort of thing."

Mrs. Mantella snorted. "That doesn't seem to be stopping the rest of 'em." She pointed her cane at the top of the rock where Pierre Jeveraux and Ben Baxter were carving into the smooth surface. "Most of our wagon train is up there." She gave Charisse a shrewd glance. "I think you're too much of a lady to clamber around on a hunk of rock."

Charisse had the distinct feeling Mrs. Mantella was referring to more than her manners. Did the old woman see through her disguise the way Sadie had? "I don't see your son," she said, hoping to change the subject.

"He ran off with the rest of them," Mrs. Mantella said with disgust. "Can't write his name, of course, but insisted he could make his mark, no matter how stupid I told him it was."

Charisse found herself feeling sorry for Robbie Mantella. "I'm going back to the wagons. Would you like to walk with me?"

"Thank you." She grasped Charisse's arm with her claw-like hand. "Are you and your husband joining the party tonight?"

"Wouldn't miss it for the world." Charisse couldn't help remembering Sadie's conviction that Mrs. Mantella was less infirm than she appeared. Where had Sadie ever gotten that idea? The older woman was moving at a snail's pace.

"I'm so glad we got here by the Fourth of July." Charisse said. "It says in my guide book you should be here by the fourth if you are going to make it through the mountains before it starts to snow. I'd be even happier if we were clear to Fort Bridger by now."

"Fort Bridger. That's where the trail splits, isn't it?"

Charisse nodded. "I think so. Close by, anyway."

"Are you and Mr. McCabe going on to Oregon, or will you be turning south toward California?"

"Oregon, of course."

"Ah," Mrs. Mantella nodded as though this cleared up some great mystery in her mind. "And how are you going to make a living once you get there?"

"I was planning on starting a school. I don't suppose there are many there yet."

"And your husband?"

Charisse realized with a shock, she had absolutely no idea what Luke's profession was. "He…we're going to take out a homestead."

"Your husband doesn't strike me as a farmer."

He didn't strike Charisse that way either, but it was the first plausible thing that popped into her head. "He was raised on a farm, and he's always missed it," she said. "The offer of free land was more than he could resist."

"Why didn't he stay on the family farm?"

That's a good question. Why exactly would he have left if he loved it so much? "His older brother took over when their father died. The farm was too small to support two families, so when Luke came of age he left."

"What did he do then?"

Blast the woman's curiosity, anyway! How the heck am I supposed to know what Luke has done in his life? "A little of everything, but nothing ever really fit." She shrugged for effect. "That's why we decided to pull up stakes and go to Oregon."

"He seems more like a soldier," Mrs. Mantella observed. "Or a policeman."

"Luke?" Charisse laughed. "He'll be delighted to hear you think so. Oh look, there's another wagon train pulling in," Charisse said, grabbing onto the diversion. "With ours and the one that came the day before us that makes three. What fun!"

"You won't think so if there isn't enough graze for all the animals," Mrs. Mantella muttered darkly. "And all this folderol because of an overgrown boulder in the middle of nowhere."

Charisse turned to look at the other woman, surprised at her vehemence. "I was under the impression you were in favor of the party."

"Oh, I am, of course. I'm just a natural worrier." Mrs. Mantella appeared to be having difficulty schooling her features into a pleasant expression. "You're sure you and your husband are going then?"

Charisse felt her lips thin with irritation. It was time to put this question and answer session to an end. "Oh, yes," she said brightly. "We're quite excited. It's our anniversary, you see. And we have"—she looked away as though suddenly embarrassed—"plans." Charisse did have plans. Plans that brought a slight blush to her face as she thought of them. Was she really preparing to lure Luke into her bed?

Mrs. Mantella peered at her closely, then nodded. "My Roberto was a lusty man too. He'd use any excuse for love-making. Liked to make a big production of it."

Charisse blushed in earnest at the old woman's frankness, and Mrs. Mantella cackled in response.

"You young people, you think you invented sex." She patted Charisse's arm. "Take my advice and enjoy it while you can. Unless I miss my guess, that man of yours will keep you busy half the night!"

Charisse knew her face had turned a bright red, and she had no idea what to say. Mrs. Mantella saved her the trouble by tottering off toward her own wagon. Charisse watched her go with a mixture of relief and chagrin.

"Looks like you were treated to some of Mrs. Mantella's acid charm," Luke observed as he came to stand beside her. "What did the old witch want?"

"Luke!" she admonished him. "I'm having a hard time convincing the children she's harmless without you calling her a witch, too."

"They call her a witch?" He grinned down at her. "Always knew my son was smart. So, what did she want?"

"Nothing. I walked her back from the rock, and she shocked me by talking about… unseemly subjects."

Luke laughed. "Got a bit warm, did she? Good for her. I like crusty old ladies who have no trouble saying what they think. Maybe she isn't as bad as I thought."

"We're going to Oregon to homestead, by the way. Your older brother inherited the family farm, and you miss farming."

"I do?"

"I had to say something," she said irritably. "She asked me what we were going to do when we got there."

Luke's gaze sharpened. "She was pumping you for information?"

"No, she was making conversation." Charisse looked up at him. "What do you do for a living, anyway?"

"This and that." He flashed her a grin. "Right now, I'm driving two yoke of oxen across the prairie for a fair lady in need. Which reminds me— do you think you could find someone to watch Toby for us tonight?"

Charisse blinked. "Why?"

"I want to take my wife dancing, that's why. You haven't had a day off since we started this charade." He traced the side of her face with his knuckle. "And I want to dance with you," he said softly.

"Oh," she said in a small, breathless voice as his lips descended toward hers. She closed her eyes in anticipation.

"Oh, no, you don't," he whispered in her ear. "You're not distracting me. We'll finish this conversation tonight." He dropped a chaste kiss on her forehead. "Wear something pretty." And then he was gone.

Charisse opened her eyes and watched him in bewilderment as he strode away.

Later that afternoon, Charisse sought out John Jessup and found him mending a halter in the shade of his wagon. "John?" she said.

"Charisse! Here, have a seat." He gestured to a three-legged stool next to him. "To what to I owe this pleasure?

"First, what are your plans for the evening?"

John looked surprised. "Taking the family to the party, maybe dancing with a pretty lady or two, then bringing the three youngest home, and putting them to bed. Why?"

"I have a favor to ask."

"Name it."

Charisse shifted, a little uncomfortable with her request. "Would you mind watching Toby for us tonight?"

"Sure. Glad to." John grinned with good humor. "One more isn't going to make a nickel's worth of difference. Besides, you've watched my brood often enough. I reckon I owe you."

"You don't owe me a thing. In fact, I probably owe you for sharing them with me." She smiled. "I'm hoping we'll all settle in the same area of Oregon so I can watch them grow up."

"I don't know that we're going on to Oregon."

A wave of disappointment washed over her. "Oh, I didn't realize you were going to California."

He looked up from the piece of tack and gazed out over the prairie. "Actually, I'm thinking of settling right here."

"Here?" Startled, Charisse followed his gaze out onto the barren landscape. "But there's nothing here."

"Nothing except miles and miles of open range. It's perfect for horses. I didn't think of it until we passed that wild herd the other day. They do very well here. There's even a market nearby." He looked at her. "There's a lot of money to be made supplying the army with horses."

"Fort Laramie?"

He nodded. "For a start. Travel along the Oregon Trail is only going to grow, and all those people are going to need protection. That means more forts. The army has already opened Fort Bridger and Platte River Station. Even those three would be enough to keep us in business, and there are bound to be others."

Charisse felt a lump form in her throat. "When will you leave the train?"

"I haven't decided that I will for sure, but I'm going to have to do something pretty soon." He grimaced and pointed his thumb back over his shoulder. "Our wagon cover didn't survive the fire."

Charisse glanced at his wagon. For the first time, she noticed it was peppered with black rimmed holes of varying sizes. "Oh my. I didn't realize…"

"We didn't have enough hands to spare during the fire. It took everything we had to keep the horses under control." He shrugged. "At the time, it seemed a small price to pay, but now I have no way of protecting our supplies."

"Surely you'll be able to buy more canvas at Fort Bridger."

"That's what I'm hoping, but the chances of us getting to Fort Bridger before it rains are pretty slim."

Charisse studied the canvas cover objectively. "I could probably mend the worst of those holes. I'll bet I could get some of the other ladies to help too."

"I never thought of that. It might even work." He smiled at her. "You are a wonder. I never met anyone so anxious to fix everyone's problems."

Charisse laughed. "I have a tendency to stick my nose in other people's business, if that's what you mean."

"You know, I've never been a particularly envious person, but I find myself damned envious right now."

"What do you mean?"

"I've never really thought about getting married again, but if you weren't so in love with that husband of yours…"

Charisse's mouth fell open in shock. "Mr. Jessup!"

"I know, I know." He held up his hand. "You needn't look at me that way. I didn't mean anything by it, only that if anything ever happens to him, you and Toby would have a place with us."

"I… I hardly know what to say."

"Say 'Thank you, Mr. Jessup. You are ever so kind,'" he said in a high falsetto. "Then go find Luke and have a good time tonight."

"Thank you, John." She stood up, then leaned over and

kissed his cheek. "Save me a dance."

CHAPTER 30

"You are the most beautiful partner I've had all evening," Luke said as he whirled Charisse around the circle of dancers.

"Flatterer!" She tapped him on the arm playfully. "I'll bet you've said the same to any number of women this evening."

"Nope, only you. That dress is enough to make a man lose his better sense."

"It's always been one of my favorites," Charisse said as she relaxed in his embrace and gave herself over to the music. In truth, it was the last of her ball gowns, and plain by comparison to the others. She loved the soft blue-green fabric and the way it belled out over her crinoline. The off the shoulder neckline had been the perfect showcase for her grandmother's pearls. Preston had hated the dress and the pearls, of course, preferring her in diamonds, rubies or sapphires. But Charisse had always wondered if his real objection was that the pearls, along with a small jointure, were her inheritance from her English grandmother and beyond his reach.

The pearls were gone now, sold to help finance the trip to Oregon, but she'd kept the dress, and tonight its magic was going to help her carry out her plan. She'd spent a long time preparing, from donning her hoops and dancing slippers to pinning her hair up in an elaborate chignon, and placing some of her precious perfume in strategic places on her body.

The music stopped and she smiled up at Luke. "Shall we sit the next one out?"

"Fine by me." He took her arm. "Tired?" he asked as they walked toward their wagon.

"A little, but it's a good tired." She sighed happily. "At least it's not from a day spent gathering buffalo chips."

He laughed. "Or dealing with the oxen and all the dust."

"Or mud." They reached the wagon and Charisse twirled around before plunking herself down on the double tree of the wagon hitch.

"I'm having a wonderful time! How about you?"

"It would have been more fun if I hadn't had to fight my way through a herd of star-struck males every time I wanted to ask you to dance."

"What an exaggeration! I only danced with John and Ben."

"And half a dozen strangers from the other wagon trains!"

"Only four or five." She found herself pleased he cared. "And you didn't exactly sit there and watch. Every time I looked up, you were dancing with a different woman."

"I had to do something to pass the time while you were smiling and flirting with every man here. Half of them will probably fancy themselves in love with you, and I'll have my hands full tomorrow fighting them all off."

She gave a gurgle of laughter. "You're the only man that doesn't think I'm a married woman."

"And they're all jealous because I'm married to the most exquisite woman this side of the Mississippi. Would you like another drink?"

"Just a little." Charisse watched as Luke poured half an inch of fine Irish whiskey into the bottom of her cup. He sat down on her right and handed her the cup.

"If I didn't know better, I'd think you were trying to get me drunk so you could take advantage of me," she said.

He wiggled his eyebrows in a sinister fashion. "What makes you think I'm not?"

"Oh, I do hope so." She gave him her most flirtatious smile.

"On second thought, I think you've had enough." He took the cup from her hand and sipped it himself.

"No fair!" She made a face at him. "The Swindells gave us that to celebrate our anniversary."

"Our nonexistent anniversary. Where do you suppose they got that idea, anyway?"

She shrugged a little. "I might have said something about it to Mrs. Mantella."

"You could have warned me. I looked pretty stupid when they all came by to give it to us."

"How was I supposed to know she was going to tell everybody on the wagon train?" Charisse smiled and brushed his forelock off his brow. "Besides, no one noticed."

"Only because you played the gracious hostess and made everyone forget by offering them all a drink."

"That was just good manners." Charisse sighed and leaned back against him, watching the dancers that stomped and twirled around the center of the wagon circle. "It's been almost like a real anniversary, hasn't it?"

"Yes, it has." He nuzzled her ear. "Did I tell you how beautiful you are tonight?"

She closed her eyes and smiled. "You may have mentioned it a time or two. You look pretty good yourself." The truth was, she hadn't wanted to take her eyes off him all evening. With her intimate knowledge of his wardrobe, she knew he lacked the finery some of the other men had hidden away in their wagons, but he'd found a crisp white shirt somewhere, as well as a beautiful brocade vest and black jacket to go with it. As far as she was concerned, he threw all the other men into the shade any time, but tonight he was devastating.

"Would you like to dance again?"

"Not really." She screwed up her courage. "I'd rather go for a walk."

"A walk?" He sounded surprised.

"Why not? It's a gorgeous night, and I want to see Independence Rock by moonlight."

He shrugged. "All right, if that's what you really want to do."

She stood, then grabbed his hand and pulled him to his feet. "Come on, let's go. We can grab my quilt out of the back of the wagon."

"Your quilt? What do you want that for?"

"To keep myself warm, of course. This dress is a little drafty, and it gets cold here after the sun goes down."

The quilt was easily found, but Luke frowned as he draped it around her shoulders. It was huge and engulfed her whole body from her shoulders to the ground. "Are you sure you wouldn't rather have your shawl?"

"Nope. This is much warmer." She gazed up at the sky. "It's beautiful out here, isn't it? Just look at those stars."

"Yes, it is. Makes me want to spout poetry. Too bad I don't know any."

She giggled. "It's probably a good thing. I can't see you down on one knee reciting flowery phrases."

His teeth flashed in the darkness as he grinned. "Neither can I."

Charisse's nervousness mounted as they strolled hand-in-hand through the black velvet darkness. Her resolve was set. She'd purposely imbibed enough alcohol to give her false courage, and she knew exactly where they were going. There was a grassy alcove toward the back of Independence Rock that would make a lovely bower.

Trouble was, Luke wasn't cooperating. She'd depended on him being carried away by passion. But so far he was showing remarkable restraint, and in a moment they would have strolled past her chosen lover's retreat.

"Luke," she said softly, "aren't you going to kiss me?"

"No."

She blinked in bewilderment. "Why not?"

"Because I know what would happen if I did."

She stopped and stared up at him. "What?"

He raised his hand to her face and ran his thumb over her cheek. "What started as a simple kiss would turn into a blaze of passion that would make the prairie fire look like a buffalo-chip ember. Once we started, I wouldn't be able to stop."

"And what would be wrong with that?" she murmured.

He groaned. "Charisse, don't do this to me. I can't make love to you."

She swallowed a gasp of shocked dismay, then blinked back her tears. Rejection was the last thing she had expected, but at least it was something she knew how to deal with. "I understand," she said, willing the hurt not to show in her voice. "I guess it's time we were getting back, anyway." She was proud of the smile she managed to give him as she turned away. It felt brittle and unreal, but she knew from experience that it would fool the most discerning eye.

"Charisse—"

"Coming?" She wrapped the quilt tighter around her and took a step back toward the wagons.

"Charisse, damn it…"

"Oh, Luke. It's all right." She smiled again and held out her hand. "Come on, let's finish our walk."

"You don't understand." He ran his hand through his hair in frustration. "There's nothing I'd rather do than make love to you right here under the stars."

"But?"

"But I can't marry you, Charisse."

She blinked in surprise. "Who said anything about marriage?"

"Oh, come on. You know as well as I do that's where this would lead."

"Why?"

"Because sex with decent women means marriage."

A surge of relief flowed through her. He wasn't indifferent after all. Charisse gave a soft laugh. "If misplaced nobility is all that's stopping you…" She took the quilt from her shoulders and flipped it out flat on the ground. "I ceased to be a decent woman a long time ago."

"That's not true."

"Of course, it is." Charisse stepped closer to him and ran her hands up his coat lapels. "The minute Preston signed his name to the divorce papers, he set me free from all of society's notions of propriety. I can't lose my good name because I don't have one. I can do what I please, and right now that means making love with you."

"You won't feel that way in the morning." His voice sounded strangled, as though he was having trouble breathing. "It's the whiskey making you feel this way."

Charisse looked up at him in surprise. "You think I'm drunk?"

His mouth twisted into an ironic smile. "I know you are. I also know the demon alcohol makes people do things they'll regret when they sober up."

"Ah, but in this case, it gave me the courage to do what I've wanted to ever since the night Toby interrupted us." She gave a laugh low in her throat. "I've never felt the things you made me feel. Preston considered strong emotion ill-bred. He didn't particularly like the way I…" Charisse shrugged. "Anyway, I want to know what else I've been missing."

"Your ex-husband has to be the biggest jackass ever created. What kind of an idiot leaves a warm, passionate woman like you curious about sex?"

"I'm not sure he knew all that much himself." She unbuttoned his vest and ran her hands over his chest. "But I think you do. Show me, Luke."

"I'll do my best not to disappoint you," he whispered against her lips.

"Mmmm," she murmured when they came up for air. "Definitely not a disappointment."

"Are you sure you won't regret this in the morning?" He whispered, softly trailing tiny kisses across her eyelids and then down her cheek.

"Not even for a second," she said breathlessly. "Consider it an anniversary present to both of us."

"One last chance to change your mind," he murmured as he kissed the corner of her mouth."

"Not on your—"

The rest of her answer was lost as he nibbled at her lips, begging entrance. She complied with a tiny sigh of pleasure. As he explored the interior of her mouth, Charisse felt as though she was drowning in forbidden delights. His hands slowly traced the curve of her back, the buttons and loops parting easily beneath his fingers. She shivered as his warm hands caressed her skin, and it had nothing to do with cold. "Oh!" her hands clutched at his shoulders as he began to trace erotic circles on her naked back. She gave a small moan as his touch sent shivers of longing through her.

With deft fingers, he plucked the pins from her hair and let it cascade down over his hands. "Lord but you have beautiful hair."

"And you have lovely muscles." She ran her hands up over his chest. Then gave him a saucy little smile and started to unbutton his shirt. "I've been wanting another peek ever since I shrank your undershirt."

"Are you always this playful when you're drunk?"

"I have no idea." Charisse pulled his shirttails out of his pants. "I've never been drunk before. Oh, my!" She sucked in her breath as the shirt gapped open and she saw what lay beneath. She touched him with tentative fingers, lightly tracing the contours of his chest. "You feel…amazing!" she whispered. *Silk on steel.* With a look of wonder on her face, she flattened her palms and ran them up over his chest to his shoulders. "I think it's time we got rid of these," she said, pushing his coat and shirt off the broad expanse.

"Anything to please a lady." Luke shed the offending garments with absolutely no thought to how Ben would feel about the mistreatment of the clothing he'd lent his partner. Within seconds, jacket, shirt, and vest lay forgotten in a rumpled pile on the ground.

"You are so beautiful," she murmured, running her hands up over his chest and down his arms. Then she leaned forward and kissed the hollow of his throat.

Luke gave a deep groan as he gathered her in his arms. This time there was nothing sweet or gentle about their kiss. It was hot and sensual. Suddenly, getting Charisse naked and moaning in his arms became as necessary as breathing. Luke slid the sleeves of her dress down her arms and undid the fastener on her skirt. The dress didn't drop to the ground as he expected. In fact, it didn't even sag beyond her waist. Puzzled, Luke did a quick exploration with his fingers but couldn't find any other hooks, buttons, or ties. After a second futile search, he broke off the kiss and stepped back to see what the problem was.

"Wh-what's the matter?" Charisse asked breathlessly.

He raised his gaze and almost stopped breathing. Tousled hair surrounded her in thick waves clear to her waist. The semi-transparent fabric of her shift did little to hide breasts that rose and fell with each breath. Her skin glowed in the moonlight and passion gleamed in her eyes. She was a vision of lust incarnate. Knowing every bit of that irresistible package was his for the taking, was almost more than he could stand.

With a frustrated groan, he ran his hand through his hair and dropped his gaze to her waist again.

"Luke, what is it?"

"I can't figure out how to get this infernal thing off," he muttered. Luke put his hands on her waist and turned her this way and that to see if he had missed something.

Charisse giggled. "You've never had any experience with hoops?"

"Hell no. I don't even know what they're for, other than to drive a man stark-raving mad."

"They enhance the female figure," Charisse said with a grin. "I had to make a few alterations since I don't have a corset. That's probably why you're having trouble. Here, let me." She fumbled with whatever held the skirt closed at her waist.

"Your figure doesn't need enhancing," he growled. "And it doesn't need a corset either."

Charisse laughed again. "If I hadn't lost so much weight on this trip, I would have never gotten into this dress without a corset." Freed at last, the dress slipped down, revealing the cage-like crinoline underneath.

"Looks like something you'd put your bird in," he

commented as she undid the tapes on either side and let it collapse around her feet. Without taking her eyes off him, she kicked off her slippers, then slowly raised her shift and reached for the drawstring at her waist. A flick of her wrist undid the knot and sent her drawers down her legs to the ground. She stepped out of the pile of skirts and petticoats and stood before him, bathed in moonlight.

She looked like a goddess standing there in nothing but a thin shift. Luke swallowed hard. Even his most lurid thoughts hadn't prepared him for the reality that was Charisse. From her long graceful legs and impossibly tiny waist to the full breasts and curtain of hair, she was easily the most beautiful woman he'd ever seen. It wasn't until his chest began to hurt that he realized he'd forgotten to breathe.

When she crossed her arms over her breasts, Luke realized she took his silence for disapproval. He stepped forward and pulled her into his arms. "Do you have any idea how gorgeous you are?" His lips traced a path down her neck to her shoulder. "You take my breath away."

Charisse braced her hands on his shoulders and stood on tip-toes to give him better access. "Make love to me, Luke," she whispered.

With a sound somewhere between a growl and a groan, he dropped his arms and stepped back. He pulled off first one boot then the other, before removing his pants in record time. Then he scooped her up and carried her to the quilt. Conscious of Charisse's lack of experience with the delights of unbridled passion, Luke concentrated on her pleasure. With lips and hands, he drove her to her limits, and she finally toppled over into an earthshaking climax without him ever possessing her.

Watching her come apart in his arms, Luke was filled with a fierce longing that had little to do with sex. Suddenly, he wanted nothing more than to spend the rest of their lives sharing this magic. He was the first to take her to the heights; he wanted to be the last.

"Oh!" She opened her eyes and gazed at him in stunned

amazement. "I had no idea. That was the most—"

"Shhh." He put his finger to her lips. "That was nothing compared to the real thing."

"You mean it gets better?"

"Definitely." He captured her lips, and began caressing her with the same single-minded determination. This time, though, Charisse refused to let him have it all his way. She began matching him touch for touch. It wasn't long before they were both on the brink.

When Luke eased his knee between hers, Charisse parted her legs in eager welcome. He poised above her, gazing into her passion glazed eyes. "Are you sure about this?"

She reached up and caressed the side of his face. "Luke," she said in a breathless voice, "I swear, if you stop now, I'm going to walk back to the wagon, get my derringer and shoot you."

"I'll take that as a yes," he said with the ghost of a laugh. He closed his eyes and sank into heaven. Their joining was as magical as all the rest. Higher and higher they spiraled until her inner tremors drove him over the edge, and he joined her in a multi-colored kaleidoscope of sensation that burst into a rainbow shower of pleasure. They lay entwined as they drifted back to earth, reveling in the feel of each other.

"I didn't know it could be like that!" She ran her hands up his back and kissed his shoulder. "We might have to try that again."

"We might at that." Luke rolled to his side, pulling her into his arms. "We've got all night," he said nuzzling her neck. "Let's see if this quilt is big enough to cover us."

"Cold?"

"Not yet, but I think I will be soon." Luke reached over her, grabbed the edge of the quilt and pulled it over them. "It's a tight fit, and my butt might get a little chilly, but the important parts are covered."

"Good." She sighed and snuggled against his chest. "I'm not ready to go back quite yet."

"Neither am I—" He broke off and listened intently. "That's all we need." He rolled over, reached into his pile of clothes and pulled out a pistol. Then he peered into the darkness and made a disgusted noise before lowering his gun. "Damn it, Ben. I nearly shot you. What the hell do you want?"

"You." Ben emerged out of the darkness and tossed a pile of clothes at him. "Get dressed. We have work to do. I'll be right back; I'm going to make sure we don't have any company." He disappeared back into the night.

Charisse sat up, clutching the quilt to her chest. "What's going on?"

"I don't know, but Ben wouldn't be here if it wasn't important."

Luke was dressed and pulling on his boots by the time his partner reappeared with an extra rifle. Ben winced when he caught sight of Charisse's wide-eyed stare. "I'm damn sorry about this, Charisse," he said looking away. "I wouldn't have bothered the two of you if there were any other way."

Luke stood and tucked his shirt into his pants. "What the hell is going on?"

"It's Simms," Ben said, tossing Luke one of the rifles. "He's finally on the move."

CHAPTER 31

"Simms is on the move?" Luke said. "Where's he going?"

Ben shook his head. "I'm not sure, but something is up."

Luke sighed, then glanced at Charisse. "I can't even begin to tell you how sorry I am, sweetheart," he said, regret visible in every line of his body. "Best get dressed so I can walk you back to the wagon."

"All right, but don't think you're going to get out of this without an explanation." She sat hugging the quilt to her chest. "Now, if the two of you don't mind…" She pointed into the darkness.

"Right." The two men meekly moved away, giving Charisse a modicum of privacy.

"All right, Ben, tell me what's going on." Luke glanced over his shoulder. "And it had better be good."

"Near as I can tell, he's headed for a rendezvous," Ben said. "Simms disappeared right after you did. I decided to see what he was up to, and cover your back if necessary. He lost interest in you and Charisse pretty fast."

Luke frowned. "How much did he see?"

"Nothing much. He followed you long enough to be sure the two of you were going to be occupied for a while, then went south. I followed him about halfway around the rock before he started to climb."

"He climbed Independence Rock in the middle of the night? Is he crazy?"

"That went through my head too," Ben said. "The part he chose to climb is tricky at the best of times, and he was doing it in the dark. Anyway, when he got halfway up he lit a lantern then started covering and uncovering the light."

"A signal?"

Ben nodded. "Morse code."

Luke was impressed in spite of himself. "Simms has all kinds of surprising skills, doesn't he? I don't suppose you could tell what he was saying?"

"Not at first. I was in the wrong place. By the time I moved around so I could see his signals, he was almost finished. All I could make out was midnight and meeting place."

"Did you see any sign of his contact?"

"Only a single flash of light. Looked like it was somewhere between here and Devil's Gate."

"How much time do we have?"

Ben took out his pocket watch. "It's eleven fifteen."

"Our best bet is to follow Simms," Luke said, "but I think we should keep an eye on the wagon, too. The message could have been about the map or even whatever he has hidden under the floorboards."

"Good point. I'll follow Simms, and you watch the wagon." He grinned and jerked his head toward Charisse. "You're going that way anyway, and unless I miss my guess you have some serious explaining to do."

Luke's mouth twisted. "I'm half-tempted to tell her the truth." He held up his hand when Ben started to protest. "I know, I can't. I'm going to have to distract her with something that sounds plausible."

"You're going to try and fool Charisse?" Ben chuckled. "I'd like to be a mouse in the sagebrush listening."

"It was people like you who enjoyed watching the Romans feed Christians to the lions," Luke said with a wry twist of his mouth. Then he sobered. "Be careful out there. I don't want to have to break in a new partner."

Ben gripped his hand. "The same goes for you, my friend. And tell Charisse I really am sorry." Then he was gone, a darker shadow sliding through the night.

Swallowing a sigh, Luke turned back to Charisse, who had almost finished dressing. She was struggling to fasten up the back of her dress when Luke reached her. "Here," he said, gently moving her hands out of the way so he could rebutton it. "Let me."

"Where's Ben?" she asked.

"Gone." He did the last button and dropped a kiss on the back of her neck. "He said to tell you he was sorry."

Charisse began to braid the hair she'd draped over her shoulder. "Are you going to tell me what's going on?"

A thousand excuses ran through Luke's head. They ranged from completely ridiculous to almost believable. But as he stared at the uncompromising line of her back, he knew he couldn't use any of them. She didn't deserve to be lied to, not by him.

"No, I'm not." He put his arms around her and pulled her against his body. "I don't want to lie to you."

"Then tell me the truth!" Charisse pushed at his arms, but he wouldn't let her go.

Luke turned her to face him, lifted her chin with his finger, and gazed down into her eyes. "If I could, I'd tell you everything from the beginning, but I can't. Lives depend on absolute secrecy."

She stopped struggling as if surprised by his words. "Ben's?" she asked after a moment. "And yours?"

He nodded, "But Ben and I are pretty unimportant in the whole scheme of things. If we fail, it could mean hundreds of innocent lives."

"Mrs. Mantella thought you might be a policeman or a soldier."

Luke shook his head.

"A U.S. Marshall?"

Luke laughed. "Not hardly."

"This is why you wrote your will, though, isn't it?"

He nodded again.

She was quiet for a long moment. "Is Joshua Simms behind all this, then?"

"We think he might be," Luke said cautiously.

"That's why you go to the poker games," Charisse said as though solving a great mystery, "and why you wanted me to befriend Caroline." She looked at him. "Is she involved? Caroline, I mean."

"I really don't know. My gut instinct is to trust her, but I can't be sure."

Charisse reached up and touched his cheek. "Oh, my poor Luke, you've been running yourself ragged this whole trip. All those late-night jaunts. You were doing...whatever it is that you and Ben do. I thought you were meeting Caroline on the sly."

"What would I do a damn fool thing like that for?"

Charisse shrugged. "She's a beautiful woman."

"If it was a beautiful woman I was after, I wouldn't have to look any farther than my own wagon."

"What a sweet thing to say." She gave him a quick kiss then started gathering up their belongings. "I suppose we better be getting back," she said. "You have work to do."

"Come here," he said softly.

Charisse walked into his arms and raised her lips to his. Their kiss sang of starlight and moonbeams, of lover's secrets shared in the night. It left them both breathless and leaning against each other for support.

"This is the best anniversary I've ever had," she said with a smile in her voice.

Luke chuckled. "Me too. I wish we had more time."

"Maybe you'll get finished with... whatever it is before morning," she said. "Toby is staying with the Jessups all night."

He sighed. "Charisse, we can't do this again..."

"I'll bet we could if we tried." She batted her eyelashes at him.

"Don't tempt me." He kissed the tip of her nose, then released her and draped the quilt around her. "We need to be getting back."

"All right."

Instead of moving away, he picked up her hands and ran his thumbs over her knuckles as he gazed down at her. "Thank you for a wonderful evening, for accepting my half-assed explanation, and — most of all — for being the amazing woman you are."

She smiled as she pulled her hands out of his grasp. "I didn't exactly accept it," she said. "In fact, as soon as all this is over, I expect a full confession."

He nodded. "Fair enough." He bent to pick up the rifle Ben had given him.

They walked hand-in-hand back toward the wagon train, vitally aware that the current between them had changed from friends to that of lovers. It was a comfortable silence, and Charisse broke it as they neared the circled wagons. "He beats her, you know."

"Who?"

"Mr. Simms. That's how Caroline and I got to be friends. I found her one day after he'd "reprimanded" her for something. She told me it was an accident, but I knew better. I used to use the same excuses, but you don't get black eyes and split lips from running into things."

Luke stopped. "What do you mean, you used the same excuses?"

"Preston used to... *discipline* me too. So, I recognized the signs."

"That son of a bitch! If I ever get my hands on that ex-husband of yours —"

"That's not important anymore." She waved her hand as though she thought the past irrelevant. "The point is, Caroline Simms is under her husband's control. If she's done something wrong, it may not be her fault." Charisse looked up at him. "Keep that in mind."

As she held his gaze, silently pleading her case, he realized with a start how much it had cost her to admit her own abuse. "All right," he said. "We will."

"Good," she said with satisfaction and started walking again. "That's all I ask."

"Take Franklin and stay in the lean-to," he said gruffly

when they reached the wagon. "There's nothing you can do, and I won't be able to focus on my job if I have to worry about you."

"I will, Luke. I promise." She reached up and caressed the side of his face. "Please be careful. I… I don't know what Toby and I would do without you." She kissed him once more, then untied Franklin and went inside the tent without ever looking at him again.

It only took a few more minutes to make his silent way to Joshua Simms' wagon. The poker game was going on as usual, but only Dempsey and Nugent were playing cards instead of the usual five. Simms, Cassex and Snyder were conspicuously absent. As he moved around to get a better view, Luke noticed something else peculiar. When they had come into camp, Simms' wagon had been right behind Jessups'. Now the two wagons were on opposite sides of the circle.

Simms had gone to a great deal of trouble to get his wagon there. Luke wasn't even surprised when he took his bearings and realized it was a straight line from the wagon to Devil's Gate.

With the party over, and the revelers all back in their wagons, the camp was peaceful. Luke settled down out of sight to wait. It soon became apparent the two poker players were only going through the motions and their conversation was desultory at best. Luke found his mind wandering to the last two hours with Charisse. Marriage was out of the question, though he knew he could easily fall into that trap with her. When Elizabeth died, he'd promised himself he would never marry again, never destroy another woman with his neglect. Charisse deserved a solid man who would stay by her side, not a will-o'-the-wisp who was here one day and off on one of McNesby's crazy jaunts the next. Irritated with himself, Luke pushed his musings aside. It was time to focus on the job at hand. A distraction like Charisse could easily make a man wind up dead.

Independence Rock and Devil's gate lay in a long flat

valley, one easily visible from the other. Though it was a day's travel from Independence Rock to Devil's Gate by wagon train, they were only about twelve to fifteen miles apart. Wagon trains tended to spread out when they came to the wide valley, so the Oregon Trail looked less like a road here, and more like a wide grassy plain that stretched as far as the eye could see toward the west. Once the moon had set and he was able to hide in the shadows, it was perfect for surveillance. He settled himself where he couldn't be seen but was close enough to the poker game to hear what was going on.

Luke fixed his attention on the two poker players. They were clearly uneasy. Both kept glancing toward Independence Rock and then Devil's Gate, so Luke did the same. Even so, he very nearly missed the signal when it came at last.

"There it is," Dempsey said, pointing toward the rock.

Luke looked up and caught the flash of light.

"They're sending a wagon," Nugent interpreted. "And they want three boxes instead of one."

The two exchanged a distinctly uneasy look. "The boss ain't gonna like that."

Dempsey shrugged. "Maybe plans changed, and Simms forgot to tell us. It wouldn't be the first time."

They went to the sleeping tent next to the wagon. "Mrs. Simms," Dempsey called. "Mrs. Simms."

There was a moment of silence, and then a light appeared in the tent. "Yes?"

"It's time for you to take a walk, ma'am."

"A walk? But it's the middle of the night."

"Joshua said you was to leave," said Dempsey. "And put that light out."

"All right. Let me get my dressing gown."

As the light went out Luke was forcibly reminded of Charisse's revelation. What kind of husband told men like Nugent and Dempsey to throw his wife out of bed in the middle of the night without even a light? Simms deserved everything he got.

A moment later, Caroline appeared in the doorway of her tent. Cringing away from the hand Dempsey extended to help her, she turned and disappeared into the night. Luke silently moved into position so he could see the back of the wagon and follow the men at a discrete distance.

The two men set to work. In a matter of minutes, the back of the wagon was gone, revealing a black hole under the floorboards. The men pulled out three long boxes and set them on the ground, then transported them one by one to the road a couple of hundred yards away. Their grunts and swearing attested to the weight of the boxes, but gave Luke no clue to the contents. There was a pile of smaller boxes and a keg already there. Where had they come from? Dempsey and Nugent finished hauling boxes, and settled themselves next to the road.

Luke lay in a small swale where he could see what was going on but was concealed in the darkness. It wasn't long before he heard the telltale rumble of wheels along the road. Dempsey demanded a password from the driver. A stranger, then.

I need to be on that wagon, Luke thought with some urgency. He moved into place while the three men loaded the wagon. Crouched low in the darkness, he knew he resembled a piece of brush and risked little in the way of detection. The critical moment would be when he started to move. At last, the driver climbed onto the seat of the wagon and slapped the reins on the backs of the horses. Luke gritted his teeth in frustration as Nugent and Dempsey stood where they were, watching the wagon drive away. The window of opportunity was closing quickly. The wagon wasn't moving all that fast, but if Simms' two cronies didn't leave soon he'd never make it. Finally, Dempsey slapped Nugent on the shoulder, and they headed back toward the wagon train.

The minute their backs were turned, Luke sprinted after the wagon. The glow of campfires from the wagon train was nearly out of sight behind him when he finally caught up with it and pull himself aboard. He settled on the floor next to the boxes and tried to calm his breathing so the driver wouldn't realize he had a passenger. Luckily, the rattle of harnesses and the noise of the wagon on the rutted road would drown out anything less than a brass band. No wonder the rendezvous had been so far from the wagon train.

The familiar smell of oil and metal rose from the unmarked boxes. He wasn't even surprised when he discovered the acrid smell of gunpowder emanating from the keg. *Of course*. It all made sense now.

Hopefully, he'd have time to sneak out before they reached their destination. He didn't know who he was dealing with yet, but he doubted they would look kindly on anyone hiding in their load of stolen guns and ammo.

CHAPTER 32

Whoa!" The driver called out, and the wagon slowed. Luke did a last-minute check of the little surprise he'd jury-rigged. All seemed secure. Praying he was hidden by the darkness, he slipped out of the wagon and ran in a crouch alongside as it slowed to a stop. He quickly scanned the immediate area, looking for a place to hide. From his vantage point on the left side of the wagon, there was nothing but open ground clear to the cliffs of Devil's Gate in the distance.

"Did you get the guns?" a voice asked in the darkness ahead of the wagon.

"Yeah, three crates plus four boxes of ammunition and a big keg of powder." The driver climbed out of the wagon. "'Course I ain't had time to look inside to see if Simms was telling the truth."

"What do you mean, if I was telling the truth?" Joshua Simms' indignant voice came from the front of the wagon.

"It wouldn't be the first time someone made the mistake of trying to cheat me," the first voice answered. "Come on, let's you and me take a look."

The thud of boots on the road galvanized Luke into action. He dove for the only available hiding place: under the wagon. He rolled out of sight as the three men walked past him to the back. There was a screech of nail as though a board was being pried off the top of a box, and the clink of metal on metal as a rifle was lifted out.

"See, the latest army issue," Simms said proudly.

The other man gave a noncommittal grunt. Luke heard the sound of another wooden lid being pried off and the sound of it hitting the wagon floor. "There isn't nearly enough ammunition here for the number of rifles."

"This was all I could get you," Simms said. "If you'll remember, the original deal was for twenty rifles, not sixty."

"We'll pay you for the extra ammunition too."

"Sorry," Simms said. "I don't have control of the powder and ammunition."

"Hey, Buck," the driver said suddenly. "Someone's coming."

"Friends of yours, Simms?" The stranger's voice was so menacing Luke almost found himself feeling a little sorry for Joshua Simms, especially when James Cassex rode up.

"Evening," Cassex said pleasantly. "It seems Mr. Simms miscounted the number of rifles he was supposed to deliver to you boys. I came to talk to you about the extras."

"There aren't any extra," Buck said. "We paid top dollar for all sixty rifles."

"Well now, see, that's the problem. Simms here overstepped his bounds. It doesn't matter how much you're willing to pay. The rest are already promised to buyers down the trail. All you get is twenty rifles."

"That's too bad," Buck said. "We paid for sixty; we're keeping sixty." Luke heard the click of a rifle being cocked and then another. "Now, if I was you, I'd turn my horse around and ride on out before you get yourself shot."

Cassex sighed. "Somehow I figured that was going to be your answer. Mind if I take Simms with me?"

"Hell, no. We ain't got any use for him."

From Luke's hiding place he saw Simms' boots stumble toward Cassex as though he'd been given a hard shove.

Buck spit on the ground. "Be glad I don't take the money back too. We got you surrounded and could kill you right now."

Cassex snorted. "I bet there aren't more than three men hid out in the dark."

Buck gave a crack of laughter. "That's one bet you'd lose. I'm going to give you to the count of five to leave. One..."

"Hurry up, Simms," Cassex said in a low voice. "We've got to get out of here."

His words sent chills up Luke's spine. Cassex wasn't the brightest candle in the box, but even he wouldn't have been dumb enough to ride in alone. An all-out war was going to commence, and Luke was trapped right in the middle of it.

"Two..."

Luke scanned the far side of the wagon. There was a small outcropping of rocks about a hundred yards away. Tall grass would make good cover for most of the distance, but there was a good twenty-five yards of open ground between him and the grass. There was a chance one side or the other already had someone hidden there, but he had no other choice. He rolled over, pulled a Lucifer match out of his pocket and lit it, then set fire to the gunpowder on the sock dangling down through a knothole in the wagon bed.

"Three..."

He crawled to the edge of the wagon and looked around. Everyone seemed focused on Simms who had his foot in the stirrup and was in the process of swinging up behind Cassex. It was now or never.

"Four..."

Luke crawled out, scrambled into a crouched position and began to run, fully expecting to hear a cry of alarm or feel a bullet slam into his back.

"Five!"

Luke dove into the tall grass as all hell broke loose behind him. The sounds of rifle fire and the smell of burnt gunpowder filled the darkness. Each side appeared to being doing its best to annihilate the other. No shots seemed to be coming from the outcropping, so Luke continued to crawl toward it. Though it was smaller than it had looked from the wagon, its protection was far better than being out in the open. He reached it at last and ducked behind the nearest rock — only to find himself nose-to-nose with a rifle barrel.

His gaze traveled up the barrel to the man behind the gun.

"Paying me back for nearly shooting you earlier tonight?"

"Nah." Ben grinned as he lowered his rifle and eased the hammer down. "I figure I deserved that one. I just wasn't real sure who was sneaking through the grass on his belly. What's going on down there?"

By the time Luke finished telling Ben what he had learned, the rifle fire had died down some.

"So that's what the mysterious cargo is," Ben said. "How many more rifles do you suppose there are?"

Luke shook his head. "There could be a couple dozen or more boxes under the floor of Simms' wagon."

"That's a lot of rifles."

"I have a feeling this isn't the first delivery."

"Probably not." Ben looked back at the tableau below. "Too bad we couldn't at least get rid of this load."

"I tried," Luke said. "I rigged a bomb out of the keg of powder and my sock. I lit the fuse when I left, but if it was going to blow it would have done it already."

"Your sock?" Ben looked at his partner in surprise.

"I tried to cover it with gunpowder." He shrugged. "I guess there wasn't enough."

"Too bad. That would have been—"

A sudden explosion drowned his words. They both ducked in reflex, then exchanged a look before peering over the rock. Chaos reigned. What was left of the wagon was engulfed in flames while bits and pieces of burning wood fell to earth over a large area.

"Slow fuse," Ben said with a grin.

As they watched, the two warring factions came out of the dark and stared at the burning wagon.

"Uh oh," Luke said. "It's not going to take them long to figure out that explosion wasn't caused by their little war."

"And when they do, they'll start looking around to see who did. Guess it's time we headed back to the wagon train."

"Just what I was thinking."

Adonis was tied a fair distance behind the outcropping, but

the glow from the fire was already starting to fade by the time they reached him.

"Do you think Simms had the whole thing set up?" Ben asked as Luke swung up behind the saddle.

"I've been wondering the same thing myself." Luke frowned. "It would be like him to try and pull a fast one. He had the money, and his men were in position to take the rifles back."

"It's a pretty good swindle, and one he could pull over and over."

"Maybe that's the whole scheme," Luke said thoughtfully.

"Maybe. On the other hand, the powder and ammunition didn't come from his wagon, and don't forget the map."

"True. It must have some importance, or he wouldn't have gone to such great pains to keep it hidden," Luke said.

The wagon train, when they arrived, had a deserted look about it. Simms and his gang had not yet returned, so Ben and Luke parted company and headed for their own beds.

The lean-to was dark, but its shadowy interior welcomed him like an old friend. *Home.* The word came out of nowhere with a blast of emotion Luke had thought long dead. It had been years since he'd thought of that word in relation to himself. Yet, this covered wagon and small buffalo-hide lean-to in the middle of nowhere did seem like home.

"Luke?" came a soft voice out of the darkness. Luke smiled.

"I'm sorry, did I wake you?"

"No, not really. I've been waiting for you."

"Is Toby still with the Jessups?" He sat down on the edge of the bed and pulled off his boot.

"Yes." There was a rustle of blankets. "I've been worried."

"Everything's fine."

"Did you and Ben have something to do with that explosion?"

Luke paused in the process of undressing. "Explosion?"

Charisse made a noise that sounded very much like a snort. "Yes, the explosion that lit up the sky and woke everybody out of a sound sleep."

"Oh, that explosion. Somebody got their gunpowder a little too close to a flame." He set his boots out of the way under the wagon. But I don't think anyone was hurt."

She sighed. "Somehow, I didn't think you were going to tell me what happened. I covered for both of you, by the way."

Luke turned in surprise. "You did?"

"The men decided to go find out what happened, and I knew they would miss the two of you eventually."

"I—thank you.

"I'm not sure why I bothered."

Luke smiled. "Because you're a sweetheart."

"More like I didn't want people to get suspicious and think I had anything to do with it. Anyway, you and Ben got into a drinking contest and passed out about an hour before it happened."

"That was poor-spirited of us."

"Yes, it was, especially on our anniversary." He could almost hear her smile in the darkness. "I managed to garner quite a bit of sympathy from the other ladies."

He turned back toward the blankets and paused in surprise. "What happened to my bedroll?"

"I spread it out on the bottom and put mine over the top. I decided we could share tonight." She sounded suddenly unsure of herself. "I... I hope you don't mind."

"Mind?" Luke crawled in and pulled the blankets over them both. "Only an idiot would mind when a beautiful woman invites him into her bed. Come here."

Charisse moved closer. "Oh, Luke, I was so scared when I heard that explosion."

"Shhh." He put his arms around her and kissed her forehead. "There's nothing to worry about." He captured her lips in a searing kiss calculated to wipe everything else from her mind. With tender words and touches, they worshiped each other in the deep shadows of the night. Afterward, they lay in each other's arms exhausted, fulfilled and completely happy.

"I wish this night didn't have to end," Charisse said, pillowing her head on his shoulder.

"Me too." He settled her closer and played with a lock of hair that curled across his chest. "We still have a few hours before dawn and we're not leaving until mid-morning."

"Why is that?"

"Jeveraux decided to stagger our departure to put some distance between the three wagon trains."

"Oh, that makes sense." She yawned, and snuggled closed. "We'll still have to be dressed when Toby shows up, but I'm too tired to move right now."

Luke smiled and closed his eyes, reveling in the sensation of her breath whispering across his skin in a feather-light caress. She was right. There would be plenty of time before Toby showed up.

But it wasn't Toby that awakened them at dawn— it was a scream.

CHAPTER 33

"Wh—?" Charisse jerked awake.

"Something's happened," Luke said, already dressing. "That scream came from Independence Rock. Wait here." He pulled on his boots, grabbed his rifle and was gone.

"In a pig's eye, I'll stay here!"

Luke had barely left the lean-to before Charisse was out of bed and throwing on her own clothes. She arrived at Independence Rock still tying the belt of her dressing gown. Though she knew she was only a few minutes behind Luke, she couldn't see him in the crowd.

"What is it?" she asked a matronly woman from one of the other wagon trains.

"Someone fell," she said.

Charisse gasped and covered her mouth with her hands. "Fell? You mean from the rock?"

The woman nodded. "That's what I heard them say."

As Charisse absorbed the horror of it, the crowd shifted, revealing Ben Baxter, grim-faced and holding a sobbing woman protectively in his arms.

"Caroline," Charisse whispered. "Oh, no!" Luke and Pierre Jeaveraux hunkered down next to a twisted body face-down in the dirt.

As she watched, Pierre raised his eyes to the crowd, his countenance grave. "It's Joshua Simms," he said, "and I'm afraid his neck is broken!"

After a short consultation, the three wagon train captains agreed Simms' death had been an accident, probably brought on by drink, and declared the matter closed. The crowd dispersed back to their wagons, and breakfast fires were soon burning all over the three camps. Luke and the others were still digging the grave when the first wagon train pulled out. By the time Joshua Simms was buried and the wagons packed, it was late morning.

Luke's gaze kept straying to Charisse as he followed Duncan's wagon down the trail. She had her hands full keeping the children under control, especially when they passed the wreckage of the explosion. All three of them wanted to get a closer look. Not that there was much left to see— only a few splinters of charred wood, the black twisted remains of the wagon wheels, and a pile of rubble which Luke suspected was originally three boxes of brand-new army issue repeating rifles.

They stopped for the night earlier than usual to put more distance between themselves and the wagon train ahead. Luke caught sight of Toby and the four Jessups off in the distance as he climbed down from the wagon. Will had taken the children hunting. Brave man, Luke thought, as he anticipated the time alone with Charisse. But when Charisse finished her conversation with Eliza she went straight to the back of the wagon and began rummaging around.

"What's going on?" Luke asked as she pulled her sewing kit out of the corner where she kept it.

"We've decided to mend the holes in Jessup's wagon cover." She glanced around, then lowered her voice. "Actually, it's more of a diversion to take Caroline's mind off her troubles. It's all Eliza and I could come up with."

"My little problem solver," Luke said with a grin. "Leave it to you to come up with a way to benefit both Caroline and John." He gave a wide sweep of his hand toward the other wagons. "Go then, fix our neighbors' problems."

Charisse gave him a doubtful look. "Are you sure? Supper will likely be late."

"Of course, I'm sure, and don't worry about supper. I'll cook up the beans you have soaking and feed Toby when he shows up. You can eat when you're finished."

"Thank you, Luke." She looked at him as if he'd just

handed her the moon, then hurried off to join the other women.

So much for exploring our new relationship, he thought as he watched her go. Supper was nearly done when Toby raced into camp.

"Pa, Pa, Will took me and Morgan hunting and we got about a hundred rabbits!"

"Is that so?"

"It was only six, but Pa's cooking them up for the ladies who are fixing our wagon cover," Will said, following Toby in. "He said to see if you want to come, too."

Luke shot the beans a regretful glance. "Wish I could but these are almost done. Seems a shame to waste them." He sighed when he saw the disappointed look on his son's face. "No reason Toby can't go though."

"Really, Pa?"

"Seems only fair since you helped get the rabbits and all. Hunters have to eat what they kill."

"Thanks, Pa!"

A sudden wave of something that felt very much like loneliness hit Luke as he watched his son run across the wagon circle ahead of Will. It was an odd feeling. He'd eaten a thousand solitary meals like this one with nary a thought of being alone. Traveling with Charisse and Toby had changed that. When had suppertime become the focal point of his day?

"Evenin', McCabe."

Luke looked up as Ben rode in. "Baxter."

"There appears to be something going on over on the other side of camp," Ben said conversationally.

"The ladies decided to fix Jessups' wagon cover, and John's feeding them."

"You're not joining the party?"

Luke shook his head. "Didn't want to waste these beans." He stirred the contents of the pan on the fire. "You eaten yet?"

"Nope. Just got back from scouting the trail ahead."

"Might as well join me then. I'm not fond of eating alone."

"Don't mind if I do," Ben said, swinging down from the

saddle.

"What can you tell me about the trail ahead?" Luke asked, jerking his head toward the back of the wagon.

Ben nodded. It was their signal to make sure they were alone and couldn't be overheard. "We're clear all the way to Split Rock," Ben said as he walked around the wagon and tied Adonis to the back. "There's a buffalo herd to the west that may cause us some trouble." He raised his voice so Luke could hear him.

"About how many, do you figure?" Luke called as Ben casually scanned the area behind the wagon and strolled up the other side.

"I don't know. Looked like thousands to me." Ben swung his leg over the wagon tongue and sat. "No sign of anybody," he said in a low voice. "And you owe me six bits."

"Oh?"

"McNesby sent a messenger."

"Sorry, that wasn't the bet. You said he'd catch up with us by Fort Laramie."

Ben shrugged. "So, I missed it by a week or two. The point is, McNesby came through."

"Never had any doubt he would. What did the messenger say?"

"He gave me a letter." Ben took it out of his pocket and handed it to Luke.

"And?"

"And it's for you."

"That's never stopped you before." Luke opened it and made a face. "It's in code."

"What did you expect? This is McNesby we're dealing with. Sure glad it was addressed to you."

Luke gave him a wry look, then reached into his pocket and pulled out a coin. "Heads or tails?"

"Heads."

Luke flipped the coin in the air, caught it and slapped it on his wrist. "Tails," he said in a satisfied tone as he handed the message back. "You get to decode it."

"Damn!" Ben made a face and slipped the letter into his pocket.

Luke chuckled. They both knew it wouldn't take Ben very long to decode McNesby's message. They had both become quite adept at deciphering the complex code, but trying to get out of it was a long-standing joke between them.

"Find out anything new while I was gone?"

Luke shook his head. "Jeveraux is convinced it was an accident."

"Any chance it was?"

"None. There were definite finger marks around his neck."

Ben sighed. "And there goes our one solid connection. Damn, this is frustrating. We find out they're selling guns and lose our main suspect."

"I've spent the day feeling like an idiot for not realizing Simms wasn't any part of that set up last night," Luke said.

"How could you have known?"

"Dempsey and Cassex were surprised when they got the message to bring three boxes of rifles instead of one, and Simms had to have been the one who sent it. They said the boss wasn't going to like it, but I was so used to thinking of Simms as the leader of this bunch of cut-throats that I never gave it a thought. Someone else is pulling the strings. Simms is dead because he overstepped his authority by selling those extra guns, and we missed it."

"After the hell he's put his wife through, I figure he deserved everything he got." Ben said with bitter emphasis. "Even if I'd been standing next to him, I wouldn't have done a thing to save the son of a bitch!"

Luke's lips curved. "You know, Charisse said basically the same thing—only she thought breaking his neck was far too quick and painless."

Ben looked surprised. "Sweet little Charisse said that?"

"She has a rather bloodthirsty side if you push her. Apparently, Simms had a bad habit of taking his temper out on

Caroline with his fists. Charisse didn't approve."

Ben made a growling noise in his throat. "I suspected as much, but it's not something you can come right out and ask."

Luke sighed. "I wish we knew who did him in."

"Any ideas?"

Luke shook his head. "All I could tell was that whoever did it had huge hands. The fingers had to be at least half an inch wide."

"The same man that killed Bartell and tried to choke you, then." Ben was silent for a moment mulling it over. "Jessup?"

"He's certainly big enough and has the strength, but I still can't quite convince myself he's a cold-blooded killer."

"No, neither can I. For one thing, he has his hands full. With a herd of horses and that passel of young'uns to keep track of, I don't see how he'd have time to be running guns. Besides, he's leaving the wagon train."

Luke looked up in surprise. "He is?"

"He's decided to settle here instead of going on to Oregon."

"That seems a little odd. There's nothing much here but Indians and rattlesnakes."

"And wild horses. John says that's what convinced him this was the best place for them to start their herd. Figures they'll sell horses to the army."

Luke frowned. "Strange none of us ever heard a word of it until now."

"On the other hand, he did cover your back with the Indians."

"True, but Morgan wasn't supposed to be there. His own daughter being involved would have changed things."

Ben gave him a wry look. "You've been thinking on this all day, haven't you?"

"Yes, and the more I think about it the more damning the evidence is." Luke started counting on his fingers. "He was the last one to show up the night Bartell died; he said he went to check his horses. Jessup rode into that Indian camp ahead of me saying his size and the string of horses he was leading would cause both interest and intimidation."

"And the Indians weren't exactly unhappy to see you," Ben put in.

"No, in fact they fell all over themselves to make a deal. Last night, Jessup left the party early to put Toby and Morgan to bed. We never saw him again."

"But you really don't think it was him, do you?"

Luke sighed heavily. "No."

"If it makes you feel any better, I don't either."

"So, I guess we keep a close watch on the guns, since that's all we have."

Ben nodded. "I think I'll see if Mrs. Simms wants me to drive her wagon for her."

"Good plan. I'm going to take a look around. It will be interesting to see where the poker game winds up."

"Those beans about ready?" Ben asked.

"I guess so." Luke scooped a spoonful out onto each plate. "I never thought I'd miss Charisse's cooking, but I do."

Ben snorted, "I don't think that's what you're missing, my friend. I've had her cooking, and trust me, yours is better."

The simple meal was dispatched in short order, and the two men went their separate ways.

The poker game was in the last place Luke expected it— right where it always had been. Snyder, Nugent Cassex, and Dempsey sat playing cards next to the Simms wagon the same way they did every night. The absence of Joshua Simms was hardly noticeable.

"Luke!"

Luke turned. Caroline stood next to Jessup's wagon, waving at him.

"Charisse is over here," she called. "Come on over."

He glanced back at the poker players, then walked toward the women. Only an idiot would choose a poker game over Charisse Jones.

The women sat in a circle with Jessup's wagon cover stretched between them, each sewing on a section. "I see you decided to have a sewing bee," he said, dropping a kiss on Charisse's forehead.

She blushed and gave him a shy smile. "Mr. Jessup needs his wagon cover mended."

"And you women can't resist a poor man in need," he said with a smile.

"Or an excuse to get together and gossip," put in Eliza Duncan. "We haven't had much time to do that out here on the trail."

Violet Swindell tipped her head to the side. "Did anyone ever find out what that explosion was all about?"

Luke shook his head. "The scout said it looked like a wagon full of guns and ammunition caught fire."

Eliza frowned. "One would think an accident like that would have killed anyone on the wagon. There would have been bodies."

Mrs. Mantella made a rude noise. "Maybe, unless the idiot blew himself to bits, and there was nothing left to find!"

Luke gave Charisse's shoulder a squeeze. "Have you got a minute?"

"Sure." She put her sewing aside. "I'll be right back."

As they walked away from the other women, Luke thought he heard someone say, "…so much in love…" and "…lucky woman…"

He looked down at Charisse and found her blushing adorably. "How's Caroline doing?

"About like you'd expect. I doubt it was a love match to start with, and he was horribly mean to her. Still, it was a terrible shock. Would you mind if I stayed with her tonight? I don't think she should be alone."

"I sort of figured you'd want to," he admitted, brushing the hair back from her face. "Just keep your eyes open and be careful."

She looked over at the card players and frowned. "Can you believe they're sitting there playing poker like nothing ever happened?"

"It does seem pretty insensitive," Luke agreed.

"I told Caroline to send them packing, but she says it's their way of mourning her husband." She looked up at Luke. "Do you think if you played with them for a while you might convince them to go somewhere else?"

"I don't play often enough to have any influence."

"Oh." She looked disconcerted for a moment. "Well, how about Ben?"

Luke doubted the game would move as long as the guns were in Caroline's wagon. "Tell you what, if they won't move, one or the other of us will play until it breaks up every night."

"All right. That's better than—" she broke off and stared across the wagon circle. "Say, isn't that Ben over there by our wagon?"

Luke frowned. He'd expected the contents of McNesby's message to be delivered at their nightly rendezvous. "Guess I'd better go see what he wants." Luke pulled her into his arms for the kiss he'd been wanting to give her all day. He'd only meant it to be light and affectionate, but that was before he felt her arms go around his waist and her hands trace the muscles of his back. Her lips parted with a soft whimper, and Luke was lost. They kissed open-mouthed, hungrily, as though they couldn't get enough. The kiss, when it ended, left them both shaken and slightly befuddled.

"I'd better go see what Ben wants," he said.

"Right... Ben," she said in a dreamy voice.

Luke glanced over her head, then smiled as he bracketed her face with his hands. "And you'd best think up a good story for the other ladies." He kissed her lightly. "They're all watching us."

"What?" She jerked out of her trance and took a quick look over her shoulder. The other women sat frozen in place, needles and good manners forgotten, as they stared unabashedly at Luke and Charisse. "Oh dear."

"Don't worry," he said, kissing her nose. "You'll think of something."

"Maybe you're trying to convince me to forgive you for getting drunk on our anniversary."

Luke chuckled as he let her go. "If that was a peace offering, I can hardly wait until we make up."

"Oh, you!" Charisse blushed, and gave him a playful slap on the arm. Then she looked back at Simms' wagon. "Don't forget about those men."

"I won't." He couldn't resist one last quick kiss and received another lighthearted swat for his pains. Then she gave him a soft smile before returning to the other women, rosy-cheeked and embarrassed.

With his hands in his pockets, Luke sauntered across the circle of wagons to his own, where Ben leaned against the frame rolling a cigarette. "Evening, Baxter," he said.

"McCabe." Ben licked the cigarette paper and rolled it over the tobacco. "Don't suppose you have a match," he said as he twisted the ends and stuck the cigarette in his mouth.

"I might at that." Luke made a show of digging through his pockets as he walked over to Ben. "Is that the best you could think of?" he said in a low voice. "Only an idiot would carry Lucifer matches in his pocket. Damn good way to catch yourself on fire."

Ben grinned as he produced one of his own and slipped it into Luke's hand. "Seems to me you had one last night."

"That's because I took it out of *your* pocket when we changed clothes." Luke struck the match and made a show of lighting the cigarette. "I take it McNesby's message was more urgent than we thought?"

Ben's grin faded. "It's about Charisse."

"What?"

"It took McNesby all this time to find her. Seems there is no record of Charisse Jones anywhere. It was as though she sprang into being when she bought her rig in St. Louis."

"I figured Jones was an alias," Luke said.

Ben nodded. "Your idea that she came from a rich family was what led him to her. Ever hear of P. J. Collingsworth the third?"

"The railroad king?"

"Right. It seems he divorced his wife Mary a year and a half ago, claiming she was responsible for their daughter's death." He paused. "Her full name is Mary Charisse Collingsworth."

"Oh, hell."

"That's what I thought too. No charges were ever brought, and the reason for the girl's death was natural causes."

"So, she isn't running from the law, then?"

"No, but someone hired the Pinkerton Agency to locate her. Until McNesby and Allen Pinkerton started comparing notes there hadn't been a break in the case. Charisse had apparently gone to great lengths to disappear."

Luke frowned. "Who's looking for her?"

"A firm of London-based solicitors called Hussets, Howser, and Brahms."

Luke was startled. "Why would English lawyers be looking for Charisse?"

"You've got me. When McNesby asked, he was told in no uncertain terms it was a personal matter they were not at liberty to discuss."

Luke gave a low whistle. "Sounds ominous."

"We have a new assignment. That's the reason I came to find you."

"Oh?"

"We're supposed to keep Charisse Jones under surveillance until Hussets, Howser, and Brahms' representative catches up with us."

"Why surveillance?"

"Hussets, Howser, and Brahms stressed there was danger involved. McNesby didn't know if they considered *her* a danger, or if they thought she was *in* danger. Whichever it is, we're supposed to proceed with extreme caution."

"Damn!"

"Exactly." Ben grinned suddenly. "Leave it to you to hire a nanny to save your backside and wind up with a woman half of England is trying to find."

CHAPTER 34

"Do you think I'll ever see them again, Mama?" Toby asked as Charisse stowed the last of the clean supper dishes in the campbox and closed the lid.

Charisse smoothed Toby's hair. "I don't know, sweetheart. You never quite know what life will bring you." She'd lost count of the number of times she'd answered the same question. The Jessups had left two days before, just as the wagon train started to climb South Pass through the Rocky Mountains. Without his playmates, Toby was lost.

"Maybe when I grow up, I'll find Morgan and marry her."

"Maybe. Anyway, Mr. Jessup said he was going to settle close to Fort Laramie, so you can write to her and the twins."

"Guess I'd better practice so I can write good enough."

"Well enough," she corrected. "Don't worry, we're going to continue your lessons."

"It won't be near as much fun without Morgan, Matt and Andy."

Charisse smiled sympathetically. "Why don't you and Franklin go find your father after you do your chores? The two of you can check tomorrow's trail."

"We're almost to the top," Toby said, his eyes brightening. "Maybe we'll be able to see it."

"You might at that." Charisse smiled as she watched him run to find Luke. Nothing kept his spirits down for long. Then she sighed. Truth be told, she felt a little lost herself. It had been as difficult for her to say good-bye to the Jessups as it had been for Toby. A dozen times a day she'd found herself looking for all four of her charges and felt a pang of loss every time.

How much worse would it be when Luke and Toby left?

There was no use deluding herself; Luke was not the marrying kind, nor was he planning to settle in Oregon. He and Ben were on this wagon train to do a job. When it was done, they would go back to wherever they came from and she would go on to Oregon and try to make a new life for herself — alone.

Maybe she should have gone with the Jessups, not as John's wife but as their housekeeper. She could have made a home for them and for herself. But she knew she'd never desert Toby, nor, if she was honest with herself, Luke and Ben. Whatever they were involved in was dangerous; two men were already dead, perhaps more. If she left the wagon train now, it would expose Luke and possibly Ben to their enemies. She'd be signing their death warrants.

But it was more than that. Nothing could change the bond she and Luke had forged during that unforgettable night of passion. Not Luke's continued refusal to tell her who or what he was. Not the realization he may well have returned to her bed moments after killing Joshua Simms. Not the suspicion the incredible kiss that had almost set her garters ablaze had been staged for the benefit of those who watched. Not even the odd way he had watched her ever since. No matter what happened, she had no choice but to see this through, for Toby, for Luke, and for herself.

Luke and Toby were late for supper, but they brought her a small chunk of ice they had found in a cave beneath a snow bank. Toby put it in her cup of water and watched happily as she took a sip. As she tasted her first cold water in months, she thought of the magnificent ice sculptures her chef had created for the dinner parties and galas Preston insisted they put on for his high society friends and business associates. There had been swans, tigers, lions and once an incredible running horse, but none as marvelous as the small piece of leftover winter floating in her cup now.

"That's an interesting smile," Luke remarked, filling his cup with coffee. "A penny for your thoughts."

"I was thinking how life changes. There was a time I

couldn't have imagined a chunk of ice being the highlight of my week."

"I know. I'll never take a roof over my head in a rainstorm for granted again."

She closed her eyes. "Or a hot bath."

"Or a bed."

Her eyes popped open and encountered a knowing grin on his face.

"Luke!"

"What? You like sleeping on the hard ground? Just think how much you'd enjoy a nice, comfortable, bouncy bed."

The image of the two of them making love in the huge heirloom bed she'd inherited from her grandmother burst into her mind, and a wave of pure heat flashed through her.

"You look a little warm, Charisse," Luke commented, his grin unrepentant.

"Nonsense!"

"Do you want to go see the ice cave?" Toby asked, bouncing up and down. "You'll love it, Mama. It's the most 'mazing thing, and you won't be hot anymore."

Luke's grin grew. "Good idea. I think Mama could use some cooling off."

"So could Pa," Charisse muttered. "Maybe he should dunk his head in the snow drift."

Toby looked concerned. "It's not deep enough for that, Mama. Besides, it's too cold."

"I can't go with you, anyway. I have guard duty tonight." Luke managed to sound regretful, but his dancing eyes gave him away. "Maybe we can discuss this fever of yours when I get home."

"I doubt it," she said, with a toss of her head. "I'm sure I'll be sleeping. Come on, Toby. If I'm going to see this marvel before dark, we're going to have to hurry."

Luke's deep chuckle vibrated along her nerve endings as they walked away. In spite of her offended air, Charisse enjoyed their banter as much as Luke appeared to, and she felt giddy as a school girl.

They reached the cave as Caroline and Ben were leaving. Charisse could almost see the current of attraction zinging back and forth between the other two. Not for the first time, she wondered if that was why Caroline had refused Ben's offer to drive her wagon and had hired James Cassex instead. There had been little love lost between Caroline and Joshua Simms, but she was probably reluctant to make tongues wag so soon after his death. Or did Caroline perhaps sense there was no future for a romance with Ben Baxter? It seemed so unfair. After what she'd been through, Caroline deserved to be happy.

So do you, said a small voice inside.

The truth of it sucked some of the pleasure out of the outing. Even the cave with its amazing deposit of ice and Toby's excited chatter failed to raise her spirits.

Luke was getting ready to leave when they arrived back at the wagon.

"I thought your guard duty started at midnight," Charisse said with surprise.

"It does, but it's also poker night. I thought I'd check on the game first."

"All right," Charisse said doubtfully. Though it wasn't unusual, and she had asked him to keep an eye on the poker players, she had an uneasy feeling, as she watched him leave. She pushed away a flutter of panic as he disappeared into the night. Calling herself seven kinds of a fool, she put Toby to bed then went to bed herself, certain it was just a case of nerves. Still, a little niggling worry kept Charisse awake for a long time.

It seemed like she had only been asleep a few minutes, when Franklin's growls broke the stillness of the night. "Mrs. McCabe," a voice whispered out of the darkness.

"Huh?" Charisse woke with a start. "Who's there?"

"It's me, Mrs. McCabe, James Cassex. Mr. McCabe needs you."

Charisse sat up in alarm, clutching her blanket to her chest. "What's happened?"

"I'm not sure, but he asked me to fetch you." He swore as Franklin curled his lip and took a step forward. "Call off your dog," Cassex said nervously.

Charisse snapped her fingers. "Down, Franklin." The dog obediently stopped growling and dropped to the ground. But his teeth were still bared and his eyes never left the intruder. "Give me a minute to get ready," Charisse said. "I can't leave my son here by himself."

There was a moment of silence as he considered this. "If you'll write a note for Mrs. Simms, I could take him to her while you get dressed."

"Thank you. That would be most helpful."

Charisse leaned over and shook Toby. "Wake up, sweetheart."

She sighed when she got no response. Toby was such a sound sleeper, he was next to impossible to wake. Finally, she put on his shoes, wrapped him in a blanket, and sent him to Caroline in his nightclothes along with a hastily scribbled note. She felt a pang as Cassex carried him off into the darkness. Franklin rose to his feet and followed.

Charisse thought about calling the dog back, but decided against it. She knew Toby would be safe with Caroline, but Franklin was a little added insurance.

Meanwhile, she needed to get to Luke. Worry curled through her mind as she struggled into her clothes. It must be a matter of life and death for Luke to risk sending someone like Cassex to get her.

She tucked her derringer into the pocket of her apron just as Cassex returned.

"Mrs. Simms said she'd keep him 'til morning. Are you ready?"

"Yes." Charisse settled her shawl around her shoulders. "Where is my husband?"

"Over yonder," he said, waving in the general direction of the trail.

"He's still on guard duty?"

"That's why he couldn't come get you himself."

It made sense. Charisse quieted her misgivings and followed him out of camp. As they walked through the darkness, she gradually realized they were going northward, away from the wagons. Hadn't Luke said he'd be on the south side of the encampment? Perhaps Pierre Jeveraux had changed the guard duty schedule and sent Luke to the opposite side.

"How did Luke find you if he was on guard duty?" Charisse asked.

"I drew first watch tonight. He was my replacement."

"Then why didn't he come get me himself before he relieved you?"

"Beats me. I ain't exactly in his confidence."

Charisse frowned. There was something not right about this. She glanced over her shoulder and was shocked to see how far they had come. The wagons were barely visible behind them. There was no way the guard perimeter was this far out.

"Mr. Cassex—" she began.

The words had barely left her lips when a calloused hand clamped over her mouth and choked off the rest.

"Hello, Eli. 'Bout time you boys showed up," Cassex said as Charisse's captor yanked her arms behind her. "She was starting to get nervous."

A large man with a bushy beard stepped out of the shadows. "You sure this is the right one?"

"Hell yes, it's the right one," Cassex said indignantly.

The other man grunted. "Just making sure the boss gets what he paid for. He said she had red hair."

"It's sorta red, when the sun shines on it."

"You best get her tied up, Sid," Eli said, handing a length of rope to the man holding Charisse.

Charisse bit down on the hand covering her mouth.

"Ouch!" the man yelped, jerking his hand away.

Charisse sucked in her breath for a loud scream, but Eli stuffed a handkerchief in her mouth before she got a chance and secured it with a bandana.

"She's a feisty one," Cassex said with a grin.

"She won't be when I get done with her," Sid growled.

"Settle down," said Eli. "The boss wants her in one piece."

"Yeah, but he said we might have to kill her so I reckon I can have my fun first."

Eli sighed. "You got a one-track mind, Sid. Best tie her hands in front so she can ride a horse."

Struggle was futile, and Charisse knew it. Her time with White Otter had taught her that. The three men would have her overpowered before she even got in a good kick, and all it would accomplish would be to make them watch her closer. Her best bet was to act frightened and subdued, to bide her time and see what opportunities might present themselves.

Cassex held her immobile while Sid tied her hands. By the time he was finished, Eli had retrieved two horses from wherever they had been hidden in the darkness.

With Eli's help, Sid lifted Charisse onto his horse, and swung up behind her. He settled himself against her back, then reached forward and squeezed her breast. Reacting without thought, Charisse drove an elbow backwards into his mid-section.

At Sid's grunt of pain, Eli glanced up and gave a disgusted sigh. "Damn it, Sid, we don't have time for your fooling around." Eli swung up on his own horse and looked down at Cassex. "How long do you figure we have?"

"He won't know she's gone until dawn, and then we'll send him off in the wrong direction. By the time he gets it all figured out, you should be ahead of him by at least two days," Cassex said. "Just make sure you keep him occupied for three days like your boss promised."

"Might mean we have to kill him."

Cassex shrugged. "Don't reckon anybody on this end would care much."

A chill of horror twisted Charisse's stomach and froze her to the marrow of her bones. Their purpose in kidnapping her was suddenly horribly clear. They're trying to draw Luke away from the wagon train. It's a trap, and she was the bait!

CHAPTER 35

The sun was still below the horizon when Luke awoke. He groaned, knowing he'd toss and turn until it was finally time to get up, the same as he had every other morning Charisse stayed with Caroline. He didn't begrudge Caroline Charisse's company, but he'd been disappointed when James Cassex came to tell him Caroline wanted Charisse to spend one more night with her.

Luke sighed and threw back the covers. Charisse would be back from Caroline's a few minutes after dawn. He might as well build the fire and get the coffee started.

Half an hour later, Luke was tired of waiting and decided to take Charisse for a sunrise walk, though how romantic it would be with Toby along was questionable. He was humming a happy tune by the time he arrived at the Simms' wagon.

"Pa! I thought you were gone."

Luke smiled with real pleasure as Toby ran up and hugged him. "What made you think that?"

"Luke!" Caroline said, coming around the side of the wagon. "I didn't expect to see you back so soon."

"Back from where?" he asked, as the first fingers of apprehension unfurled.

"Why, from where ever the Jessups are."

Dread skittered down his spine. "Caroline, where's Charisse?"

"Isn't she with you?"

"I haven't seen her since supper last night."

"Mr. Cassex said John Jessup rode in late last night to get Charisse because Morgan and the twins are very ill. He said she wanted me to watch Toby. Luke, what's going on?"

"I'm not sure yet. Would you keep an eye on Toby until I get back?"

"Of course."

Luke hunkered down in front of Toby. "Son, I need you to stay here with Mrs. Simms while I go get Mama."

"Can't I go too?"

Luke shook his head. "Not this time. I'll be traveling too fast. I need to have you here where I know you're safe so I can focus on finding Mama."

"Ok, Pa," Toby said. "I'll stay here and help Mrs. Simms like I do Mama."

"I knew I could count on you, son. Mama and I will be back as soon as we can." Luke gave Toby a hug, then went to find James Cassex.

Cassex was still sound asleep when Luke kicked him out of bed.

"Hey," he grumbled as he rolled out of his blankets. "Whaddya think you're doing?"

"Where's my wife?"

"How the hell should I know?"

"You told me she was going to stay with Caroline Simms, and you told Caroline John Jessup came to get Charisse."

"All I know is what your wife told me," he said sulkily as he sat up. "I was walking back to my camp about midnight when John Jessup comes gallopin' in and goes right to your wagon." Cassex said. "Then Mrs. McCabe calls me over and asks me to go tell you she was going to Mrs. Simms."

"So why hasn't Caroline seen her?"

Cassex shrugged. "Mrs. McCabe wanted to wait for you, but Jessup was pressuring her into going right then 'cause his three kids was sick. He's the one that suggested I take your son to Mrs. Simms. So, I did. Then I come back here and went to bed."

"What time did this happen?"

"I don't know," Cassex said sullenly. "But it was after midnight 'cause that's when the poker game broke up."

Luke nodded. "Thanks." Though he made the rounds and talked to everyone in camp, Cassex was the only one who had seen Charisse or John Jessup.

He managed to signal Ben, and they met unobtrusively down by the river. "Don't know if this has to do with Charisse's mystery or the guns, and there's no way to tell for sure."

Ben sighed. "Not unless they are one in the same."

"That thought occurred to me, too. Her being right there when I needed a nanny was pretty coincidental, not to mention the accidental meeting with Toby."

"Except that no one knew you needed a nanny, did they?"

Luke sighed. "Who knows? I don't think Simms was on to me yet, but I had signed on with the wagon train, so it is possible."

"Or maybe Charisse is an innocent pawn." Ben rubbed his face. "It appears we were wrong about Jessup, though."

"Yes, and this is probably a trap."

"But you're going anyway."

It was a statement, not a question. Luke nodded. "Wouldn't you?"

"Without hesitation. Do you want me to go with you?"

"Hell yes, I want you with me!" Luke sighed. "But there's a good chance the whole purpose of this is to draw me away from those guns so they can attempt another delivery, and you need to be here if they do."

"Take Adonis. He's fast, and he's up to carrying both of you if he has to."

"All right, but we need to cover our tracks. As far as we know, you're still in the clear, and we don't want to jeopardize that."

"Good point." Ben thought for a moment, then began to grin. "I lost rather heavily at poker last night, so I might be inclined to take a job I wouldn't otherwise."

"You mean like driving my wagon while I go after my wife?"

"Precisely."

"I suppose you're planning on putting on a good show?"

Ben's grin broadened. "You betcha. Be warned, this is going to cost you."

For the first time all morning, Luke grinned back. "It's going to cost McNesby, you mean."

Ten minutes later Luke made his way to the cluster of single men who were seated around the campfire they shared at mealtimes. Everyone, including Ben, was eating breakfast and drinking coffee.

"Good morning," Luke said. "I need someone to drive my wagon for a few days." Silence greeted this pronouncement, though Cassex gave him a wary look. "John Jessup's children are sick," he continued, "and my wife and I are going to help out." More silence. Ben grabbed the coffee pot and poured himself another cup before going back to his plate of beans.

"I'm willing to pay," Luke said.

"There you go, Baxter," Snyder said with a snicker. "You can pay off your gambling debts."

Ben gave him a surly look then glanced at Luke. "How much?"

"Four bits a day."

"Not worth my time."

Luke frowned. "How much is your time worth?"

"A dollar a day."

"Are you out of your mind?"

Ben shrugged. "Take it or leave it."

Luke thought about it for a moment then gave a resigned sigh. "All right, but I'll need to borrow your horse, too."

"That will cost you an extra four bits," Ben said.

"That's highway robbery!" Luke was practically sputtering. "The Jessups need help."

"Look, McCabe, I'm sorry about Jessup's problems, I really am. But it's not my business. Not exactly yours either, come to that." He ate the last of the beans on his plate. "And frankly," he said around a mouthful, "I'd rather not drive those oxen of yours."

"Fine!" Luke said with ill grace. "A dollar fifty a day then, and I hope you choke on it." He turned and stalked away.

"And if anything happens to my horse, you'll replace him," Ben called after him.

Luke raised a hand in acknowledgement and kept walking, hiding the smile that tugged at the corners of his mouth. Leave it to Ben to put on a show. I'm surprised he didn't demand payment in advance.

A long hug from Toby, a change of clothes, a sack of food from Caroline, and he was off. Adonis's ground-eating stride left him with little to do but think.

Charisse didn't know how long they had been riding, but it seemed like forever. The sun beat down on her unmercifully, her muscles ached as her jaws stretched around the gag in her mouth, and her body fought to maintain its balance in the saddle she shared with the repulsive man behind her. Only her ferocious grip on the saddle horn with her bound hands kept her from falling off.

"We'll be stopping pretty soon, honey," Sid whispered in her ear. "Maybe we can have us a little fun." She tensed as he ran his hand down her thigh. "Got somethin' real special you're gonna like a lot." The way he rubbed himself against her left no doubt as to his meaning.

Charisse shuddered, fighting the nausea that threatened to overwhelm her.

At long last, Eli called a halt next to a small stream. Three scraggly cottonwoods—the first trees they had seen all morning—grew there, surrounded by a variety of tall plants and a small patch of grass. It wasn't much but it looked like a veritable oasis to Charisse.

Sid slid her to the ground and chuckled as her exhausted legs gave out, and she crumpled into the dirt. "Looks like we ain't gonna have to worry about you running away." Dismounting next to her, he grabbed her bound hands, jerked her to her feet, and led her to a log.

Charise sat down with a thump. The rape he had been promising all morning loomed large in her mind, and she prepared herself to fight with everything she had.

With a look of disgust at Sid, Eli set about hobbling the horses so the animals could graze on the grass. It was clear the two men had no fear of pursuit.

Sid settled back against the log, and pulled a strip of jerky out of his pocket. "Hungry?"

Eating was about the last thing Charisse wanted, but she nodded — she knew he'd have to remove the gag to feed her. Instead, he glanced toward Eli as though checking to make sure the other man's attention was elsewhere. "Reckon you and me can work something out to pay for it," he said quietly. With a lascivious grin, he ran his hand under the hem of her skirt and up her leg.

Eli came out of the bushes buttoning his pants. "Sid, what the hell are you doing?"

Sid jerked his hand out from under her skirt. "Nothing," he said.

Eli grunted and shook his head. "Remember, Sid, she has to arrive in one piece or we don't get paid."

Sid looked sulky. "Don't reckon the boss will care if we use her a bit first."

"You don't know that. Could be he wants her for himself." Eli untied the bandana and removed the gag from her mouth. "We don't need this anymore. Ain't nobody to hear no matter how loud you scream."

"C-can I have some water?" Charisse croaked. The inside of her mouth felt as if she'd been sucking on a bale of cotton.

Eli held his canteen to her lips, then handed her a piece of jerky, and attached his lariat to the rope binding her wrists, before tying it to a tree. "There, that should keep you out of trouble." He lay down in the shade where she couldn't reach him and put his hat over his face.

Sid settled down next to a rock where he could watch her. Charisse pretended to ignore him as she ate her meager meal.

Charisse was still chewing her jerky when the sound of a snore reached her ears, and she glanced over her shoulder in surprise. Sid was sound asleep against the rock. She turned to look at Eli, who appeared not to have moved.

Carefully, Charisse slid her hands down her thigh until her fingers felt the outline of the derringer in her pocket. The small pistol only had a single shot, and wasn't much good unless the target was at point-blank range. *Still, you never know when an opportunity might present itself.* She spent the entire time Eli and Sid were napping trying to get her gun out of her pocket, but she finally had to admit defeat. With her hands tied together at the wrists the way they were, she couldn't reach into her pocket far enough to get it out.

Finally, Eli yawned, stretched and rolled to his feet. "Come on Sid. It's time we hit the trail. Don't want McCabe catching up before we get back to camp."

Sid made a face, then stumbled into the bushes. He still hadn't reappeared by the time Eli caught the horses, removed their hobbles and hoisted Charisse back into the saddle.

Sid!" he called. "Hurry up. We haven't got all day."

"Ouch—what the hell?" The air was suddenly filled with the sound of cursing and someone thrashing around.

"Sid, what's wrong?" Eli asked.

"I don't know. Ow! Something's stinging the hell out of me! Ow!"

Eli closed his eyes and shook his head, then made his way into the thicket. "For hell's sake, Sid, that's stinging nettle."

"What is?"

"Those tall green plants you're in the middle of. Leave it to you to take a piss in a patch of nettles." Eli sighed. "Reckon it's going to be uncomfortable riding, but I don't see as we have any choice." He mounted his horse, then glanced at Charisse. "At least he won't be giving you any grief."

As they waited for Sid, an idea burst into Charisse's mind. Sid wasn't the sharpest rock in the road. It might just work.

Charisse forced herself to stay calm as she prepared for the part she was to play. Sid finally appeared, looking most uncomfortable and walking gingerly.

Charisse bit her lip as she watched him climb painfully onto the horse. He seated himself behind the saddle instead of sharing it with her. He had little to say.

Checking to see if Eli was out of earshot, Charisse allowed herself to slump slightly in the saddle. "I'm so, so sorry," she said softly. "I didn't mean for that to happen."

"What are you talking about?"

"Your… problem. With the poison ivy."

"It was stingin' nettle, and it ain't your fault, anyhow."

"Actually, it is." She gave a dramatic sigh. "You see, I'm a jinx."

CHAPTER 36

It was nearly dark when Luke finally caught up with the Jessups. They were sitting down to supper when he rode in. All looked hale and hearty.

John Jessup rose to his feet and came forward, a welcoming smile on his face. "Luke, what—"

"Where the hell is she?" Luke swung down off his horse. "What did you do with Charisse?"

"Charisse? What are you talking about?"

"You tell me." Luke grabbed John's shirtfront. "You're the one that showed up in the middle of the night with a sad story and took my wife."

John reached down and grasped Luke's wrists in a crushing grip. "I haven't seen your wife or anyone else from the wagon train since we left you three days ago."

"And you're a damned liar!" Luke wrested his hands from John's grip and punched him hard in the stomach. It was like hitting a brick wall. He had the momentary realization that this was not the man he had fought behind Simms' wagon before a sudden white-hot pain exploded in his jaw and everything went black.

"Pa, he's coming around."

Luke opened his eyes and thought for a moment he was seeing double, then his eyes focused, and he realized he was looking at the twins. His head swam as he sat up and looked at John who appeared to be waiting for him to wake up. "We've never fought before, have we?" he said, fingering his jaw.

John frowned. "Hell, no we haven't. Up until ten minutes

ago, I thought we were friends." He looked at his younger children. "I think it's time you three got ready for bed."

"What about Charisse?"

"If she needs your help, I'll let you know."

"But, Pa—"

John pointed toward the wagon. "Bed!"

As the children left grumbling, Luke decided it was time to trust his gut instinct. John had the strength to kill with his bare hands, but he was not the man Luke had fought. That man was powerful, but hitting him hadn't been like plowing into Independence Rock. John might even be able to help him figure all this out if Luke trusted him with the truth. "I think I owe you an apology."

"Or at the very least an explanation."

"Charisse is gone."

"I gathered that. What made you think I had anything to do with it?"

"She disappeared last night. James Cassex said your children were sick and you came to get Charisse."

"That is something I might have done," John agreed, "but I'd have let you know."

Luke sighed. "I overheard your proposal the night of the party at Independence Rock. It occurred to me you might have decided to give her a little stronger coaxing."

A dangerous light entered the other man's eyes. "I ought to bust your other jaw! I'd never steal another man's wife, and I sure as hell wouldn't take her against her will."

"The thing is, I wasn't sure she'd be unwilling."

"What the hell are you talking about? That wife of yours."

"We're not married," Luke said quietly.

"—loves you and Toby with every ounce— what?"

"She's not my wife." He shook his head at John's scandalized expression. "It's not like that. She needed a driver, and I needed someone to take care of Toby. We posed as husband and wife because...well, frankly to avoid reactions like the one you're having right now. It's a business arrangement, nothing more."

"You expect me to believe that?"

Luke shrugged. "It's the truth. You offered her security with a family she already loves. She'd be a fool not to take it."

"What about you?"

"Charisse and I will go our separate ways once we get to Oregon."

John gave him a long look. "Then you're an idiot." He frowned. "But Charisse didn't come to us — so, where is she?"

Luke ran his hand through his hair. "I'm afraid she may have been kidnapped."

"Kidnapped! Why?"

"I'm not exactly sure, but I think someone may have paid Cassex to send me in the wrong direction."

"Damn!" John sighed. "I wish I could go with you, Luke, but I can't leave my kids or the horses. I can't even spare you Will."

"I know, and I wouldn't ask it of you." He stood and brushed the dirt off his clothes. "I could use a couple of good horses, though."

"Take your pick."

In a short time, Luke was on the trail again, just as a full moon rose in the east. He rode a long-legged roan and led a string of two more horses and Adonis. All four horses were built for speed and endurance. Luke prayed it would be enough.

The storm hit on the afternoon of the second day. It came howling out of the north to blast them with heavy winds and blinding rain. Charisse was drenched within minutes and freezing cold. Lightning flashed and thunder growled all around them. Charisse's only consolation was the knowledge that Sid blamed it all on her, just as he had the swarm of mosquitoes that had arisen from the grass as they rode through a marshy area. The voracious insects feasted on humans and horses alike until all were nearly driven mad. That was when Sid started whining about her being a jinx.

Charisse smiled even as she hunched forward against the rain and the shrieking wind. If the mosquitoes had made Sid nervous, this storm was going to scare him to death!

"We've got to get down somewhere away from that lightning." Eli yelled as he veered off to the left. They were almost upon the gully before Charisse saw it.

Eli dismounted and looked over the edge then came back to Sid's horse. "There's a rock ledge that will give us some protection," he shouted. "Hobble the horses, Sid. I'll take care of the prisoner."

Eli helped her down from the horse then cut the rope around her wrists. "Follow me."

Charisse slipped twice in the morass of mud as she made her way down to the meager protection of the rock ledge. "What about the horses?" she yelled as Eli reached up to help her down the slippery slope to the dubious shelter of the ledge. "They could be struck by lightning."

"There's no room for them under here, even if they could make it down the hill."

Shivering with cold, Charisse glanced back up as Sid started down. He was nearly to the ledge when his feet went out from under him. With arms and legs flailing, he slid clear to the bottom of the gulch, bouncing from sagebrush to sagebrush as he went. He finally crashed at the bottom and lay there unmoving.

"Sid!" Eli yelled. "Sid, are you all right?"

Sid groaned and lifted his head. "Help," he called weakly. "I don't think I can get back up there by myself."

"Well, I ain't comin' down after you."

Charisse peered down at Sid and frowned. "You're just going to leave him there?"

Eli hunkered down. "He'll make it," he said as he handed her a chunk of jerky.

Charisse soon saw Eli was right. By grabbing on to the

sagebrush, Sid began slowly hauling himself up the hill.

"You going to Oregon or California?"

"Oregon," Charisse said in surprise.

Eli sighed. "Me and Sid thought about going to California to see if we could strike it rich, but this is as far as we got."

"What exactly is it you do out here?"

He shrugged. "Work cattle, catch horses, whatever someone hires us to do."

Charisse blinked. "So, you were hired to kidnap me?"

"Yep." He looked at her. "It ain't personal, you know. Hell, I kinda like you. You're gutsy."

Charisse forced a smile. "Thank you. So… who hired you to kidnap me?"

"Fella by the name of Sam Jackson."

"What does he want with me?" Charisse couldn't imagine any reason anyone would want to kidnap her. There was no one who would pay a ransom.

"I never asked." He sighed. "It would've been better if the Indians had kept you, though."

Charisse was startled. "The Indians were Mr. Jackson's idea?"

"Nah, it was mine. Jackson just wants you out of the way. I figured you'd be safe with the Indians. Probably would've been a slave for a few months then one of them would've married you." He shrugged again. "Better than bein' dead." He grinned and pointed toward the slope below them. "Looks like Sid made it."

Charisse was thoughtful as Eli helped Sid up the hill. They were mere hirelings with no particular loyalty to the man who had hired them. Perhaps she'd be able to use that.

"She's a jinx, I tell you, Eli." Sid gasped as his brother pulled him into the shelter.

"Ain't no such thing," Eli said with disgust.

"Then how do you explain the stinging nettles?"

"Stupidity."

Charisse hid her smile by staring down at the bottom of the

gulch. Then she frowned. Surely that stream of water hadn't been there before. Something niggled at her mind, something she'd read in The Prairie Traveler.

"What about the mosquitoes, and the storm, and me falling down the hill?" Sid said.

Charisse surged to her feet. "Oh, my Lord! We've got to get out of here!"

"It's raining fit to drown a man," Eli pointed out.

"I know, that's why we have to leave. This gully is going to flood." Charisse pointed to the water in the bottom of the gulch. "That water has risen a good two feet in the last few minutes."

The men stared down at the rapidly growing stream. "It's only a little water," Eli said, "and it's a long way from reaching us."

"Fine, you stay. I'm getting to higher ground." Charisse began climbing the hill.

"You can't leave," Eli called after her. "You're our prisoner."

"Then you better come get me," she said under her breath, "because if I get to the horses first I'm leaving you both here."

The hill was so slippery she had to use her hands to get anywhere. By grabbing sagebrush when she could and sticking her hand into the mud when she couldn't, she managed to fight her way up the hill. She fell more than once but kept going until she finally crawled over the top. She lay on the ground gasping for breath as the rain pelted down on her.

After a few minutes, she sat up and listened. An unfamiliar roaring filled the air. With a feeling of dread, she got to her feet and peered over the edge of the gulch. The water had risen dramatically and roared down the gully like a rampaging river. The ledge had already disappeared.

Sid clung to a large sagebrush as the water swirled and eddied around him. It was only a matter of time before he would be swept away. Above him on the hill, Eli was caught in a dilemma. He could make it to safety or try to save Sid. If he did the latter, there was a good chance they would both die. If he didn't, Sid almost certainly would. Charisse was surprised to find it bothered her.

She pushed the thought away. This was her chance. She could take the horses and leave the brothers to their fate. Even if they did survive, they'd never catch her on foot. Then she remembered her conversation with Eli. He wasn't all bad, just misguided. "Damn," she muttered to herself. *Stupid conscience!*

The horses stood with their backs to the storm and had barely moved from where Eli left them. It only took a minute to remove the hobbles from the piebald gelding, then grab Sid's rope and loop it around the saddle horn. She led the horse over to the edge. "Here!" she yelled, tossing the coil of rope to Eli who had worked his way back down the hill. He looked up at her in surprise, then grabbed the rope and frantically started working the end of it.

The water had risen until the sagebrush Sid was holding onto had disappeared beneath the surface, and only his head was visible. As she watched, something gave way, and Sid swirled out into the stream with a frightened yell.

Charisse's stomach lurched and her hands flew to her mouth. Sid was going to drown right in front of her eyes. Much as she disliked the despicable little toad, she found she didn't want to watch him die. Suddenly a lasso sailed through the air and settled on the water in front of Sid. As he made a grab for it, Charisse snapped back to reality. She was wasting time here.

With one last look at the brothers, she turned and ran to the bay mare. Without a side-saddle, she had a difficult time mounting with her heavy, sodden skirts. She'd never ridden astride before and felt rather unstable as she turned the reluctant horse back the way they had come. As she urged her mount to move at a faster clip, she called herself seven kinds of an idiot for leaving the other horse. She'd probably thrown away her one chance at escape. Even so, she couldn't regret her choice.

Though the rain still poured down so heavily it veiled the hills across the valley, the clouds started to lift as the sun set.

They rose until a small ring of blue sky showed on the western horizon. The sunset reflected off the clouds, turning the whole sky a vivid red as the last rays of the sun shone through the rain, gilding everything with gold. As she rode, the beautiful shower of golden rain beneath reddish-pink sky seemed like a good omen. Perhaps it was God's way of telling her he was pleased with her decision. Now if she could just find a place to hide so the brothers couldn't find her, she might be pleased with it herself.

Charisse had ridden a couple of miles when the rain stopped, and she saw a cave in the rocky hill nearby. It probably wasn't much more than a hole back into the hill, but it looked large enough to conceal her and the horse. The shadows of night would do the rest. She turned the horse toward the cave with renewed hope. About fifty yards from the cave, the horse shied, and she nearly lost her hold. Charisse managed to get the animal under control, but it still seemed a tad skittish, as they continued on their way.

When they reached the bottom of the hill, Charisse dismounted and untied the bedroll from the back of the saddle. Suddenly, the horse snorted and reared, knocking her to the ground. Charisse was nearly trampled underfoot as the animal turned and fled into the gathering darkness.

Stunned, Charisse lay there for a moment, taking inventory of her body parts. She had a few scrapes and bruises, but nothing was broken. Gingerly, she sat up and looked around. The horse had disappeared, leaving her on foot.

Sid and Eli were surely searching for her by now and would be here soon. Her best bet was still to climb up to the cave and hide. The hill wasn't nearly as hard to navigate as the side of the gully had been, and she was soon safely inside. She wrinkled her nose at the heavy, slightly rancid odor that permeated the place, but wrapped up in the blanket and sat down to pass the interminable night.

Her shivering had just started when she heard a voice outside. "You may as well come out, Missy!" yelled Sid. "We know you're in there."

Charisse's stomach sank to her toes. They had found her!

"Damn it, Sid. What did you have to go and do that for? We could have snuck up on her." Eli sounded even more exasperated than usual.

Charisse was frantically trying to decide what to do when she heard an odd snuffling sound from the cave directly behind her. *What in the world? It must be some kind of animal.* She didn't know what it was, but she could tell it was big by the amount of noise it was making coming toward her. The noise of a small landslide of rocks and gravel clattering against the floor of the cave galvanized her into motion. Whatever it was, she had no intention of staying around to make its acquaintance. Charisse scrambled to her feet and dashed out of the cave.

"There she is," yelled Sid in jubilation. A second later his eyes widened in shock. "Holy hell, look at that!"

Charisse turned as a huge grizzly bear lumbered out of the cave and stood sniffing the wind. She froze as the huge head swiveled to look at her. A moment later she fumbled for her pocket. The tiny derringer felt ridiculously small in her hand as she brought it up and aimed for the bear's eye. Praying the powder wasn't wet, she held her breath and squeezed the trigger.

Even though she was expecting it, the blast made Charisse jump. The bear roared in pain and anger. As it pawed at its head, Charisse realized her one precious shot had done little more than anger the bear—and made it that much more dangerous. Panicking, she threw the derringer. She heard it hit with a solid thunk as she turned and ran.

CHAPTER 37

The sound of a shot from over the hill brought Luke up short. *What the hell? That's a small caliber*, he thought. *Charisse?* Deciding to investigate, he galloped to the top of the rise, and looked down on a scene of complete chaos. With her skirts hiked to her knees, Charisse was tearing down a hill just ahead of a huge grizzly. The bear was having trouble navigating the downhill slope but would easily catch up with her when they reached flat ground. Two men sat on horses at the base of the hill. For some reason, they hadn't pulled a gun to shoot the bear even though Charisse was running right toward them.

With his heart in his throat, Luke jerked his rifle from its scabbard and spurred his horse. Charisse didn't even slow down as she reached the bottom of the hill, but continued in a straight path toward the two men. She momentarily disappeared as she ran between the two horses and raced out across the prairie.

The bear followed her as far as the horses. Confronted by a new menace, he stood up on his hind legs and roared. The horses blew sky high. With snorts and high-pitched squeals, the terrified horses began rearing and pawing the air, trying to escape the huge predator. One of the men hit the ground, and his horse took off at a high lope in the opposite direction.

Charisse stopped and stood with her hands over her mouth as she watched the pandemonium she had wrought. She didn't realize the bear might still come for her. Luke wanted to yell at her to keep running, but he knew she'd never hear him.

Though he was probably still too far away to hit his target, Luke lifted his rifle, took aim, and shot. The noise brought Charisse's head around as he'd hoped it would. She took one look, lifted her skirts and ran straight for him.

Luke galloped toward her, the need to reach her blocking out any other consideration. And then he was there, sliding to a stop next to her, jumping to the ground and pulling her into his arms. He felt as if his heart might explode as he ran his hands over her, assuring himself she was all right.

"Oh, Luke," she sobbed into his chest.

"Shhh," he crooned. "I've got you now. You're safe." Over her shoulder he could see the two men riding double, hell bent for leather across the prairie, with the bear right behind them. The other horse was running just as fast in the opposite direction. Luke closed his eyes and pulled her closer, a feeling of fierce protectiveness surged through him. When her tears subsided at last, she wiped her eyes and then leaned her head against his chest.

He hugged her again. "I've been half crazy worrying about you."

"You got here just in time," she said. "I was about to be eaten by a bear."

He chuckled. "Looks to me like you had everything well in hand. I almost feel sorry for those two."

"Oh dear, I forgot all about them." Charisse turned to look behind her. "Oh my!"

Across the prairie Eli and Sid were still visible as they tried to outrun the giant predator.

"Do you think the bear will catch them?" Charisse asked.

"Probably not. He might be able to outrun the horse over a short distance, but he'll likely give up before long."

"Then we don't have time to deal with them." She waved her hand dismissively. "It was all a trick to get you away from the wagon train," she said. "Maybe we can get back in time."

"In time for what?"

"I thought you might know," she said. "I supposed it had to do with whatever you and Ben are up to. Where's Toby?"

The blood in his veins seemed to turn to ice water. He'd been so focused on Charisse that he hadn't even stopped to think about Caroline Simms and her wagon full of illegal guns. If Charisse was right, Toby was right in the middle of it. "Time to switch horses," he said. "Can you ride astride?"

"I managed earlier today when I stole Eli's horse."

Luke pulled the saddle off John's roan. "You stole his horse?"

"It seemed like a good idea at the time."

"You never cease to amaze me," Luke said. He threw the saddle up onto Adonis. "If I'd gotten here any later you'd have probably figured out how to get one of their rifles and hold them at gun point."

"Oh! I forgot my derringer."

"Your derringer?" He paused in the middle of tightening the cinch and looked at her again. "I'm almost afraid to ask."

"It's probably still up by the cave. I shot the bear, but it didn't do much good so I threw it at him."

"You tried to shoot a grizzly with your little popgun?" he asked faintly. "Did you actually think it would protect you from a bear?"

"All right, it probably wasn't all that smart, but it was all I could think of. And you're right, all it did was make him mad."

"It wasn't all wasted. I heard the shot and came to investigate. Otherwise I'd have ridden right by." He shuddered to think what would have happened if he had. Luke grinned suddenly. "I'm beginning to wonder what those two cowpokes would pay me to take you away. They might even top White Otter's tipi cover."

"Very funny! That reminds me. They were responsible for the Indians taking me. Eli said a man named Sam Jackson paid them to get rid of me."

"Sam Jackson?" Luke frowned as he remembered his encounter with the man at Platte Bridge Station. "That name mean anything to you?"

Charisse shook her head. "No, should it?"

"I don't know. Can you think of any reason why somebody would want you out of the way?"

"No. There's not a soul that cares anything about me one way or the other."

Mounted on fresh horses, they picked up her derringer and were on their way. By then Charisse's abductors and the bear had disappeared. Luke thought he probably should have gone after them, but Toby and whatever was going on back at the wagon train were far more important.

They stopped several hours later to eat a bite and rest the horses. Charisse was all for pushing on as soon as they could, but Luke hadn't slept a wink in the two days since he'd discovered Charisse was gone. He knew he was at the end of his endurance and needed sleep if he was going to be any good to anybody.

Luke rolled up in his blanket and lay down on the hard ground. Seconds later Charisse cuddled next to him, rolled in her own blanket.

When he woke, she was in his arms with her head tucked into the curve of his neck. It felt natural and right to wake next to her that way. He smiled down at her, wishing he could take time to savor the moment. But worry about his son and an overwhelming sense of urgency overrode the pleasure. When he kissed her awake, she smiled and stretched, soft and sexy. Luke would have liked nothing better than to take her up on her unconscious invitation, but he knew they didn't have time. Whatever Cassex and the rest had planned might already be happening.

Charisse watched as he saddled two horses. "I never asked where you got the extra horses."

"John Jessup."

"The Jessups came back to the wagon train?"

"No, I caught up with them about Split Rock. I thought that was where you went."

She gave him a dumbfounded look. "Whatever gave you that idea?"

"James Cassex said Morgan and the twins were sick and John had come to get you."

"That lying snake told me you needed me, and then delivered me straight into Eli's and Sid's hands!"

"I assume that's the two that were being chased by the bear. They're Sam Jackson's hired hands. He's apparently calling the shots. Did you happen to find out why he wants you?"

She shook her head. "All I know is what I heard when James Cassex turned me over to them. It sounded as if they had two different bosses who had struck a bargain. Cassex said he'd send you off in the wrong direction to give Eli and Sid a two-day head start, and then it was up to them to keep you busy for another day at least. But I don't know why."

"They want me gone because I'm sticking my nose where they don't want it," Luke said, tightening the cinch on her horse. "What about you?"

"No idea."

He put the stirrup down and glanced over his shoulder at her. "Do you stand to inherit anything?"

She shook her head. "I already inherited everything I'm ever going to. Since I'm a woman, Preston got it all, except a small jointure from my grandmother that he couldn't touch."

Luke boosted her up into the saddle. "You're sure there wasn't anything else?"

"Positive. Anybody who wanted my inheritance would have to go after Preston."

He sighed. There was only one more thing he could think of. "What about your daughter?"

Charisse stiffened. "What about her?"

"How did she die?"

"Diphtheria," she said in a strangled voice. "It was her tenth birthday. Annabelle wanted a big party, so we invited everyone she knew. Her best friend, Charlotte, came down with diphtheria the very next day." Charisse's eyes filled with anguish and tears. "They all got it, Luke, every single child at that damnable party, and four of them d-died."

"God, Charisse. I'm sorry."

"They all blamed me, even Charlotte's mother, and I didn't

care. All I could think of was my sweet little girl and how very sick she was. When she died in my arms, I wanted to die too."

He reached up and gripped her hand, wishing he could take the pain from her. "Was anybody mad enough to want revenge?"

"Two years later in the middle of the wilderness?" Charisse gave a small laugh. "None of them would waste the energy. Besides, my divorce was revenge enough. As far as those people are concerned, I'm dead."

There seemed no reply to that.

When they reached the wagon train, the camp looked as it always did shortly after dawn: all the wagons were circled with the livestock safely corralled inside. Luke stopped atop a small rise and surveyed the bucolic scene with narrowed eyes. "Something doesn't feel right," he said.

"Nobody's cooking breakfast," Charisse said suddenly, "and none of the campfires are burning."

"You're right. We'd better picket the horses where no one can see them," he said as they turned and rode back down the hill. "Then I'll go in on foot."

"We'll *both* go in on foot," she corrected him.

"It will probably be dangerous."

"So? Those are my friends in there, Luke McCabe, and the closest thing I have to a family. You can leave me here if you want, but I'll just follow you."

He took in the stubborn tilt of her jaw and sighed. "All right—but you'll do as I say, understand?"

She nodded. "Of course. You know what you're doing."

"I wish I was sure of that."

The horses were soon safely hidden behind a large outcropping, and Luke and Charisse began their approach. Though a sense of urgency drove them, they worked their way around the camp, getting the lay of the land. Dempsey seemed to be the only guard. Luke gestured for Charisse to stay in the shadows as he sneaked up behind the man and easily overpowered him. They left him behind, bound and gagged, then moved closer to the camp. They crept in from the north through a small depression in the earth and lay on the ground between Duncan's wagon and their own.

It was immediately clear why there was none of the usual early morning activity around camp. The livestock had been pushed to one side of the enclosure and were milling around. There was no sign of Caroline, Toby or Franklin, but Pierre Jeveraux, the Duncans, and the Swindells were bound and tied in a group next to one of Swindell's wagons. They were all still in nightclothes as though the camp had been roused during the night. The men sported a variety of cuts and bruises, and the women looked mussed, as though they had been manhandled. It appeared none of them had been captured easily. Nugent, Snyder and Cassex stood guard over them all, though their attention—like everyone else's—was fixed on the center of the encampment and the drama taking place there.

Ben Baxter stood with his hands tied behind his back, barefooted, bare-chested, and covered with bloody weals. His nemesis walked briskly back and forth, flicking a lethal-looking quirt. There was no doubt that the quirt had caused most of Ben's injuries, just as there was suddenly no doubt who the mastermind behind the whole operation was. And Luke could hardly believe his eyes.

CHAPTER 38

"You know, Mr. Baxter, being stubborn isn't going to get you anywhere." Mrs. Mantella's voice was almost gentle. "Who do you and McCabe work for?"

"I keep telling you, I don't work for anybody except Captain Jeveraux, and the only thing I know about Luke McCabe is that he hired me to drive his wagon."

The quirt cut across his shoulder with a vicious slash. "The next one will be across your face," she snarled.

Mrs. Mantella looked years younger. Gone was the stooped, frail body. Instead of hobbling, she strode, and her feeble voice was strong and vigorous. The change was so complete, it was hard to believe it was the same person.

"If you think I will let you destroy everything my husband worked for, you're sadly mistaken," she said, glaring at Ben. "He was a true patriot and this, his last great plan, will win back what was stolen from us."

"Oh, hell," Luke murmured under his breath. "Roberto Mantella! How did we miss it?"

"Who?" Charisse asked.

"Roberto Mantella was a general during the Mexican War. When Mexico lost, it ceded its northern territory to the United States. A lot of folks living there still think it should be part of Mexico. Unless I miss my guess, Mantella's land was part of Mexico's concessions in the peace treaty, and that's his widow." Luke pursed his lips to warble out the call of the meadowlark, counted to ten, and then called again.

"Do you know how to use this?" Luke whispered, patting his rifle.

Charisse nodded. "I'm not very accurate, though."

"Doesn't matter. Ben knows we're here, and he's going to distract them while I go get help. Your job is to make sure he stays alive. Understand?"

Charisse stared at Luke in disbelief. "You think he can distract them?"

"I know he can. If you have to use that, shoot to kill."

"You're leaving?"

"Don't have a choice. I'm a little outnumbered." He nodded toward the inside of the circle where Cassex, Snyder, and Nugent were standing with their backs to the prisoners. "I need to get things set up a bit more in my favor."

Luke gave Charisse a quick kiss, then left her there, hidden behind a box under a wagon, hoping, he was sure, that she wouldn't have to shoot anybody. While he crept along the backside of the wagons, he considered his options. What he needed was a diversion—something to keep the guard's attention away from the prisoners.

"Luke!" Caroline whispered as she slipped around the back of her wagon, and grabbed his arm, the frantic expression on her face emphasized by swollen red eyes and tear-stained cheeks. "Thank heavens you're here!"

"Where's Toby?" he asked in a sharp whisper.

"Still asleep in my wagon. This morning, Franklin wouldn't let them in, so they left him alone."

"You're sure he's safe?"

"Positive. I checked him right after Franklin bit James Cassex. Toby just smiled and went back to sleep. I don't think he fully woke up." She tightened her grasp on his arm. "Luke, you have to save Ben!"

"What's going on?"

"Robbie found Ben just before dawn and started beating the daylights out of him. The noise woke everyone else and when the Swindells and Captain Jeveraux tried to stop it, his mother ordered her men to round everybody up and tie them to the wagon. She's been interrogating Ben ever since."

"Why?"

"At first I thought it was because they found him outside my tent." She bit her lip. "We'd been...together."

Her blush said more eloquently than words what they had been doing. Damn, what had Ben been thinking? He wasn't above using seduction to find out what he wanted to know, but not with someone like Caroline, and he never became so involved he got careless.

"Robbie's very protective of me, and I thought that was why he was upset, but then Tía Lucia started asking all kinds of strange questions."

"Tía Lucia?"

"Lucia Mantella is my tía — it means aunt in Spanish — and Robbie is my cousin. Look, I know this is all very confusing, but I don't have time to explain right now. They're going to kill Ben if you don't do something!"

Luke wondered if he could trust her. She was untied, which meant the guards hadn't considered her a threat. On the other hand, she was clearly distraught. If it was an act, then she was as talented an actress as ever graced the stage. The biggest factor in her favor was that she hadn't revealed his presence. "I think I can get him out, but I need a distraction."

"A distraction?"

"Something to keep their attention away from the wagons." Caroline looked thoughtful. "For how long?"

"As long as we can manage."

"All right, I'll do my best."

"Good girl. Get that diversion going as soon as you can." Caroline nodded and disappeared.

Luke crept underneath the wagon to where Jesse Swindell was tied to the wagon wheel. "Jesse, it's Luke." he said quietly as he touched the other man's shoulder. "Don't say anything — just listen." Luke explained the plan. The milling oxen provided a perfect cover for any noise he might make, though Mrs. Mantella was so intent on interrogating Ben, Luke questioned whether she would have noticed him anyway.

Ben was doing his best to hold everyone's attention, but it

was hard to say how much more abuse he could take. Lucia Mantella was becoming more agitated by the moment.

"Why were you snooping around last night?" she demanded, swishing her quirt menacingly.

"I wasn't snooping. I was out taking a walk."

"Without your boots?"

"I wasn't going that far."

This time the quirt sang through the air and slashed down across his face. Ben fell to his knees with a groan. "All right," he murmured. "I'll tell you what you want to hear."

"Good!" Mrs. Mantella stepped back. Luke could hear the self-satisfaction in her voice.

After a moment, Ben looked up at her through bleary eyes. "Well?"

"Well what?"

"What is it you want me to say? Tell me what you want, and I'll say it."

She backhanded him and knocked him flat on the ground. "Get him up," she barked.

Robbie Mantella grabbed Ben by the shoulders and jerked him to his feet. "Want me to take care of him, Madre?"

"Nooo!" Caroline ran past Mrs. Mantella, and dropped to her knees beside Ben. "Please, Tía. He can't tell you any more because he didn't do whatever it is you think he did. He's trying to protect me."

Mrs. Mantella raised her brows. "Protect you from what?"

"He...he was with me." Caroline looked down. "That's why he was at my tent, and why he isn't wearing any boots. He doesn't know anything about... about the secret cargo in my wagon."

Mrs. Mantella frowned. "What are you talking about?"

Caroline gave her a wry smile. "Tía, please. You aren't the only one in the family with brains. Your guards have been with that wagon since we left Independence. I knew there was something going on from the beginning. After I realized Robbie had killed Joshua, I decided to see what he had hidden that was important enough to die for." She shook her head. "But Ben doesn't know anything about it. He came to see me, and..." She trailed off and hung her head again.

"Your husband is barely cold in his grave, and you gave yourself to another man?"

"Joshua was your choice for me. Ben is mine." She looked up. "I'm not ashamed of what I did."

"You little fool. I suppose you even thought he was falling in love with you." Mrs. Mantella gave a derisive laugh. "He's been using you. All he cares about is finding out what's in your wagon."

"Don't listen to her, Caroline!" Ben called out. "I didn't— umph!" Robbie's fist plowed into his gut, and Ben crumpled to the ground again.

"Think about it," Lucia continued. "He spent every night playing poker at your wagon and never paid you a bit of attention until after Joshua died. You're an idiot if you think he loves you."

"That's not true. I—"

Caroline winced as Robbie gave Ben a hard kick and he curled into a fetal position on the ground. Then she stiffened her spine and lifted her chin. "It doesn't matter. He saved my life, and I won't let you kill him. You owe me, and now I'm calling it in."

"You're what?" Mrs. Mantella's voice held a note of disbelief.

"You heard me." Caroline stood up and brushed off the front of her dress.

"Our deal was for your father's land."

"No, our deal was that if I married Joshua Simms and convinced him to play your game, you would give me what I wanted. I've changed my mind about keeping the ranch. Ben is what I want now."

Mrs. Mantella stared at her. "If I let Baxter live, you'll walk away from your father's ranch?"

Caroline shrugged. "As you have pointed out over and

over, it was my grandfather's ranch first, and if your sister hadn't married my greedy gringo father, it would have been yours."

"You're willing to give it up for a man who doesn't love you?"

"Give me two horses so we can ride out of here, and I'll sign the deed over to you right here and now."

"What about when he laughs in your face and walks away? You'll come crawling back to your family then."

"Even if I did, you'd still have my father's ranch—which is all you care about anyway. Even the revolution is secondary to that."

Mrs. Mantella drew herself up to her full height. "You know nothing about it," she said indignantly. "The revolution was my dear Roberto's final wish. He died a broken man, deserted by the country he loved."

"The truth is, General Montoya promised you my father's ranch if the revolution is successful," Caroline said.

Mrs. Mantella smirked. "Then I'll get it anyway, won't I?"

"No, because if you don't give me what I want, I'll marry General Montoya's good friend Señor Flores, and you'll never get your hands on the ranch. It will be divided up between Manuel's five sons."

The smile disappeared from the widow's face. "You'd never marry Manuel Flores! You refused his suit out of hand. What was it she said, Robbie?"

"That she wouldn't marry him if he was the last man on Earth." He looked at Caroline with guileless blue eyes. "Don't you remember, Caro? You said he was old and smelled of garlic."

"That was before your madre married me to that slimy toad, Joshua Simms. Compared to him, Señor Flores is a prince."

"You cried when Joshua died," Robbie pointed out.

"Only because of you, dearest. It was what your madre made you do that made me cry." She turned back to Mrs.

Mantella. "That's the worst of what you've done. How could you turn your own son into a murderer?"

Mrs. Mantella shrugged. "It isn't murder — it's patriotism. I only have him take care of enemies of the revolution."

Caroline gave a humorless laugh. "Enemies of the revolution? Joshua was your partner, or have you forgotten the Confederacy? How are you going to explain killing their representative?"

"Our alliance will not be affected," Mrs. Mantella said with a toss of her head. "The wheels are already set in motion in Georgia, just as they will be here as soon as General Montoya arrives."

Luke never lost track of the scene taking place in the center of the wagon ring as, one by one, he set the four men free. Any sound they made was effectively covered by the nearby cattle, and the guards were so involved in Caroline's interaction with her aunt they never spared a glance for their prisoners. Jesse Swindell was able to retrieve the two rifles they kept under the seat of their extra wagon. Then he and his brother went to guard the road while Pierre Jeveraux and Henry Duncan set about freeing the women.

That left Toby and Franklin. Simms' wagon was on the far side of the wagon circle, and everyone except Caroline was facing the other direction. With any kind of luck, they'd stay that way. Luke cautiously made his way around the circle. He couldn't shake the feeling that all eyes were upon him, but reached Caroline's wagon without incident.

"Toby," he whispered, "It's me."

"Pa?" Toby's voice was very quiet, and Luke could hear him moving inside the wagon. He touched the canvas and felt the imprint of his son's hand against his palm almost immediately. "I'm here, son. We need to get you out of there," Luke whispered. "I'm going to make sure it's safe, then I'll be back to get you and Franklin."

"Ok," Toby whispered with a slight quaver in his voice.

Luke knelt out of sight next to the wagon wheel, and peered

at the tableau near the center of the wagon circle. Little had changed except Mrs. Mantella seemed to be ranting about the future of the revolution. He hoped Ben was able to take it all in. It would probably solve their entire investigation for them.

Luke pulled his knife as he rose to his feet. It only took a few moments to cut the rope that tied down the wagon's canvas cover and pull it out of the way. Toby was waiting right inside with Franklin plastered to his side as though guarding him from any danger that might present itself.

"Pa," Toby said, hugging his father for all he was worth. "Oh, Pa, I was so scared."

Luke buried his face in his son's neck. "Me too, son." He took a deep breath and raised his head. "All right. We'll have to take Franklin out first, then you," Luke whispered. "Can you lift him up to me?"

"I think so." Toby put his arms around Franklin's middle and grunted as he hefted the dog as high as he could. "He's really heavy, Pa."

Luke reached over the side and took the dog from Toby's arms. "I've got him." He resisted the urge to grunt himself, as he lifted the surprisingly substantial dog over the edge and set him on the ground. Franklin sat by the wheel and watched Luke lift Toby down too. Then Luke commandeered enough guns from the wagon to double arm everyone. In all, the whole process only took a few minutes, but it seemed much longer to Luke. The women were gone, hopefully already hidden in the rocky outcropping where he and Charisse had left their horses.

Luke was taking Toby to them when Jesse Swindell caught up with him.

"I stopped two riders," he said. "They claim they want to talk to Charisse or the man who rescued her."

Oh, great. It was probably the messenger McNesby said was coming to find Charisse—just what they needed right now. "Where are they?" Luke asked.

"Waiting about three hundred yards from camp, around the corner, out of sight."

Luke nodded. "All right, take Toby to the women, and I'll go see what they want." He made sure his rifle was loaded and that he had extra ammunition. But when he rounded the corner he stopped in surprise. He'd only seen them from a distance, but the piebald horse one rode was unmistakable. It was the two men who had abducted Charisse. Luke lifted his rifle and pointed it at them.

"If you boys have any intelligence at all, you'll ride out of here and forget you ever heard of Charisse."

"You the one who rescued her?" asked the taller one.

"Yes, and I'll kill you before I let anyone touch my wife again. You can take that message to your boss."

"She's your wife?"

"Damn right she is!"

The man nodded in satisfaction. "See, Sid, I told you he'd be willing to pay."

"Ain't said he would," Sid pointed out. "This is plumb crazy, Eli. Let's ride out of here while we still can."

"Pay for what?" Luke demanded.

"The man who hired us to kidnap your wife."

Luke raised his eye from the rifle sight. "What?"

"For two hundred dollars, we'll deliver Sam Jackson."

Luke raised his eyebrows. "You're willing to switch sides for two hundred dollars?"

"We sort'a figure since this is the second time we lost the woman, he ain't likely to come through with the money he owes us. That and the fact we figure we owe you and the missus both."

"Why's that?"

"She saved Sid from drowning by throwing us a rope, and you killed the bear."

"I didn't kill the bear."

"Not outright, but you nicked it on the neck, and it bled to death. If you hadn't shot him, he'd a killed us when the horse bucked us off."

Sid glowered. "I still say we was jinxed."

"Don't mind him," Eli said. "He's just sour because the bear fell on him when it died."

Luke blinked. "And now you want to work for me?"

Eli shrugged. "We spent most of the summer working for Jackson and ain't seen a dime. I figure this is the only way to make it pay."

They weren't exactly a trustworthy pair. On the other hand, Luke wasn't one to overlook an opportunity when one presented itself. "So, for two hundred dollars, you'll deliver Sam Jackson to me?"

"That's right."

"Would you be willing to do another little service for me if I paid you an extra hundred?"

Eli's eyes took on a distinct gleam as he grinned from ear to ear. "For three hundred dollars, we'll kill him for you if that's what you want!"

Luke gave a slow smile. "All I need you to do is cause a little diversion."

CHAPTER 39

Conscious of the weight of the rifle in her hands and the responsibility Luke had firmly set on her shoulders, Charisse hadn't moved since she'd hidden beneath the wagon. But, like the guards, she hung on Caroline's every word, unable to believe what she was hearing, as Caroline faced her aunt.

"Just think of it, Tía. For two horses, you'll get two thousand acres of prime ranch land," Caroline reminded her aunt.

Mrs. Mantella appeared to consider it for several long minutes, then nodded. "All right, I'll give you Baxter and the horses, but you can't leave until General Montoya arrives with the Indian chiefs. I don't want anything ruining the gun transfer."

"You're selling guns to the Indians?" Caroline's shock was evident in her voice. "That's treason!"

"Only if you are an American. I am a citizen of Mexico, and this is war. The unfriendly tribes I've supplied with rifles will keep the army busy, and when the South secedes, so do we." Mrs. Mantella gave her niece a smug look. "The United States won't have enough men to fight wars on all three fronts. Our success is assured."

"I think you're underestimating the United States army. You'll be out-gunned and out-manned."

"We might be out-manned, but we won't be out-gunned." Mrs. Mantella smiled an evil smile. "That was your dear departed husband's job. He diverted shipments of rifles that were destined for the western forts and falsified the records. The government will send men out here to fight, thinking there are plenty of weapons for them."

"But there won't be because you gave them to the Indians," Caroline murmured.

"Exactly," Mrs. Mantella said triumphantly. "The United States will be defeated before they can unravel the mess Joshua made of things. They won't even be able to find their supplies, which are scattered from Canada to Texas. Joshua even made sure lead for bullets and gunpowder went in opposite directions."

"And when it's all over? What then? Your little country won't be big enough to support itself."

Mrs. Mantella shrugged. "We won't have to. Mexico will annex us as soon as we've won our independence. General Montoya already has that promise."

"Mexico will risk another war with the United States?"

"The United States will be too busy fighting a civil war with the South to take on Mexico."

Caroline shook her head in wonder. "You really have this all planned out, don't you?"

"Roberto had it planned. I just put it together."

"What about the deaths of George Bartell and Joshua? Even revolutionaries take a dim view of murder."

"They were executed, not murdered. George was clumsy and alerted Luke McCabe, and Joshua got greedy. He was responsible for the loss of three full boxes of rifles and the defection of a small army who had agreed to keep the soldiers from Platte Bridge Station busy."

"Riders coming in!" Cassex called out.

Mrs. Mantella smiled with satisfaction. "General Montoya is two hours early. All the better."

When Eli and Sid rode in, Charisse felt her stomach dropped to her toes. What were they doing here? Suddenly, her gaze snapped back to the wagons. The prisoners were gone! All three of the guards were as oblivious as she had been. Like her, their eyes had been focused on the players in center ring.

"Did General Montoya send you?" Mrs. Mantella asked as

the two men rode up.

"No," said Cassex, "These are the men who took care of the McCabe problem."

Mrs. Mantella raised her eyebrows. "Then why are you here?"

"Our boss thought you might like to know what happened," Sid said with a sullen look at his brother.

"Well?"

"McCabe is dead," Eli said. "And so is that wife of his."

Caroline gasped. "Oh, Tía," she said. "What have you done?"

Mrs. Mantella shrugged. "It was a business proposition. I met a man who wanted Charisse, and was willing to take out McCabe in the process."

A frisson of awareness skittered through Charisse. Sam Jackson, whoever he is. What in the world does he want with me, and how is that connected to all this? She was still trying to make sense of it when Luke slipped in beside her.

"We're all set," he whispered. "We got everybody out."

"Where's Toby?"

"With the other women, back where it's safe. It's time for you to go there, too."

"I don't think so. Caroline and Ben need me."

Luke sighed. "I don't suppose it would do any good to point out that my son needs you too."

"Nope. Sadie and Violet will keep him under control, and Franklin will protect him better than I could."

"I was afraid of that." He handed her his shot bag and powder horn. "Do you know how to load that gun?"

"Is it like my derringer?"

"Yes."

"Then yes, I can load it, but I'm really slow."

"Then stay back and make that one shot count. All the men are armed and have a prearranged target. When I give the signal, we're going to charge from all sides. I'm going to get Ben. You cover me. Understand?"

"Yes." She frowned. "But what about Eli and Sid?"

"As long as the money holds out, they're on our side. We needed another distraction, so I paid them to ride in and report us dead. Caroline drew it out as long as she could, but I figured she'd about reached her limit."

Charisse was shocked. "You sent her in there?"

"She volunteered. I had no idea what she was going to do. I was as surprised as you were."

"Then your world tipped on its side, too?"

He smiled. "That pretty much describes it. You ready?"

Charisse swallowed hard and nodded.

"For luck!" he said, as he leaned over to give her a quick kiss. Then he turned away, pursed his lips and cooed like a dove.

For luck. Charisse was still basking in the unexpected glow of Luke's words when she saw Ben tense, as though bracing himself.

"Six, seven, eight, nine, ten," Luke said under his breath, then jumped to his feet as all hell broke loose on the other side of the camp.

Surrounded by the sound of gunfire and the smell of black powder, Charisse focused on Luke and Ben, steeling herself to shoot Robbie Mantella if she had to. She needn't have worried. As soon as the commotion began, Ben uncoiled from his fetal position like a spring. His leg flashed out and swept Robbie's feet out from under him. He went down like a felled oak.

By the time Robbie had struggled to his feet, Luke had cut Ben loose. They both tackled the giant again. This time when he went down, he stayed down.

The whole fight was over in a matter of minutes. Sid and Eli were binding Mrs. Mantella, though she was screeching at them like a banshee. Cassex, Nugent and Snyder lay on the ground, their blood soaking into the dirt. Luke went to see if the guards were dead and to collect their weapons, while Charisse went to get Toby and the women.

By the time everyone returned to camp, Mrs. Mantella and

her hulking son were tied to their wagon much as they had done to the others. Cassex was still alive, but barely. Eli and Sid were digging graves in the soft dirt next to the trail for Snyder and Nugent.

"You fools," hissed Mrs. Mantella. "You haven't won. General Montoya and his army will be here with our Indian allies to pick up those guns. There's no way you can fight them all."

"She's right, you know," Luke said to the group gathered inside the wagon circle. "We need to figure out what to do."

"Why don't we leave?" suggested Jesse. "There are five wagon trains within two days of us on either side. They won't know which one to stop."

Luke shook his head. "They'll stop and search them all if they have to. There are several hundred guns in Caroline's wagon." Gasps and murmurs of surprise rose from the members of the wagon train.

"How far are we from Fort Bridger, Pierre?" Luke asked.

The Frenchman looked thoughtful. "I'd say a week at least. There's no way we can outrun them. Men on horseback could make the same trip in two or three days."

Lucia Mantella laughed. "Why don't you give up and surrender? You don't stand a chance against an army. You'll all die." A crafty light entered her eyes. "But if you leave the guns and ammunition here they will have no reason to follow you."

"I think Mrs. Mantella is right." said Charisse. "We'll leave the guns here."

"Charisse—" Luke began.

"No, hear me out. This will work. They won't follow us if they have their guns, right? What if we disable the guns somehow? They won't know until they go to use them, and by then we'll be to Fort Bridger."

The men exchanged looks. "You know," said Jeveraux, "that just might work. But how do we disable them? Most parts are interchangeable on army rifles. They'll just replace what doesn't work."

Ben nodded. "And if we tamper with the sights they'll know immediately."

"Pour melted lead down the barrel," Caroline said suddenly. "When Robbie and I were little, we did that to one of my uncle's rifles. We ruined it completely and couldn't sit down for a week."

Luke raised his eyebrows. "And there wouldn't be any sign of tampering. Simple, but effective. Mrs. Mantella said they'd be here in about two hours, right?"

"I'm not sure," said Caroline. "Her men were coming to unload the guns when they caught Ben, just before dawn."

"Where were they taking them?" Luke asked.

"I don't know," said Caroline, "but it couldn't have been too far away. They weren't planning on taking the wagon."

Luke glanced at Lucia Mantella. "She'll never tell us the pick-up point."

"No," said Caroline, "but Robbie might."

"Robbie doesn't know!" hissed Mrs. Mantella. "He's too feeble-minded to understand what I was saying even if I were stupid enough to tell him."

Caroline gave an inarticulate cry and ran to him. "Don't listen to her, Robbie." She stroked his arm comfortingly and she gave her aunt an angry look. "Why do you say things like that, Tía? You know it hurts him."

Lucia just shrugged and turned away.

The men searched Mantella's wagon until they found the lead. As they built up the fire and began melting the metal, Caroline knelt next to her cousin, trying to discover what he might know. "Do you know where you were going to take the rifles?" she asked.

He nodded. "A safe place."

"Think Robbie, did you hear them say where the safe place was?"

Robbie frowned as though he were concentrating very hard. Finally he shook his head sadly. "I don't know."

Caroline hugged him. "It's all right, sweetheart." She

dropped a kiss on his forehead and joined the others. "Tía Lucia told the truth. Robbie didn't know where he was supposed to take the guns."

Ben ran his hand through his hair. "If we leave them in the wrong place, Montoya won't find them, and they'll come after us."

"What if we took the guns to them?" Charisse said. "We could load everything in a wagon and go out to meet them."

Henry Duncan nodded his head. "And if we say there is cholera on the wagon train, they won't even think of following us."

"Won't they be expecting her to be with us?" Pierre nodded toward Mrs. Mantella. "They'll be suspicious of any deviation of the plan."

"Not if I'm with whoever goes," Caroline said. "General Montoya knows me."

"Hmph! He also knows I don't trust you as far as I can throw you." Mrs. Mantella said scornfully. "You're wasting your time."

"She could be right," Caroline admitted. "I was never included in any of the planning."

"Would they accept a note from Mrs. Mantella if they thought she was too ill to come herself?" Henry asked thoughtfully.

"Probably," Caroline said, "but they've been corresponding for months. He'd be sure to recognize her writing."

Silence fell as they all considered her words.

"It's time to start hauling out guns," Pierre said finally. " The lead is nearly melted."

As the others moved toward the Simms' wagon, Henry took Eliza's hand and squared his shoulders. "Luke, Ben, Mrs. Simms, if I might speak with you alone for a moment..."

Caroline, Luke and Ben exchanged puzzled looks, but walked away from the others with him.

When they were alone, Henry turned to Caroline. "Do you

have a sample of your aunt's writing?"

"I know where her journal is."

"Oh, Henry, no!" Eliza cried. "It's not worth it."

He lifted her hand and kissed her knuckles. "Eliza, my darling, don't you see? It may be the only time in my life that it is worth it. For once I'll be using my talent for good."

"But we don't really know who they are," she said in a low voice as she glanced toward Luke and Ben. "What if they arrest you?"

"I'm not doing anything illegal." He shrugged. "Besides, I'm not going to spend the rest of my life running every time I see a police officer." He looked at Luke and Ben. "I don't think they're policemen, anyway."

Luke shook his head. "No. We have temporary jurisdiction to make arrests, but you're not part of our investigation. If you have something you can contribute, we'd appreciate it."

Henry nodded. "I can write a letter to General Montoya in Mrs. Mantella's handwriting."

"Forgery?" Luke said in surprise.

"It was a sideline."

"A sideline to what?"

"Counterfeiting."

"You're a counterfeiter?"

"Former. I've given it up." He smiled fondly at Eliza. "I found something more important in life."

Ben looked thunderstruck. "You're Henry Holland!"

"You've heard of me?" Henry asked in surprise.

"Heard of you! My, God! Luke, don't you remember the Boston counterfeiting ring they busted up about ten years ago? He's the best there is!"

Luke looked at Henry with dawning respect. "They couldn't tell your bills from the real thing. If it hadn't been for someone turning you in, they'd have never caught you."

Eliza straightened her spine. "That was me, and he's served his time!"

Henry smiled. "Eliza waited ten long years for me to get

out." He took in their stunned expressions and shrugged. "She said she loved me too much to let me remain a criminal. When my old colleagues showed up and tried to force me back into the business, she's the one that came up with the idea of posing as brother and sister and leaving everything behind."

"So, you can forge a convincing letter for us, then?"

"Find me some of Mrs. Mantella's handwriting, and I'll give you a letter so perfect even she wouldn't be able to tell she hadn't written it."

Luke looked thoughtful. "You know, Ben, maybe Henry should take a look at the map, too."

"That's not a bad idea. We can leave a copy of it hidden under the water barrel for Montoya and take the original back to McNesby."

Luke smiled. "That's what I was thinking. Caroline, I'd appreciate it if you could get Henry that journal and some paper."

"I'll get the map, and then help him compose the letter," said Ben.

By the time Luke rejoined the others, they had fallen into a routine. Violet and Sadie dipped molten lead out of the pot and poured it down the gun barrels as the others moved the rifles to the two women and back to the side of the wagon where they leaned the worthless weapons to cool.

They were about half finished when Ben called out, "Stop right there!" As one, everyone by the wagon turned and gasped.

Though Luke couldn't tell how, Mrs. Mantella and Robbie were both free and Ben Baxter held them at gun point with only Charisse's derringer.

"Kill him, Robbie!" Mrs. Mantell shouted.

Robbie took a step forward, knocked the gun from Ben's hand, and grabbed him around the throat.

"Robbie, no!" Caroline screamed. "Don't hurt him!"

"Don't listen to her," Mrs. Mantella yelled. "Kill him!"

The big man looked back and forth between them,

confusion written across his face.

Caroline grabbed his arm. "Please, Robbie, I love him."

He looked down at her tear-streaked face, then loosened his hold.

"Roberto Carlos Mantella, don't you dare let him go!" his mother snapped. "He's going to take everything away from us."

Robbie frowned, then smashed a fist into Ben's jaw. Ben crumpled to the ground and Caroline rushed to his side.

"It's all right, Caro," said Robbie. "He isn't dead. I just made him go to sleep."

Before Caroline could respond, Lucia Mantella grabbed her by the hair, and jerked her to her feet. Caroline's scream was cut short by the knife her aunt held to her throat.

"Tía!" Caroline whispered.

"Don't call me 'Aunt,' you little traitor. I've hated you since the day you were born, whole and perfect. My son was born first—he should have been the heir. The minute Papa saw you he forgot all about Robbie."

"That isn't true," Caroline cried. "Grandpapa loved him! He always said Robbie was a special gift that—"

"Shut up!" Mrs. Mantella pressed the knife tighter against Caroline's throat. A spot of blood appeared where the sharp blade nicked the skin. "I've waited years for this. I'm going to cut your throat and watch you bleed to death in the dirt."

Mrs. Mantella was suddenly jerked off her feet and whirled around. "You don't hurt Caro," Robbie said angrily. "You don't hurt her!"

Mrs. Mantella thrust the knife at Robbie just as he squeezed his hands around her neck. The sickening sound of snapping bones could be heard all around the camp. Mrs. Mantella gave an odd gurgle, then slipped from her son's hands to the ground. At first, Robbie stood there staring down at the knife protruding from his chest, then he too crumpled to the earth.

"Oh, no, no, no!" Caroline fell to her knees beside Robbie and felt frantically for a pulse. Pierre Jeveraux finally stepped forward and examined both bodies. Then he looked back at the other members of the wagon train and shook his head. "They're both dead," he said in a solemn voice.

The sound of Caroline's sobs filled the dusty summer air.

CHAPTER 40

"No sign of them yet?" Violet asked, coming to stand next to Charisse by the road.

Charisse shook her head. "But Luke said it might be after dark. I'm sure they'll be here soon." She sighed. "Did you and Eliza finish laying the Mantellas out?"

"Yes."

"The graves are dug. Do you think we should wait until Caroline gets back or bury them now?"

"It's hard to know, isn't it? I can't think she'd care much about her aunt, but she seemed awfully fond of Robbie."

"I know. Almost like he was her brother."

Violet sighed. "Five graves in one day. It's kind of odd. Every other wagon train has been beset by sickness and accidents since the beginning, and we've been traveling under a lucky star. Now this."

"I know. It's a good thing we're close to Fort Bridger. Our train never was very big, but it's dwindling fast."

They glanced at each other, neither saying what was on her mind. If their plan didn't work, they'd be short three more members of their party. They looked toward the road, searching the distance, but there was still no sign of Luke, Ben, or Caroline.

While the rifles were being disabled, Eliza, Charisse and Toby had sabotaged the gun powder by dumping one quarter of each barrel and mixing the remaining powder with sand. Then, as soon as they'd reloaded everything in Caroline's wagon, Luke, Ben and Caroline had left, traveling east to meet General Montoya.

The rest of them had buried Snyder, Nugent, and Cassex in

the graves Eli and Sid had dug, then loaded up their wagons and pushed on to the west with all the speed they could muster. They hadn't taken time to dig additional graves for the Mantellas in their rush to get away. Even Dempsey, who seemed terrified of having to explain to General Montoya why he was the only survivor, was anxious to put as much distance between them as possible. Sid and Eli had disappeared by then, but only Charisse noticed.

They had made camp far later than usual. Violet and Eliza had prepared the Mantellas for burial while the men dug the graves. Now they waited, unsure what Caroline would want to do when she arrived, if she ever did.

In the end, Pierre made the decision, saying it was his job as captain. Lucia and Robbie Mantella were buried in two unmarked graves next to the trail. No one was inclined to say anything over them, leaving the actual funeral until morning if Caroline was so inclined.

It was full dark before anyone got around to thinking of supper. No one seemed to want to be alone. By tacit agreement, they lit a large fire in the middle of the camp and huddled together in its cheery light while the men took turns standing guard. Charisse sat with Toby cuddled up against her and Franklin at her feet. Eliza and Sadie filled their Dutch ovens with biscuits and buried them in the coals. As everyone waited, they passed around hard tack and jerky and told stories of their lives before, trying to ignore their unease and the fact that more than two thirds of their number was missing.

The Dutch ovens were pulled from the coals, and the first one opened. The delicious smell of baked biscuits was still wafting through the air when Frank Swindell yelled, "Riders coming in!"

They all exchanged a look. Charisse gripped the derringer in her pocket, and Pierre reached for his rifle.

A moment later, everyone gave a glad cry as Ben, Caroline, and Luke rode into camp. Before they could even dismount, they were surrounded and besieged with questions.

"It worked?" Charisse asked as Luke swung down off his horse.

"Thanks to Caroline and Henry, it did. Montoya didn't become a general by being careless."

"He questioned the delivery, then?"

"He questioned everything about it." Ben winced as he eased himself down from his horse. "It's a good thing Pierre had the idea of leaving some of the rifles untampered with, or Montoya would have figured it out."

Luke nodded. "Even so, I think it was the note from Mrs. Mantella and Ben's less than-healthy appearance that finally convinced him."

"But he looks like he got beat up, not like he's coming down with cholera," Charisse protested.

"Caroline told them I got most of the bruises from trying to subdue a delirious Robbie. Pretty sure he figured I'd be dead if Robbie hadn't been sick, and that convinced him as much as anything."

"He offered to take us back to Mexico with him," Caroline said. "I thought we were in for it then, but Ben saved the day by pointing out that our not returning would make the other members of the wagon train suspicious."

Luke grinned. "He promised us we'd be heroes of the revolution. I hope we're long gone before he figures out what we did."

The crowd pulled the three to the fire and plied them with food, coffee and more questions as Pierre took care of their horses and returned. Ben and Caroline left to tend his wounds as soon as they finished eating, leaving Luke to answer the rest of the questions. Eventually everyone's curiosity had been satisfied, and the euphoria had faded. That's when worry began to set in.

"What about when General Montoya finds out we ruined his rifles?" asked Eliza. "Won't he come after us?"

Luke sighed. "It's a distinct possibility. That's why we have to get to Fort Bridger as soon as we can."

"What about when we leave there?" Violet wanted to know.

"We discussed it, and I think we may have come up with a viable solution," Luke said. "We'll split up. That way Montoya can't trace us."

They all exchanged surprised glances. "Split up?" Henry said. "You mean join other wagon trains?"

"Exactly. When we get to Fort Bridger, we'll separate and each leave with a different train. There are wagon trains pulling in and out every day, so it shouldn't take more than a few days for everyone to be on their way again, with nothing to tie us to the guns or Lucia Mantella."

They all stared at each other in silence for a long moment. At last Jesse nodded. "It makes sense. Half of us are going to California and the other half to Oregon anyway. We'll just be taking leave of each other a few days earlier."

"What about him?" Violet asked, pointing to Dempsey, who was tied to a wagon.

"I'm leaving tomorrow morning for the fort," said Luke. "I'll take Dempsey with me and turn him over to the authorities."

"You're leaving?" Charisse couldn't quite keep the quaver out of her voice.

"I have no choice," he said ruefully. "We have to let the army know what's going on. By the time we get to Fort Bridger in the wagons, it might be too late."

"But you haven't slept more than two hours in the last four days! Couldn't someone else…"

He cupped her cheek with his hand. "There is no one else," he said softly. "Ben's about done in, and we don't have the right to ask any of these good people to take on a mission like this."

Charisse glanced around the circle of faces and realized what he said was true. She also knew with sudden clarity that she and Luke needed to have this conversation in private. "It's time you went to bed then. You'll need a good night's sleep before you leave."

"Yes, ma'am," Luke said meekly as he rose and took the sleeping Toby from her arms. "There's no reasoning with her when she uses that tone," he told the group around the campfire. "If I don't get back before you get to the fort, I'll see you all there, and thanks for your help today."

There were murmurs of thanks and well-wishes as they left the cozy circle and walked back to their wagon.

"Today was the whole reason you came on this trip, isn't it?" Charisse said as soon as they were out of ear-shot.

"Yes, this is what Ben and I were sent to investigate."

"You knew all about those guns and Caroline and everything?"

"No." He shook his head. "All we knew was Joshua Simms had been tampering with the supply records."

Charisse digested this. "And that's why you went out every night, isn't it? You were trying to figure it all out."

"That's right, and Ben was sent to help me. We could have used a few more men, though. It was touch and go today." He smiled at her. "I guess my lucky streak is holding."

For once Charisse ignored the warm feeling the words gave her. "Luke, who are you?"

He sighed. "Have you ever heard of the Pinkerton Detective Agency?"

"Yes, they catch clerks who embezzle money from the railroads."

Luke grinned. "That's one of our jobs. Basically, we investigate anything anyone hires us to."

She blinked as she digested this. "You and Ben are Pinkertons? But that doesn't make any sense. Who would hire you to investigate something like this?"

"The United States Government." They had reached their wagon, and Luke raised his eyebrows. "You got the tent up all by yourself!"

Charisse shrugged as he eased Toby down on the bedroll closest to the wagon. "I've watched you often enough. It wasn't that hard."

He straightened. "I need to go check on Ben," he said. "Do you mind?"

"Of course not. He and Caroline got the worst of it today."

"I won't be long." His voice was a deep sexy rumble as he tipped her chin up with his finger. The kiss was sweet and warm, a light touching of lips filled with promise. "Hold that thought," he whispered. Luke was aware of her gaze following him as he made his way between the wagons.

The glow of a lantern showed through the canvas of the Mantella wagon. All of Caroline's possessions had been moved here when the gunpowder was loaded into her wagon. He couldn't help but think how difficult this day had been for her. The last thing he wanted to do was bring her more pain.

He raised his hand to his mouth and hooted like an owl. Two calls thirty seconds apart, then a third.

"I'm here, Luke," Ben called. "If you don't mind, I'd rather not get up and come out."

"No problem," Luke said, moving to the back of the wagon. "I wanted to check in. I probably won't see you before I leave in the morning."

Ben was bare to the waist and stretched out on a mattress on the floor of the wagon as Caroline dressed the last of his wounds. He struggled to sit up. "I should be going with you."

"You're in no shape to go anywhere," Caroline said, pushing his shoulders down. "It's a miracle you made it to the rendezvous with General Montoya and back."

Luke smiled. "She's right, you know. Besides, this wagon train isn't out of the woods yet. We need you here to keep an eye on things and make sure everyone gets to Fort Bridger."

Caroline looked back and forth between them, then stood. "You know, Luke, if you don't mind staying with him, I need to leave for a few minutes."

"Sure." He helped her out of the wagon, then looked at Ben. "What was that all about?"

"I guess she realized you and I haven't had a chance to talk privately all day."

"Ah. I have been wondering what you were thinking this morning."

Ben grimaced. "I wasn't thinking at all."

"They did sort of catch you with your pants down," Luke said with a grin.

"You might say that. Still, if I hadn't been with Caroline, we'd probably have missed the transfer, and would never have figured out what happened or who was responsible."

"You have a point there," Luke said. "The Mantellas were the only people on this wagon train I never suspected. I assume Robbie Mantella is our mysterious killer?"

Ben nodded. "I'd say so. Looking back on it, I wonder how we missed it. What about the two men who kidnapped Charisse?"

"They work for Sam Jackson. Apparently someone had spotted him following the wagon train a couple of times, so Cassex approached Jackson to find out what he was up to. He and Mantella made a deal. If Mantella's men delivered Charisse, then Jackson and his underlings would distract me long enough for the transfer of guns to take place. It almost worked, too."

"So where are Jackson's men now?"

"On their way to capture him."

Ben was startled. "What?"

"They figured he wouldn't pay them after they let Charisse get away twice, so they offered to switch their allegiance. For two hundred dollars they're going to bring Sam Jackson to Fort Bridger for me."

"And you trust them?"

"No, but I didn't have much choice this morning—Lucia Mantella was making mincemeat out of you, and I had to mount a rescue with bartenders and shopkeepers for backup."

"I never thanked you for saving my neck."

Luke grinned. "That makes us even again, doesn't it?"

Ben nodded. "I think so, but we aren't finished with this assignment yet."

"No." Luke gave Ben a speculative look. "I take it you weren't trying to gather information last night?"

"Hell no! I'd never use Caroline that way. It just...happened, you know?"

Luke thought of Charisse and nodded. "Yeah, I know. So, what now?"

"I'm not sure. I've never met a woman like Caroline before. What about Charisse?"

"That's a good question. I still don't know what is going on with her, but I'm pretty sure it's separate from this mess with the Mantellas. That's the other reason I need you to stay with the wagon train. That messenger McNesby told us about hasn't arrived yet, and someone needs to keep an eye on Charisse and Toby."

"Keeping an eye on Charisse is always a pleasure," Ben said with a grin. Then he sobered. "How much are you going to tell her?"

"I already told her we were Pinkertons. It seemed to startle her, though."

"Guilty conscience?"

"I don't know. It almost seemed like it."

"Can I come back now?" Caroline's voice came out of the darkness.

"Are you sure you want to?" Luke asked. "He's usually a pretty bad patient."

"I guess I'll have to take my chances. He's taken possession of my wagon, and I don't have anywhere else to sleep."

"You're a brave woman." Luke helped her into the wagon. "Take care of him," he said softly.

She smiled down at him. "I will."

"What are you two whispering about?" Ben demanded.

"I was giving her advice on how to keep you under control."

Ben's eyes widened in mock fright. "Don't believe a word he says!"

"Ah ha, clearly good advice then," said Caroline

triumphantly. "Thanks, Luke."

Ben shook his head then reached out his hand. "Be careful out there, Luke."

"You too, Ben." The two men shook hands, a wealth of emotion expressed in the hard grip. They were both facing danger, only this time there wouldn't be anyone there to watch their backs.

Luke felt and unusual heaviness as he walked back to his own wagon. He rarely gave his partings from Ben a second thought, yet for some reason this one bothered him. Was it a premonition? Or was it the thought of leaving Charisse alone for so long?

She was asleep, her hair curling softly around her in the moonlight, so breathtakingly beautiful it almost hurt to look at her. As if she felt his gaze, she opened her eyes and smiled up at him. "Luke." Her voice was almost a caress as she put out her palm to pull him into bed.

Instead, he grasped her hand and pulled her to her feet. "Come here."

She walked into his embrace and twined her arms around his neck. "How was Ben?"

"Fine." His voice sounded rough and ragged even to his own ears. "We need to talk," he whispered against her mouth.

"Mmm hmm. Later." Her lips opened under his, and he was lost.

Luke caressed the silken interior of her mouth with his tongue as his hands explored the supple curves beneath the simple cotton nightgown. The buttons at her throat parted one by one under his nimble fingers until he could slip his hands inside to the soft skin beneath. She moaned into his mouth as his thumbs brushed the hardened nubs of her nipples.

"Luke," she whispered breathlessly as his hands slid down to her waist and pulled her against him. "We can't do this here in front of God and everybody."

"You're right." He scooped up a blanket and draped it around her shoulders, then took her hand in his. "Let's go."

"What about Toby?"

"We aren't going that far. Franklin will watch over him, and we'll hear him if he wakes up. Besides," he lifted her hand and kissed her knuckles, "we really do need to talk."

As they walked to a patch of willows nearby, Luke tried to decide how to broach the subject of her past. He had to discover what she was hiding, to ferret out her secrets and find out where she fit into the picture before he left.

In the end, he never asked a thing. Instead, he made passionate love to her and fell asleep with his head pillowed on her chest.

CHAPTER 41

"Mama, I miss my Pa," Toby said mournfully.

Charisse sighed. "I know, sweetheart, so do I, but we should see him the day after tomorrow when we get to Fort Bridger."

"He said he was going to try to meet up with the wagon train before we got there," Toby pointed out.

"I know, but something probably came up that kept him at the fort longer than he thought."

"Maybe he'll come tomorrow."

"Maybe he will." Charisse smiled at him. "In the meantime, go get me a bucket of water so I can fix your supper."

Toby grabbed the bucket and took off like a shot. Charisse watched him, love expanding her heart until she felt like it might burst. Then she sighed again and turned back to the job of setting up camp.

Luke had ridden away before dawn nearly a week ago. Ben said it would have taken him at least five days to reach the fort and get back. Only now he'd been gone six, and Charisse was worried. What if Dempsey had somehow gotten loose? Luke had been exhausted when they left, and Dempsey was well rested and angry. The image of Luke lying out in the middle of the prairie with his blood soaking into the dry earth haunted her day and night.

Determined to put the morbid picture out of her mind, she dwelled instead on their last night together. Charisse smiled as she put up the lean-to. He'd wanted to talk, but she'd refused to give up the chance to make another precious memory in Luke's arms for a conversation she didn't want to have.

Not that it had been all that hard to distract him. A few

kisses in interesting places, some creative finger play, and a little skin-to-skin contact had turned him to putty in her hands. Or maybe she'd been the putty. At any rate, the result had been the most incredible bout of loving she had ever experienced. When they were finished, his exhaustion had taken its toll, and he'd fallen asleep almost immediately. She'd spent the long night holding him in her arms, smoothing his hair, tracing the lines of his face and body with gentle fingers and storing up enough memories to last her a lifetime.

The conversation would still have to happen, of course, but why ruin their last night together? Delivering the last of the gang to Fort Bridger and taking the news of the planned rebellion to the army would bring Luke's assignment to an end. That meant he and Toby were about to leave her. Annabelle's death had taught her the importance of living every day to its fullest. Rather than dwell on the fact she wouldn't have a lifetime with them, she thanked God for the time she'd had. If her heart was breaking, at least the memories of this summer would forever be a bright spot she could look back on.

"Charisse?"

Charisse stuck her head out of the lean-to. "I'm over here, Caroline."

"Someone just rode into camp looking for Charisse Collingsworth," Caroline said.

"What?" Charisse's stomach dropped at the name. This can't be anything good, she thought. "Did he say why he's here?"

Caroline shook her head. "Only that he had important news for Charisse Collingsworth. Is that you?"

"It used to be. I suppose I should go see what he wants."

"He's at Eliza's wagon." Caroline gave a smile of sympathy. "He couldn't make it any farther, though he said he'd be fine after a cup of tea. I take it the poor man doesn't travel well."

Charisse found him perched on a stool drinking tea with Eliza Duncan. Somehow the delicate china cup and saucer in his hand didn't look as incongruous as it should have. The man was dressed in a brown suit of superfine. His umbrella and derby sat on a chunk of wood nearby. Even covered with a layer of travel dust and looking uncomfortably disheveled, he exuded an air of refinement.

"Here she is now," said Eliza, taking the empty cup from his hand.

The gentleman looked up, then surged to his feet, his face alight with pleasure. "It is you!" he said. "I can't tell you how glad I am to see you at last." His clipped British accent was almost as much of a shock as his words. "You are the very image of your late grandmother, God rest her soul."

"You knew my grandmother?" Charisse asked in surprise.

"Yes, and your grandfather, the earl, as well. Hussets, Howser and Brahms have served the Earls of Brentwood for nearly a hundred years."

"I see," said Charisse, very conscious of Caroline and Eliza staring at the two of them in open-mouthed astonishment. "And you are…?"

"Oh, pardon me." He bowed. "Isaiah Brahms, at your service."

Now it was Charisse's turn to be astonished. This wasn't some low-paid underling from her grandfather's solicitor's office. This was one of the partners. What in the world was going on? "My cousin…?"

"The earl was enjoying his customary good health when I left England. I'd be glad to take a letter back, if you'd like."

"Perhaps." The truth was, she couldn't care less about cousin Bertie. She'd only met him once as a child, and he'd been a self-important bully then. People changed when they grew up, of course—but not Bertie, apparently. She'd been so desperate when Preston divorced her that she'd written to him, as the head of her mother's family, asking for help. He hadn't even cared enough to have his secretary send her a rebuff. He had simply ignored her.

"Is there some place we could speak privately, Mrs.

Collingsworth?"

"That isn't my name any longer," she said.

He colored. "Oh, of course not. Such an unfortunate incident… but then it appears… ah…"

Charisse decided to put the poor man out of his embarrassed misery. "We can talk at my wagon," she said. "It's right over there."

"Excellent, let me get my things."

As he retrieved his bowler and umbrella, Charisse turned to her friends, who were staring at her as though they had never seen her before. She swallowed a sigh. "Caroline, would you mind intercepting Toby for me?"

"S-sure. I'll be glad to."

Charisse could hear them whispering as she walked away with Mr. Brahms. She caught "…granddaughter of an earl…" and "…first husband…" So much for hiding her past. Not that it really mattered—they would all be parting ways in a few days anyway.

"Have a seat," she said, gesturing to one of the chunks of wood they used for stools. "I'm sorry I don't have any real chairs," she said as she sat on the other.

"Quite all right," he said, giving it a cursory brush with his handkerchief before sitting. "I've endured much worse on this hellish trip."

"You're a poor traveler, then?"

"Unfortunately, yes, though never this bad before. I have a little trouble with sea sickness, but these primitive roads…" He gave a delicate shudder then appeared to collect himself and smiled happily. "Be that as it may, I have found you at last."

Charisse smiled back. "Surely you didn't come all this way to tell me I look like my grandmother, and that my cousin is well."

"No, of course not." He straightened his shoulders and took on such a professional manner, Charisse could almost imagine she was sitting across a desk from him in his London office. "It's about your grandfather's will."

"But that was all settled when he died, wasn't it?"

"We thought so. However, there has been a new development."

"So dear old cousin Bertie found a way to break the will?" Charisse shook her head. "I'm sorry, Mr. Brahms. I'm afraid you've come all this way for nothing. I no longer have access to my inheritance. It belongs to my ex-husband. My cousin will have to fight it out with him."

"No, no, it's nothing like that. Lord Brentwood is the one who suggested we come after you when none of our letters received a reply. He suspected your... rather... that Mr. Collingsworth might be intercepting them."

Charisse blinked. "You sent me letters?"

"Quite a number, in fact. As you may recall, your grandfather left you everything not entailed to the estate, which was his personal fortune as well as your grandmother's rather sizable dowry. All of the property went to the new earl."

"Has that changed?" Charisse asked.

"No. However, there was a codicil to your grandfather's will."

"A codicil?"

"Yes, an addition he added shortly after your parents were killed. He had reason to believe your... uh... husband had something to do with it."

Charisse was thunderstruck. "Grandfather thought Preston had something to do with my parent's accident?" Her heart squeezed at the thought.

"It was only a suspicion, you understand. He thought their deaths a mere six months after your wedding was a bit too convenient for Mr. Collingsworth."

"I never thought of it before, but you're right. Preston went from a fairly minor position to the head of the railroad overnight."

"The earl thought the nature of your parents' deaths a trifle odd as well."

"That's true, too," Charisse said slowly. "My father was an

excellent sailor, and he knew that lake like the back of his hand. To have their sailboat sink like that on a clear day with no warning was very odd. Everyone said so."

"Precisely, which is why your grandfather added the codicil."

Charisse blinked. She'd forgotten the codicil for a moment. "What was in it?"

"Essentially, it says your grandfather's fortune could not pass out of your control."

Shock ricocheted through her. "You mean Preston couldn't touch it?"

"Exactly."

"My grandfather has been dead for eight years. Why am I just now hearing this?"

Mr. Brahms sighed. "This is rather embarrassing, but true nonetheless. You see, none of us knew the codicil existed."

"What?"

"My partner, Felix Hussets, was your grandfather's executor. He wrote the codicil shortly before his own death. Because it was a fairly straightforward document, we speculate he gave it to a clerk to file with the original will and never mentioned it to the rest of us."

"So, what happened to it?"

Mr. Brahms looked pained. "I'm afraid it was stolen."

"Stolen! I don't understand."

"Once we knew about the codicil, we began an investigation inside our company and found the culprit. It seems Mr. Collingsworth had paid one of our clerks a rather large sum of money to make the codicil disappear. Unfortunately for Mr. Collingsworth, his accomplice wasn't satisfied with one payment and has continued to extort money to keep it quiet."

It serves that slimy toad right! I had to sell my clothes just to survive, and he knew it. Here it was my money all the time!" Charisse gave her head a little shake, "Wait a minute. If the codicil disappeared, how did you find out about it?"

The Earl of Brentwood brought it to our attention. Apparently, you wrote to him after your… ah… that is…."

"My divorce."

"Right. Brentwood knew all about the codicil since your grandfather kept a copy in his personal papers. He found it very strange you were destitute, so he sent you a letter and a bank draft with a courier. When the courier never returned, and he didn't receive a reply to his letter, he came to us."

"I thought he had washed his hands of me like everyone else."

"Hardly. I'm here at his request."

Charisse raised her eyebrows. "You are?"

"Yes, indeed. Once he found out there was chicanery afoot, he insisted one of us should come in person to find out what was going on."

"So that's why you're here rather than a minor employee."

"Exactly. He felt he could only send someone he trusted completely."

"And you've traveled across an ocean and half a continent to find me." Charisse shook her head in wonder. "I'd say the earl's trust was well-placed."

"Thank you," Mr. Brahms said modestly. "But the earl deserves a great deal of the credit. He alerted your father's solicitors, and by the time I arrived, they had discovered your father's will had been tampered with."

"What do you mean tampered with?"

"One small part had been changed slightly."

"Let me guess—it gave everything to Preston, right?"

"Nothing so blatant. The document stated you would always hold the controlling shares of the railroad and all decisions had to be approved by you, unless you chose to sign your control over to someone else. In the original document, there was no provision for you to sign your shares over to anyone."

"I suppose a document was found that said I had done that?"

"Yes, and it was dated within days of your parent's death. Your father's lawyers never questioned it, since you appeared to take no interest in the railroad. However, when the earl asked for a full investigation, they compared signatures and discovered yours had been forged. He also asked we find you before formal charges are filed against Mr. Collingsworth. We were afraid that if he were alerted to what was going on, he might try to hurt you. The authorities agreed."

"It seems the Earl of Brentwood is a powerful man," she murmured.

"He is indeed."

"Charisse!" Ben suddenly burst around the side of the wagon.

Charisse's stomach gave a sickening lurch. "What's happened, Ben? Is it Luke?"

"No." He looked from Charisse to Mr. Brahms and back again. "Are you all right?"

"Yes, of course. Why wouldn't I be?"

Instead of answering her he fixed a menacing stare on Isaiah Brahms. "You're the messenger from Hussets, Howser and Brahms?"

"I...yes, but how did you know—?"

"I work for Allen Pinkerton."

A look of relief crossed his face. "Ah, then you must be Mr. McCabe."

"Uh... no." Ben gave Charisse a wary look. "I'm actually Benjamin Baxter. Luke's my partner."

"What does Luke McCabe have to do with this?" Charisse asked, confused.

Mr. Brahms looked surprised. "Why, if it hadn't been for his investigation, we would never have found you."

"Investigation?" Charisse's confusion morphed into anger, and she gave Ben a dangerous look. "What investigation was that?"

"It's not what you think, Charisse," Ben said quickly. "When you and Luke first met, he wrote to our superior and asked him to check your background. That's all. It's our job to be suspicious, and you'll have to admit you showing up when you did was a very lucky coincidence."

"All right, I guess that makes sense, but how did you know Mr. Brahms was coming?"

"We got a message from our superior."

"And when was that?"

Ben shifted uncomfortably. "Independence Rock."

"That was weeks ago! Why didn't you tell me?"

"Charisse, in our job we can't afford to take chances. We knew we were dealing with a revolution that could destroy the country, two men were dead, we'd lost our prime suspect, and here comes a message that tells us you are the subject of a manhunt and there was danger involved."

"But you know me. You knew I wasn't dangerous."

"We didn't think Lucia and Robbie Mantella were, either. Luke and I have learned to play our cards close to our chest. It's the only way to stay alive in this business."

"I can perhaps shed some light on this matter," said Mr. Brahms. "I was the one who told Mr. Pinkerton to include a warning. We had every reason to believe you might well be in danger."

"That's kind of what Luke and I figured it meant, too." Ben admitted. "There had already been at least one attempt on your life. That's why I'm here, instead of with Luke." He looked at Mr. Brahms. "We thought the danger might be from the messenger. It appears that was wrong."

"She is in no danger from me," Mr. Brahms assured him. "In fact, I've come quite a long way to protect her interests."

"He came on business," Charisse said, with a toss of her head. "Business we have yet to complete, so if you don't mind…"

Ben grinned. "All right, but I'm going to keep a look out anyway. You may not be afraid of Luke, but I am. The last thing he said before he left was to keep you safe, and I intend to do it."

Charisse stamped her foot, "Darn you, Ben Baxter! I'm trying to stay angry at him, and you keep placating me!"

"You have no reason to be angry with him about this."

"I don't understand why he doesn't trust me."

"Charisse," Ben said softly, "If he hadn't trusted you, he wouldn't have left his son with you." He gave her a slight smile then withdrew to a rock about twenty feet away. There, he sat down and rolled a cigarette as though he had nothing better to do.

Charisse rolled her eyes and turned back to her visitor. "I'm sorry about that, Mr. Brahms. You've come a long way. You deserve better than suspicion and dramatics."

"Quite the contrary, I appreciate his help and that of your Mr. McCabe. When I left England, none of us could have guessed how difficult you would be to find."

"You've been looking for me for a long time, then?"

"I left England eleven months ago. You have not been easy to track, I don't mind telling you. If it hadn't been for the Pinkerton Detective Agency, I would still be looking."

"I haven't been trying to hide."

"Perhaps not, but changing your name made it quite difficult to pick up your trail. Charisse Jones is rather different than Mary Collingsworth. If I hadn't known your childhood name of Charisse, I never would have found you."

Charisse shook her head. "Preston again. He insisted I go by Mary, though I've never liked it. When we divorced, I went back to Charisse, and Jones seemed an innocuous-enough last name." She sighed. "I suppose it will be a long court battle trying to separate Preston's money from mine before I can reclaim any of my inheritance."

"On the contrary, it appears Mr. Collingworth's entire fortune was fabricated."

"What does that mean?"

"He lied. When you met him, he was as poor as a church mouse."

"But his house in the country, the racing stable. My parents and I spent a week there before Preston and I were married. He sold it since he was going to focus his attention on helping my father with the railroad."

"Actually, he was only the caretaker there while the owners toured Europe. Your grandfather had him investigated shortly after your parents' death."

"Why didn't he tell me?"

"I understand he came to America with every intention of doing that, but he found you apparently very happy. You and your husband seemed deeply in love and you had a beautiful daughter that you both doted on. He decided to leave well enough alone."

"I remember that visit." Charisse sighed. "I guess I did a bit too well with the play-acting."

"Maybe not." He made a palms-up gesture. "After all, he went home and added the codicil to his will."

"So, what does all of this mean?"

"It means that everything is yours: the house, the railroad, all the money." Mr. Brahms beamed at her. "In a nutshell, it means you are a very wealthy woman."

CHAPTER 42

"You sure this is where you were supposed to meet Sid and Eli?" Ben asked. "It isn't even big enough to be called a one-horse town."

Luke swung down from his horse and tied it to the hitching rail. "That's because Fort Bridger hasn't been an army fort for a year yet. These little towns outside the forts have a way of growing as the fort does. Eli probably thinks it's safer to meet here than at the fort."

"I suppose our friends might have reason to avoid the army," Ben observed. "You want me to stay and watch your back? The wagon train is only a few miles away, and Jeveraux won't expect me back for a while yet."

Luke shook his head. "Sid and Eli won't want to cause trouble this close to the fort. Besides, I made it very clear that the two hundred dollars I'm giving them is all I have. They'd have no reason to kill me."

"Unless Sam Jackson offered them more money."

"They don't trust him anymore. He hasn't paid them a dime, and I've already shown I pay up when the job is done."

"Has it occurred to you two hundred dollars is all the money you have to get home?"

"It's worth it to know Charisse will be safe. Besides, I have the fifty-dollar reward for Dempsey. Too bad we buried Cassex, Nugent and Snyder. They were worth a hundred each."

Ben grinned. "I guess we could go dig them up and bring them in."

"No thanks. I don't think I'll get that desperate."

"The wagon train should be here sometime this afternoon," Ben said, leaning on the saddle horn. "Charisse isn't exactly in charity with you right now."

Luke sighed. "Do you think she's telling the truth about what the messenger had to say?"

"That he came all the way from England to straighten out a problem with her grandfather's will?" Ben shrugged. "It makes sense, and Brahms didn't deny it. He even smiled and nodded when she said she'd discovered she had a bit more money than she realized."

"It seems like an awfully long trip for a few dollars."

"I imagine it was more like a few thousand. Anyway, it all seemed on the up and up to me. If Brahms is anything other than an English lawyer, I'll eat my hat."

"So, where does Sam Jackson fit into all this?"

Ben shrugged. "You've got me."

"I suppose you'd better be getting back to the wagon train. When are you going to be ready to head back to civilization?"

There was a long pause as Ben pondered this. "I don't think I'm going back."

"What?"

Ben gazed off into the distance. "I think I might take up ranching instead. I've asked Caroline to marry me, only she doesn't want a husband who's gone all the time." He smiled. "The funny thing is, I find I don't really want that any more either."

"You don't know anything about ranching."

"No, but she does. Her aunt was so caught up in the revolution and revenge, she never noticed Robbie and Caroline were running both ranches." He grinned. "Besides, I think she's marrying me for my skills as a defender of justice and right. The first thing she wants me to do is set up a line of defense. There's still the possibility General Montoya will get the revolution off the ground. Even if he doesn't, there's a good chance he'll come looking for revenge."

"Aren't you the man who spent the last ten years bouncing from one adventure to another, laughing in the face of danger, and scoffing at anyone who would choose another way of life?"

Ben smiled softly. "Turns out Caroline is the only adventure I need."

Luke grinned. "I've been waiting for the day some woman caught you napping."

"You might do well to consider settling down yourself," Ben said, turning his horse away. "Somehow, I can't see you letting Charisse Jones walk out of your life in less than a week. See you in a few hours."

Luke watched him go. He was right. The thought of leaving Charisse was almost more than he could stand. Then there was Toby. What would it do to him to lose another mother, one he loved even more than his own? Toby wasn't the only one who loved Charisse. He did too, with his whole heart and soul—too much to put her through the hell he'd put Elizabeth through. The question was, did he love her enough to let her go? It was a question he had asked himself a hundred times.

He sauntered into the saloon and found a table next to the wall where no one could sneak up on him and ordered a whiskey. Luke was still pondering the best method of making enough money to get himself and Toby home again, when Sid sidled in the door. After a furtive look around, he spied Luke. His face lit up, and he crossed to the table.

"You still want Jackson?"

"Do you have him?"

"Right outside the door. Eli says for you to come with me, and have the money out where he can see it."

Luke frowned. "Is this some kind of trick?"

"No—not to you, anyways. Eli's plannin' to trick Jackson, but he wants to see the color of your money first on account of we ain't giving up Jackson until we're sure we're gettin' paid."

It made sense. Trusting wasn't something Eli did and probably with good reason. "All right," Luke said. "But you walk in front of me, and keep your hands where I can see them."

"You bet, Mr. McCabe." Sid whirled around and made for the door with his arms out to his sides. He stepped through the swinging doors and stopped. "Take a look, then hold the money up so Eli can see it."

Curious now, Luke stepped up to the door and looked out. Eli and Sam Jackson stood next to the hitching rail, relaxed and waiting for something. Jackson leaned on the rail with his back to the saloon. Eli stood right next to him leaning on one hip as he smoked a cigarette. Standing sideways like that, he could see the door without alerting Jackson.

"I assumed he would be tied up," Luke said. "What's to keep him from running?"

"Don't you worry none about that. Just hold up the money where Eli can see it."

"All right." Luke fanned the bills in his left hand and put his right hand on his gun as he lifted the money above the door.

Eli nodded, then calmly pulled his pistol and struck Jackson on the back of the head with the butt. Jackson crumpled to the ground without a sound as Sid grabbed the money out of Luke's hand and sprinted for his horse. Eli already had both horses untied and was in the saddle as his brother stuffed the money in his saddlebag and swung up onto his own horse.

Eli tossed a length of rope toward Jackson's body, then tipped his hat to Luke. "It's a pleasure doing business with you, Mr. McCabe. Give the missus my regards." With that, he wheeled his horse, and the two brothers galloped down the short street out of town.

Luke stood there stunned for several seconds, then started to grin. Damn, but he had to admire the two of them. If he hadn't come through with the money, they'd have still had Jackson. He pushed through the doors and strode across the walk.

Jackson's appearance hadn't improved much since Platte River Station. His nose and forehead were still peeling, though most of the sunburn had turned to tan and some of the blisters on his palms had become calluses. His clothing was torn and filthy, and he had quite a variety of scratches and bruises.

"You've had a pretty rough time of it, haven't you?" Luke

muttered. "Now what am I going to do with you?"

The first order of business was to get him off the street. Luckily, everyone had been inside during the heat of the day, so there were no witnesses to Eli's perfidy.

In the end, he decided the best bet was to get his prisoner out of town. Luke removed Jackson's saddle, slung him across the horse's back face down and tied him on. He wouldn't be terribly comfortable when he woke up, but as far as Luke was concerned, the man deserved it for what he'd put Charisse through.

Rather than find a place to hide his prisoner, Luke decided to ride out and meet the wagon train. Unmindful of the burden on the horse he was leading, he covered the distance in record time. The urge to see Charisse and Toby was irresistible.

His timing was perfect. The wagon train had stopped for the noon rest, and everyone was relaxed in the shade of the wagons. Jesse Swindell was the first to see him.

"McCabe's back!" he yelled, as Luke dismounted and tied his horse to the nearest wagon.

Suddenly he was surrounded with everyone asking questions at once. Luke did his best to answer until he glanced up and saw Charisse. Their eyes met and held. The next minute they were both moving toward each other, only vaguely aware of their friends and neighbors grinning and getting out of their way.

Then she was in his arms, kissing him. He lifted her and swung her around without ever breaking contact. It went on and on until a voice finally broke through their haze of preoccupation.

"Pa, Pa!" Toby was pulling on Luke's shirt, demanding attention. "Franklin and I want a hug too."

They broke apart with a laugh, and Luke scooped him up in his arms. "Did you miss me, Sprout?"

"Bunches and bunches. I'm glad you're back."

Luke hugged him tightly. "Me too, son, me too."

"Hey, Luke," yelled Ben, "The load on your pack horse is

moving. Don't you think you should cut him loose?"

Luke put Toby down. "He's waking up?"

"Looks like it. I figured he was dead. Scared me half to death when he started moaning!"

"No, not dead." Luke pulled his knife as he walked to the packhorse. "Just knocked out. I suppose he's got a devil of a headache, but he has a lot of explaining to do." He cut through the ropes, and let Jackson slide off the horse.

Jackson groaned as he landed face down in the dirt. "Sorry about that," Luke said, but he wasn't sorry at all. He reached down and rolled him over, then glanced up in surprise when he heard Charisse's gasp. Her face had turned chalk white as she stared down at the man on the ground.

"What is it, Charisse?"

She looked up at him, wide-eyed and shaken. "I-it's Preston!"

CHAPTER 43

"What are you doing here, Preston?" Charisse demanded, refusing to take pity on the pathetic creature perched on the chunk of wood before her.

"I...I've been trying to find you," he said mournfully. "After you left, I realized how much I love you. I want you to come home so we can start all over."

"Nice try. I've already talked with my grandfather's lawyers—I know the truth."

"Don't you think we should have this conversation in private, Mary?" he said with a meaningful look at Luke, Ben and Isaiah Brahms, who stood in a semicircle behind her.

"My name isn't Mary, it's Charisse. Luke, Mr. Brahms, Ben, I'd appreciate it if you'd stay, since this affects you, too."

Mr. Brahms nodded. "Of course, my dear."

"Wild horses couldn't drag me away," Ben assured her.

Luke gave Preston a wolfish grin that caused the other man to flinch.

Charisse smiled at Preston. "There isn't anything they don't already know about me."

A sly look entered his eyes. "Are you sure about that?"

"All right, I'll play your silly game." Charisse turned and faced the three men. "I was married to this slimy toad for twelve years until he divorced me in the most publicly humiliating way possible. Then he threw me out on the street with only my clothes and a small pittance my grandmother left me that he couldn't touch." She turned back to Preston. "There, now they know. I'm going to ask you again, Preston. What are you doing here?"

He gave her a mulish look. "I only came to find you and

take you home, and you can't prove any differently."

Luke yanked Preston to his feet. "I think Eli and Sid would be willing to testify about what you hired them to do. There are some hard feelings there. You never paid them for all the work they did. In fact, I don't think they like you very much."

"You're bluffing," Preston said. "They know which side their bread is buttered on."

"They sure do," Luke agreed. "How do you think I got hold of you?"

"It was pure luck. You snuck up behind me and hit me over the head."

"Nope. Eli did it. They brought you to Fort Bridger like I asked them to, and set you up. All I had to do was show him the money, and he hit you over the head without a qualm."

"I don't believe you."

"No? Then where are they, and how did I, one man alone, manage to overpower two men without you even knowing I was there?"

Preston frowned as he thought this over. Then he looked up. "What are you going to do with me?"

"If you don't give Charisse her answers, you're going to jail for kidnapping, and four counts of attempted murder."

"I never tried to kill her!"

"Really? A judge and jury might not see it that way." Luke started counting off on his fingers. "You had her kidnapped by Indians. When that didn't work, you tried to use my son to get to her at Platte River Station, only I came along and messed up your plan, whatever it was. Then you started a prairie fire and—"

"That was an accident," Preston protested. "My campfire got away from me. As soon as I realized where it was going, I tried to warn you, but it was moving too fast."

Luke snorted. "More like you were going to see if the fire had succeeded where you'd failed. It almost worked, too. If I hadn't been right there, Charisse would have burned to death when her dress caught fire. So, you tried to shoot her. Lucky you're such a piss-poor shot."

Preston hung his head. "I... I don't know what came over me. Jealousy, I guess. The sight of my darling melting in someone else's arms, kissing him..."

Charisse laughed. "As if you cared one jot who I kiss. There's not a soul who believes you were motivated by jealousy, least of all me."

"Then how do you explain that it never happened again?" he said belligerently. "I had plenty of other opportunities to shoot you."

Luke snorted. "It didn't happen because after the first attempt, I started watching her more carefully, and you couldn't get close anymore."

"Not to mention you left your ram rod behind and couldn't load your gun," Ben said, stepping forward to stand by Charisse..

"You can't prove any of it!" Preston cried desperately.

"Oh, but you see, I can. You're in even deeper water than you realize. I can easily implicate you in several acts of high treason."

"What? I never —"

"Maybe not, but your partners did."

"Partners, what partners? I'm not responsible for anything Eli and Sid —"

"I'm not talking about those two penny-ante criminals," Luke said. "I mean your other partners, the ones who helped plan your nefarious schemes and who gave you the guns to trade with the Indians."

"Do you really think it's possible he didn't know who he was dealing with?" Ben asked.

"I don't see how anybody could be that stupid," Luke said. "On the other hand, I have said more than once that the man is an idiot. Maybe you'd better tell him."

Ben put an arm around Preston's shoulders as though he were sharing a confidence with a good friend. "You see, Preston, Luke and I aren't quite the foot-loose cowboys we seem. We're Pinkerton Detectives working undercover for the United States Government. We were on this wagon train tracking a faction of militants who were trying to start a revolution and throw the United States into a civil war. The very same people you made a deal with to kidnap Charisse. Didn't you wonder when they provided you with guns to give the Indians?"

Preston shrugged. "How was I to know what they were planning?"

"Surely you know selling guns to enemies of the United States is treason." Ben took his arm away and put his hand up in a helpless gesture. "Anyway, they're all dead now, so we really don't have anyone to take in."

"Except for you, Preston," Charisse added. "You who promised guns to the Indians if they kidnapped me."

"And don't forget all the charges Hussets, Howser & Brahms are prepared to bring against you for extortion, forgery and embezzlement," said Mr. Brahms.

"And the murders of George Bartell and Joshua Simms," Luke added. "Put that together with a charge of treason, and you'll surely hang."

Charisse crossed her arms and looked at him with raised eyebrows. "So, what's it going to be, Preston? Are you going to jail for your own crimes, or those of Lucia Mantella and her band of criminals?"

The starch seemed to go out of him, and he slumped. "I never planned to kill you," he admitted. "I... I didn't know what to do. They were closing in from all sides." He looked up at Charisse. "I was desperate. That's when I realized you were the only one who could help me solve my problems."

Charisse was stunned. "After everything you did to me, you thought I'd help you?"

"You always had before. Even when I had to discipline you."

"When you beat me, you mean!"

He hunched one shoulder, then continued on as though she

hadn't spoken. "You were always better with money than me. I decided to tell you there had been a mistake and the divorce wasn't real. I figured you'd forgive me and straighten it all out if you thought we were still legally married."

"You thought I'd just forgive and forget?" Charisse nearly strangled on the words. "You…You…" She took three deep breaths and forced herself to calm down. "So, you decided to come after me yourself?"

"I had to. I couldn't trust anyone else. That's how I got in this fix in the first place. At first it was hard to follow your trail, then I figured out a simple way to do it."

"How was that?"

He looked inordinately proud of himself. "Franklin. Anybody who sees him remembers him. I asked about a woman with a dog that had ridiculously short legs and no tail, and people knew exactly who I was talking about."

At the sound of his name, Franklin came trotting out from behind Caroline's wagon. When he caught sight of Preston, he started barking at the top of his lungs. He charged between Charisse and Preston and growled. The hair on his back bristled in a threatening manner and his lip curled back over his teeth.

Preston took a step back. "Down!" he ordered. He snapped his fingers and Franklin dropped to the ground, defused but still watchful.

"I see Franklin's attitude toward you hasn't changed," Charisse said.

Luke chuckled. "Always did like that dog."

Preston eyed Franklin warily. "That animal is a menace!"

"Only to you, Preston. Now, as you were saying…"

"I found out you'd left for Oregon with a man and his son. At first, the fact you were remarried threw me. But then I thought if I could convince you the divorce wasn't real, and your new marriage vows weren't legal… I caught up with your wagon train at the Big Blue River."

"How did you know it was ours?" Luke asked.

"I saw Charisse from a distance. She was talking to him."

He pointed at Ben. "The minute I saw the ground crumble under his feet, I knew I'd found her."

Luke frowned. "That makes no sense."

"Of course, it does. She's a jinx! Who else could cause such a thing?"

Luke stared at Preston in astonishment, then burst into laughter. "A jinx! Are you out of your mind?"

"That's why I divorced her," Preston said defensively. "I couldn't put up with the bad luck anymore."

"You know, the more I hear about it, the more I think Charisse's divorce was a stroke of good luck for her. A jinx, of all things!"

"Everybody in St. Louis knew it! Why do you think she left?"

Luke's eyes narrowed ominously. "Funny how easy it is to make people believe something so completely ridiculous. All you had to do was suggest it, and every bit of bad luck that befell anyone instantly became Charisse's fault."

"It's true," Preston insisted. "Look at all the bad luck you've had."

"What bad luck?"

"I heard her mules almost dragged you to death in Independence."

"*Almost* is the key word there. I *should* have been dead, but not only did I live to tell the tale, I haven't got a single scar to show for it. I call that uncommonly *good* luck. I've lost track of the number of times I've survived dire situations since I met her." He gave Charisse a soft smile. "She's my very own good luck charm."

Charisse blushed slightly and returned his smile. Then she turned back to Preston, the smile disappearing into a frown as she did. "So, you caught up with us at the Blue River. Then what?"

That's where I met Eli and Sid, and they introduced me to James Cassex," Preston said. "We made a plan for the Indians to kidnap Charisse so I could talk to her." He gave her a pleading look. "That's all I ever wanted. I never meant for you to be hurt, and I certainly never planned to kill you."

"All you wanted was to destroy her life once again." Luke had finally had enough. His eyes looked as though they were shooting fire as he grabbed the other man's shirtfront and jerked him off his feet. "You bastard—"

"Luke, stop it!" Charisse's voice was sharp. "Put him down. You forget I was married to the man for twelve years."

Luke looked at her in surprise, but set Preston back on his feet and stepped away.

"Thank you." Charisse and Franklin walked up to Preston. "You're willing to take me back in spite of everything?" she asked sweetly. "I could pick up my old life just like it was, with my beautiful house, my pretty clothes and all my cultured friends?"

"Of course, my darling." He straightened his clothes and threw a superior smirk at Luke, then smiled down at her. "Just like it was before."

"That's what I thought." Charisse doubled up her fist and punched him in the stomach as hard as she could.

Preston fell to his knees, gasping for air and clutching his midsection.

"Be glad I don't have my derringer on me, or I'd shoot you in the kneecap." As he struggled to his feet, Charisse snapped her fingers and pointed. Franklin darted forward to grab Preston's pant leg. With a couple of sharp tugs, he dumped the hapless man back on the ground.

"Good dog!" Charisse said. "Be glad he's not a biter, Preston. That's what you deserve." She turned and walked away with Franklin at her heels. "He's all yours, Luke," she called over her shoulder.

"I always did admire that woman," Ben said. "She's got a good head on her shoulders."

"And a killer right hook," agreed Isaiah Brahms with a touch of pride. "Just like her grandmother."

"You don't know what you're letting yourself in for,"

Preston gasped. "She's a jinx, I tell you! I should know — I was married to the bitch."

"I'm really glad to hear you say that," Luke said pleasantly, as he pulled the other man to his feet. "I've been itching to teach you a lesson from the first day I heard your name, and you just gave me the excuse I was looking for."

CHAPTER 44

Charisse pulled the box containing Granny's dishes from the back of the wagon and set it on the ground. Hopefully the contents would get her back to St. Louis. What a day! When she'd gotten up this morning she dreaded their arrival in Fort Bridger, for she knew she'd be saying good-bye to Luke and Toby tomorrow. Then Isaiah Brahms and Preston had turned her world upside down, and she caught a glimpse of a second chance. But what if she couldn't persuade Luke to fall in with her plan? Her heart clenched. All the money in the world wouldn't heal the hurt of losing them.

"Mama, Pa and I have been looking all over for you!" Toby ran up and gave her a big hug.

"I've been right here, unloading the wagon for the night," she said. "Why were you looking for me?"

"'Cause me and Pa have a prop… prop…"

"Proposition?" she supplied.

"Yeah, and a present too."

"Really?" Charise glanced over his head and saw Luke walking toward them.

"Pa says he can do it by himself, but I wanted you to know it was my idea, too."

"Toby!" Caroline's voice floated across the parade ground where she and Ben stood. She lifted her hand and gestured for Toby to join them.

Toby glanced over his shoulder. "Oh yeah, Ben and Caroline asked if I could go to the sutler's store with them. Can I, please?"

Charisse frowned. "Are you sure they asked you, or did you invite yourself?"

Toby's eyes opened wide, and he shook his head. "Oh no, Mama. You teached me better manners than that."

"I taught you. All right, but don't be a pest."

"I won't, Mama. I'll be the bestest boy they ever saw."

"I'll bet," she muttered as she watched him and Franklin run off.

"And there he goes," Luke said with a wry look over his shoulder. "I'm almost afraid to ask what he told you."

"Mostly that Ben and Caroline invited him to go to the store with them, though I haven't a clue why."

"Because I asked them to. They're keeping him until further notice." He brought his hand out from behind his back and presented her with a large bouquet of wild flowers.

"Oh, Luke, they're beautiful! It must have taken you all afternoon to pick them."

"Nope, it took Toby about fifteen minutes. I finally figured out a way to harness that energy."

Charisse laughed. "All right, now I'm suspicious. You send Toby off with Ben and Caroline and you bring me flowers. What are you up to?"

"It turns out there's a hotel here at the fort for travelers, and I rented you a room."

"A room?" Charisse squealed. "With a real bed?"

"Yes, indeed, and I ordered a hot bath too."

"Oh, Luke!" She threw her arms around his neck and gave him a big kiss.

He grinned. "I can't wait to see what I get when I tell you the rest of the surprise."

"There's more?"

"Certainly. There's also a small restaurant, so I figured we'd have supper."

"I won't have to cook?"

"Nope."

She grinned. "And you won't have to starve."

"That did occur to me." He looked at her expectantly. "Well?"

"Well what?"

"Well, what's my reward?"

"Hmm. If you never went to pick Toby up, would Ben and Caroline keep him all night?"

"Yes."

She walked her fingers up his chest. "Then why don't you come share that bed at the hotel with me?"

"That's all?"

Charisse blinked. "That's not enough?"

"I was sort of hoping to share the bath too."

She laughed and gave him a hug. "Oh, I suppose!"

"Don't you care what happened to Preston?"

She sighed and let him go. "No, not really. I knew he was a cad, but never realized how truly despicable he is until today."

"I left him in the guard house. The colonel sent for a U.S. Marshal to come pick him up and take him back for trial."

"Good. I hope he rots in prison."

"I don't think you're going to have to worry about that. Isaiah Brahms is planning to wait for the marshal and go back with him. He says he's not leaving Preston until he's sure the scoundrel gets what he deserves."

"I knew I liked that man," Charisse said. "Do you know why Mr. Brahms is here?"

"Something about your grandfather's will. I take it old Preston was involved in a bit of embezzlement, right?"

"Among other things," Charisse said with a grimace. "I'm going to have to go back to St. Louis and straighten it out."

"I had heard you were going back. What a coincidence! Turns out we're headed that direction as well."

"Is that so?"

"I need to return John Jessup's horses, not to mention that my boss is waiting for a full report. It does put me in a bit of a quandary, though."

"Really?"

He nodded. "Yes. You see, I need someone to take care of my son on the way back."

"Hmm. This seems vaguely familiar," Charisse said with a grin. "It just so happens I need a driver for my wagon. Have any ideas?"

"As a matter of fact, I do."

"I'll bet this is the proposition Toby mentioned the two of you had for me," she said with a smile. "He said it came from both of you."

"Oh, that son of mine!" He put his hand over his eyes and shook his head in exasperation. "It wasn't a proposition, it was a proposal. And that's precisely why I sent him with Caroline and Ben."

"Why? Aren't you proposing to hire a nanny for the trip back?"

"No, I wasn't planning on a nanny for him."

"You weren't?"

"I was thinking more of a mother."

"A-a mother?" Charisse's heart turned over in her chest. "You mean, you're *proposing* proposing, as in getting married?"

"That's exactly what I mean. Toby thought we should propose together and include Franklin and Petey."

"Oh my!"

"Yes, that's what I thought, too. Anyway, there's a post chaplin here at the fort who says he'll be more than happy to marry us. The more, the merrier."

"What does that mean?"

Luke chuckled. "It means Ben Baxter and Henry Holland got there before me."

"Good heavens!"

"The chaplin was a tad suspicious when a third man from our wagon train requested his services. I think he wondered what was going on."

"I imagine." Charisse grinned. "Maybe we should all get married together."

"Caroline said the same thing. Sadie and Violet heard about it and decided we should all have a big party afterwards."

Charisse gave a happy sigh. "I can't think of a group I'd

rather celebrate my wedding with."

"Nor can I." He smiled down at her. "I was thinking the trip back will serve pretty well as a honeymoon."

"A two-month honeymoon?"

He put his arms around her and kissed the tip of her nose. "That's right. No investigations, no midnight assignations with Ben, and no interminable poker games. It will be just the two of us."

"The two of us and Toby."

"And Franklin and Petey. Oh, the oxen, too. I expect Toby won't be able to part with them by the time we get back, and we'll have to figure out a place to keep them."

"It sounds wonderful." Charisse sighed and snuggled closer. "I thought you weren't the marrying kind. What changed your mind?"

"You did, when you sucker-punched Preston."

She pulled back and looked up at him. "Are you crazy?"

"No, just blind—or at least I was. You see, I've blamed myself and my dedication to my job for Elizabeth's death. As I stood there listening to that jackass you were married to, I realized you'd been through a hundred times more than Elizabeth ever had, and you never took the easy way out."

"Poor Elizabeth. She had the perfect family, and it wasn't enough."

"Ah, so now we're perfect? That bodes well for my mission." He smiled softly as he traced the curve of her cheek. "It's you and your love that makes us perfect."

"Oh, Luke!"

"I love you, and I want to spend the rest of my life making love to you every night, falling asleep in your arms, and waking up to your smile every morning." He tipped her chin up with the crook of his finger. "Will you marry me?"

"Aren't you forgetting something?"

He frowned. "I don't think so."

"Your proposal was supposed to include Toby."

"Oh."

"And Franklin and Petey," she said with a grin.

He sighed and rested his chin on top of her head. "All right, let's see. Will you, Franklin and Petey do Toby and me the honor of marrying us?"

Charisse giggled. "When you put it like that, how could I refuse? Of course, I—uh, we—will marry you. I love you too, and have almost since the beginning." She stood on her tiptoes and kissed him. "You and Toby are my-happily-ever-after."

"We can even go to Oregon Territory next year if you want to."

"What about your job?"

"I've had enough cloak-and-dagger intrigue to last a lifetime. Besides, I'm getting a little old for it, anyway. I'm ready to try something else."

"And you want to be a farmer?"

"Not really, but I've always had a head for business. Maybe I'll start some kind of company."

Or maybe learn to run a railroad, Charisse thought happily to herself. "What if I don't want to go to Oregon anymore?"

"It doesn't matter. As long as I have you and Toby, we could live on the moon for all I care."

"So, when do we leave? As soon as the oxen are rested up?"

"It might take a little longer than that. I'll need to find a job so we can restock for the trip back."

"Why?"

"We're out of money."

Charisse shook her head. "No, we're not. We'll sell Granny's dishes."

"The hell we will! You're not giving up your grandmother's dishes."

She chuckled. "Even if the whole plan was to sell them anyway?"

"What are you talking about?"

"Come on, I'll show you." Charisse took him by the hand and led him to the back of the wagon where the familiar crate sat on the ground. "I knew I'd need to restock supplies on the trip and would need money to get started when I got to Oregon, so I invested my cash to make it stretch. There was a little bit of a risk, but thanks to your packing ability, and the distance we've come, it will net me a huge profit."

"Charisse, I don't think china is going to sell all that well out here on the prairie."

She grabbed the pry bar from the back of the wagon and handed it to him. "Go ahead—open it."

He gave her a quizzical look, then knelt down and pried off the lid. "Lard?"

"Partially." Charisse scooped some of it out of the way. "But this is the real treasure."

"Well, I'll be damned. Eggs!"

Charisse smiled and reached over his shoulder to pick one up. "The crate is lined with tin and the eggs are packed in lard to keep them fresh and unbroken. Both lard and eggs are scarce out here. I got the idea when I read about eggs costing as much as two dollars apiece in the mining camps. They paid me a dollar and a quarter each for them at Platte River Station. I haven't approached the sutler here yet, but I imagine there are enough to get us clear back to St. Louis. We could probably even afford to take the stage."

He looked up at her and shook his head. "You never cease to amaze me. Any more surprises?"

Charisse thought of the fortune waiting for them back in St. Louis and smiled. "A few, but they'll wait until morning. There's a delightful evening waiting for us."

"You're right." Luke put the lid back on the crate and set it back in the wagon. "So, what will it be first?"

"First I need to get these beautiful flowers in water. They might turn out to be my bridal bouquet."

"And then?"

"The logical course would be the bath first, the meal next, and finally the bed."

"That's true."

"On the other hand, we might want to check out the bed to

make sure it's bouncy enough."

"If we do, we may never get to the bath or the meal."

"Life is full of risks," Charisse said with a wave of her hand.

"We do have several hours before the restaurant closes," he said. "And I guess it will still be there in the morning if we find we can't get away."

"Mmm. They'll probably even serve us eggs for breakfast if we bring the eggs."

"Eggs and coffee. That's worth waiting for."

"Sure is."

They grinned at each other, then strolled off into the gathering darkness hand in hand.

AUTHOR'S NOTE

Warning: Spoilers Ahead!

In the writing world, I am what is known as a *pantser*. Most historical authors start with a neat little outline of the plot, character charts, and folders bulging with research. Not me. As soon as I know my two main characters and where the story begins, I jump in and start writing. I go where the story takes me, following whatever path presents itself, and discovering the plot along the way. In other words, I write by the seat of my pants!

When I started this novel, all I knew was that it was set on the Oregon Trail, that my hero was a Pinkerton Detective, and that the heroine was a jinx. All right, I'll admit it, *jinx* is an anachronism in this book. The word, which refers to someone who brings bad luck to others, wasn't coined until the 1920's. The concept was around, of course, but not in a recognizable word. It's never established if Charisse really is a jinx, but odd things begin happening to my hero from the moment he meets her. That's when I realized it was all a matter of perspective. Luke is an incurable optimist. Instead of deciding he's living under a cloud of disaster like Preston, he considers it a stroke of incredibly good luck whenever he survives a close call, and he starts to think of Charisse as his personal good luck charm.

I knew Luke was in Independence, Missouri to investigate something, probably a simple case of embezzlement by a railroad clerk, because that's what Pinkertons generally did. But that wouldn't take long and certainly wouldn't send him on a 2000-mile trek across the wilderness. Enter Matthew McNesby. McNesby is a rather useful character who has a habit of popping into my books unannounced. From Murphy's Rainbow, where he first appeared, I knew McNesby was the head of Union espionage during the Civil War. What I didn't know was that job was actually held by none other than Allan Pinkerton, who, among other things, foiled a plot to assassinate President Lincoln. Obviously, McNesby and Pinkerton worked together during the Civil War, so it wasn't much of a stretch for them to be associates before the war, who traded resources and men back and forth.

Which brought me to the question of what exactly was going on. I didn't have to look far. Manifest Destiny, or the idea that the United States should stretch from sea to shining sea, was the buzzword of the mid-nineteenth century. President James K. Polk was such a *huge* fan that one of his campaign promises was to bring Texas into the Union, which he did. Then, he offered Mexico 25 million dollars for what is now California, New Mexico, Nevada and an area claimed by both Mexico and Texas. Mexico refused, and both countries sent troops into the disputed area. When Mexican cavalry fired on American dragoons, President Polk declared war, and the U.S. Army invaded Mexico.

I'll spare you the gory details, but the United States eventually won. On February 2, 1848, the Treaty of Guadelupe-Hidalgo was signed. Mexico relinquished all claim on Texas, and for 15 million dollars, ceded over a third of its territory to the United States. If you draw a line from California's northern border all the way over to Texas, you can see how large of an area it is. Though it wasn't as densely populated as it is now, there were many Mexicans living there who suddenly found themselves U.S. citizens. It's not hard to imagine that a military man like Roberto Mantella, who had spent most of his adult life fighting skirmishes with the United States, might consider staging a rebellion.

Meanwhile, tensions between the North and South were heating up. Though Mexico was staunchly anti-slavery, the two groups had quite a bit in common. I have no doubt there was talk of secession on both sides. Banding together against a mutual enemy and hatching a plot like the one in The Jinx and the Pinkerton could easily have happened.

Then there was the Native American population. When white men offered them trade goods for the land, they readily agreed, especially in the beginning, because they had no concept of owning the land they inhabited. In the mid 1850's, many, like Cougar Tail's band, were still content to trade with the white settlers travelling through their hunting grounds and would have jumped at the chance to obtain state of the art rifles. But some had begun to understand that matters were not so benign as they seemed and would have gladly used those rifles to fight the white invaders who were driving off game.

If the people living in the lands bought from Mexico had seceded at the same time as the Confederate States, and there had been a sudden Indian uprising in the West, the United States would have been fighting on three fronts. Success for both groups of rebels would have almost been guaranteed. Luckily for the United States, no such plot existed. At least as far as we know. Maybe it did, and would have changed the course of history if not for two intrepid Pinkerton detectives and a wagon train full of misfits.

Sneak Peek

Book 2 of the Pinkerton Trilogy

THE WASICU
(working title)

(Wyoming Territory 1868)

CHAPTER 1

"Morgan, open the damn window!"

Morgan blinked sleepily. Why was her brother making such a racket in the middle of the night? *You're dreaming,* she thought to herself and snuggled back down to sleep. *So nice to have a real bed again after all those weeks traveling in one bone-jarring stage coach after another.*

"Morgan!" This time the voice was accompanied by the sound of rapping on the glass.

Morgan sat bolt upright and stared at the window. It wasn't a dream. There was someone there.

"Come on, wake up. This is no time to be sleeping."

"No, of course it isn't," she muttered as she threw back the covers and got out of bed. "Who sleeps in the middle of the night? All right, I'm coming." Morgan crossed the room, wondering why Andy was here now instead of this afternoon when she had first come home. She unlocked the window and tugged at the bottom. It jerked open and her brother's head and shoulders filled the aperture.

"It took you long enough," he said, hefting himself up onto the sill.

"Oh, I *am* sorry." Her tone was sarcastic as she put on her dressing gown. "I suppose you have a good reason for not using the front door?"

"Too dangerous."

"Dangerous! Since when?"

"We were afraid we'd be seen."

Morgan snorted. "Oh right, that makes all kinds of sense since Sadie and Sam are the only ones around for miles. I suppose Matt's with you too?"

"Where else would he be?"

"Funny, that's what I wondered when I came in on the stage yesterday. Silly me, I thought my brothers might be there to meet me, since I haven't been home for two years!"

"Something came up."

"Whatever it was had better be good."

"It was." He turned back to the window. "All right, Matt, let's get Will inside."

Morgan straightened. "Will's with you, too?"

"That's why we're here. Easy now," he said, reaching back through the window. "That wound could start bleeding again."

Morgan's heart lurched in her chest. "Wound? Andy, what's happened?"

"Will took a bullet in the chest. Steady now, Matt, ease him over the sill."

Horrified, Morgan didn't even take time to watch Andy and Matt lift the injured man through the opening. She hurried over to her trunk and grabbed her medical bag. Then she lit the lamp and yanked the blankets off the bed. Andy and Matt carried the limp body to the bed. His feet stuck out over the end, and the broad shoulders took up a goodly portion of the mattress, but he looked pathetically vulnerable. His twin brothers, who were fully as large, stood looking down at him with identical expressions of helpless dismay.

Morgan pushed between them. "For heaven's sake, get out of the way. I can't do anything with you two standing in my light." Anxiety lent a sharp edge to her words as she stood beside the bed. "Pull yourselves together. I'm going to need your help. There's no way I can move this big ox by myself."

"I better go take care of the horses," Matt murmured. "You

stay here and help Morgan."

"Oh, for heaven's sake." Morgan glanced up in irritation. "This is no time to be worrying about the horses, Matt. Go get the doctor."

"No doctor," Matt said emphatically then disappeared out the window.

Morgan stared at Andy. "What's going on?"

Andy avoided her eyes. "It's a long story. Don't you think you should concentrate on Will? He's lost a lot of blood."

"All right," she said with a frown. "But as soon as I'm done here, you're telling me everything."

Andy just nodded. The next few minutes were filled with trying to get their brother out of his blood-soaked clothing without hurting him any worse. "The bullet missed his lung and went straight through, thank goodness." Morgan pulled a small pair of sharp scissors out of her bag and snipped away Will's undershirt. "I can clean and pack a wound, but I'm not sure I could take a bullet out."

"Open up!" A strident male voice accompanied by insistent pounding on the front door echoed through the house.

Startled, Morgan looked up in surprise. "What in the world—"

"Oh hell." Andy's gaze darted around the room in panic. "We've got to hide Will!"

"Hide Will? But—"

"Look, Morgan. I don't have time to explain. Just help me get Will out of sight. If they find him here, they'll kill him."

Morgan didn't understand her brother's urgency, but she didn't waste time questioning it. Her gaze darted about the room looking for somewhere big enough to hide a man of Will's size. The room she'd always considered a cozy sanctuary suddenly seemed stark and barren.

"What about the wardrobe?" Andy asked.

Morgan shook her head. "Not big enough. Besides, he's too weak to stand up. The root cellar?"

"No time, and I don't think we could get him down there

without Matt's help."

"We know you're in there, Jessup. You might as well give up and come out." The voice was louder than before and the pounding on the door more insistent. "Give me a minute," Morgan yelled. "I'll be right there!"

"I'll figure it out," Andy whispered. "You go stall them for as long as you can."

Morgan grabbed a handful of bandages from her bag and thrust them at Andy. "Put these on the wound and apply pressure. With a hole that size, he could bleed to death," she whispered back. She glanced uncertainly down at Will.

"Just go!" Andy said. "And take the lamp with you."

With one last look at her brothers, she snatched up the lamp with one hand and closed the door behind her with the other.

"Open up or we'll break down the damn door!"

"All right, all right. I'm coming." She hurried down the hallway and across the kitchen, wondering who in the world it could be. Their ranch was miles from the nearest neighbor except for Sam and Sadie, the elderly couple who lived and worked there.

"This is your last chance," the voice barked.

"Oh, for heaven's sake," she said, jerking open the door. "What do you want?"

The man outside was a short, slightly pudgy stranger. His expression was of shocked surprise. He blushed furiously and snatched the hat off his head. He apparently hadn't been expecting a woman. "Uh… sorry, ma'am, but we need to search your house."

"Search my house?" She stared at him in disbelief. "It's the middle of the night!"

"Yes, ma'am, I know, but—"

An angry voice came out of the darkness. "What's the problem, Boone?"

The man at the door looked over his shoulder and shifted nervously. "No problem, Sheriff James, but—"

"But what? I told you to search the house." A tall man

carrying a rifle strode out of the darkness from the direction of the barn. "Why are you still standing outside?"

"She just now opened the door."

"What dunderhead told you to knock?"

"No one, I just thought—"

"Thought you'd give them time to hide the evidence?" The sheriff gave him a look of pure disgust. "The whole point was to catch them red-handed." Sheriff James pushed the other man out of the way. It was probably a trick of the moonlight but Morgan saw a menacing gleam lurking in the dark eyes as he loomed over her. "Move aside unless you want to be arrested for interfering with the law."

Morgan hadn't spent her life around huge older brothers without learning how to deal with intimidation tactics. She straightened to her full height and stared him right in the eye. "You're not coming through this door until you give me a darn good reason."

Sheriff James's eyes narrowed. "Who are you?"

"I'm Morgan Jessup, and this is my home. The question is, who are you?"

"Huh," Boone said. "Didn't know any of the Jessups was married."

The sheriff leaned forward threateningly. "Are you going to let us in or are we going to have to move you out of the way?"

Morgan held her ground. "You still haven't told me who you are, and why you woke me up in the middle of the night to search my house."

"I'm the law around here," the sheriff said, "and I can damn well search any house I want, any time I want."

"We're looking for a gang of desperate outlaws," Boone said quickly.

Morgan was startled. "Outlaws?" *They think my brothers are outlaws?*

"They robbed the bank in town."

"And you think they might be hiding in my house?"

"We *know* they are," the sheriff said with a growl. "We

followed the trail of blood."

"Good heavens!" Morgan put her hand to her mouth as though shocked by the mere thought. "Are you sure? I never heard a thing."

"Probably slept through it," Boone muttered. "Took forever for her to wake up enough to answer the door."

The sheriff's eyes narrowed even further. "Why *did* it take you so long to come to the door, Mrs. Jessup?"

Morgan figured she had more clout as a wife than as an old maid sister so she didn't bother to correct the name. "My room is at the back of the house," she said, "and I sleep very soundly." She could almost see the suspicion forming in Sheriff James's mind. To delay any longer would only serve to convince him she had something to hide. Morgan gave a nervous glance over her shoulder at the shadowy kitchen. "D-do you think they're still here?"

"No place else they could be," the sheriff said. "We've got the place surrounded."

"Are you sure you have enough men?"

"I deputized half the town."

"Thank goodness for that," Morgan said, resisting the urge to roll her eyes. Like most of the tiny towns that grew up close to frontier forts, the town of Fort Laramie was barely big enough to make a wide spot in the Oregon Trail. James would have been lucky to find more than five men for his posse. "Where are they?"

"Look, we really don't have time to stand around here talking all night while those criminals are getting away."

"I thought you said they were in my house."

He sighed in exasperation. "We're pretty sure they are, but there's always the chance that they aren't. That's why we have to search. Now if you'll just get out of the way—"

"Sheriff!" An excited voice came out of the darkness. "I found one of them sneaking around the back with a rifle."

Morgan's heart jumped to her throat. Matt! They must have caught him as he came back from taking care of the horses. A second later relief flooded her as she heard Sam's familiar voice filled with righteous anger. Matt was safe, at least for the moment.

"I ain't no confounded bank robber. I live here, damn it. Now let me go!"

"Sam!" Morgan said as the two men appeared out of the darkness. "What's wrong?"

"Some men got me and the missus out of bed. Said they was deputies and was looking for a gang of bank robbers. They was searching the house when I left. Sadie sent me up here to make sure you was all right." He glared at the man who had him by the arm. "This dadgum idiot jumped me out back."

"He was sneaking around," the deputy repeated. "Acted like he was up to no good."

Sam gave an indignant snort. "'Course, I was sneaking around. I never go into a dangerous situation without studying it first!"

The sheriff's eyes narrowed. "Who are you and what are you doing here?"

"He's our hired hand," Morgan said quickly. "He and his wife live in the small house near the barn."

The sheriff gave Sam a speculative look then shook his head. "He's too old to be one of them." Turning back to Morgan, he raised his rifle slightly. "I'd rather not shoot you, Mrs. Jessup, but unless you step aside, I will."

"Oh, sorry." Trying to look as though she'd forgotten she blocked the door, Morgan stepped out of the way.

"Go alert the others, and make sure you have every window and door covered," James said to the man holding Sam. "Boone and I are going to search the house. Keep your guns ready in case they try to escape. They'll be armed and ready to shoot their way out if they have to." He glared at Morgan as though he thought she'd be able to sneak his quarry out of the house while his back was turned. "You'll come with us, Mrs. Jessup. What's behind that door?" he asked, nodding toward the far wall.

"The pantry."

"Good place to start," he said. "Hold that lantern up high so we can see."

Morgan obediently lifted the lantern then glanced at Sam. Five years ago, he'd have been exactly the ally she needed, but time had taken its toll. While she'd been back East, he'd become so forgetful that he was more of a liability than an asset. He was still bristling and glaring at the sheriff and his men. The last thing they needed right now was another confrontation. As gun-happy as the sheriff appeared to be, who knew what would happen?

"Why don't you go home and make sure Sadie is all right," Morgan said quietly.

Sam frowned. "Don't rightly like to leave you alone with the likes of that trumped- up sheriff and his men!"

"They won't do me any harm. They'll soon realize there's nothing here for them to find and they'll leave. I need you near the barn to make sure they don't bother any of the horses."

Sam looked doubtful. "If you're sure—"

"Positive." Morgan patted his arm and pushed him toward the door. "Tell Sadie not to worry, everything's fine here. I'll see you both in the morning." She watched him shuffle outside then turned back to Sheriff James and Boone.

She winced as the sheriff shoved the carefully arranged contents of the pantry out of the way so he could tap the walls with the butt of his rifle. Sadie was not going to be happy when she saw the mess he was making. When he finally finished, there was a look of disappointment on his face.

Morgan swallowed a smile. The man had a taste for melodrama. He'd clearly been hoping to find a secret room concealed behind the walls. As he stepped away, his boot heel hit the floor with a slight hollow sound.

The sheriff's expression sharpened, and he stomped on the floorboards again. "There's a hidden room under this floor," he said triumphantly.

"It's the root cellar," Morgan said.

"A root cellar," he repeated in a disbelieving tone. "Where's the door to it?"

"Right there under your feet," she said, pointing to the throw rug that covered the trap door into the cellar.

Sheriff James' eyes brightened as he kicked the rug out of the way to reveal a large iron ring set in the floor. He stepped off the trapdoor, then nodded to Boone. "Open it."

Boone did as he was told, and the door swung up on silent hinges. Boone peered down into the blackness. "Can't see nothing. It's darker than the pits of hell down there." He looked at Sheriff James. "Smells like a root cellar."

"There's a ladder just inside the hole," Morgan said helpfully.

He practically snatched the lantern from her hand.

Morgan hid another smile as she watched them descend through the trap door. She hadn't been down into the root cellar since she'd been home, but was pretty sure they'd find the tail end of last summer's vegetables and precious little else.

Sure enough, the two men emerged empty-handed several minutes later, liberally coated with dust and cobwebs. Sheriff James did not look happy.

They made a quick search of the kitchen and parlor, then moved down the hall toward the bedrooms. The first had originally been their father's, but now belonged to Will. The twins slept across the hall in a room all three of her brothers had once shared, and Morgan's was at the far end.

It took little time to search the first two rooms. Each contained only neatly made beds, a chest of drawers and pegs on the wall where several articles of clothing hung. "Seems too damn neat," James muttered. "Not what you'd expect from a bunch of men."

"It's our housekeeper's doing," Morgan said. "If it were left up to the three of them, the place would be a wreck."

James gave her a suspicious look, then moved down the hall to the last door.

"This is my room." Morgan's stomach lurched as she

realized her mistake. "Mine and my husband's," she corrected, praying that Andy had somehow managed to hide Will. "You don't think they could be hiding in there do you? I'd surely have heard them."

Sheriff James stared at her for a long moment as she tried to maintain a look of frightened apprehension, which wasn't all fake. Lord only knew what lay behind that door. Boone pushed it open and stepped aside so the sheriff could enter.

The room appeared just as one would expect. Her riding clothes were draped across the top of her trunk and the blankets thrown aside as though she had risen in a hurry. There was no sign of her brothers or her medical bag. The sheriff's gaze barely touched the rumpled bed as he focused on the wardrobe, but Morgan's froze on the place she had last seen her brothers. A spot of blood was visible just under the edge of the blanket Andy had hastily thrown back on the bed.

"Well, well, look what we have here," Sheriff James said in a soft voice. "The perfect hiding place."

Morgan took an unobtrusive step toward the bed, then another as James and Boone pointed their guns at the wardrobe.

"We know you're in there, Jessup," the sheriff said. "Come out with your hands up." He lowered his voice. "On the count of three, Boone."

Morgan kept her eye on the two men as she sidled up next to the bed.

"One." Both James and Boone tightened their grips. "Two." Morgan reached down for the blanket.

"Three!" Both guns fired just as Morgan let out an involuntary screech of surprise and yanked the corner of the blanket over the incriminating spot.

"Mrs. Jessup." Sheriff James's tone was so menacing that Morgan thought for a moment that he'd seen her hide the blood on the bed. Then she realized he was gesturing toward the wardrobe. "Open it."

"My wardrobe!" she cried, staring at the shattered wood in

dismay. "You destroyed it."

Sheriff James gestured toward the door with the barrel of his gun. "And anyone who was standing inside. Open the damn door!"

Morgan stalked to the ruined cabinet and threw open the door. "See, it's empty except for my clothes." She fingered the bullet hole in one of the two gowns hanging there. "Congratulations," she said sarcastically. "You killed my best dress!"

The sheriff pushed her aside and peered into the nearly empty cupboard himself. "Damn, I could have sworn—"

"Sheriff, look!" Boone said suddenly. "There's somebody under the bed."

James spun around and stared at the patch of white just visible under the edge of the quilt where it didn't quite reach the floor. Morgan winced inwardly. It hadn't been visible until she moved the covers. It had to be Will and Andy—there was simply no other place they could have hidden. Fighting panic, she looked around for something to use as a weapon. If she could keep one of them occupied, then Andy might be able to take the other by surprise.

Boone bent over and pulled a froth of cotton and lace out from under the bed. "My petticoat!" she said, color flooding her face as she remembered changing into her riding clothes that afternoon and kicking the female trappings under the bed in disgust. Boone bent again and pulled out her corset.

"Give me that!" she said, snatching her underwear out of his hand.

Sheriff James glanced from her scarlet face back to the bed. "Anything else under there, Boone?"

Boone lifted the edge of the quilt and peered underneath. Morgan held her breath and mentally prepared herself to smash the heavy whalebone corset into Sheriff James's head.

"Just some more petticoats and a dress. Looks like she keeps her clothes under her bed instead of the wardrobe," Boone said with a snicker.

"It's my laundry!" Morgan snapped. "Now, if you don't mind —"

"Sheriff James!" An excited voice called from the hallway. "Sheriff James, where are you?"

"In here, Avery. What's the problem?"

"It's all a trick!" Two men Morgan hadn't seen before rushed into the room. "They only made it look like they stopped here. The men you sent to scout down near the river found their tracks."

Sheriff James frowned. "Are you sure?"

"Yes!" The second man nodded emphatically. "We found where they'd laid the wounded one on the ground while they doubled back and covered up the trail to make it look like they'd come up here!"

"From the amount of blood, it looks like the one you shot must be near dead," the other man added.

The sheriff glared at Morgan. "And you kept us here searching the house so they could get away."

"I did no such thing," Morgan said indignantly. "You're the one who insisted there was a gang of criminals hiding in my house. I told you it was utter nonsense —"

But the sheriff and his men were already leaving; she practically had to run to keep up with them.

"Mount up, men," the sheriff called as he walked out the front door. He untied his horse and swung up into the saddle, then leaned on the horn and looked at Morgan with narrowed eyes. "Nice try, Mrs. Jessup. Lucky I figured out what you were up to before it was too late. I have half a mind to arrest you for obstructing justice." With that, he wheeled his horse and led the posse thundering out of the yard.

Morgan stared after them. "Of all the —"

"Morgan!"

She jumped and whirled around as a voice hissed in her ear. "Andy!"

"What was that all about?"

"Darned if I know." Morgan glanced outside just as the last

of the horsemen disappeared down the dark road. She shook her head and shut the door. "How's Will?"

"Not so good. I think you'd better come."

"Right, put some water on to heat while I go get my instruments ready." Sheriff James and his motley crew were forgotten as Morgan hurried down the hall, mentally preparing herself to battle for her brother's life.

ABOUT THE AUTHOR

Carolyn Lampman has won several industry awards for her previous novels, including the National Reader's Choice Award and the Coeur Du Bois Heart of Romance award. She was also a finalist for RWA's coveted RITA and a two-time finalist for EPIC's prestigious EPPIE. Carolyn lives in a small town in Wyoming with her husband, a Welsh Corgi, and a herd of grandchildren who come and go.